AS A MACHINE AND
PARTS

AS A MACHINE AND PARTS

a novella by Caleb J. Ross

Originally published by Aqueous Books, 2011, 2nd edition, 2013
Viscera Irrational

Cover design and internal layout, Caleb J. Ross
Cover image CSA Images

ISBN: 978-0615824116

Produced in the United States of America

O, to be a machine

O, to be wanted

to be useful

               --*Menomena*, Evil Bee

01000100 01101111 01101110 00100111

01110100 00100000 01100101 01101110

01110110 01111001 00100000 01101101

01100101

               --*Toshiba*, Satellite 1805-S207

As a Machine

Eric tosses night-glow emergency phone number magnets at a 1970's retro avocado-green refrigerator, hard enough to rattle the rebuilt compressor. "Rebuilt" used loosely; he brags weekly of having fixed the botched part, defending his neophyte mechanic's talents by blaming subsequent failures on untouched pieces. Marsha has owned this fridge for years, since we first met. We've shared many reheated carryout steakhouse dinners, and for that to continue I pray Eric gets smart soon. The magnets, comped from his part time at KCPL Energy, he handles with dirty fingers and perpetually-grimed knuckles; this makeup seemingly imperative to his skill; he's good. The magnets rarely reflect. A hit, and a loose coil somewhere vibrates applause.

"Heard you and my mom this morning." He breathes this revelation through the widened gaps of his clenched, yellowed teeth. He doesn't smoke cigarettes. The hue has always baffled me.

"Which part? The moans or the screams?"

A magnet ricochets. A rare miss. Eric has a shaggy-haired, hunched-shouldered look somewhere between flea market redneck and barefooted hippy, with the mental disposition of both extremes to keep him at a constant verge of Red v. Blue political explosion. For as long as I've known him he's sworn to one day "get back at this fucking world." For what, he never addresses. Possibly for giving him the ever-scent of sun-baked urine and rubber. I keep Marsha's windows open when he's home.

 This morning's post-coitus exchange warrants all the more mutual antipathy considering our close ages. Eric and I share nostalgic referents: G.I Joe cartoons and china-made cereal box toys. We even shared a classroom once in fourth grade, but only briefly, as Eric ultimately traded education for paint fumes and carburetors. His then neighbor, still his neighbor, now a friend, Ferret, embraced the role of teacher. By the end of what would be fourth grade, Eric knew how to lynch a smooth joint. I like him for this. So far, only this.

 I break his magnet's fire line for a slice of cheese and some mayonnaise. The refrigerator door handle stinks of spilled milk, long forgotten, but fitting to the kitchen's organically-upholstered decor. Things spill. Things stay. Bread crumbs decorate mildewed counter tile grout. Aerosol degreaser overspray lacquers the walls, the oven, and the dying plant leaves to a spotty, reflective patina. The daytime home remodeling TV shows that Eric calls "school" would name this style vagabond Rustic. I let the door swing hard against its deteriorating gasket and make a show of wiping my greased hand on a nearby towel. "You should major in house cleaning. And fix this gasket."

"Do me a favor and hit her harder tonight. I like that." He grins, gathering magnets from the door.

"That's your *mother*." It's the only threat I have. I'm not his father. I'm his peer. Marsha and I will never marry. She's too old. I'm too smart. It's a shame Eric and I can't bond. Grade school clique residue keeps us forever apart: he, an angry deadhead: torn jeans and Metallica t-shirts his uniform; me, intelligence and a taste for sweeter sounds. Perhaps if something were to change we could all come together as a family. A hastily-soldered yet solid family.

"If you listen hard enough, you'll hear me moan back from my room," Eric says. A magnet cuts the air.

His mother's sudden appearance curbs my rebuttal, breaching the kitchen in a shirt I left on her floor weeks ago.

I think I originally took it from Eric's closet in a hurry to escape Eric's inconvenient return home. This was before his mother and I decided to out our relationship. We've since grown comfortable with him as we've grown comfortable with ourselves.

"How're my boys this morning?" Her skin smells of copper and her hair of headboard woodstain; we redecorated earlier this week.

"It's three thirty in the afternoon," Eric says, but smiles like he's delivering genuinely helpful information.

"You know I'm great," I say.

"What's for breakfast?" she asks, reaching for a mug from the delicate stack of clean-enough dishes filling the sink.

"Sausage." I smirk. An angry magnet shaves my earlobe, whapping to the fridge door. I'm impressed. The compressor reports with a tinny vibration.

"I thought you fixed that, Eric." She fills the cup with yesterday's coffee and sets the microwave for a full minute.

"Probably the cylinder block this time. I'll get to it tomorrow."

"Have you checked the mechanic?" Another missile, this one hard into my back, then drops to the ground. "Watch it, son."

Another magnet, to my neck, then the ground. I kick the felled weapon under the refrigerator.

"Can it, Eric. Mitchell's back isn't right. You know that." She turns to the cabinet for bread. I leverage her turned interest to pantomime sex, hips and ass slaps. Eric takes the bait and throws an entire stack at my chest.

"Fuck!" I yell, genuine pain.

Three days ago Ferret asked Eric and I to help him sleeve a dead llama, with an understood-beer-and conversation payment. Ferret's first words upon our arrival were an unprovoked insistence on the animal having been found dead; *"I didn't kill it,"* which means, in Ferret-speak, that he did kill it. Ferret would kill anything if it meant keeping the skin.

I don't know if *sleeve* is his word or legitimate taxidermy jargon; he says it with such nonchalance that I'd argue for the former. It means the opposite of skinning; replacing the treated hide over the stuffed mold, post-gutting. The term *sleeving* misleads a textile-savvy layman such as myself, implying a simple loose wrap with zero mess. But the fit is tight and produces plenty of mess. They should call it socking "or Marsha stuffing" I said to Eric during our visit, choking back a laugh. I blame his subsequent animosity and hesitancy to help after my fall on this beautiful comment.

Two things: 1) blood is slick, and 2) Ferret is not a professional. I took the low end when transporting the freshly "found" body to Ferret's basement, and slipped, landing sandwiched between the greasy concrete and 300 lbs. of warm llama.

The resulting pain wasn't muscular entirely, nor a skeletal thing. Ferret said he had experience in blunt force trauma and elected to inspect the contact point with a stethoscope he kept to "ensure death, when it isn't so obvious." I hoped he meant the animals. After awkward minutes and additional strange jargon (these words I'm positive are his: congetudinal breakage, suede abrasion, 100 lb test line stitches), he gave me the okay and assured me that I was still good to sleeve. I worked well, too, impressing both him and myself. He called me a machine, and welcomed my help anytime. Eric and I, as best we've ever done before, bonded-over blood. I fear what that means.

"They're fucking magnets," Eric says, prying more weapons from the fridge. "Don't tell me they hurt your back."

"They hurt my back."

Marsha removes her coffee from the beeping microwave, intercepting another magnet. "Eric Charles," she yells.

That sweet mother's tone, using a middle name works for me in a dangerous way. "I'm sure he didn't mean it," I say, embracing the moment, nodding toward the bedroom. She grins. Eric fumes.

I catch Eric digging under the fridge through filth for my kicked magnet. His audible disgust warns me of the impending projectile, but I have other things on my mind, other positions and scents already clouding my brain.

The magnet cuts the air, contact with my neck. But this time the smack against the sticky linoleum doesn't happen. I rip the projectile from my skin and rotate to return it, but the magnet won't leave my hand.

"I'll keep it then," I say, sex and sweat on the brain, and escort Marsha to the back room, her coffee left steaming on the kitchen counter.

An ambulance ride later and I'm tracking strangers like barcodes. I've cataloged the entire waiting room in sortable, delimited rows and columns. Thirty-six percent blond or blond derivatives. Forty-two percent brunette or brunette derivatives. Ten percent too bleached white to know. Twelve percent other. I don't normally think like this, in numbers and charts. But for the last week, equations have been my air.

A mother across this fluorescent bio-dome warns her eight year-old boy in long-tail threats, slowly bottlenecking into terse commands. He's using a red marker to color his left earlobe. From my position, his ear appears vibrant with blood. The child obeys once the haggard woman reaches single-syllable threats, but he pouts in defeat, refocusing his crimson dye to the webbing between his fingers. His sister, sick, a 101 degree temperature I can read for no apparent reason. The boy and I commiserate. *I don't want to be here either, friend.* We end up here only when nothing else works. We're broken machines.

"That's a fine mother/son relationship," Eric says, noting the exchange. "Yelling and teaching. That's the way it should be."

"Your mom is not my mom."

"Good thing. I'd hope you wouldn't break your own mother's leg."

Eric drove himself, opting out of the inevitable awkward conversation regarding his mother's new injury. Something like this was bound to happen. Over the last week, I've gained one-hundred seventy pounds, most of it in broken spurts, though I've lost three inches from my waist. My shoes ceased to accommodate the shifting shape of my feet, so I wear boots made for thyroid freaks. I've already lost two toes. I fear metal detectors. A crushed femur during sex was bound to happen.

It started last Tuesday. I awoke from unsettling dreams, as they say, to find my left elbow replaced by a rotational hinge joint. Unsettling may be grandiose, as I suffered no more than a repeating nocturnal saga involving numbers, vivid fractions to infinity that I hang on to like a fable. During sex, I dream numbers. The dream isn't, as it once was, fear-inducing; I've crossed that divide between conscious visuals and unconscious imagery. As soon as a dream starts, I recognize the ruse and have learned to enjoy the ride. But

=

when I awoke, and the articular surfaces of my humerus and ulna had shed skin to reveal metal, waking life too, had crossed that divide.

My chair moans under my weight. I move the floor, taking a worry-abused copy of *Good Housekeeping* with me. I have trouble thumbing through the pages. "Who's the one with questions of respect, here? You want me to hit her next time."

"I don't really love my mom like that," Eric says in an effort to retract his earlier oedipal comment from the kitchen (7,268 characters back). "The situation isn't something I know how to fight against. Sorry."

He insists on calling his mother and me a "situation," while offering no restraint of hostilities otherwise. As far as he's concerned, we're fucking daylight away from jaundiced infants. "But look at that kid, Eric. He's never going to learn. He's a lost cause, a witch's asshole in a coalmine, and there's nothing that can be done. With a sister like that, sick eight days a week, the world doesn't have time for him. The only reason he came is that the babysitter's busy getting arrested and let go, both by way of indecent exposure. That woman's not raising him. She's tolerating him."

"How do you know the girl is sick that much?" he asks.

"People are products."

A family of brunette derivatives herds into the waiting room, shifting the air's equation.

"People are people. Nothing more."

"Then what am I, Eric? I'm massaging my arm like it still houses muscle, letting *Good Housekeeping* fall to the ground. I'm not sure yet, but I think my phalanges are socket cap bolts now. They swivel. And as I knead my unfamiliar arm, the bolts meld. Think now, of all the things that once gave your life its tale. Your history. The existence to your essence. So many of these things depend on your evolved human form. Grasping, articulating, organic movement bound only by the constraints of the brain's will. Imagine now, a flipper. Imagine a claw, lacking the nervous function to maneuver a magazine page, let alone a pen. Unfamiliarity will always presume devolution. Am I worse without a pen?

"You're a mother fucker, Mitchell."

That's fair.

I can smell the hallway latex and colostomy plastic pumping through the hospital vents. Dr. Fielding would call my still-healthy olfactories a good thing. He's a doctor, not a mechanic, so of course he's interested in keeping me human.

"So why do you say it?" I ask back to Eric. He sits behind me with a geriatric topics magazine, his heart beating faster than it should (98 bpm). "If you didn't mean it?"

"To gross you out. What you're doing is sick."

"It's not sick."

"Explain it to me, then."

"It's love," I begin, but catch myself. The word feels so foreign against my tongue, tangential at best. Marsha and I used to dance around the concept of love like verbalizing it didn't matter. Dr. Fielding said the first to go would be my fingers, and that the brain would ultimately succumb, but that I should have some time before I fail. Just last week I gazed in awe at stars. Now I count them. "Love..." I start again, but a nurse interrupts.

She tells us that Marsha's casted, then asks our relation. I let Eric go without me, forgoing an explanation. I use my time alone to catalog the popcorn speckles in the ceiling paint by size.

Dr. Fielding wanted to be a vet. Now he works to give animals a chance by taming humans through a loose prescription pad. Mad Lib a body part, mention pain, and the pills flow. All pets really want is a warm lap, and Fielding's rationale is that enough sedation will turn any busy pet owner into an adequate bean bag chair.

His receptionist's name is Kitty. Hand to god.

Hang in There cat posters, yes plural, paper his walls like he's peddling last resort-medicine. Hang in There is a fitting mantra for a man whose practice thrives on addicts and terminal cases. *Hang in there, and surely things will work out. That'll be a thirty-dollar co-pay, see you next month.* I'm neither addicted nor terminal. So how did I get here? Marsha.

"I heard Marsha had a stay with us last night." Fielding slips a plastic cover over a candy cooking thermometer. I broke his scale last week, so he dives right into the internal assessments now, sitting on the floor in front of me. Once someone attains four-hundred pounds, precise weight doesn't matter much anymore.

"She's still here. Just upstairs. Broken leg."

He tells me to open. "How'd that happen?" A mouthful of thermometer gives me permission to mumble through the embarrassing tale. When he yanks the thermometer from my under my tongue, I spit metal filings to the ground. My tongue doesn't bleed, but still I taste rust. He checks the reading. "Two-hundred thirteen. You're running hot today."

Marsha made me start seeing Dr. Fielding as soon as my first toe fell away. She sees auras, said mine wasn't its usual vibrancy, gray when it used to be yellow. She had been visiting Fielding for years, and I blame him for the shit she sees. Some of his pills could make a corpse see colors. Marsha's no match for those pills. She swears by the man, so as a testament to my faith in our relationship I owed her the visit. And I've taken to him. Any other doctor would try to cure me. I need treatment.

"Anything new?" he asks, a tiny flashlight stressing my iris.

"Claws." I drum them against the linoleum floor. "And I'm down to one toe. My hair is falling out. I think I'm evolving. Nobody loses body parts and feels fine about it." *Did I ever feel bad about it?*

"Any fever? Has your back pain continued?"

"So you're dismissing evolution?"

"I can't write a prescription for evolution, Mitchell."

"Back pain is still there. Must be I still have a back. That's good news."

"Be thankful you can still move. Some aren't so lucky."

Fielding has a colleague out west who diagnoses from an office papered in parchment degrees. I've seen pictures, Fielding and the hotshot shaking hands in a 1970s sepia-paneled office, the framed certificates looming like specters. Fielding speaks fondly, but refers to the man only as a professional associate. *Hang in there, Doc. You've got fine wallpaper.*

The hair-plugged aging prodigy, Dr. Something, tried to steal me away from Fielding during my initial diagnostic sessions. Desperate for answers, Fielding phoned Dr. Something with a list of symptoms in-hand. Fibrodysplasia Ossificans Progressiva, Dr. Something said. "He's a Stone Man." Turns out, the villain doc was doing a study on F.O.P., and felt tweaking a few symptoms for the benefit of a research grant and a new wrap-around deck for his kept mistress's corner condo was worth skewing a patient. The Stone Man gene is responsible for a slow morphing of muscle tissue into bone tissue, until finally the lungs solidify and the patient suffocates from the inside. F.O.P doesn't account for my missing toes, a shoulder that plateaus at the top like a table, the disappearing hair, my weight gain, the claws, or my vanishing skin. There are charities for F.O.P. Where are the Mitchell charities?

I stayed with Fielding, not because he's unmotivated by research money and hi-life accoutrement, but because Marsha would kill me if I pissed off her dealer.

Dr. Fielding works my elbow's hinge joint with nonchalance, almost distain. "How's Marsha dealing with everything?"

"It's crushing her." I hide a smile.

"You've got a good one with her—"

"How much longer do you think I have?"

"Does she like machines?"

"To stay human...how much longer will I be human?"

Dr. Fielding allows me to drop my arm, my hip's remaining skin cushioning the blow to a soft metallic thump. I don't bruise anymore. I dent. "Your deterioration reminds me of frostbite. The non-essential extremities die first in order to keep the important cogs spinning and actuators pumping. You are streamlining for survival."

"To survive what?"

He shrugs. "The human condition?"

"I should be upset by this. But honestly, I'm not sure I am capable of feeling upset anymore." I offer him my other arm; as of this morning, also a beautiful hinge.

"Running with the frostbite comparison, I'd think your brain would go last."

"So if I'm already apathetic?"

"At this rate, you'll be welded to an assembly line by month's end."

I've got a résumé befitting such a life. I once worked at a wholesale bakery, pearling cupcakes with a dangling white icing gun, its cords wired through the ceiling to tanks the size of bloated whales. My co-workers and I gave our tools names, theirs having been assigned years before I arrived. I named mine Mr. Freud. Theirs had female names. Sometimes an icing gun is just an icing gun. Nobody got the reference.

Mr. Freud and I were a good team. I only as capable as he, and he as capable as me.

"Marsha's disability checks should kick in about that time," I say. "Maybe she'll fund my WD-40 baths and rust-proofing."

"Maybe you won't need the extra lubricants," he says with a smile. "As long as you still have emotions, you should still have tears. Though you may cry oil."

Fielding falls back onto his wheeled stool. He slides to a counter organized by jars containing various sterile instruments. The glass clanks from the force of his impact. He grits his teeth. I miss pain like that. "Try hanging on to that human side," he says rubbing his ribs. "Work through what you're feeling. Maybe talk to some other people in your position."

"Cyborgs? I'll give Van Damme a call."

"Honestly," he shakes his head. "I'm thinking transsexuals."

I search for a smile, but find nothing. "You're joking."

"You're right, *I'm* crazy. Find a toaster to talk to."

If only a toaster could sign a prescription pad.

Mr. Freud, on the line back at the bakery, offered our only dialogue. Anything outside my head drowned in the industrial hum. He had a family, bolts mostly, a few nuts, married to a German automobile injection-unit machine with hip joints that could brace a full semi-trailer chassis. He was happy. Monotony was enough excitement for that family man. I wonder if Mr. Freud knew any fun toasters.

"Maybe a tranny with a toaster *and* a doctor's handwriting?" I say.

"*You're* joking, now?"

I'm not sure.

Fielding checks the clock above my head and claims to have another appointment.

"Humans wait," I say. "Machines make their own time."

"If only you were a clock, Mitchell. I could use a few more hours." He closes a paperclipped manila folder stuffed with my half-month worth of observation and interpretation. I've seen him coin new words and draft essays on the spot. I've got a *condition*, that's about the clearest he's been with me. Years from now they'll find a cure for rust and obsolescence, but until then I endure inaugural change.

"You think I'm contagious?"

Fielding tosses my folder to the counter. "No. I've been inhaling your exhaust for a couple weeks, and as far as I can tell, I'm still human."

I still love. That's about all the human I need. Which reminds me, "Marsha's got joint pain. She's out of Percocet."

"Muscle pain?"

"That's the one."

Fielding pulls a pad from his chest pocket and decorates a sheet in his personal scribble. He places the prescription slip between my claw. "She'll have plenty from the doctors upstairs. Keep these for yourself. While you still have muscles to hurt."

This morning I woke with barely a remaining lock of hair, a situation I remedy with masking tape, layered as the low-grade gauze of a frugal head trauma patient. I've got an angle-flow globe valve for a nose, can smell sweet smoke nearby. The floor creaks and bows as I lumber from room to room, searching for the source of such beautiful smoke. Eric knows better than to leave a roach within reach. In a rush to grab Marsha from the hospital, leaving me a note mortared by angry misspellings, he left the air curtained in fog. So while I still have lungs to hurt, Herr Doktor? Inhale.

I am not car-friendly anymore, and Ferret's busy with his truck, hauling home pose- and sell-able road kill. One of his vagrant scouts phoned in a tip, a felled cow at the edge of town off 51 Highway. City's usually pretty good about scraping even outskirt bodies from the road before the stink interferes too much with the town's edge-drifter population, though those guys (us guys) seem to have adapted to infected air. Marsha has stories, ripped from her daily work to-and-froms through their trailer parks and corner congregations, rife with vagabond children playing in dirt-colored auras. The smoke from Marsha's OLEAN factory mixed with the burned blood stench of the BWP plant could assimilate any pair of lungs into breathing noxia. So, when a call comes, Ferret drops all else, afraid of missing out to those as morbid as himself.

If I didn't have pot, I'd feel like a shut-in. It's just me and the settled debris: car magazines and Eric's ashtrays mostly, the couch arm straddled by a few spread grocery store paperbacks. Marsha dares me to read just one, that I'd be hooked if I gave them a chance. They're crap; *Romancing the Gypsy Turd,* covers adorned with faultless human specimens. Oddly, strong as steel, like machine-chiseled.

Two months in his house and I'm still not entirely convinced of my welcome. Eric, he radiates animosity. Marsha, though, we've got it good with each other, but I have yet to claim a patch of real-estate for myself. The couch accepted me well enough, as did Marsha's bed— now I'm relegated to the floor for weight reasons—but I still feel the part of an abstraction in a world of realism. Marsha and I started dating after a friend dared me to fake a purse-snatching. Our life together seems melded by these coy provocations; she invites me to live with her, but through a quivering lip.

Eric announces his and Marsha's arrival with a cough and a swift yank of his ashen joint from my mouth. Marsha is asleep, riding stacked wheelchair cushions and Percocet by judge of her drool's swell; Vicodin spit drips rather than bloats.

"The fuck you doing?" He tries for a final hit, but inhales only a few secondhand spirals. "I can't fucking leave anything out with you here." Nerves move him to a stack of KCPL magnets sitting on a corner table. He aims.

"How is she?"

Eric mocks a few tosses while extracting what he can from the dissipating smoke, flexing his lungs until his cheeks take on a red hue, before answering. "Seriously. I had some time carved out for that roach." He lets the nib stick to his lower lip as he moves to Marsha's handles.

"How is she?"

I see myself in her spokes, in the x-brace beneath the propped cast. She is a used chair, ramp-worn yet stable—support a guy could get used to. Marsha's flaccid arms burn against the handrim as Eric wheels her to a sunny corner reserved for this homecoming. My lungs deflate. The sun shines upon every exposed metal surface, celebrating her arrival with reflected mirror ball confetti along the Formica paneled walls and dropped ceiling.

Give credit to simple mechanics. Four wheels. An axle (though weakened and stressed). Two forked casters. Then a chair for comfort, dressed in vinyl. We could have grown up together, the same block, the same factory even. A nymphet machine, no need for motors or oil. Her name, Invacare, is etched into her side.

"...I said she's fine. Wake the fuck up." A magnet hits my head, shaking my final strands of hair to the floor. Who needs dead protein? "What the fuck does she see in you?"

I peel the magnet from my scalp. "You know I didn't mean to do that to her, right?"

"Condescension aside, yes, I know." He pulls the magnet from my claw and returns it to the stack.

"So why not let up about it?"

"We're the same age, dick. We played spin-the-bottle in the same circles."

"And that age is twenty-nine. We're beyond crushes."

Eric pulls an alligator clip from his pocket and secures the fading roach. He re-lights, inhales, extinguishes. "A mom is supposed to have more sense than her son." Exhales.

"You're talking like she just caught you inside a soggy cantaloupe. Grow the fuck up."

"She told you about—"

"What's your mom's favorite food?"

"Why?"

"Chocolate chip pancakes from Chubby's. Her favorite album?"

"Van Halen's—"

"Superbird by Neil Sedaka."

"Nobody's favorite anything is Neil Sedaka."

"Sure, fucking write *me* off, that's fine. But *she* likes me. Love your mom enough to respect that."

"Shouldn't you be fucking a forklift or something?" Eric detaches from the smoldering joint, lets it sparkle to the carpet. In one motion, he pulls a baggie from his pocket and rips the globe valve from my face. "This should make a good pipe," he says turning toward the front door. "I'll be at Ferret's stuffing the llama."

He slams the door behind him. The horizontal blinds rattle against the door's window, shaking Marsha awake. She wipes her mouth and gathers the scene through her narcotic haze. "Your nose is gone," she says.

A forklift, or perhaps, Invacare. "How are you feeling?" I ask, concerned more for Invacare's poor axle.

Ferret exists so far demographically and socially removed from the rest of us that one would be pressed to call him a neighbor. Though proximity to Marsha's own two-bedroom ranch-style abode might suggest otherwise, Ferret's bomb-shelter of a residence, like its occupant, doesn't share the neighborhood's genetic makeup. Half of his home is a converted industrial storage container, the other half a tin trailer displaced by a government initiative to replace factory dilapidation with residential promise. Ferret claimed the garbage, and the city obliged, stipulating only that he not use the material for a residence. He agreed, with intentions of doing just that. This pilfered config sits atop a disrepaired cellar left from his original, legitimate house after a vengeful storm stole away the structure. Ferret welded the two halves with a borrowed torch. He bought a stained couch from Marsha for ten dollars and half a bottle of Yellow Tail.

Ferret is a vet of some mild, decades-old skirmish that few remember and even fewer admit to even happening. In the proper company of VA soldiers he's boasted that his actions are the very reasons for its continued secrecy. In the improper company of civilians, he's claimed not to think much about the past. But immersed dependence breeds apparent disregard; how often do people think of the air they breathe? This man *is* a war. For all these reasons, I think he may be the one to help me understand my foreign body.

A man like this *has* to operate on dead animals. He treats his lawn as a taxidermy showroom, offering nightmares to kids since late '91 when he revealed his first showpiece: a housecat he named Meowser, displayed with a wooden placard. Today he's up to two bobcats, a horse, and a few dogs, all posed and weather-worn into stylized mange.

I arrive, and taped to his front door, beside a Seirra Club decal, is a flyer—fresh by judge of its crisp edges—pleading for information on a "Missing" llama. Her name is/was Daisy. *Any information, please contact. Reward.*

I take the flyer and round the home toward a detached garage out back. I receive both the stink of acrid pot and the sight of Eric with my displaced *nose* to his mouth. He tells me, glassy-eyed excited, that "it came with its own screen."

I raise the flyer. "Someone's on to you," I yell to Ferret, past Eric, trying to ignore my part in his mouth. The screen is likely the mechanized version of my nostril hairs. I don't tell him this, not because it would make him sick—I'd love to see that—but because in his current condition, morbid interest would just make him inhale deeper.

Ferret, who hasn't seen me but for perhaps a bedroom-window glimpse since my fall down his stairs, rushes to me. He accepts the flyer, giving it only a casual glance, before refocusing on me. "Eric said you had changed. Damn, I thought he meant emotionally, like you took to beating Marsha, or something?" He takes me in through his blood-splattered plastic goggles. "He says you put her in a wheelchair."

"That was an accident. You can ask her, once she fully wakes up."

"No need. Eric's not much of a liar. You're not a wife beater."

"Wife. Thanks for thinking of me that way."

Ferret lifts the goggles to his forehead, revealing eyes, bloodshot like tiny versions of his garage floor's cracked red foundation. "What are you?"

"I think something between a terminator and one of those machines that caps bottles at a beer factory." I pantomime an opened glass bottle to my lips.

"No," he says. "You've got blades, see," he leans into my claws, moving up the steel plate, once a nippled and hairy chest. From there, my collar bone, now a simple rubber belt, turning my shoulders, my arms, my claws which, according to Ferret, are more adept for cutting than grasping, though I've managed so far to leverage them for the latter. And everything else could be any industrial machine in any factory to eyes like mine, which are more accustomed to file cabinets and hanging folders than to rotary whatevers. "This flat area where your chest was, I'd say that's a bed for steel blanks, like you're a punch press for those single serving office coffee machines." He walks around to check out my backside. "Yep. The backs of your knees are spot welders for base panels. Marsha manned one of those for a while down at OLEAN. I went in once for an interview. Failed the drug test. Her boss, Dickfuck Rogers, doesn't like me much anyway. Not since I fucked his daughter." He drops to his knees, mumbling something about serial numbers. "Damn, you could sell well for scrap. How is Marsha, anyway? The way Eric tells it, she's five feet under."

"I haven't talked much to her yet."

"Why?"

"I don't know. She's got a great looking chair though. Invacare. Sleek thing."

Ferret stands. "Alright." He turns away, revealing behind him, Llama Daisy, standing Frankensteined with human dentures and a balsawood horn fastened to her forehead. Her coat drips with wet drab green and brown paint, an attempt at camouflage, as everything in Ferret's world tries to be. She's got a saddlebag without a saddle, the sack supporting what appear to be mortar tubes for makeshift RPG missiles; everything to Ferret is either a weapon, or has the potential to be one. All this atop a wooden frame and four casters, with a cord running from her left-rear leg. Most days, I'm more relieved than happy to have him call me friend.

"She's in quite a bit of pain," Eric offers from his clouded corner.

I ignore Eric. "The fuck is this?" My head meets Daisy's shoulder; she is risen to the height of a wild elk.

"According to your flyer, she's a missing llama named Daisy. But to me, she's a unicorn hybrid, with some artillery for safety. Haven't named her yet."

I note the cord from her leg.

"My first dabble in animatronic taxidermy. I could have kept her hollow and made her a tank, I guess."

"A Trojan llama. What do you have hiding in there?"

"A motor and a few simple actuators. She's not battle-ready. I said my *first* dabble."

"May I?" I touch. What fur should feel like: coarse, slight give, doesn't happen. Have my nerves withered? I look to Daisy's cord, the open patches of skin and fur revealing joints and bolts below, back up to the brilliant white porcelain teeth, the crude facial hair, and the eyes. The empty eyes. "What's wrong with the eyes?"

"Those are the hardest to get right," Ferret says. "There's a reason those are the most expensive part. The fur, the skin, all of that is taken right from the animal. But the eyes have to be custom made. Life drains out of the eyes, and it's near impossible getting it back."

"A bit scary, no?" I lean in close enough to read my distorted reflection in the glass.

"Lot of room you have to talk," Eric says from his corner seat atop a workbench. He's crushing walnuts in a vice, chewing the meat, spitting renegade shell shards into the air with fervor. "You looked at your eyes lately?"

"Pot and motor oil gets Eric sympathetic," Ferret says, shaking his head. "And if there isn't a soapbox to stand on, a few puffs and he'll build one."

My eye in Daisy's eye, reciprocated hollow. "Is it more animal or machine?"

"The word is *empathetic*, you dick," Eric corrects Ferret. He throws a whole walnut to the back of my head, rattling my vision like a broken refrigerator compressor. "I feel like I'm the one standing on four wheels, full of wires and metal."

"Strange," I say. "*I* feel nothing."

"You should." Eric passes the smoldering joint to Ferret, who inhales quick, then drops down to a loose nut anchoring Daisy's right-front leg. He summons a wrench and tightens.

"Really, you don't feel anything. Human or machine?"

I suppose I should. But no. I'm just like Daisy, parts and wires, and a couple glass eyes. "*Apathetic*, I suppose would be the word. Maybe *neutral* would be better."

Eric hops down from his workbench seat, slipping on congealed blood. "Could you kill a person?" he asks, checking his balance.

"As much as I could unplug a machine, I suppose."

Ferret stands and measures me with his eyes, hushes to conspiratorial whispers. "I could get you some skin. Maybe even human skin."

I shrug. "Maybe some wheels?"

Eric walks between us, the sebaceous oil on his face close enough to lubricate my eyeballs. "You need to find out what you are, Mitchell. If a human, be a human. If a machine, figure out what assembly line you belong to."

I back away. An assembly line. Marsha used to come home from OLEAN, assembly-line gossip spilling, happy just to open up to a kindred. Those hours of giddy secrets— simmered at the factory line, frothing for my eventual consumption—this was our communion. Am I the only resident of a new limbo. "Okay. But can you help? Both of you?"

"I can get you some skin," Ferret says.

"Keep that on the list," I joke, "but Fielding has a different idea." I tell them about the tranny support group, gauging their reactions, finding the expected. Ferret, despite riding his garage hot-boxed mellowed high, steps back and vehemently shakes his head. Eric feigns repulsion, but poorly; I see a spark of interest there and know just what will pull him the rest of the way. "You guys help, and this is yours." I reveal the prescription Fielding had written for me.

Eric swipes the paper and agrees, already drooling. Ferrett asks, "Why do you need us?" An honest question, deserving of an honest answer: "Moral support."

Eric jumps. "So you *do* still have morals."

"All the more reason to embrace other struggling humans, right?"

Eric slinks back to the bench vice, crushes a walnut. "*Both* of you could use the empathy."

Ferret busies his hands with an oiled rag. "Do I have to wear a dress?"

"You'll get to pick it out," I say.

A walnut ricochets off of my head. "I get mom's red spaghetti strap," Eric yells and rushes out the garage door.

By the time Ferret and I catch up, Eric is already holding Marsha's red Fuck Me dress up to a full-length hallway mirror. She wears it when prepping for a night beneath me (sans an unplanned crushed femur). I should warn Eric not to hold the article so close to his skin, for fear of contamination; knowing Marsha's nil dry-cleaning budget, that thing is saturated. But I won't warn him. Chances are good that he has had contact with my protein spillage at some point, anyway. Marsha and I love love.

She remains in the sunlit corner, conscious, though wet with spittle. She's managed to lift the TV remote but without strength enough to surf beyond daytime infomercials. Ronco has a new version of the set-and-forget rotisserie. I envy its curves.

Eric eagerly calls Ferret to the back bedroom, and Ferret accepts with an exaggerated sign. "That prescript had better be real," he says to me through clenched teeth.

I grab Marsha by the chin and turn her face toward Ferret. "Look at this drool," I say. He retreats back to the bedroom, grinning with the promise of an evening medicated stupor.

Marsha falls back when I release. She works her jaw with a limp wristed, gnarled hand. "I may have taken too many," (4) she says and rattles her pill bottle (15 remaining). Her leg, casted and propped by a perfect metal rod, throbs shades darker than her healthy limbs. She's scrap. The chair wheezes under the burden of Marsha's every struggling breath; given emotions, Invacare would opt for pity.

"Maybe you'd be better on the couch," I say. She agrees, and works her flaccid arm around what remains of my neck. She once latched to this part, happy to have me carry her drunk weight home from a Friday night Eagle's Club party or a daytime neighborhood welfare-rat rally. A few missed attempts to hook me confuses her, though the misjudgment passes with little more ceremony than an exhausted sigh. Once secure, I heave her dead weight from

Invacare and rotate to the couch. Maybe I belong in a meat packaging plant. "How are you feeling?"

Ferret shouts from the back room. "Can I be a woman dressed as a man?"

Eric answers, "shave your beard, then," knowing that Ferret would sooner feign gender confusion than discard his chin's forested bramble. He started growing the bush in junior high to impress his father. After that, he used it to leverage authority with his mother's boyfriends. Eric tried the same tactic once, but his patchy growth didn't intimidate. I echo, "You're going as a woman."

"You've changed," Marsha says, taking my frame in full from her position on the couch. She's beautiful, and I thank the ether that I still recognize that.

"I've been working out." I smile, teeth faded to slate gray, en route to steel, I assume, but the lips around them still stretch for these struggling human emotions. Happiness, still surging, pivots joints and turns wheels. I sweat smog and breathe exhaust. But I still know enough to smile. Smile = happiness.

Marsha reciprocates, hers dampened by the pills but honest. "I mean your body. You're looking less like Mitchell every hour, it seems."

"You haven't seen me for nearly a day."

She nods. "How do you think I'll survive without work for the next two months?" She brings back the smile, an invitation to share in her sarcasm. Humor is something we'll always have; should I break down or crumble to rust, I'll save some grease for belly laughs.

"If you start to miss it," I say, "you can work with me. Ferret says I might be a punch press, like from OLEAN."

"Who will play the part of Dickfuck Rogers?" she says. "Can't be a day at work without his morale-destroying ass."

"Eric. He seems quite the thespian," and at that perfect moment, Eric steps from the hallway in full Marsha garb, accessories wrapped around his neck, his wrists, and tight around his suffocated shame. A pair of strapped white heels gives him the awkward poise of a newborn giraffe. Ferret follows with a weaker attempt, pleated "mom jeans" complete with fupa pouch, from Marsha's postpartum days, and a ruffled blouse that, in the context of a pirate menagerie, could pass for a man's.

"Any respectable tranny would wear this, yea?" Eric says, thrusting a red satined hip toward me.

Marsha blinks away any possible medicinal hallucination and settles on the truth: her son has metamorphosed into a woman. "I can't deal with *both* my men changing on me."

"It's temporary," Eric says, suddenly hostile. "Besides, Mitchell wanted me to."

She meets my glass eyes. I defend: "Fielding said it might help my transition if I were to visit some other transitory types."

"Try next door," Marsha says with a brow furrowed beyond simple annoyance. "Ferret's yard is full of animal machines. A night out with a stuffed bobcat, maybe."

Ferret takes the cue: "Tried that. Believe me; I'm not happy about being in your pants either." Eric forces a comb on him. Ferret accepts, whispering a question regarding the correct side of the head to part tranny hair.

"You're embarrassing," Eric says to Ferret and pulls him back to the bedroom.

I slide closer to Marsha. "You've been fucking a machine for the past week. I figured you of all people would show some acceptance."

"That is willful. You're problem isn't." Marsha lets a few beats pass. "Isn't it?"

"I'm not ready to stop being human," I assure her. "But I'm slipping. What do you imagine I think when I look at you, bandaged and broken, here on the couch?"

"I hope a bit of sympathy."

It's my turn to let a beat pass.

"You don't?" She says, propping herself with her elbows.

"I want to care that I did this to you. Truly. But I don't. And it's empathy, I need. Not sympathy."

She reacts in a way that I recognize as anger, but a disaffecting anger. My joints still move, and it seems such articulation is my sole reason for having been born. Marsha turns from my eyes, lifting herself from the couch, then hops over to Invacare who waits patiently for her captain.

Secured and settled, Marsha manages her way from the living room to the open hallway. She shouts for Eric. He arrives, wearing the same red dress, but an exchanged set of black flat-bottomed shoes. "Why are you still here, if you don't have emotions anymore?"

"I have emotions. I think. I guess I just don't have the capacity for responsibility anymore."

Marsha rides over to her jacket, tossed limp over the kitchen partition banister, and nods toward her son. "You mind taking me to Grandma's before going to your little party?"

Eric stares through me. He answers, never parting from me. "Sure. We'll go right now." He calls for Ferret who follows through the front door, though defensive about going out in his transposed attire while "the sun can still call us out." The door slams shut and all I can wonder is how many more of those before vibrations through the doorknob's screw post rattle the spindle loose.

That, and I muster strength for a few oily tears.

My wig, a bleach-blond version of something Marylyn Monroe might have sculpted had Norma Jean Baker opted for a trailer park instead of Hollywood, reacts to the highway evening breeze in hypnotic algorithms. I'm no longer able to feel the strands whip against my face, but my reflection in the glass of the cab's rear window proves this anthropomorphic wave. My disgust has also waned, and with thanks; this wig has entire gnat colonies squatting within the polyester threads. What more to expect from accoutrement gained through a source Eric reveals only as "a friend with connections."

I ride as the freight on the back of Ferret's flatbed truck, stressing his shocks as his erratic driving stresses my remaining equilibrium. Eric jerks open the sliding cab window and yells above the wind's whistle to "stop being so dramatic." I'm a dog trying to gain footing, the way I glide between wheel hubs.

"Tell Ferret to put a liner on this thing, then."

Ferret takes a break from his stewing anger to acknowledge that, "I didn't expect to cart around a machine capable of bitching."

And ever so appropriately, I respond, "I wasn't expecting to be the machine," but his hand reaches back and slams the widow shut before the retort fully escapes.

"Deer," he yells, barely audible behind the glass. He swerves, suddenly, not to avoid the animal, but to attack it head on, sending me from the truck, rolling into the county road ditch. I'm calculating damage as the earth passes in slow-motion below me. Nothing scrap-worthy results from the impact. The truck screeches to a stop 34 feet ahead before reversing for its prize.

Ferret's truck is outfitted for just this sort of quick-nab product accumulation. An iron grid full of tie downs and bungee cords, and even a floor drain welded at the center of the bed for quick cleaning. He pursues roadkill the way hi-income neighborhood trash days beacon for furniture refurbishing startups. His dining table, once simply too out of style for modern Leawood families, came from just such an event. He's had it for over a decade, and still claims it as the defining anchor to his, as Eric has coined, "Up-tempo Trash" décor. He exploits discarded kitchen cabinets as tool storage and stripped ottomans for taxidermy bases.

From the side of the fallen deer, Ferret yells for me to help him heave the body to his truck. I obey, the way a machine should, I suppose. I have only so many points of articulation, though, and ask Eric for a hand. "I don't help assholes." Ferret removes fur and bits of escaped organ from the radiator grill.

I release the deer's head, prompting Ferret to warn me that cracking an antler will cost me.

"You've never liked me," I say. "Why?"

"This is about my mom, not you."

"Your mom likes me."

"Exactly." He steps from the truck, his mother's wardrobe clashing against the scene: a dead deer, Ferret's beard, and a rusted truck with particle effect smoke billowing from the hood. His wig, a higher quality brunette, obeys the same wind as mine, but with more complex equations manipulating its finer strands. "She told me that you don't care about her anymore."

"This is about your mom, not me."

"You really don't care that you crushed her leg?"

"Bring me the compressor," Ferret says from somewhere in the falling evening dark.

Eric unlatches the air compressor's tank from the back of the truck, stepping over.

"I want to care. Did she tell you that part?"

"Then care."

"Think about it this way: you're dressed like a woman, but you aren't really a woman."

He lugs the compressor toward Ferret's cursing grumble.

"Why were you born a man? Chance, right? Well, I don't even have the idea of chance to explain what has happened to me."

"How did this happen to you?"

"That's not the point."

"Just throw the fucking thing in the truck," Ferret yells above air blasts. We fall silent, lift and secure the body amid a web of quickly-wrapped bungee cords. Our dissidence makes for a shoddy job, one Ferret inspects, regrets, and corrects within the span of a single aggravated breath leaving two tie-downs unlatched. "Get in the cab," he says to Eric. "Snuggle up next to the body," he says to me. I climb up and cradle the limp deer. He secures the remaining tie-downs around me, and we're back on the road before the opening verse of a Winebox song fades. All of this, seemingly simultaneous.

The body and I share the road's rhythm in different ways. Her succumbing to pot holes with a gelatinous acceptance. Me, matching every bump in form and depth, with only the truck's shock absorbers to cushion my sway. I still have some pliable skin, but only in concept; call it a rubber veneer. "I'm Mitchell," I tell the deer, name her Molly. In a shared assembly line, manufactured deco way, I am her, that limp meat on its way to a dog bowl. And like Daisy, Molly houses stoic eyes, already glassy and dead. "Do you know Daisy, the llama?"

A dangerous swerve rocks her head *no*.

"I caught her at the end. Unfortunately, I suspect, as she seemed a fine specimen. She's a machine now, like me in reverse. Like you will be. But life is gone, not to come back. I wish you could have been warned to hold on to those eyes, but they are already gone. Machines can create a semblance of life." Eric and Ferret harmonize the *I miss the old girl in the frame* chorus, a first shared smile since our stop. "But *you*, the you your family, your drinking buddies, your girlfriend knew, is gone." As the song winds down, camaraderie has patched their hostilities. What I wouldn't give for the capacity to forget. In my head, every scene is a complex schematic with rules and procedures, etched forever as an infinite basis for comparison. Eric will always have yelled, and from that outburst I'll compare future outbursts. Ferret will always have killed Molly; how much more will he kill? The world becomes referent files, archived for use as emotional interpretation. Yelling. Anger

What is that?
Which one We squeal into the lamp-lit St. Patrick's
Any of them What are they? Hospital parking lot, where in the basement awaits a collection of transgender and cross-dressing specimens the three of us have convinced ourselves will certainly share in our costumed appearance. Though, out of the truck and into the light, we exchange a sudden realization that perhaps we will be the night's freaks. Eric, the cleanest of all of us, appears barely formatted for a frat party Halloween. He's satisfied, though, by comparison. Ferret's white blouse is camouflage-patched in mud and deer blood, with his beard and cheeks dyed to compliment. I'm a three-hundred pound punch press with a spaghetti-strapped satin shirt draped around a couple flywheels. For the first time, in the imminent eyes of supposed kindreds, I've grasped a complex. "I can't do this."

Ferret ducks back into the truck with a laugh buried in his tattered beard. Eric interrupts his friend's relief with a simple, "You have to."

"I'm a fucking machine," I say.

Ferret calls from the cab: "I've seen pornos like that. You could do one of those."

"If you don't do this, you're scrap."

I could rust in a junkyard as well as anywhere, I suppose. But I've still got a nagging human purpose buried somewhere within these bolts and rivets. "But I empathize enough to be embarrassed. That's got to count for something."

"It does. But I'm not letting you get by with mere embarrassment. Remember the fundamental commonality here. We're all pre-op, en route to something different."

"The Sybian, it's called," Ferret yells. "Check yourself for a rubber cock."

"What are you saying?" I ask.

"We're all changing, I mean. Child to adult. Student to teacher. Son to brother-in-law.

Man to woman. You've got a tougher journey, sure, but we've all got the journey."

"To brother-in-law?" I regret the question even as it leaves me. But Eric, for my sake or his, feigns deafness and allows a breath for me to cover. "I already have these clothes. We're already here. I suppose we should keep going."

Ferret yells from his widow. "Can I wait out here?" Who the hell are these guys?

"And forfeit the prescript, yes."

He steps from his truck, shame still turning down the corners of his mouth. Eric and I receive him with amused welcome. The three of us, together, slink through the damp parking lot night toward a sliding door manned by a lone podium-stationed security guard. He's armed with a roll of pink nametag stickers, primed to attach them to our chests, but we part the night, claiming his rapt attention. He drops the roll. "Hurry," he says, excited by our blood, it seems, rounding to the front of the podium. "Emergency room is around the other side, but I can escort you through the halls." He grabs for Ferret's arm, a true Good Samaritan in his dismissal of our dress and my weight. It's the blood that fuels him.

Ferret pulls away. "It's not ours, jackass. Just point us to the basement."

I still know laughter. We indulge in this boisterous communal grease en-route to the basement, spilling along the way our individual fantasies regarding the blood's origin. Eric imagines having fought a stranger, something he claims he's always wanted to do. Me, I imagine Ferret dying, though I don't know why; he reacts to my faux attribution with a shallow "fuck you." We arrive before Ferret has time to retaliate.

From behind the door, structured conversation halts our nonchalant approach. Voices murmur in turns while a single, smooth voice, governs the exchanges. "This feels like school," Eric says. "I don't like it."

You're being who you are

Who I think I am

I turn the doorknob and force him through. "We're here to learn," I say.

Who do you think you are

That's why I'm here

Our barrage freezes all remaining chatter, these masculine voices belied by feminine dress held fast behind confused Adam's apples, waiting for even a single syllable from us intruders. "Gender confusion?" Eric asks.

This is the Transupport Group," says the smooth-voiced man, spackled in beige makeup, but wearing a conservative pantsuit in stark contrast to the flamboyance around him. He looks fresh-picked from a downtown Hubert loft. The radiating bits of solemn performance art around him are planted in metal folding-chairs, holding coffee and interrupted tears. "We're not the confused ones. Please, have a seat."

We approach the huddle, our heavy steps echoing against the Formica paneled hospital basement walls. Elmer's craft paste and janitorial sweat stain the air. A bookshelf stuffed with spines, none wider than a number four machine screw leans against the far wall, atop a rug patterned with Ark animals. Some sanctuary. A hospital basement used as a Sunday School. Eric divides Ferret and me for an open chair next to a bloated, glittered specimen, name tag:

Dynasty. I follow, and Ferret behind me, like skittish animals wary of the dinner table.

Dynasty smiles, then looks to the pantsuited leader for address.

"I'm Tom," the leader says.

A brief AA tour three years ago taught Eric and me to rouse group morale with exaggerated, choral greetings. Our "Hi Tom," though lacks the backing of the group, so we suffer an awkward, spotlit silence. All eyes shift back to the leader, unable to navigate themselves out of our apparent faux pas.

Tom gestures toward open chairs. "You aren't very late, but we have already introduced ourselves. How about the three of you go. Tell us your names and anything else you'd like to share."

Colored construction paper scraps decorate the ground, the shrapnel from an earlier Bible study, no doubt. Eric leverages the lead and begins: "I'm a kindergarten teacher by day. But at night they call me Majesty." He pronounces his ridiculous name with a practiced flourish. The room, largely offended by his and our quickly-fading ruse, waits for more. But he retreats.

Eyes fall to Ferret. "I'm Ferret. And I don't want to be here."

Back to the leader. "This isn't a twelve-step thing, Ferret. This is a community. You don't have to be here."

"Thanks," and as Ferret leaves he whispers to Eric and I that he will be waiting in the truck, stripping wig, blouse, and shoes as he escapes the circle.

Eric and I fall back to Tom, who allows Ferret's exit before speaking. "People like us are maligned daily. This is our place to be safe and open. We don't appreciate ridicule."

"We're maligned," I say.

Tom settles, surprised, it seems, to hear me speak. Eric, too, awaits elaboration.

"Until recently, I lived as any number of others. I was normal. But what is normal, right?" The overt sympathy card weasels a few slow nods from the crowd. "But against my will, perhaps by the will of society, perhaps by the will of some other invisible hand, I changed. But I wasn't meant to change. I want to go back to who I was."

Deep nods resound. Tom asks me to continue, says "We're listening. We don't judge appearance here." Like an ear is all I've ever needed. "You're not the first one like you that we've had here."

Tom's approval coaxes me further. "I have a friend in the same situation. Molly. She describes it like getting hit by a highway truck at 70 miles per hour."

Eric sneaks a knowing grin my way.

"One day, she has life planned. She's fine with day-to-day monotony, content with simply existing, the only intrusions being on her terms. Then, she's hit, blood everywhere. Hospital and therapy imminent. She knows she won't be the same. But still, she knows there are options. One: accept whatever is coming to her. If she's a vegetable for the rest of her life, so be it. If some maniac wants to stuff her full of gears and actuators, let it happen." Eric widens his grin, slowly morphing from a nod to a subtle head shake. "Or Two: remember who you were before and try like goddamn to keep that spark. I'm here because I want option two." The words pour as if born from those feelings I thought had fallen away. Most heads continue their shallow nods, and those that don't are frozen in search. They are me, and I, somewhere, am they.

"Exactly," Tom says. "We're all trapped, against our own terms, and yearning to be ourselves. On that, let's break."

Eric rises before any other and whispers that he's "hitting the can before a freak contaminates the toilet," disappearing through a hallway door, grasping a nervous handful of his dress's hem. I'm left with the echo of Molly's story still lingering. Cliques congregate around me, without me, in small whispered huddles. High School did the same, though with less overt gender confusion.

Content enough with the simple act of sharing, I make my way toward the toilet as

What is it?

Male, I guess.

No, species

You're better than that, Arthur.

well; if anything I can at least mock Eric from the hallway for pissing in a dress. Though I shouldn't push him too hard; he did stick around for the humiliation.

Vending machines illuminate the otherwise dark hallway, beckoning evening cravers into sodium and sucrose comas. I've had little taste for sweets since the start of my transformation, a strange reaction I credit to my streamlined need for oil only. Fats work for me. Sugars just gum up the works. I could use some coffee, though, which feels strangely cannibalistic.

Adjacent the neon soda vendor sits a per-cup Brio coffee machine. A strange sense of pride overwhelms, a sense that this very machine could have come from me. The logic falters, but the kindred embrace smoothes over such simple chronological inaccuracies. I match its edges against my elbow's antecubital pit. The selection button holes meet my die-casting finger clamps. The bean grinder shelf, my own shoulder. My chest, when I lean close enough to caress, takes in the subtle convexed façade as an equal species. I could have made this.

"**How about a cup?**" I turn quick, Dynasty grins a mouthful of stained gray teeth. I release the Brio and stammer for an explanation.

"**Mitchell, right?**"

The voice carries a confident history, its tone and pitch wisdom-saturated. This voice isn't like any other, but at the same time reeks of every voice I have ever heard.

Man or woman, I can't tell. Where most of Tom's emotionally-vested clientele are obvious, this one traffics in a delicate limbo. It looks, it smells, and when I shake its hand, feels androgynous. "Dynasty?"

"**Not my real name. But trust me, it's a step up. Those parents of mine have a sense of humor.**"

"I could use a laugh. What is it?"

Dynasty grins. "**What about that cup of coffee?**"

"I think I *am* this machine," I say and pretend to search non-existent pockets for change. This burgeoning friend rescues me with a dollar and together we wait, the steam spilling. "Needs a tune up," I say.

The tranny pulls my cup of Spanish roast and sips before releasing it to me. **"I'll go for something more delicate,"** and punches a few quick buttons for a new cup. **"Tell me more about this Molly,"** heavy breath rolling the steam.

"She chose option two." Eric's linoleum-echo whistle creeps from under the bathroom door, shoe taps and off-key hums to the tune of radio pop comfort. I think of Minneapolis airport bathrooms and imagine a laugh. Whispers of other trannies float, seemingly oblivious to human ears.

"I worked on a farm once, most of my life, really," Dynasty says, steam gathering into bulbs of beige foundation at the forehead. **"Out there, I could do pretty much anything I wanted, with only my father, maybe my mother to piss on me. Then I move to the city. At home, on the farm, I didn't heed a**

support group. There're a lot more fingers to point at me in the city."

"So you would have taken number one?"

"I won't say that. It's just important to remember that there are always two options."

The toilet gargles. Eric escapes the bathroom, whispers of olfactory warning on his lips, before noticing Dynasty standing beside me. The neon vending machines camouflage the tranny's comparatively dim makeup and uniform. Eric smiles, then turns to me. "Who the fuck is Molly?"

Dynasty, not yet one I'm urged to impress, hears me straight: "The deer."

"You gave it a name?" Eric says, still adjusting his pantyhose.

"And a back-story. What's with the disbelief? You're the full human, here. Understand me."

Dynasty sips the coffee before pitching in. "That explains the blood." S/he motions toward our costumes, forces our self-examination. "Tom isn't buying the routine. And it is a routine. You aren't the first citizens to voyeur for a sniff of the Other."

"Edward Said?" I say, impressed by the reference.

"Sarte's application is a bit more apt, here. But yeah, when there is the Other, there is self-consciousness. If only we could all live on desolate farms. Without the judgmental family, of course."

Dynasty's apparent knowledge of the mind invigorates the idea of an emotional reconnection. It's tactile. Possible. "How do the Others reconnect with everyone else?" I ask.

"Why Molly?" Eric says. "Give it a better name if you're crazy enough to give it a name in the first place."

"It's not about reconnecting, sometimes. It can be about connecting for the first time, to a new group. Transupport, for example."

"But Molly wants to stay Molly."

"Bambi," Eric hunts the vending selection, mutters disapproval. Though, I'd be surprised if he had any money, let alone the intent to purchase. "Bambi isn't original, but it makes sense at least."

"Molly," Dynasty says with a knowing facetiousness, **"she may have to revisit those needed connections personally. Go back to something from before the change."**

"Bruce. Bruce is a good name."

"Daisy."

Eric shakes his head. "That was the llama, right? Don't recycle."

"No," I take another sip of the Spanish blend and let the oils lubricate my vessels. "I could take Daisy back to her owner."

"Good luck tearing that thing away from Ferret."

"He turns living things into machines. I have some authority with that."

"Just the llama. All the others are inanimate." Finding nothing, he takes to stabbing random buttons in hopes for treasure.

"I think it could help."

"Don't go fucking PETA on me. You've already got blood on your clothes."

not going to make it long
how long?
not long

"I loved Marsha. Then I became a machine. Now I don't. You can't argue that I didn't fall apart somewhere in there. What about the owner of the llama? I'm sure the llama cares for him."

Dynasty drops to a chair hidden in the hallway corner. **"You've got to try things. We get ideas for a reason."**

"I once imagined fucking a cantaloupe." Eric presses a final button. "Fuck," and kicks the lit front panel dark, splitting the plastic from top down to dispense slot. A few panicked curses later and Beige Tom appears, insisting first that the two of us leave, and asking second if we are hurt. Dynasty rips a malignant bolt from my leg and lies about a slick floor and spilling blood. She ushers us past Tom on an implied emergency room mission, swearing that she will ensure our health. Tom is a fading memory by the time we meet Ferret at his truck, and Dynasty too is a long forgotten nothing. Where are my memories going?

Ferret has annexed the parking lot as a mortician's table, ripping into Molly already, bookending the carcass with piles of organ and bone. He's dyed his blouse brown and red, and displays a sloppy carnivore's beard. "You guys are quick," he says.

"Likewise," Eric toes around the estuaried blood puddles radiating from under the truck.

I stay smart and silent, thankful that of all the things I'm losing, I'm at least growing in the ability to rationalize my decisions; an argument now would be hard theft later tonight. Besides, Eric and I are going to play this robbery like family.

Last night I dreamt of Twinkies. It was my job to inject the crème filling. I think it was a wet dream.

The couch accepted me well enough, as did Marsha's bed—now I'm relegated to the floor for weight reasons—but I still feel the part of an abstraction in a world of realism.

When Dr. Fielding first consulted his Dr. Something nemesis for a gulped pride session and a few ounces of direction regarding my curious condition, I sat back and daydreamed in comfortable repetition. My head straddled an edge between human and machine, floating amid the mutual appreciation of ambient loops and their mathematical logic. The air vent hum, a distant car alarm, and layers of wind-rustled leaves appeasing both halves of my schismed brain.

Dr. Something, his voice loud through the phone or perhaps my hearing attuned, assured Fielding that my head would break down as an Asberger's patient, swollen by logic and zapped of any social dictionary. Fielding thanked the man and hung up with yet another pilfered diagnosis on his lips. Fielding wanted to be a veterinarian. I just wanted to stay human. Things happen and we react as well as we are programmed to. Hang in there, Mitchell.

This morning I search to regain that relaxed monotony hidden in the outside wind, in the window unit air conditioner hum, in the dying refrigerator compressor, perhaps beneath layers even my attuned, though still transitory being cannot permeate.

Like a statistical spike, Marsha's head peeks above the couch back. She controls the TV in fixed bursts, color, black transition, color, black transition... Her pattern pulls me from the search for my own.

She spins. A frown to most would mean sadness. A frown to me should mean nothing. So when I approach Marsha's frown I do so with a contradicting smile, happy that I still understand her anger.

The night shed my feet for riveted base plates and my ribs for rubber belts. I'm still wearing Marsha's camisole shirt, making for a machine fetishist's dream incarnate. Marsha tempts with an amused grin, a sign I anticipate as a gesture of wanted forgiveness. "Do you care yet?" she asks. She holds a dripping spoon above a bowl of soggy cereal, the TV remote dropped to her lap.

I'm not programmed to lie. "No."

She takes a bite, slurping the milk through terse lips. Forgiveness dissipated.

"But I have an idea. Give me this last one." I slide to Invacare's base, the floor's planks bowing beneath me. The stressed house wheezes at my every shift. Invacare is war-torn already, dressed in the battle scuffs and dents of a learning cripple. Marsha's fingers bleed and her palms reflect a Neosporin shine. Her cast, an ancient plaster model, holds the inscriptions of well-wishers, most names I don't recognize, likely known but now forgotten. "You should be more careful," I say, on behalf of Marsha or Invacare, I don't know. yeah, he still lives there

"The idea," she says.

"I'm going to return Ferret's llama to its owner."

"I've seen the posters." Marsha tips the cereal slush to her mouth and slurps to bloated cheeks before swallowing. "I betcha the reward's not money."

"All I need is a reaction. Maybe I've just forgotten how to empathize. An instant turn from stale sadness to absolute horror may be just the shock I need. Like, a child is proud to display living room wall crayon drawings until a parent's reaction makes him understand how shitty the picture is."

"I could fake that."

"Crushing your leg didn't fix me. Pantomime won't either."

"Ferret says we should sell you for scrap." She exchanges her empty bowl for the TV remote. With her free hand she picks a forgotten refrigerator magnet from the couch and flings it my way. The dull, metallic thump punctuates the stale air between us."

"When did you talk to Ferret?" I leave the magnet.

"He's been saying it for days. Said we could get a lot out of you. Hundreds."

"Hundreds?"

"He says you're full of some pretty desired parts." The TV flickers, brightens to a home remodeling program.

I slide to interrupt Marsha's already zombied TV stare, forcing her gaze to my glass orbs. "If this doesn't work," I say, finding my grayed face in her eyes, "maybe you could sell me, instead, to the OLEAN plant. They might put you back on the line. I'd like to know we'll still be together."

She treats the gesture with a malaise I have come to recognize in other machines. "Just like a machine can't care about me, I can't care about a machine. If this doesn't work, I'm trading you in for a plasma TV."

"Wait for me," I plead and take her hand. She screams. I've clamped hard, torn the skin. I pull away, watch blood fill the gaps among my metacarpal bolts.

Eric bursts through the front door, no concern, only news that Ferret is awake and likely itching for a morning bowl. "Let Operation: Take Back the Machine commence."

He drops back to the porch, letting the screen door slam shut behind him. I credit Eric's 180 to a breakthrough at Transupport...or the dime bag I promised him.

Marsha's eyes pool. She measures my concern by the depth of my facial nuances, what facial muscle I have left to manipulate. I replicate sadness, but not well enough. "Leave," she says, and wheels to the kitchen for an icepack.

I still know your smell, Marsha. You do not need a hard hat around me yet.

Through the cracked back door I peek over to Ferret's property. Eric already has him distracted with a front porch roach and a promised lead on parts for his other projects: a golf cart drive shaft for a rolling St. Bernard found dead in a cross town ditch, and a pump value for a bird bath built with the birds' corpses, neither of which exist, but Ferret takes the news with absolute conviction. I wait at Marsha's back step for the agreed sign of abandon: a brisk cough, which hacks through the air on the ruse of a sharp inhale.

I leave Marsha alone and move toward Ferret's shed in hopes that this departure will not become abandonment. She inhales tears and mucus, sending her sad echo into the outside, as I carve a grass path to our mechanized llama. Those sobs mingle amid the laughter now spewing from Ferret's front porch. Laughter = happiness. Sob = sadness. See also *frown*, *tears*.

The shed air smells of rust and oil. Or perhaps me. I'm part of the ambient lifelessness, frozen wrenches, still sockets, a stiff saw nailed to the wall. Awaiting purpose. *Stay human, Mitchell.*

Daisy sits center stage, surrounded by discarded tools and stripped wire sheaths. She is the armored nucleus, sure to soon be shrapnel under Ferret's pyrotechnic direction. She grows fuses. She sprouts cannons. I have seen Ferret destroy buildings with less.

Her fur gives, but I feel no skin. I remember the sense coarse hair should allow, but I feel nothing. No ground, no weight, no air. And the smell too has suddenly disappeared.

Human, Mitchell.

I repurpose a mud-lacquered garden hose and hitch the statued body to my own. Our escape comes clean, trekking through backyards and concrete overflow ditches, cloaked by the reliable disinterest neighborhood of stoners. Ferret laughs a dying wail. The llama follows behind me, obedient to the tether and graceful despite the pebbled ground and recycled casters (from shopping carts, the best I can tell). Its armaments entice ignition at every jarring step. Weathered posters measure my journey, most devoid of the llama's likeness, washed of all ink, just flimsy flaps of paper advertising nothing. The neighborhood too appears withered.

The llama's home just nicks the periphery of our neighborhood, a positive x coordinate to Marsha's negative. And as the opposing geography would imply, the home's crisp landscaping and pristine blue paint job contrast Marsha's weed garden and stripped wooden siding. I wonder how Ferret got as far as he did without rousing suspicion. A home like this keeps motion lights for people like Ferret. Likewise, how am I so invisible? And at that thought, just as I spot the house at the end of the block, a young girl rides up beside me on a yellow bike with patriotic handlebar streamers, limp despite the subtle breeze. I guess age nine by her boyish chest and willingness to engage a stranger. "Hey," she says, pedaling softly to maintain pace with my increasingly rigid gait. Is this what it feels like to rust? I check my frame, no rust anywhere. Is this then, what it feels like to lose a heartbeat? I ignore her; I do not need further suspicion. But she persists, riding now in front of me and craning back. "What are you doing with that?"

A few words cannot hurt. "Bringing it back to its owner. Do you know the owner?"

"What is it?"

"A llama. A dead one."

She slows her pedal at 'dead.' "Ms. Gregor use to have a llama. But it ran away."

"Does she live there?" I say, and motion toward the blue house.

The girl nods. "Why are you bringing it back?" She circles me now, a curiosity devoid of social tact favoring questions upon questions upon—"Did you kill the llama? What happened to it? Why are you metal?"

"It died. Have you ever had a pet die?"

She ponders. "I dropped a frog once, in the toilet. Mom says he's probably still alive."

"He is dead," I say and search her face for reaction.

"It's not dead," she says, less dread and more anger in her voice.

I push. "What if I could show you the dead frog? Would you believe me?"

"That wouldn't be the same frog."

I push harder. "What if I found your frog in the toilet, pulled it out, and then stomped on it myself? Then how would you feel?"

She considers the thought but shrugs. "I didn't really like that frog, anyway."

My knees are locking, letting only my hips push forward. "What about me? Do I scare you?" The house taunts me.

She shakes her head. "I've seen machines before. My mom's boyfriend works on trucks."

"Grab this hose for me," I say and flex my right clamp. As I meld into streamlined inevitability, all superfluous joints fading, I enlist the help of the girl. But, as one machine surveying the workings of another, I am conscious now of her weak-shouldered youth. I instead bend down to her bike and tie the hose. "Can you pull this to that house?" She nods. "Ring the doorbell, too." And she is off, sweating for the sake of a machine, like a perfect assembly line station.

She breaches the entrance gate, the llama trailing behind on surprising bearings. The entire yard, so obvious now, exists as a home for the llama. A shelter, treated wood and felt-underlined shingles. A trough, packed with hay. I still recognize what should be love. *Stay human, Mitchell.*

Suddenly, a desperate "hey" calls from behind. Ferret vibrates the ground at my rear, huffing a poorly-paced trot, intelligible commands robbing his weak breath. "You're scrap!" it sounds like.

I tell the girl to hurry. I think it, perhaps. My jaw hardens to an elbow bracket. She turns back, her eyes questioning motivation, but furious Ferret scares her forward. She is at the door. Presses the doorbell. Paralyzed, as I am, for a reaction.

The door opens to a woman, her friendly grin interrupted by the trailing llama. "Daisy." She cries. No reaction more human.

"Scrap!" Ferret yells, and all the world dissolves to schematics.

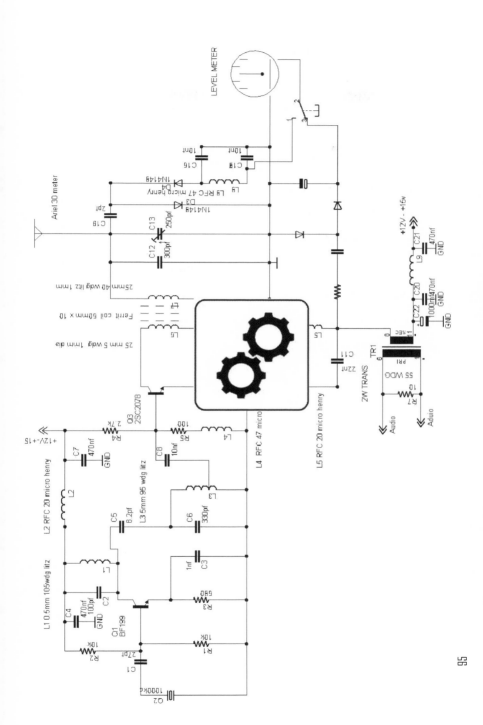

LEVEL METER

Ariel 30 meter

Ferrit coil 50mm x 10

25mm 40 wdg litz 1mm

25 mm 5 wdg 1mm dia

L4

L6

Q3
2SC207B

2.7K
R4

100
R5

10nf
C8

L4 RFC 47 micro

L4 RFC 47 micro

C11
22nf

L5 RFC 20 micro henry

L5

1N4149
D3

L9 RFC 47 micro henry

L9

1N4149
D4

10nf
C16

10nf
C18

2pf
C19

250pf
C13

300pf
C12

C7
470nf
GND

L2

L2 RFC 20 micro henry

C5
8.2pf

L3 5mm 95 wdg litz

L3

C6
300pf

L1 0.5mm 105wdg litz

C4
470nf
GND

100pf
C2

L1

C3
1nf

Q1
BF199

R3
680

R1
10K

R2
10K

27pf
C1

Q2
1000Kc

TR1
2W TRANS

SS WDG

PRI

SEC

R7
10

Audio

Aduio

C22
1000nf
GND

C20
470nf
GND

L9

C21
470nf
GND

+12V - +15v

+12V - +15

E: I assure you mom, he tried

M: But did he assure me?

E: It was Ferret. Mitchell was afraid to ask for the llama.

M: And this, this is all you could get from him? A piece of metal...what is this?

E: A screw or something. Ferret would be pissed if he knew I had this much.

M: I'll hang a picture with it.

E: Mom.

M: Eric.

E: Did you do this to him?

M: I don't know how to be human any more than you do or he did. Maybe he simply failed...I could have. Sure. Maybe.

E: How's your leg?

M: This chair is a godsend. I wouldn't feel human without it.

Parts

globe valve

These downtown Hubert Lofts hijacked my young horizons. Two renegade weeds from an otherwise clean, though admittedly barren, lawn split the earth years ago to strangle the clouds and occupy our family photograph backgrounds; pictures rendered good enough for Mom's wall, but always heavy with commentary. "I'd love to have raised you downtown, Eric," she said too often. "We're not even cultured enough for the suburbs to claim us." Seeing the towers reminded us that we didn't live in them.

From Tom's loft balcony, my mother's home doesn't exist. The tree canopy and church steeple distractions erase that life, leaving a view washed of all but green and stone. Tom uses words like *quaint* and *dismal* when measuring to my mother's distant horizon.

"I don't know," I tell Tom. "Distant maybe. But I wouldn't say quaint." I inhale from my converted globe valve pipe, let the smoke waft beyond the railing. A breeze tangles my blond cancer wig, my mother's. Tom inhales, denies the smoke from escaping our contrived conversation. I'm not gay, neither am I a habitual cross-dresser, but for a chance to walk these lofts I can pretend. Mom always wanted to know how these people lived. So far, mom, I'd use words like *aromatic* and *chic*. "That's a nice pipe you have there," Tom says.

"I stole it from a friend. He's got a nose for things like this."

Tom lifts a highball from a table at his knee. "Must have been a good friend." He drinks.

"I stole it."

Silence from each neighboring wall saves the moment. The only sound to fight our discomfort and the steady winter air is Tom's own stereo, spewing ambient jazz he calls "superb."

"I don't know," I tell him. "Annoying maybe. But I wouldn't call it superb."

He touches the highball to his lips, considers it but returns the glass to the table. "Why even agree to come up here?"

"Honestly? My mother and I have a bet. She says people who live in lofts are artistic types with good taste."

"And…"

"So far, I'm winning."

He plants into one of the two metal-worked chairs behind us and reaches back to power on a dim overhanging bulb. The light reflects against the textured metal, camouflaging his balcony nook with the same stars haunting over us. We are floating, defying gravity and ascension alike. "Owning a loft *is* in good taste, wouldn't you say?"

I can feel his eyes against my back. Another inhale, exhale leaves acrid smoke hovering thick in front of us, a limbo between the asphalt below and the spotted night above. "Owning a loft for the right reasons is in good taste, yes. Owning a loft to fuck rookie trannies is not."

Tom swats a mosquito at his neck. "Since when is fucking a wrong reason?"

"This," I gesture with my chin toward his living room, a sweeping motion to describe the aging bachelor's entire life, "should be a perfect existence. You've got a couch upholstered in rabbit fur, walls filled with artists only other perfect people know, and a view that could kill lesser men. Why can't you see this?"

"Are you saying I'm one of those lesser men?"

"Do you call this perfect?"

"I've lived with better views," he says. "And I don't have a pipe that nice."

"There are no better views. Have you ever truly looked out there?" I extend my arm over the railing, the pipe at my clenched fist, and sweep the black skyline. "Have you ever envied—"

but I'm stripped of the pipe by a falling body, a blur of skin and fabric piercing the blanket of smoke. Within a single heartbeat, a body goes from being one of the Earth's residents to just one of its craggy imperfections.

Tom knocks his drink to the ground as he rushes to the railing. "Shit," he says, no taste, no art to his reaction "Did he jump?" I swear I met the body's eyes, received a wink and a confident smile. I still feel his cotton collar, his belt buckle, his laces against my fingertips. "Who the fuck was that?" Tom says pacing the balcony, this neck still craned over the edge. "You live here," I say.

Fresh light from the first floor neighbor's deck illuminates Tom's face. He's sneaking a grin amid his concern. "I don't know everybody," he says. "Should I call an ambulance?"

I keep my seat to maintain poise. "Do you know anybody?"

The first floor light flicks off. No observance beyond that simple dismissal. The darkness releases Tom back from the edge. He a claims the opportunity for a lesson: "See, this lifestyle isn't perfect. It drives some people mad." I pull away. "Yes it is. Those people just don't live it right." "I'm calling an ambulance," he says and kicks aside his fallen highball as he enters the loft.

Should I look? I have never seen a dead human, not outside my head, and morbid curiosity can be a persuasive demon. After all, I'm enduring this loft, aren't I? The smoke has dissipated entirely,

leaving not even a fog to mask the stars. Even that man's final destructive wake has died. I wonder how long he spent aiming for these lofts only to one day aim for its ground.

Tom pokes his head outside. "Ambulance is on its way." He pulls back in but stops. "I'm going down there. If your pipe survived, can I have it?"

I shrug, nod, and watch him leave with this still smuggled tiny grin. On the way out, I steal a painting from his wall—Mother's Day approaches—and head to the stairwell for a rear exit.

Figure 9a. A Fable | **Figure 9b. Cup Stacks**

I once worked alongside a piece named Frank. Something the service text called a spot welding bit, but he preferred Frank. We worked well together. In sync, in fact **(See Figure 9a).**

Frank had himself a minor family. A wife who supported him from above **(See Figure 9b)**. A child who supported him from below **(See Figure 9c)**. Per programming, he was perfectly content amid daily repetition. He had hopes, as most parents do, that his child would match his steps, would find contentment amid the world's hums and cranks and rubber belts. "A child," he said, as often as his greased joints culled the factory line, "is our next generation" **(See figure 9d).**

Frank met his wife here, long after having already embraced a cyclic life. He was happy, and having a wife only made him more efficient. Then came the child, and Frank whirred like a brand new model. A nuclear

A child is
generati
child is o
generati
is our ne
our next
A child is
child is o
next gen
is our ne
A child is
generati

Figure 9d

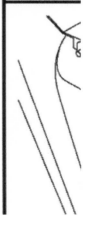

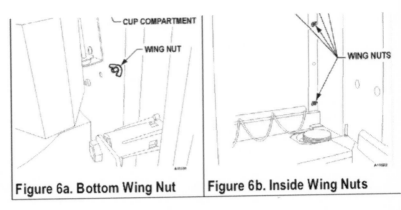

| Figure 6a. Bottom Wing Nut | Figure 6b. Inside Wing Nuts |

family, if you will, Frank v2.5. So this neighbor, he lost all bachelor rationale. Even those old bolts of his shined once the next generation arrived.

But one morning, after powering on, I passed the day's first component down the line, not to Frank, but to a version of Frank who called himself Sam. "I am Sam," he said without hesitation, as though I shared his first-day disorientation, his fresh ambition.

This version shined **(See Figure 6c)**. Sam lacked the grizzled, dusty morning makeup of most the line. Standard, or seemingly so, cobweb and grease accoutrement resisted his perfect veneer. Peel that surface away, and I assume even greater efficiency. "I am early generation," I told him, passing along components 20 and 21. "What happened to Frank?"

Sam received the components, processed them, and fed them further down the line. "I do not know

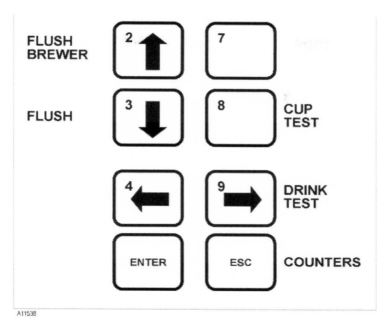

FLUSH BREWER [2 ↑] [7]

FLUSH [3 ↓] [8] **CUP TEST**

[4 ←] [9 →] **DRINK TEST**

[ENTER] [ESC] **COUNTERS**

A11538

Fig 2.1

a Frank, to be frank." He manufactured a joke. "But truly, I do not know Frank." He awaited more parts.

I met Frank my first day, after having been installed as part of a selective upgrade. He asked me where Clyde went. I never knew a Clyde. He told me Clyde was first generation, had sat at this very line even during the original product launch. The way Frank described him Clyde could very well have paved life for all of us. Clyde had no family. "Frank had a family. A wife and a child. Do you have any family?"

Sam received components 40 and 41. "I never gave it much thought. You?" He awaited more parts.

"No family." Frank's and my relationship endured our

initial animosity. Though I replaced Clyde, Frank swore he had never worked with anyone as well as he worked with me. I am not ready to see that off. "Frank was like family to me."

Clyde accepted components 50 and 51. "I can be your family. We can be brothers." He awaited more parts.

"Father and son," I said.

"Sure." Sam hesitated for two beats. "But hurry it up, old man." He claimed another joke, awaiting more parts.

"I am moving as fast as programmed," I said, and immediately realized the inevitable.

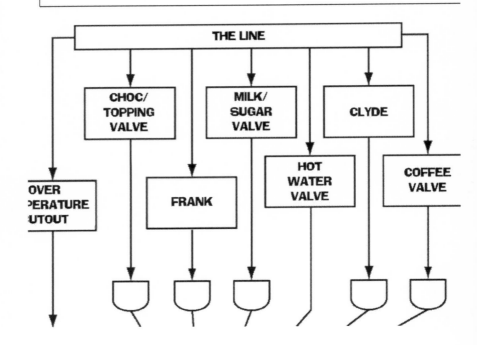

Popular theory supports that you created us in order to satiate an inherent desire for automation. But who created your desire? In a two-level hierarchy, we are the same, one step below God. But of course, you will not settle for just two levels. So you created a third: God, human, tool. We do not mind. We are not programmed to mind, after all.

But we are not so different. Limbs. Articulation points. Manuals. Yours: biology texts. Mine: service texts. The truth is that neither of us knows much of our own composition, despite the mountains of literature that attempt explanation. We simply act according to the maps of previous generations and hope that we will be the parts to patch genetic/schematic faults. Your cancer is our rust. Your death is our obsolescence.

Sam had not yet known what I eventually realized, and that following day I awoke not along my OLEAN home, but along the line of a startup baking factory that specialized in off-brand, crème-filled pastries. My neighbor asked me where Mike was. "I do not know a Mike," I said. This neighbor dusted rust from his façade and passed parts 1 and 2 my way.

Fig 5.
Maxims:
1 - Family is a valid contribution. Never underestimate human capital.
2 - Lock
3 - Coin slot
4 - Never forget that what you do today influences tomorrow.
5 - Alphanumeric display
6 - Spaces for instruction labels
7 - Selection menu
8 - Morning can bring you anywhere. Get to know your neighbors.
9 - Free vend and jug facilities key
10 - Coin return
11 - Prearrangement for payment systems or labels

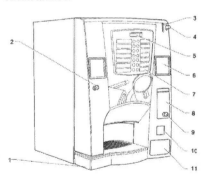

Fig. 5

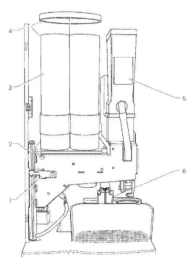

Fig. 6

malignant bolt

(ding)

Twenty-five years, and you've[1] had the same fucking[2] golf balls on your[3] wall. Too many. [4]

I think my family[5] finally got the hint that I[6] don't collect golf balls[7].

Maybe if I get you[8] another display case[9], they'd start up again[10]. Your birthday is coming up.[11]

Don't make me[12] shave your head.[13] Have a seat. [14]

Twenty-five years. How many times[15] have you heard "just[16] a trim"[17]?

From you? Too many. [18] Time for you to get rid of that mane. [19] In a dark bar, I[20] would mistake you for an[21] ugly woman[22].

≡

The less you cut, the less[23] work you have to do[24]. Not too many people can operate[25] scissors for a few minutes[26] and get away with twenty dollars[27].

Not too many people are going to[28] tolerate someone like you[29], even for those few minutes[30].

Just cut. [31]

(snip)

This shit keeps growing. [32] Why is that? They[33] teach you the biology[34] of hair in[35] barber school?[36]

I'm a stylist. [37]

They teach it to you? [38]

No other animal grows[39] hair like we do[40]. You don't see monkeys [41] chopping locks [42] with sharpened stones[43].

Do monkeys even[44] sharpen stones[45]? Humans do. [46]

I don't know[47], they didn't[48] teach it to me[49].

(snip)

When someone sits down and says[50], "just a trim,"[51] does it even register anymore? [52] You're a barber [53] to everyone. Just a[54] guy who cuts hair[55]. You're programmed for it.[56]

I'm a stylist. [57]

(snip)

How do you know the moment you cease to be human?[58] They teach you that?[59]

It's too early for that shit.[60]

(snip)

Listen to us, even we sound the same.[61]

That's too scary.[62]

(snip)

I've sat in this chair for twenty-five years. [63] The coroner will have to [64] scrape my scalp [65] from under your fingernails[66].

I have upgraded my chair[67] three times in that time.[68]

Maybe it's the[69] acknowledgement of repetition[70] that makes us human? [71] When we no longer recognize [72] the repetition, that's[73] when we stop being human.[74]

Not now.[75]

So what are we? [76] We're machines.[77] Except[78]…

Except? [79]

Except nothing. [80] If we recognize the repetition [81], but choose to ignore it[82], we are no better than machines[83].

Or monkeys. [84]

Neither is a human. [85]

(snip)

I got fired today. [86] I've been leaving a [87] single screw out of the [88] toasters for years [89]. Assembled, packed, and shipped [90], minus one screw [91].

Years? I've heard of the [92] plant letting [93] lifers go for [94] much less. I have an [95] aunt [96] who was fired for laughing [97]. She worked there for twenty-three years. [98]

And no one ever complained about the missing [99] screw. So I [100] ask you, what's the purpose of [101] this screw [102]?

Why did you work there? [103]

I like machines. [104]

Maybe the screw [105] is an aesthetic thing [106].

Whose aesthetic? [107] No one ever complained. [108]

(snip)

You cut my hair, but [109] I keep going. So [110] what is the purpose of hair [111]? To keep your elbows [112] from rusting [113]?

To pay my ex's mortgage. [114]

You're divorced? [115]

As of yesterday. [116]

(snip)

Why? If you don't mind. [117]

Said the spark died. [118] Things got tedious...[119]

Well, at least we know she's human. [120]

I am, too. I see[121] the tedium, but I[122] choose to bear it[123]. I could do something new. [124]

(snip)

Could you? Step [125] **far enough away from the minutiae**[126]**, and everything's been done** [127]**. It's all repetition.** [128] **There is nothing new under the sun.** [129] **Even this conversation** [130]**, philosophers have been having** [131] **it for years**[132]**. Sartre. Said.** [133]

Has someone really talked about[134] monkeys chopping locks with sharpened stones[135]?

I'm sure someone has. [136]

(snip)

Easy on the mane. [137] **I have plans for this.** [138]

Unless those plans [139] are to look like a woman[140], you are apt to fail. [141]

...[142]

Really?[143]

I can have conversations[144] **here with you, and have the**[145] **same conversation tonight**[146]**, but as a woman. I'm**[147] **a**

different person. So [148] something new comes of it [149]. I'm living twice[150].

You hang out with[151] tranny stylists[152]?

In theory, dick! [153] I could say the same words[154] but get something different[155]. A changed context is a [156] changed experience[157].

Why tell me this? [158]

The best way to find out if you can trust somebody is to trust them. [159] I'm sure it wasn't easy to [160] bring up your divorce [161]. You can call it [162] raiding each other's closets[163].

It was quite easy. [164] I like structure. [165] She doesn't. [166] Fucking alimony. [167]

(snip)

All done. [168] Take look in the mirror. [169]

No need. Nothing trivializes progress more than a reflection. [170]

I like that. Who said that? [171]

You. [172]

Really? I guess I don't need[173] fake tits and long hair[174]. Old age[175] seems to work just fine[176].

You want me to get you some phone numbers? [177]

Some of the trannies[178] clean up quite well[179].

Let me be single one weekend.[180] Then you can fuck off.[181]

(ding)

---

[1] Kim Antieau, *Coyote Cowgirl* (New York: Forge, 2003), p.256.

[2] Mark Haskell Smith, *Delicious: a Novel* (New York: Grove Press, 2005), p. 228

[3] Tim Knox, *Everything I Know about Business I Learned from My Mama: A Down-Home Approach to Business and Personal Success* (New Jersey: Wiley & Sons, Inc, 2007), p.179

[4] L. A. Banks, *The Wicked* (New York: Macmillan, 2008), pg.377

[5] Allen Flaming, Kate Scowen, *My Crazy Life: How I Survived My Family* (Willowdale, ON Canada: Annick Press, 2002), p.103.

[6] Michelle Valentine, *Nyagra's Falls* (New York: Simon and Schuster, 2003), p.211.

[7] John Paul Newport, "Balls in the Basement", *The Wall Street Journal Online*, http://online.wsj.com/public/article_print/SB120129464123117695.html (January 28, 2008)

[8] Cornell Woolrich, Night Has a Thousand Eyes (Pegasus Books, 2007), pg.24

[9] Amy Tan, *The Bonesetter's Daughter* (Random House, Inc., 2003), p.358.

[10] Brian Garfield, Christopher Creighton, *The Paladin* (New York: Simon and Schuster, 1979), p.335

[11] Patricia A. Marx, *Him, her, him again, the end of him* (New York: Simon and Schuster, 2007), p.46

[12] Robert Shapard, James Thomas, *Sudden Fiction* (Gibbs Smith, 1987), pg.51

[13] Sheng Yen, Kenneth Wapner, *Footprints in the Snow: The Autobiography of a Chinese Buddhist Monk*, (New York: Random House, Inc., 2008), pg.99

[14] George Singleton, *Work shirts for madmen*, (New York: Houghton Mifflin Harcourt, 2007), pg.20

[15] Michael McGarrity, *Under the Color of Law*, (New York: Onyx, 2002), pg.311

[16] Barbara Ann Kipfer, *Field Guide to Happiness for Women*, (Guilford, Connecticut: Globe Pequot, 2009),pg.95

[17] Robert Ludlum, *The Icarus Agenda*, (New York: Bantam Books, 1989), pg.364

[18] Victor Barnouw, *Wisconsin Chippewa Myths & Tales: And Their Relation to Chippewa Life*, (University of Wisconsin Press, 1979), pg.55

[19] "Dita Von Teese: She Certainly Has This Look Down!", *My Hair Style: The Latest Hair Trends*, http://www.my-hair-style.com/2009/04/21/dita-von-teese-she-certainly-has-this-look-down/ (April 21, 2009)

[20] Joanne Fluke, *Cherry Cheesecake Murder*, (Books, 2008), pg.180

[21] Lawrence Block, *Hit List*, (New York: HarperTorch, 2000), pg.134

[22] Patrizia Bettella, *The Ugly Woman: Transgressive Aesthetic Models in Italian Poetry From the Middle Ages to the Baroque*, (University of Toronto Press, 2005), title

[23] Jamie Doeren, Dennis Roghair, *Chainsaw Carving an Eagle*, (East Petersburg, PA: Fox Chapel Publishing, 2005), pg.3

[24] Mitch Albom, *For One More Day*, (New York: Hyperion, 2006), pg.134

[25] Martin Bauer, *Resistance to New Technology*, (Cambridge University Press, 1997), pg.268

[26] Edward Everett Hale, "The Happy Island: Chapter One", *Harper's New Monthly Magazine*, (June-November 1879), pg.209

[27] Sepand S., *iBegin*, Rev. of Red Lobster, http://toronto.ibegin.com/restaurants/red-lobster-restaurants/reviews/ (March 2, 2006)

[28] Bob Cullen, Robert Cullen, *A Mulligan for Bobby Jobe*, (New York: Perennial, 2002), pg.3

[29] David Lozell Martin, *The Crying Heart Tattoo*, (Simon and Schuster, 2008), pg.210

[30] Mary Higgins Clark, *I Heard That Song Before*, (New York: Simon and Schuster, 2007), pg.193

[31] Michael Gruber, *Tropic of Night*, (New York: HarperTorch, 2003), pg.81

[32] Prince Love, "Jasmine Bryne In Da House!", *Pimps & Playaz*, http://pimpsandplayaz.com/archives/320 (May 5, 2009)

[33] Nanamoli, Bodhi, *The Middle Length Discourses of the Buddha*, (Boston: Wisdom Publications, 1995), pg.580

[34] Princeton Review, Judene Wright, *Cracking the SAT Biology E/M Subject Test*, (New York: The Princeton Review, 2005), pg.17

[35] Howard Eilberg-Schwartz, Wendy Doniger, *Off With Her Head!*, (University of California Press, 1995), pg.53

[36] Jack L. Cooke, *Getting By in a Silent World*, (The History Press, 2005), pg. 190

[37] Debra Ginsberg, *The Grift*, (New York: Crown Publishing, 2008), pg.38

[38] Rosellen Brown, *Half a Heart*, (New York: Picador, 2001), pg.312

[39] John William Donaldson, *Exercises Adapted to the Complete Latin Grammar*, (BiblioBazaar, LLC, 2008), pg.8

[40] Ray Reece, *Abigail in Gangland*, (Budapest: La Ventana, 2007), pg.144

[41] Susan Martins Miller, *The Latest Mrs. Furst*, (RiverOak, 2006), pg.125

[42] Eric Schelkopf, "Chopping locks to raise some bucks", *The Chronicle*, http://www.kcchronicle.com/articles/2009/06/03/11471843/index.xml (June 3, 2009)

[43] Dan Simmons, *Hyperion*, (New York: Random House, Inc., 1990), pg.55

[44] Sarah Deveau, *Sink or Swim*, (Toronto, Ontario: Dundurn Press Ltd., 2003), pg.81

[45] Peter Dechert, *At Lagunitas*, (Santa Fe: Sunstone Press, 2007), pg.46

[46] Richard Swinburne, *The Existence of God*, (Oxford University Press, 2004), pg.170

[47] Yann Martel, *Life of Pi: a novel*, (Houghton Mifflin Harcourt, 2001), pg.312

[48] Suzetta Perkins, *Ex-Terminator: Life After Marriage* (New York: Simon and Schuster, 2008), pg.431

[49] Robin Hobb, *Assassin's Quest* (New York: Random House, Inc., 1998), pg.132

[50] Charles A. Murray, *Losing ground: American social policy, 1950-1980* (New York: Basic Books, 1994), pg.291

[51] Caleb J. Ross, *As a Machine and Parts* (Viscera Irrational, 2013), pg111

[52] Jamie Brown, "Yeasayer" Glasgow's Kin Tut", *Is This Music?*, http://www.isthismusic.com/yeasayer (March 30, 2008)

[53] Uwe Timm, Peter Tegel, *Midsummer Night* (New York: New Directions Publishing, 2000), pg.50

[54] Civacankari, Uma Narayanan, *Tyagu: Oru manithanin kathai* (University of Michigan, 2007), pg.2

[55] Patricia Armstrong, *Kate* (New York: Harlequin Enterprises, Limited, 1995), pg.93

[56] Mike Fleetham, Roanne Charles, Kate Sheppard, *Multiple Intelligences in Practice*, (Stafford: Continuum International Publishing Group, 2006)

[57] Debra Ginsberg, *The Grift*, (New York: Crown Publishing, 2008), pg.38

[58] Brian Evenson, *Last Days* (Portland, Oregon: Underland Press, 2009), p. 186.

[59] Nancy Bond, *A String in the Harp* (New York: Simon and Schuster, 2007), pg.196

[60] Gary Hardwick, *Color of Justice* (New York: HarperCollins, 2002), pg.33

[61] Gordon Highland, email to the author (paraphrased), 6 September 2009

[62] John Irvin, *A Prayer for Owen Meany* (Random House, Inc., 1997), pg. 54

[63] Jerry Horne, "Franklin Police Get Lubed", *Aimlessly Unbalanced*, http://aimlesslyunbalanced.blogspot.com/2007_06_01_archive.html (June 2007)

[64] Charles Dickens, All the Year Round (Charles Dickens, 1866), pg. 366

[65] Loung Ung, *Luck Child* (New York: HarperCollins, 2005), pg. 63

[66] Chuck Palahniuk, *Survivor*, (New York: W. W. Norton & Company, 1999), pg. 27

[67] wahoo, "Report UFO or Alien Experiences or Dreams", *Alien UFOs*, http://www.alien-ufos.com/1974-Charelston-SC-sitting-Update-merged-t6811.html (April 27, 2005)

[68] Lawrence McNally, *Cajun Conspiracy* (iUniverse, 2002), pg. 126

[69] Charles Martin, *Wrapped in Rain* (Nashville: Thomas Nelson Inc, 2005), pg. 14

[70] Abraham Sagi, Batya Stein, *Albert Camus and the philosophy of the absurd* (Amsterdam: Rodopi, 2002), pg. 81

[71] David Walsh, *The Growth of the Liberal Soul* (University of Missouri Press, 1997), pg. 262

[72] Ann Belford Ulanov, Barry Ulanov, *Religion and the Unconscious* (Philadelphia: Westminster John Knox Press, 1985), pg. 171

[73] Jonathan Kalb, *Free Admissions: Collected Theater Writings* (New York: Hal Leonard Corporation, 1993), pg. 59

[74] Bruce Dawe, K. L. Goodwin, *Bruce Dawe: Essays and Opinions* (Longman Cheshire, 1990), pg. 49

[75] Stephen Graham Jones, *Bleed into Me: a Collection of Stories* (University of Nebraska Press: 2005), pg. 29

[76] Will Christopher Baer, *Penny Dreadful* (San Francisco: MacAdam/Cage Publishing, 2004), pg. 201

[77] Peter David, *Sagittarius is Bleeding: a Battlestar Galactica novel* (New York: Macmillan, 2006), pg. 33

[78] Paul Eckert, "Saturn Passed By", *Dogmatika*, http://dogmatika.wordpress.com/2009/05/01/saturn-passed-by, (2009)

[79] Caleb J. Ross, *As a Machine and Parts* (Viscera Irrational, 2013), pg113

[80] Vassiliki Kolocotroni, Jane Goldman, Olga Taxidou, *Modernism: an anthology of sources and documents* (University of Chicago Press, 1998), pg. 422

[81] Lothar Honnighausen, *Faulkner: Masks and Metaphors* (Univ. Press of Mississippi, 2006), pg. 118

[82] Reza Aslan, *No god but God: the origins, evolution, and future of Islam* (New York: Random House, Inc., 2005), pg. 170

[83] Pheng Cheah, *Spectral Nationality* (Columbia University Press, 2003), pg. 35

[84] Jaap Goudsmit, *Viral Sex: The Nature of AIDS* (Oxford University Press US, 1998), pg. 180

[85] James Griffin, *On Human Rights* (Oxford University Press US, 2008), pg. 58

[86] Patricia A. Marx, *Him, Her, Him Again, the End of Him* (New York: Simon and Schuster, 2007), pg134

[87] Elizabeth Sinclair, *Angel Unaware* (Medallion Press, Inc., 2008), pg. 15

[88] Alden Hatch, *Franklin D. Roosevelt*, (Read Books, 2007), pg. 12

[89] Michael Wolff, *Autumn of the moguls: My Misadventures with the Titans, Poseurs, and Money Guys Who Mastered and Messed Up Big Media*, (New York: HarperCollins, 2004), pg. 215

[90] Ian Graham, *Alfred Maudslay and the Maya: a biography*, (University of Oklahoma Press, 2002), pg. 130

[91] Industrial Fasteners Institute, *Fastener Standards* (Industrial Fasteners Institute, 1970), pg. 34

[92] United States. Congress. House. Committee on Energy and Commerce. Subcommittee on Health, Timothy J. Muris, *Examining issues related to competition in the pharmaceutical marketplace* (U.S. G.P.O., 2002), pg. 96

[93] Liberty Hyde Bailey, *Botany: An Elementary Text for Schools* (Macmillan, 1909), pg13

[94] Bruce E. Altschuler, *Running in Place: a Campaign Journal* (Nelson-Hall, 1996), pg. 40

[95] Richard B. Brandt, *Ethical Theory: the Problems of Normative and Critical Ethics* (Prentice-Hall, 1959), pg.229

[96] Douglas Coupland, *Hey Nostradamus!* (New York: Random House, Inc., 2004), pg.173

[97] Judith Stepan-Norris, Maurice Zeitlin, *Talking Union* (University of Illinois Press, 1996), pg.86

[98] Anna Haebich, Doreen Mellor, National Library of Australia, *Many Voices: Reflections on Experiences of Indigenous Child Separation* (National Library Australia, 2002), pg.180

[99] Tananarive Due, *Blood Colony* (New York: Simon and Schuster, 2008), pg.165

[100] George Meredith, *Evan Harrington: A Novel* (Scribner, 1900), pg.318

[101] Paul Bortolazzo, *The Coming of the Son of Man: After the Tribulation of Those Days* (Tate Publishing, 2007), pg.166

[102] Edgar Allan Poe, Stephen Marlowe, *The Fall of the House of Usher and Other Tales* (Signet Classic, 1998), pg.3

[103] Linda Randall Wisdom, *Twist of Fate* (Harlequin Sales Corp (Mm), 1996), pg.127

[104] John Steinbeck, *Of Mice and Men* (New York: Penguin Books, 1994), p. 78.

[105] Isaac Bashevis Singer, *A Friend of Kafka* (Macmillan, 1979), pg.131

[106] Hugh Black, *Culture and Restraint* (BiblioBazaar, LLC, 2009), pg.49

[107] Alan Singer, Allen Dunn, *Literary Aesthetics: a reader* (Wiley-Blackwell, 2000), pg.335

[108] Caleb J. Ross, *As a Machine and Parts* (Viscera Irrational, 2013), pg.69

[109] Anne Paton, *Some Sort of a Job: My Life with Alan Paton* (Viking, 1992), pg.138

[110] Paul Zakrzewski, *Lost Tribe: Jewish Fiction From the Edge* (New York: HarperCollins, 2003), pg.425

[111] William Boyd Logan, Helen M. Moon, *Facts about Merchandise* (Prentice-Hall, 1962), pg.129

[112] Paul D'Arezzo, Nathanael Letteer, *Posture Alignment: The Missing Link in Health and Fitness* (Marcellina Mountain Press, 2003), pg.178

[113] George Burton, *Chemical Storylines* (Heinemann, 2000), pg.173

[114] Morris Lindsay, "Child Support and Shared Care", *Masculinist Evolution New Zealand* http://menz.org.nz/2007/child-support-and-shared-care/comment-page-1/, (February 13, 2008)

[115] John Ventura, Mary Reed, *Divorce for Dummies* (Hoboken: Wiley Publishing, Inc, 2009), pg.5

[116] Tony Hillerman, Otto Penzler, *The Best American Mystery Stories of the Century* (Houghton Mifflin Harcourt, 2001), pg.87

[117] Lucy Finn, *Careful What You Wish For* (Signet Classic, 2007), pg.151

[118] Donald Moffitt, *Second Genesis* (E-Reads Ltd, 1999), pg.225

[119] Clive Cussler, Craig Dirgo, *The Sea Hunters: True Adventures with Famous Shipwrecks* (New York: Simon and Schuster, 2003), pg.201

[120] Kim Louise, *Falling for You* (Kensington Books, 2002), pg.31

[121] Brian Johnston, *Sicilian Summer: A Story of Honour, Religion and the Perfect Cassata* (Allen & Unwin, 2006), pg.262

[122] Sergeï Khrushchev, *Memoirs of Nikita Khrushchev* (Penn State Press, 2004), pg.299

[123] Catherine Coulter, *The Heiress Bride* (Jove, 1993), pg.123

[124] Debbie DiGiovanni, *Reality Queen* (New York: Simon and Schuster, 2005), pg.271

[125] Toyoko Yamazaki, V. Dixon Morris, Two Homelands (University of Hawaii Press, 2008), pg.187

[126] Canfield, "James Cameron to Actually Make a Feature Film in April!!", *Twitch* http://twitchfilm.net/archives/008676.html, (January 8, 2007)

[127] Joseph Morris, St Clair Adams, *It Can Be Done* (BiblioBazaar, LLC, 2007), pg.122

[128] John H. Goldthorpe, The Affluent Worker: Industrial Attitudes and Behaviour (Cambridge University Press, 1970), pg.13

[129] New International Version Bible, *The Quest Study Bible* (Grand Rapids, Michigan: Zondervan Publishing House, 1994), pg.912, Ecclesiastes 1:9

[130] Arthur F. Kinney, *Critical essays on William Faulkner: the Compson Family* (University of Michigan, 1982), pg.68

[131] John Leslie, *Universes* (Routledge, 1996), pg.195

[132] Nathaniel Starkey, *Things which must shortly come to pass... For the time is at hand* (Oxford University, 1879), pg.14

[133] Paul A. Bové, *Edward Said and the Work of the Critic: Speaking Truth to Power* (Duke University Press, 2000), pg.209

[134] Crackedpleasures, "Greenlandic club in Danish league?", Xtratime.org http://www.xtratime.org/forum/showthread.php?t=240112, (February 14, 2009)

[135] Caleb J. Ross, *As a Machine and Parts* (Viscera Irrational, 2013), pg.112

[136] Janet Evanovich, *Three Plums in One* (New York: Simon and Schuster, 2001), pg.281

[137] J A Madrid, *Tales of Beastly Behaviors* (iUniverse, 2004), pg.48

[138] S. E. Hinton, *Hawkes Harbor* (Macmillan, 2005), pg.72

[139] Pamela Vesta Meredith, Nancy Mathes Horan, *Adult Primary Care* (University of Michigan: Saunders, 1999), pg.30

[140] University Film Producers Association, *Journal of the University Film Producers Association*, v. 7-19 (New York: Syracuse, 1954), pg.13

[141] John Rood, *Sculpture in Wood* (U of Minnesota Press, 1973), pg.61

[142] Thomas Pynchon, *The Crying of Lot 49* (New York: HarperCollins, 1966), pg.10

[143] Richard Thomas, "Paying it Up", *Colored Chalk*, issue 8, http://coloredchalk.com/uploads/pdf/ColoredChalk08.pdf, (2009), pg.8

[144] Michael Chorost, *Rebuilt: How Becoming Part Computer Made Me More Human* (Houghton Mifflin Harcourt, 2005), pg.44

[145] Dana Fuller Ross, *Utah!* (G.K. Hall, 1984), pg.227

[146] Jack Kerouac, *Visions of Cody* (McGraw Hill, 1990), pg.158

[147] Lynn Peril, *Pink Think: Becoming a Woman in Many Uneasy Lessons* (W. W. Norton & Company, 2002), pg.50

[148] Peter Robinson, *In a Dry Season: a Novel of Suspense* (HarperCollins, 2000), pg.107

[149] Martin E. Marty, *The Hidden Discipline* (Concordia Pub. House, 1962), pg.90

[150] Franz Wright , *Ill lit: Selected & New Poems* (Oberlin College Press, 1998), pg.179

[151] Adrienne Maria Vrettos, *Skin* (New York: Simon and Schuster, 2007), pg.92

[152] Forrest Mallard, "New Life -- October 1, 2006", *MySpace.com Blogs*, http://blogs.myspace.com/index.cfm?fuseaction=blog.view&friendId=1310256&blogId=182425577, (October 1, 2006)

[153] Phineas Garrett, *Dramatic Leaflets: Comprising Original and Selected Plays for Amateur Clubs* (P. Garrett & Co., 1887), pg.193

[154] Ewald August Koenig, Mary A. Robinson, *Wooing a Widow: A Novel* (R. Bonner's Sons, 1894), pg.25

[155] Aristotle, *On Friendship: Being an Expanded Translation of the Nicomachean Ethics* (The University Press, 1940), pg.91

[156] Jonathan Hollowell, *Britain since 1945* (Wiley-Blackwell, 2003), pg.290

[157] Lesley Rogers, *Sexing the Brain* (Columbia University Press, 2001), pg.28

[158] Tracy Anne Warren, *The Wife Trap* (New York: Random House, Inc., 2006), pg.308

[159] Ernest Hemingway, quote: origin unknown

[160] Keith Raffel, *Dot Dead: A Silicon Valley Mystery* (Llewellyn Worldwide, 2006), pg.185

[161] April Masini, "Breakup Advice, Divorce Advice", *Ask April*, http://www.askapril.com/divorce-advice-breakup-advice-10-3/index.html

[162] Stephen L. Carter, *Palace Council* (Random House, Inc., 2009), pg.239

[163] Lesley Pratt Bannatyne, *A Halloween How-To: Costumes, Parties, Decorations, and Destinations* (Pelican Pub. Co.,2001), pg.75

[164] Edith Nesbit, *Five Children and It* (Digireads.com Publishing, 2005), pg.69

[165] Donald Burton Kuspit, Jimmy Ernst, *Jimmy Ernst* (Hudson Hills, 2000). Pg.128

[166] Andy Warhol, *a: A Novel* (Grove Press, 1998), pg.156

[167] John Westermann, *Sweet Deal: a Novel* (Soho Press, 1992), pg.66

[168] Charles Dickens, *A Christmas Carol* (Kessinger Publishing, 2004), pg.45

[169] Korn, Alfred Publishing Company, Incorporated, Hemme B. Luttjeboer, Colgan Bryan, *Take a Look in the Mirror* (Warner Bros. Publications, 2004)

[170] Caleb Ross, "The Barber Who Calls Himself Ferguson", *Bust Down the Door and Eat All the Chickens*, issue 7, http://www.absurdistjournal.com/pdf/issue7.pdf, (2007), pg.21

[171] Anabel Donald, *Smile, Honey* (Consortium Book Sales & Dist, 1990), pg.246

[172] Thomas Pynchon, *Gravity's Rainbow* (Penguin Classics, 1995), pg.137

[173] Lance P. Perticone, *The Tangled Web* (iUniverse, 2003), pg.112

[174] urbanaesthetic, "How Can I Compete...", *I Make It All Up*, http://urbanaesthetic.livejournal.com/82107.html, (July 14, 2009)

[175] Betty Carter, *My Little Mountain Home (and Me)* (Trafford Publishing, 2004), pg.96

[176] Jerald Silverman, *Managing the Laboratory Animal Facility* (CRC Press, 2008), pg.10

[177] Gorman Bechard, *Balls* (Plume, 1995), pg.58

[178] Patrick Moore, *Tweaked: a Crystal Meth Memoir* (Kensington Books, 2006)

[179] Maureen Kahl, *The Touchstone* (Tate Publishing, 2007), pg.124

[180] Steven Plakcy, *Mahu* (Harrington Park Press, The Haworth Positronic Press, 2005), pg.208

[181] Glyn Hughes, *The Rape of the Rose: a Novel* (New York: Simon & Schuster, 1993), pg.190

a screw or something

Two months with an elevated leg trains blood to reroute in all sorts of strange ways. Marsha's elbow throbs. Her thigh pulses. Inside, her veins and capillaries swell to the disarrayed tidal backflow of confused arteries. Her body narrates its deterioration in sore joints and labored breath, comforting decline by casketing her healing bones with swollen muscle and taut ligaments. This is the kind of pain Mitchell swore to have wanted for himself, toward the end, when all that was left of him was a numb desire to stay alive. While she wanted her pain to stop, he wanted his to start. The comatose and the injured, neither completely human and neither completely machine.

They had plans, no kids in mind, just eyes toward the downtown Hubert Lofts. Their bedroom window opened to the loft buildings which split the distant horizon in a perfect golden mean, anchored at the corner by a terracotta flowerpot Mitchell stole years ago from a neighbor's porch. She had in mind all the art and culture she'd use to decorate. Mitchell had a strong eye and knew where pieces should hang. Together, they were a chemical bond. But then the metal took him. An accident, likely, but nonetheless gone.

The factory parking lot smells of hot asphalt. An unfamiliar late-model Chevy Something occupies her parking space, a spot tenured as the unwritten, but understood fringe benefit of her twenty-odd-year loyalty to the OLEAN plant. Skateboard decals hide cracks in the windshield glass. Summer's here, school's out. Kids are back to their careers.

Once inside, she recognizes only a single lifer clique on the factory floor. All others seem to have dispersed in the two months since her injury and Mitchell's death, either leaving entirely or assimilating into fresh micro communities. Sparse pockets of gossip exhaust and rumor bellow from the group. She tries smiling a hello, but her heavy, medicated lips distort her good intention. She shouldn't be here, with pills in her blood, but the worker's comp has run out and her leg still throbs. According to her boss, her boss's boss, that boss's boss, she's only to take Ibuprofen, leaving anything stronger at home. According to that same hierarchy, a fractured leg really isn't all that bad, and truthfully she shouldn't have been allowed the full two months. And honestly, *"if you don't come back now, I have a kid who's more than happy to have your job."*

There's a new time clock outside the break room. She asks a young stranger for help, perhaps the scab responsible for her stolen parking space. She treats her impromptu instructor with that assumption, seething as he points and mumbles about being careful not to slide her badge too slowly. He stinks of pot. Mitchell would have invited this kid over for dinner. She inhales, sidestepping the boy for the break room, for her safety goggles from a wall locker. She remembers birthday party potlucks back here, quick card games, dominoes during lunch hours. Now, the foreign air seems capable only of misery, like she's missed out on a schism.

She ducks the clique's gaze for her returning pass through the factory floor, limping en-route to her seat at the welding station. The cushion wheezes. Three sad attempts before she has the tool running; even the machines treat her differently. Is this what it feels like to lose a heartbeat?

She watches her welder through cobwebbed goggles, airgunning away its shrapneled debris with a returning monotony, and almost smiles to have finally settled into something familiar. But before her lips can turn, a tap on the shoulder pulls her from the trance.

"Time to hit your throne," a large woman says, her name somehow forgotten, but her face easily culled from the floor's clique; mascara eyes like tribal paint behind her safety lenses. Marsha never wore makeup; Mitchell said that shit made her look methed out. "Rogers says it's mandatory." Marsha rises and limps away. With distance between them, the woman tosses a caustic whisper: "What I wouldn't give to be forced to take a break."

Marsha checks her watch. Two hours already gone.

Workers covet any additional breaks for the injured. Marsha's been there, tossing wide-mouthed asides above the factory's yell and grind. Her insults could pitch above even the lathe decibels, saturating its dusty air with the envy afforded by a coworker's welding burn, or bone fracture, or head trauma. Officially, a broken finger gets two weeks. A stitched cut, barely a day. A damaged leg, two months and an thirty days worth of mandatory fifteen-minute rests. "I wish you could take it," Marsha yells back to the woman, but she's either too far gone or too unsympathetic to respond. *I wish you were the one with a crushed leg and an empty bed*, she means to say.

She limps from the factory floor, but by the break room's staked clique territory, decides instead to follow the hallway toward the atrium exit at the distant Shipping and Receiving dock. *Atrium.* A grandiose name for Smoker's Area. The white paint has dulled to a dirty yellow. *Atrium.* The ironic harm these people do to a room with such a name brings Marsha to the day's closest smile. The people, foreign, but indentured, like Shipping and Receiving is its own country. "Have one," a thin man with knotty knuckles says, cigarette extended to Marsha's face. She declines, but thanks him. "You're smart," he says. "Probably boring. But smart. First day?"

Marsha explains her situation, cropping the story at the hows and whos, but still she forfeits enough to appease the smoker, sighing at every mention of Mitchell. The man dodges discomfort. "It wasn't me that took your space," he says. "I got dropped off."

Marsha smiles away the man's overt insistence. Everyone's a suspect, and will be until she's regained equilibrium. "Sure you don't want a smoke?" the man says. "Seems this Mitchell guy's death is reason enough to start."

"This leg is enough. I've got so many pins and patches in there that I might as well be part metal. You ever felt like that?"

"I've been at this factory a long time, Marsha. By this time, if I didn't think of myself as a cog, I'd be committed. And I'm not going that route; the company insurance plan doesn't cover psychiatric treatment. I've looked." He smiles, something wistful, almost *what could have been*. Smoke seeps from the gaps between his teeth.

"Maybe I will take one," she says and accepts a cigarette from the man's dwindling pack. She pinches the filter with her lips and leans in to receive the man's flame. She's never smoked on crutches before. Strangely, it takes focus.

The man pockets his lighter. "I've got a cousin that makes those bone pins. North only two-hundred or so miles, in Brakeford. Someone gets hurt bad enough there and you can bet that a part of the factory literally becomes that person. That's an extreme example, sure, but think of eyeglasses and tooth fillings and arthritic braces, all that stuff made by machines to keep us people as close to perfect as possible." He inhales. "There's really only two levels in all of creation: God and everything else."

"You sure that's a cigarette?" Marsha smiles, a glint of affirmation to her eyes.

"Unfortunately. I've got nothing but thinking time here," he turns to his smoking companions, "cause these fuckers can't do anything but shit and make my life hell. And half of them don't even shit that well." They retort with lazy, but good-natured grunts.

"Any of them good at making a cast that doesn't itch like hell?" Marsha leans against the wall and worms her index finger down into the top lip of her cast, dusting the concrete floor with cigarette ash.

"If we can send a man to the moon..."

Marsha pulls a long drag and drops her cigarette to an ashtray. "I should be getting back. The foreman over there is notorious for bullshit regulation."

"So he's notorious for being a foreman?" He stamps out his cigarette. "Let's rig something up for you, real quick. Something for that itch."

Marsha checks the clock on the wall. "I can be a little late."

The smoker ushers Marsha out of the atrium and through back docks, careful to navigate her around forklift paths and other areas of potential sudden movement. They land at a metal workbench, covered with random tools and aborted makeshift solutions to all the unexpected breakdowns of factory life. A few metal slabs wired together, the smoker calls "the only way to get the trash compactor working most of the time." A flattened screwdriver he says "keeps the dock bay door open when it's raining out." He pulls out a plastic wand, like a set of riot cuffs, only wider, and wraps four inches at one end in black electrical tape. "A leg-scratcher with my patented comfort-grip handle. Enjoy."

Marsha slides the tool down into her cast. "Perfect," she says. "It's hardly worth complaining about anymore." She smiles and thanks the man, before asking for return directions to the assembly floor.

Back at Assembly, the painted clique leader at Marsha's welding station has been replaced by a boy, seventeen maybe, with a black tattoo peeking above his collar. Rogers intercepts Marsha's limp, pulls her into his office, and tells her to sit. "I thought you said 'no visible tattoos,'" Marsha says, tracking the boy through Rogers's Plexiglas window.

"He's not your concern," Rogers says. "In fact, starting now, nothing to do with this factory is your concern." He waits a few beats, giving Marsha time to react, unaware of the paralyzing effect of her Percocet. "I have reason to believe that your injury did not happen on company property, and that you have been illegally reaping our benefits. Misrepresentation like that is grounds for termination."

"The compensation ran out days ago," she says, and wills a grin. Failing a returned smile she asks, "who told you it didn't happen here?"

"We're a family here," Rogers begins, but already Marsha has faded. Maybe it's the Percocet; all the world's hues have settled to a mute gray. She belongs with metal. Every motor, every gasket, every moving danger. She'd say that a day without rust is a day forgotten. And she'd mean it; this place has for so long been her home. The assembly line, her table runner. The concrete floor, her stained linoleum. But maybe it's not the pills.

"Not directly, perhaps. But fuck you if I can't blame this factory for tearing me and Mitchell down."

Rogers recoils, his furrowed brow reddening. "Box up your locker, Marsha—"

"How do you like living in the lofts?" She says, making no move to stand. Getting no response, she elaborates. "Mitchell and I wanted to live there, once. You know, we have to look at those fucking buildings every night as we go to sleep." With every word, her lips enliven, but her pain grows. "There is god, and there is everyone else. It must be lonely being a god."

Rogers reaches for a telephone, but Marsha stands, surrendering to a smooth exit. A security guard, someone Marsha recognizes from her crowded neighborhood, helps her from the office, taking in her limp with his shoulder. "Thanks," she says, smiling, but heavy with pain. Her pills have worn off, letting her nerves breathe, and goddamnit Marsha, that's something.

ABOUT THE AUTHOR

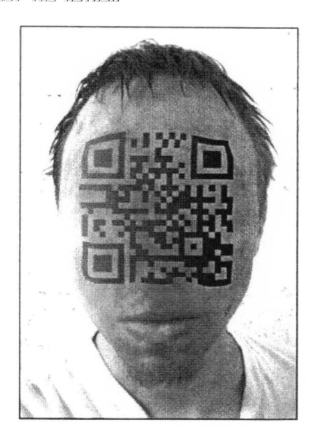

ACKNOWLEDGMENTS

www.calebjross.com would like to thank www.emporia.edu/emlj/english/webb.html for the original architecture that would eventually support the author's factory line. www.orangealert.net deserves thanks for the initial rivets and girders, www.gordonhighland.com for the first (of many) line edits and continual praise (and year-round Sam Adams Oktoberfest), www.welcometothevelvet.com (RIP) for keeping the author greased, and all the www.write-club.org cogs for keeping the author moving.

Made in the USA
Monee, IL
28 May 2020

Library of Congress Cataloging-in-Publication Data

Coffman, Ken.
    Real world FPGA design with Verilog / Ken Coffman.
    p. cm.
    Includes bibliographical references.
    ISBN 0-13-099851-6
    1. Field programmable gate arrays--Computer-aided design. 2. Verilog (Computer
hardware description language) I. Title.

TK7895.G36 C64 1999   99-046369
621.39'5--dc21

Editorial/Production Supervision: *Joan L. McNamara*
Acquisitions Editor: *Bernard Goodwin*
Marketing Manager: *Lisa Konzelmann*
Editorial Assistant: *Diane Spina*
Cover Design Director: *Jerry Votta*
Cover Designer: *Talar Agasyan*
Cover Illustration: *Alamini Design*
Manufacturing Manager: *Alexis R. Heydt*

© 2000 by Prentice Hall PTR
Prentice-Hall, Inc.
Upper Saddle River, New Jersey 07458

Prentice Hall books are widely used by corporations and government agencies for training, marketing, and resale.
The publisher offers discounts on this book when ordered in bulk quantities. For more information, contact: Corpo-
rate Sales Department, Prentice Hall PTR, One Lake Street, Upper Saddle River, NJ 07458 Phone: 800-382-3419;
Fax: 201-236-7141; email: corpsales@prenhall.com

Trademarks: Verilog is a trademark of Cadence Design Systems, Inc. OrCAD is a registered trademark of OrCAD
Systems Corporation. Silos III is a trademark of Simucad Inc. Altera is a trademark and service mark of the Altera
Corporation in the United States and other countries. MAX, FLEX, FLEX 10K, FLEX 8000, AHDL, MegaCore,
and Altera device part numbers are trademarks and/or service marks of Altera Corporation in the United States and
other countries. Xilinx is a registered trademark of Xilinx, Inc. Hardwire, LogiBLOX, VersaBlock, VersaRing are
trademarks of Xilinx, Inc. LeonardoSpectrum, LeonardoInsight, HDLInventor, FlowTabs, and Power Tabs are
trademarks of Exemplar Logic. All other product names mentioned herein are the trademarks of their respective
owners.

Printed in the United States of America
10   9   8   7   6   5   4   3

ISBN: 0-13-099851-6

Prentice-Hall International (UK) Limited, *London*
Prentice-Hall of Australia Pty. Limited, *Sydney*
Prentice-Hall Canada Inc., *Toronto*
Prentice-Hall Hispanoamericana, S.A., *Mexico*
Prentice-Hall of India Private Limited, *New Delhi*
Prentice-Hall of Japan, Inc., *Tokyo*
Pearson Education Asia Pte. Ltd.
Editora Prentice-Hall do Brasil, Ltda., *Rio de Janeiro*

*T*his is my first book to reach publication and I dedicate it to my wife, Judy Coffman. In May of 1972 we were married. Since then, she has (mostly) patiently watched me play in rock bands, get my Bachelor's degree at night school, go to a hundred concerts with my friends, do countless moonlighting projects, write a novel (with my partner Mark Bothum), promote rock shows (with my partner Craig Ranta), and now write this technical book. During these years, of course, I was working a day job to pay the bills. All this while the weeds were growing in the yard and the honeydew list was gathering dust.

Thanks for hanging in there, babe. I'll finish the landscaping as soon as I finish my next book, I promise!

Modern Semiconductor Design Series

Contents

Foreword—Notes on the Current State of the Art

When I graduated from the Université du Québec à Chicoutimi with my Engineering degree, then later from the University of Waterloo with my Master's degree, I thought I was ready to take on the world's toughest design challenges. Little did I know that the Real World of design had little to do with the ideal laboratory conditions where we bread-boarded our academic designs. For example, once in the Real World, I found it had little use for the ripple-through FIFO with asynchronous control logic I'd spent hours trying to understand. The ripple binary counters, implemented by using the Qbar from the previous bit as the clock input for the next bit, were nowhere to be seen. I think I had heard of metastability, but I was not taught where to pay attention to it, nor how to minimize the problems it causes. I should have learned how to properly implement an edge detector. I thought I knew what a glitch was, but I did not understand when glitches are a problem nor how to eliminate them. I naively believed that designs were implemented using perfect manufacturing processes. As a result, my designs were never functionally correct the first time!

The Real World of design was about to undergo a transformation for which my formal education left me ill-prepared: the apparition of logic synthesis. Minimizing logic using Karnaugh maps was being relegated to the electronic equivalent of the Stone Age. Selecting JK or T flipflops to minimize decode logic was becoming just as relevant. The little green plastic template I used to draw schematics in countless lab reports and final exams was going to join the manual typewriter in the obsolescence paradise.

The skills that turned out to be the most useful I had not learned as part of my engineering curriculum: typing (which my mother forced me to learn throughout high school on our IBM Selectric typewriter) and computer programming (where I was self-taught and still had more to learn). What my engineering background gave me was the ability to learn new tricks and discern work patterns that could be rendered repeatable, then later automated.

This book is all about what I learned through the hardware-design school of hard knocks. Many mistakes could have been avoided, and many hours of mentoring eliminated, if I had had such a textbook *and* heeded its advice. This book is not just about the Verilog language, and that is its greatest contribution. There are already numerous books about the details of the language. This book is about hardware design in the Real World, where Verilog is simply the implementation tool. I hope that the next edition will feature VHDL as well as Verilog: both are equally capable of (I would even say equally poor at) implementing designs that will meet Real World constraints. This book is also unique in describing in detail the entire FPGA design process: from HDL coding to verification to synthesis to device selection to fitting and place-and-route. Too many books satisfy themselves in showing only the HDL coding aspect.

The most important advice that this book gives is *to understand what needs to be done before you start coding.* The biggest sin this book commits is in understating the verification task: expect to spend 70% of your design time writing test fixtures and debugging the function of your design before implementing it. Both of these points underscore the importance of planning as well as investing as much effort as possible as early as possible in the design process. In hardware design, progress is not measured by how far along in the design process you are. Progress is measured by how close you are to producing *working* hardware.

Today's buzz is about IP and design reuse. This book can be considered to be about design reuse: it is about excellent and safe design practices, not only for FPGAs but for ASICs, too. Even though I have never worked with the author, I would feel confident in reusing his designs in my own. They would be trustworthy. Design reuse is about creating designs that are trustworthy in the Real World. This book should be mandatory reading for every novice FPGA (and ASIC) designer.

Janick Bergeron
Qualis Design Corporation
janick@qualis.com

Preface: Digital Design in the Real World

The world of digital design is changing quickly. At a breathtaking rate, devices are becoming faster, smaller, and denser. Ten years ago the mainstream digital designer was manipulating a few thousand gates using schematics with an occasional ABEL-HDL module tossed into the mix. Now we have programmable devices with a million gates in tiny packages. On the horizon, we see devices with many more millions of gates. It is not practical for the mainstream designer to create systems on chips with schematics (how would you like to deal with a 1,000-page schematic?), so Hardware Description Languages like VHDL and Verilog have come into their own. In spite of strong opinions on both sides of the fence (including my own), the current designscape is bilingual—multilingual if you include the work of those translating C code into hardware and the work of others on more advanced and hybrid languages.

> My own opinion of the fundamental reason for Verilog's staying power is that Verilog had a very large head start in [the] number of engineers who knew Verilog before VHDL really got out of the blocks, and Verilog is easier to learn than VHDL. Thus, the established designers already knew Verilog and had no reason to learn VHDL, and the new designers could pick it up easier than they could pick up VHDL.
> John Sanguinetti
> C2 Design Automation

> I always thought that VHDL was the bloated/bureaucratic/design-by-committee deal, and Verilog was the KISS/lean-and-mean/hippy/West Coast approach, and that the usual rules-of-engagement required us to perpetuate and widen the rift between them ☺
> Jonathan Bromley
> School of Engineering
> Oxford Brookes University

SURVIVAL SKILLS

Regardless of personal opinions, the practical designer will make sure that both VHDL and Verilog skills are present on his or her resume. The current half-life of engineering information is about four years and gets shorter every day. This means that half of what you know today will be obsolete in four years. In order to survive, we weary designers have to do two things:

1. Master the parts of our skill that are timeless. This includes physics (the analog aspects of digital design, transmission-line theory, conservation of energy, antenna theory, and power management) and design concepts like synchronization, metastability, and propagation delay.

2. Keep up with the changing technology. Take advantage of free seminars, try to read some of the tidal wave of trade magazines that pile up every month, buy as many books as your Significant Other will tolerate, and pay close attention when smart people are speaking.

> 80% of all embedded systems are delivered late.
> Jack Ganssle
> The Ganssle Group

The world of digital design is deeply divided. The elite 10%, the ASIC designers, use hardware and software tools that cost hundreds of thousands of dollars a year to maintain. They earn their living creating specialized high-volume designs. If the FPGA designer uses 50K gates, the ASIC designer uses 500K gates. If the FPGA designer is accustomed to four nanoseconds of delay through a primitive, the ASIC designer is accustomed to delays of less than a nanosecond. The ASIC designer is very careful, methodical, and does extensive planning. Errors can cost hundreds of thousands of dollars in silicon turns and schedule delays. The ASIC designer simulates, simulates, and then simulates some more.

By contrast, we FPGA designers are sloppy and impatient. There is little or no cost to experiment, so we program a part and try it. We use tools that are cheap or free on Windows-based PCs. By comparison to ASIC designers, we are a brutish and undisciplined mob, an unruly 90%. I have written this book for those who would like to join me in this mob.

> There's also the human element—stress—to the reprogrammability equation. ASICs aren't reprogrammable; the foundry casts their functionality into silicon. Making the final decision to commit a design to an ASIC can be extremely stressful for the entire design team. Once it makes the final decision, the team can't go back without incurring lots more NRE and lots more time. Erring at this stage, thus, is definitely a Career-Limiting Move (CLM). FPGAs, on the other hand, offer engineers a greater comfort zone midway through the project, giving them the ability to go back and revise a design without paying the NRE and time penalties. Reprogrammability alone may well be responsible for much of the success of the FPGA marketplace in the last decade.
>
> Rockland K. Awalt
> "Making the ASIC/FPGA Decision"
> *Integrated System Design*, July 1999
> Reprinted by permission

This is an FPGA synthesis book. It will not make the reader into an ASIC designer, though it does address issues associated with converting an FPGA design to an ASIC. This book is for the newbie FPGA designer who wants a quick and dirty guide to creating FPGA designs that actually stand a chance of surviving in the Real World.

The CD-ROM includes the evaluation version of the Silos III simulator. This software includes a project/file manager, waveform viewer, and full-featured Verilog support. The CD-ROM also includes the demonstration version of David Murray's excellent Prism Editor. This editor includes an automatic commenting/uncommenting feature, smart indentation, color coded Verilog keywords, printing of keywords in bold, column editing, and handling of Verilog code templates. A special price of USD $40.00 was negotiated for purchaser's of this book for those who choose to register the Prism Editor. Also on the CD-ROM is a fully-functional evaluation version of Emath-Pro for Windows, an electronics formula tool with over 300 useful formulas in 19 categories.

I worked hard on this book, but it is not perfect. If you find an error or want to argue about some of the points that are arguable (of which there are many), I look forward to hearing from you.

Ken Coffman
Mount Vernon, Washington
kcoffman@sos.net

Acknowledgments

I have had the honor of working with many people who were kind enough to shine some of their brilliance in my direction. People who reviewed the manuscript and made many outstanding suggestions (including some I actually took) include Janick Bergeron, Dr. Sajjan G. Shiva, and David Graf. David Pellerin introduced me to our patient editor Bernard Goodwin; without Dave's timely guidance and inspiration, this book would not exist. Joan McNamara patiently guided me through the production editing process and Bob Lentz did a great job copy-editing my fractured prose.

Influences in my colorful but not-all-that-illustrious career include Craig Ranta, Rick Penn, G. Scott Bright, Jerrold Gray, Bruce Dippie, Paul Swanson, Dock Brown, Jim Neumiller, Larry Liu, Gary Croft, Mike Kahn, Hal Bridges, Jeff Sanders, Paul Maltseff, Tom Dickens, Michael Irvine, Steve Swedenburg, Tom Dillon, Donn Gabrielson, and Ed Millett. Thanks: Lisa Vartanian, author of metric.c included on the CD-ROM.

The usual suspects on the Usenet newsgroups (see the Resources section) contributed to my thinking and advancing the state of FPGA synthesis. These folks include Paul Menchini, Peter Alfke, Ray Andraka, Edward Arthur, Rajesh Bawankule, Stuart Sutherland, Tom Coonan, Ben Cohen, Steven Knapp, Austin Franklin, Utku Ozcan, and John Cooley.

Many thanks to the folks who provided software and support: Dave Pfost, John Bennett, Patrick Kane of Xilinx, Tom Feist of Exemplar Logic, Richard Jones of Simucad, and Dennis Reynolds and Dave Kresta of Model Technology.

A special nod in the direction of William M. McDonald and Robert Craig (Coolbob) Slater, RIP brothers.

## CHAPTER 1

Verilog Design in the Real World

The challenges facing digital design engineers in the Real World have changed dramatically as technology has advanced. Designs are faster, use larger numbers of gates, and are physically smaller. Packages have many fine-pitch pins. However, the underlying design concerns have not changed, nor will they change in the future. The designer must create designs that:

- are understandable to others who will work on the design later.
- are logically correct. The design must actually implement the specified logic correctly. The designer collects user specifications, device parameters, and design entry rules, then creates a design that meets the needs of the end user.
- perform under worst-case conditions of temperature and process variation. As devices age and are exposed to changes in temperature, the performance of the circuit elements changes. Temperature changes can be self-generated or caused by external heat sources. No two devices are exactly equivalent, particularly

devices that were manufactured at different times, perhaps at different foundries and perhaps with different design rules. Variations in the device timing specifications, including clock skew, register setup and hold times, propagation delay times, and output rise/fall times must be accounted for.

- are reliable. The end design cannot exceed the package power dissipation limits. Each device has an operational temperature range. For example, a device rated for commercial operation has a temperature rating of 0 to 70 degrees C (32 to 160 degrees F). The device temperature includes the ambient temperature (the temperature of the air surrounding the product when it is in use), temperature increases due to heat-generating sources inside the product, and heat generated by the devices of the design itself. Internally generated temperature rises are proportional to the number of gates and the speed at which they are changing states.

- do not generate more EMI/RFI than necessary to accomplish the job and meet EMI/RFI specifications.

- are testable and can be proven to meet the specifications.

- do not exceed the power consumption goals (for example, in a battery-operated circuit).

These requirements exist regardless of the final form of the design and regardless of the engineering tools used to create and test the design.

SYNTHESIS
The translation of a high-level design description to target hardware. For the purposes of this book, synthesis represents all the processes that convert Verilog code into a netlist that can be implemented in hardware.

The job of the digital designer includes writing HDL code intended for synthesis. This HDL code will be implemented in the target hardware and defines the operation of the shippable product. The designer also writes code intended to stimulate and test the output of the design. The designer writes code in a language that is easy for humans to understand. This code must be translated by a compiler into a form appropriate for the final hardware implementation.

WHY HDL?
There are other methods of creating a digital design, for example: using a schematic. A schematic has some advantages: it's easy to create a design more tailored to the FPGA, and a more compact and faster design can be created. However, a schematic is not portable and schematics become unmanageable when a design contains more than 10 or 20 sheets. For large and portable designs, HDL is the best method.

As a contrast between a Verilog design found in other books and a *Real World* design, consider the code fragments in Listings 1-1 and 1-2.

Listing 1-1 Non *Real World* Example

```
// Transfer the content of register b to register a.
    a        <=      b;
```

Listing 1-2 *Real World* Example

```
/* Signal b must transfer to signal a in less than 7.3 nsec in a -
3 speed grade device as part of a much larger design that must
draw less than 80 uA while in standby and 800 uA while operating.
The whole design must cost less than $1.47, pass CE testing, and
take less than two months to be written, debugged, integrated,
documented, and shipped to the customer. Signal a must be
synchronized to the 75 MHz system clock and reset by the global
system reset. The signal b input should be located at or near pin
79 on the 208-pin package in order to help meet the setup and hold
requirement of register a.*/

    a        <=      b;
```

To illustrate the design process, let's follow a trivial example from concept to delivery and examine the issues that the designer confronts when implementing the design. Don't worry if the Verilog language elements are unfamiliar; they will be covered in detail later in this chapter.

TRIVIAL OVERHEAT DETECTOR EXAMPLE

Sarah, the Engineering Manager, writes the following email to Sam, the digital designer:

To: sam@engineering
From: sarah@management
Subject: Hot Design Project.

```
The customer wants a red light that turns on and stays on if a
button is pressed and if their machine is overheating. They want
it yesterday, it needs to be battery operated, and has to have a
final build cost of $0.02 so the company can make money when
they sell it for $9.95.
```

First, Sam estimates the scope of the design. From experience, she determines that this circuit is very similar to a design she did last year. She counts the gates of the previous design, factors in the differences between the two designs, and decides the design is approximately 20 gates. She considers the speed that the design must run at and any other complicating factors she can think of, including the error she made in estimating complexity of the previous design and the fact that she's already purchased airline tickets for a week of vacation. She knows that, overall, including design, test, integration, and documentation, she can design 2000 gates a month without working significant overtime. She counts the number of pins (the specification lists a pushbutton input, an overheat input, and an overheat output, but Sarah realizes that she'll need to add at least a reset and clock input). From the gate-count estimate and the pin estimate she can select a device. She picks a device that has more pins than she needs because she knows the design will grow as features are added. She picks an FPGA package from a family that has larger and faster parts available so she is not stuck if she needs more logic or faster speed. Now she sends a preliminary schedule and part selection to her boss and starts working on the design. Her boss will thank her for her thorough work on the cost and schedule estimates, but will insist that the job be done faster to be ready for an important trade show and cheaper to satisfy the marketing department.

Keep in mind that rarely will your estimates be low. Even when we know better, engineers are eternally optimistic. Unless you are very smart and very lucky, your estimate will not allow enough contingency to cover growth of the design (feature-creep), the hassles associated with fitting a high-speed design into a part that is too small, and the other 1001 things that can go wrong. These estimating errors result in overtime hours and increased project cost.

Now that Sam has taken care of the up-front project-related chores, she can start working on the design. Sam recognizes that a simple flipflop circuit will perform this function. She also recognizes, because of the problems she had with an earlier project, that a synchronous digital design is the right approach to solving this problem. Sam creates a Verilog design that looks like Listing 1-3.

Listing 1-3 Overheat Detector Design Example

```
module overheat (clock, reset, overheat_in, pushbutton_in,
overheat_out);
input      clock, reset, overheat_in, pushbutton_in;
output     overheat_out;
reg        overheat_out;
reg        pushbutton_sync1, pushbutton_sync2;
reg        overheat_in_sync1, overheat_in_sync2;

// Always synchronize inputs that are not phase related to
//  the system clock.
// Use double-synchronizing flipflops for external signals
//  to minimize metastability problems.
```

```
// Even better would be some type of filtering and latching
//   for poorly behaving external signals that will bounce
//   and have slow rise/fall times.

always @ (posedge clock or posedge reset)
begin
    if (reset)
            begin
            pushbutton_sync1      <=      1'b0;
            pushbutton_sync2      <=      1'b0;
            overheat_in_sync1     <=      1'b0;
            overheat_in_sync2     <=      1'b0;
            end
    else    begin
            pushbutton_sync1      <=      pushbutton_in;
            pushbutton_sync2      <=      pushbutton_sync1;
            overheat_in_sync1     <=      overheat_in;
            overheat_in_sync2     <=      overheat_in_sync1;
            end
end

// Latch the overheat output signal when overheat is
//   asserted and the user presses the pushbutton.
always @ (posedge clock or posedge reset)
begin
    if (reset)
            overheat_out  <=      1'b0;

// Overheat_out is held forever (or until reset).
    else if (overheat_in_sync2 && pushbutton_sync2)
            overheat_out <=      1'b1;
end

endmodule
```

This seems like a lot of typing for such a simple circuit, doesn't it? The first always element appears to do nothing and looks like it could be deleted. In a previous design, Sam had problems (which will be discussed in Chapter 2) with erratic logic behavior, so she always double-synchronizes inputs from the *Real World*. The second always block asserts pushbutton_out when overheat_in_sync and pushbutton_sync are asserted.

LINES OF CODE

A useful method estimating the size of a design is to count the semicolons. A utility called *metric*, which counts semicolons in a module, is included on the Real World FPGA Design with Verilog CD-ROM. This method should be used informally to avoid designers developing a semicolon-rich coding style :^).

Sam has done the fun part of the design: the actual designing of the code. She quickly runs her compiler, simulator, or Lint program to make sure there are no typographical or syntax errors. Next, because writing test vectors is almost as much fun as designing the code, Sam does a test fixture and checks out the behavior of her design. Her test fixture looks something like Listing 1-4.

Listing 1-4   Overheat Detector Test Fixture

```
// Overheat detector test fixture.
// Created by Sam Stephens

`timescale 1ns / 1ns

module oheat_tf;

reg clock, system_reset, overheat_in, pushbutton_in;

parameter clk_period        =       33.333;

overheat u1 (clock, system_reset, overheat_in, pushbutton_in,
overheat_out);

always       begin
    #clk_period clock   =       ~clock; // Generate system clock.
             end

initial
begin
             clock          =       0;
             system_reset   =       1; // Assert reset.
             overheat_in    =       0;
             pushbutton_in =       0;
#75          system_reset   =       0;
end

// Toggle the input and see if overheat_out gets asserted.
always
      begin
#200         overheat_in      =       1;
#100         pushbutton_in =       1;
#100         pushbutton_in =       0;
#200         overheat_in      =       0;
#100         $finish;
      end

endmodule
```

Sam invokes her favorite simulation tool and examines the output waveforms to make sure the output is logically correct. The output waveform looks like Figure 1-1 and appears okay. Generally Sam will write and run an automated test-fixture program (as described in

Chapter 5), but the design is simple and the boss has ordered her to quit being such a fussbudget and get on with it.

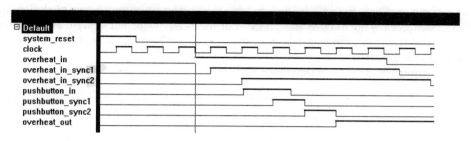

Figure 1-1   Overheat Detector Design Output Waveforms

Sam assigns input/output pins and defines timing constraints for her design. She knows that the system does not have to run fast, so she selects the lowest available crystal oscillator to drive the clock input. This gives the lowest current consumption to maximize the life of the battery. Sam submits the design to her FPGA compiler and gets a report back that tells her that the design fits into the device she chose and that timing constraints are met. From experience, she knows that a design running this slowly will not have temperature or RFI emission problems. She checks the design into the revision control system, sends an email to her boss to tell her the job is complete, and takes the rest of the day off to go rollerblading.

This probably seems like a lot of work to complete a job that consists of six flipflops, but Sam was lucky. The design fit into the device she chose, the design ran at the right speed, the design did not have temperature/EMI/RFI problems, the specifications didn't change halfway through the design, the software tools and her workstation didn't crash, and she avoided the 1001 other hazards that exist in the Real World.

ENGINEERING SCHEDULE

Too often, a management tool for browbeating an engineer into working free overtime. Engineers, even when they should really know better, are generally too optimistic when creating schedules, thus, they are almost always late.

We have to be mature about this subject: without a deadline, nothing would ever get finished. Still, most jobs should be completed with little overtime.

Some problems can be avoided by doing thorough design work up front. Sam was careful not to start coding until she completely understood the requirements of the design.

GIGO

There is a great temptation to start coding before the product is well understood. After all, to an engineer, coding is fun and planning is not.

    I don't care how much fun the job is, don't start coding the design until you know what the end result is supposed to be.

    This book emphasizes design approaches that minimize problems and unpleasant surprises.

SYNTHESIZABLE VERILOG ELEMENTS

Verilog was designed as a simulation language, and many of its elements do not translate to hardware. Verilog is a large and complete simulation language. Only about 10% of it is synthesizable. This chapter covers the fundamental properties of the 10% that the FPGA designer needs.

    Exactly which Verilog elements are considered synthesizable is a design problem faced by the synthesis vendor. Generally, an "unofficial" subset of the Verilog language elements will be supported by all vendors, but the current Verilog specification does not contain any minimum list of synthesizable language elements. An IEEE working group is writing a specification called IEEE Std 1364.1 RTL Synthesis Subset to define a minimum subset of synthesizable Verilog language elements. Whether this specification is ever released—and, once released, is embraced by users and synthesis tool vendors—remains to be seen at this writing.

    Verilog looks similar to the C programming language, but keep in mind that C defines sequential processes (after all, only one line of code can be executed by a processor at a time), whereas Verilog can define both sequential and parallel processes. Listing 1-5 presents some sample code with common synthesizable Verilog elements.

    Listing 1-5   Example Verilog Program

```
module hello (in1, in2, in3, out1, out2, clk, rst, bidir_signal,
output_enable);// See note 1.
/* See note 2.
Comments that span multiple lines can be identified like this.
*/
input       in1, in2, in3, clk, rst, output_enable; // See note 3.
output      out1, out2;
inout       bidir_signal;
reg         out2;                        // See note 4
```

```
wire          out1;

assign out             = in1 & in2;  // See note 5.
assign bidir_signal    = output_enable ? out2:1'bz;// See note 6.

always @ (posedge clk or posedge rst) // See note 7.
   begin                              // See note 8.
      if (rst) out2      <=      1'b0;          // See note 9.
      else out2          <=      (in3 & bidir_signal);
   end
endmodule
```

Note 1: The first element of a module is the module name. Modules are the building blocks of a Verilog design. In this book, the module name will be the same as the file name (with a .v extension added) and each file will contain a single module. This is not required but helps keep the design structure intelligible.

The port list follows the module/file name. This list contains the signals that connect this module to other modules and to the outside world. Signals used in the module that are not in the port list are local to the module and will not be connected to other modules. Note the use of a semicolon as a separator to isolate Verilog elements. One confusing aspect of Verilog is that not all lines end with a semicolon, particularly the compiler instructions (always statements, if statements, case statements, etc.). It takes the Verilog newbie some time to get comfortable with Verilog syntax.

Note 2: Comments follow double forward slashes or can be enclosed within a /* Comment here */ pair. The latter type of comment delimiting can't be nested. The detection of a /* following another /* will be flagged as an error.

Note 3: The port direction list follows the module port list. This list defines whether the signals are inputs, outputs, or inout (bidirectional) ports of the module. All port list signals are wires. A wire is simply a net similar to an interconnection on a printed circuit card.

Note 4: Signals are either wires (interconnects similar to traces and pads on a circuit board) or registers (a signal storage element like a latch or a flipflop). Wires can be driven by a register or by combinational assignments. It is illegal to connect two registers together inside a module. Verilog assumes that a signal, unless otherwise defined in the code, is a one-bit-wide wire. This can be a problem; the synthesis tool will not test vector width. This is one good reason for using a Verilog Lint tool.

Note 5: The assign statement is a continuous (combinational) logic assignment.

Note 6: The bidir_signal assignment uses a conditional assignment; if output_enable is true, bidir_signal is assigned the value of out2, otherwise it's assigned the tristate value z.

Note 7: Always blocks are sequential blocks. The signal list following the @ and inside the parenthesis is called the event sensitivity list, and the synthesis tool will extract block control signals from this list. The requirement of a sensitivity list comes from Verilog's simulation heritage. The simulator keeps a list of monitored signals to reduce the complexity of the simulation model; the logic is evaluated only when signals on the sensitivity list change. This allows simulation time to pass quickly when signals are not changing. This list doesn't mean much to the synthesis tool, except that, by convention, when certain signals are extracted for control, these input signals must appear on the sensitivity list. The compiler will issue a warning if the sensitivity list is not complete. These warnings should be resolved to assure that the synthesis result matches simulation.

The sensitivity list can be a list of signals (in which case, any change on any listed signal is detected and acted upon), posedge (rising-edge triggered), or negedge (falling-edge triggered). Posedge and negedge triggers can be mixed, but if posedge or negedge is used for one control, posedge or negedge must be used for ALL controls for this block.

Note 8: The begin/end command isolates code fragments. If the code can be expressed using a single semicolon, the begin/end pair is optional.

Note 9: We're using nonblocking assignments (<=) in the always block. If blocking assignments (=) are used, the order of the instructions may cause unwanted latches to be synthesized so that a value can be held while earlier variables are updated. Generally, the designer wants all elements in the sequential (always) block updated simultaneously, hence the use of the nonblocking assignment, which emulates the clock-to-Q delay. The clock-to-Q delay assures that cascaded flipflops (like a shift register) operate as expected. They are called nonblocking because updating an earlier variable will not block the updating of a later variable.

The rst input, when coded in this manner (i.e., a nonsynchronous signal used in a synchronous module), is interpreted as asynchronous reset. This is not Verilog requirement per IEEE Std 1364 but is an accepted convention.

Verilog language elements are case sensitive (X and x are not equivalent, for example). Like the C programming language, Verilog is tolerant of white space. The designer uses white space to assist legibility. It's legal to combine lines as so:

```
a = b&c; d = e&f; g = h | i; j = k^m; n = o&p;
```

but designers who write hard-to-read code like this are subject to the loss of their free sodas.

PORTABLE VERILOG CODE

It is desirable to write code that can be compiled by any vendor's compiler and implemented in any hardware technology with identical results. Unfortunately, to write high-performance (where the design runs at high speed) and efficient (where the design uses minimum hardware resources by targeting architecture-specific features) code, the designer often must use architecture- and compiler-specific commands and constructs. Portability is often not a practical or achievable design requirement. It's a great goal even if we never reach it.

We're not going to cover operator precedence. If you have a required precedence, then use parenthesis to be explicit about that precedence. The reader should be able to read the precedence in the source code, not be forced to memorize or look up the built-in language precedence(s). Don't create complicated structures; use the simplest and clearest coding style possible. Listings 1-6 and 1-7 illustrate equivalent coding structures with implicit and explicit 'don't-cares'.

Listing 1-6   Casex (Implicit Don't Care) Code Fragment

```
// Indexing example with implicit 'don't cares'.
reg         [7:0] test_vector;
Casex (test_vector)
8'bxxxx0001:
    begin
// Insert code here.
// This coding style results in a parallel case structure (MUX).
    end
endcase
```

Listing 1-7   Explicit Don't Care Code Fragment

```
// Indexing example with explicit 'don't cares'.
reg         [7:0] test_vector;
if (test_vector[3:0] == 4'b0001)
    begin
    // Insert code here.
    // This coding style results in priority encoded logic.
    end
```

One feature of Verilog the designer must conquer is whether a priority-encoded (deep and slow) structure or a MUX (wide and fast) structure is desired. Nested if-then statements tend to create priority-encoded logic. Case statements tend to create MUX logic elements. There will be more discussion of this topic later.

Do not assume a Verilog register is a flipflop of some type. In Verilog, a register is simply a memory storage element. This is one of the first of the features (or quirks) the Verilog designer grapples with. A register might synthesize to a flipflop (which is a digital construct) or a latch (which is an analog construct), a wire, or might be absorbed during optimization. Verilog assumes that a variable not explicitly changed should hold its value. This is a handy feature (compared to Altera's AHDL, which assumes that a variable not mentioned gets cleared). Verilog, with merciless glee, will instantiate latches to hold a variable's state. The designer must structure the code so that the intended hardware construct is synthesized and must be constantly alert to the possibility that the latches may be synthesized. Verilog does not include instructions that *require* the synthesizer to use a certain construct. By using conventions defined by the synthesis vendor, and making sure all input conditions are completely defined, the proper *interpretation* will be made by the synthesizer.

VERILOG HIERARCHY

A Verilog design consists of a top-level module and one or many lower-level modules. The top-level module can be instantiated by a simulation module that applies test stimulus to the device pins. The top-level device module generally contains the list of ports that connect to the outside world (device pins) and interconnect between lower-level modules and multiplexing logic for control of bidirectional I/O pins or tristate device pins. The exact way the design is structured depends on designer preference.

Module instances are defined as follows:

```
module_name instance_name (port list);
```

For example, the code in Listing 1-8 creates four instances of assorted primitive gates and the post-synthesis schematic for this design is shown in Figure 1-2.

Listing 1-8   Structural Example

```
module gates (in1,in2,in3,out4);
input      in1, in2, in3;
output     out4;
wire       in1, in2, in3, out1, out2, out3, out4;
and u1 (out1, in1, in2); // Structural (schematic-like)
or u2 (out2, out1, in3); //  constructs.
xor u3 (out3, out1, out2);
not u4 (out4, out3);
endmodule
```

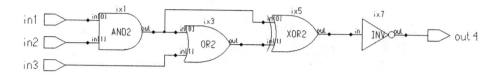

Figure 1-2   Gates Example Schematic

This example uses positional assignment. Signals are connected in the same order that they are listed in the instantiated module port list(s). Generally, the designer will cut and paste the port list to assure they are identical. A requirement for a primitive port listing is that the output(s) occur first on the port list followed by the input(s).

The module port list can also use named assignments (exception: primitives require positional assignment), in which case the order of the signals in the port list is arbitrary. For named assignments, the format is .lower-level signal name (higher-level module signal name). The module of Listing 1-9 includes examples of both named and positional assignments.

Listing 1-9   Named and Positional Assignment Example

```
module and_top;
wire        test_in1, test_in2, test_in3;
wire        test_out1, test_out2;

// Named assignment where the port order doesn't matter.
user_and u1 (.out1(test_out1), .in1(test_in1), .in2(test_in2));

// Positional assignment.
user_and u2 (test_out2, test_in2), (test_in3));
endmodule

module user_and (out1, in1, in2);
input       in1, in2;
output      out1;

assign      out1  =       (in1 & in2);
endmodule
```

BUILT-IN LOGIC PRIMITIVES

Tables 1-1 through 1-12 describe Verilog two-input functions. The input combinations are read down and across. Verilog primitives are not limited to two inputs, and the logic for primitives with more inputs can be extrapolated from these tables.

and	0	1	x	z
0	0	0	0	0
1	0	1	x	x
x	0	x	x	x
z	0	x	x	x

Table 1-1   AND Gate Logic

nand	0	1	x	z
0	1	1	1	1
1	1	0	x	z
x	1	x	x	z
z	1	x	x	z

Table 1-2   NAND Gate Logic

or	0	1	x	z
0	0	1	x	x
1	1	1	1	1
x	x	1	x	x
z	x	1	x	x

Table 1-3   OR Gate Logic

nor	0	1	x	z
0	1	0	x	x
1	0	0	0	0
x	x	0	x	x
z	x	0	x	x

Table 1-4   NOR Gate Logic

xor	0	1	x	z
0	0	1	x	x
1	1	0	x	x
x	X	x	x	x
z	X	x	x	x

Table 1-5   XOR Gate Logic

xnor	0	1	x	z
0	1	0	x	x
1	0	1	x	x
x	X	x	x	x
z	X	x	x	x

Table 1-6   XNOR (Equivalence) Gate Logic

input	output
0	0
1	1
x	x
z	x

Table 1-7 buf (buffer) Gate Logic

input	Output
0	1
1	0
x	x
z	x

Table 1-8 not (inverting buffer) Gate Logic

bufif0	control = 0	control = 1	control = x	control = z
data = 0	0	z	x	x
data = 1	1	z	x	x
data = x	x	z	x	x
data = z	x	z	x	x

Table 1-9 bufif0 (tristate buffer, low enable) Gate Logic

bufif0	control = 0	control = 1	control = x	control = z
data = 0	z	0	0 or z	0 or z
data = 1	z	1	1 or z	1 or z
data = x	z	x	x	x
data = z	z	x	x	x

Table 1-10 bufif1 (tristate buffer, high enable) Gate Logic

notif0	control = 0	control = 1	control = x	control = z
data = 0	1	z	1 or z	1 or z
data = 1	0	z	0 or z	0 or z
data = x	x	z	x	x
data = z	x	z	x	x

Table 1-11 notif0 (tristate inverting buffer, low enable) Gate Logic

notif1	control = 0	control = 1	control = x	control = z
data = 0	z	1	1 or z	1 or z
Data = 1	z	0	0 or z	x or z
Data = x	z	x	x	x
Data = z	z	x	x	x

Table 1-12 notif1 (tristate inverting buffer, high enable) Gate Logic

The code fragment in Listing 1-10 illustrates the use of these buffers and Figure 1-3 is the schematic extracted from the synthesized logic.

Listing 1-10 Example of Instantiating Structural Gates

```
module struct1 (out1, out2, out3, out4, in1, in2, in3, in4, in5,
in6, buf_control);
output     out1, out2, out3, out4;
input      in1, in2, in3, in4, in5, in6, buf_control;
```

```
bufif0 buf1(out1, in1, buf_control);
and and1(out2, in2, in3);
nor nor1(out3, in4, in5);
not not1(out4, in6);
endmodule
```

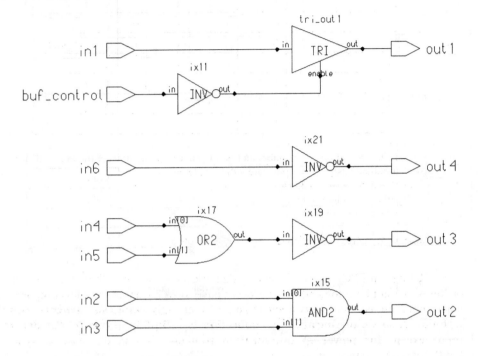

Figure 1-3   Schematic of Structural Gates

LATCHES AND FLIPFLOPS

Technically, a flipflop is defined as a bistable multivibrator. Not a very helpful definition, is it? A multivibrator is an analog circuit with two or more outputs, where, if one output is on, the other(s) will be off. Bistable means an output is binary or digital and has two output states: high or low. We will extend the output states to include tristate (z).

There are various flavors of flipflops, but generally we will be discussing the clocked D flipflop in which the output follows the D input after a clock edge. Table 1-13 shows the function table of a common edge-triggered D flipflop. Note that Table 1-13 Set and Reset inputs are active-low.

/Set	/Reset	Clock	Data	Q	/Q	
0	1	x	x	1	0	
1	0	x	x	0	1	
0	0	x	x	1	1	Note 1
1	1	r	1	1	0	
1	1	r	0	0	1	
1	1	0	x	n	n	
1	1	1	x	n	n	

Note 1: This condition is not stable and is illegal. The problem is, if the /Set and /Reset inputs are removed simultaneously, the output state will be unknown.

x = don't care (doesn't matter).

r = rising edge of clock signal.

n = no change, previous state is held.

Table 1-13   Logic description of a 7474-style D flipflop

The typical FPGA logic element design allows the use of either an asynchronous Set or Reset, but not both together, so we won't have to worry about the illegal input condition where both are asserted. **This book is going to strongly emphasize synchronous design techniques, so we discourage any connection to a flipflop asynchronous Set or Reset input except for power-up initialization control.** Even in this case, a synchronous Set/Reset might be more appropriate.

A latch is more of an analog function. It's helpful to bear in mind that all the underlying circuits that make up our digital logic are analog! There is no magic flipflop element. Flipflops are made with transistors and positive feedback: they are latches.

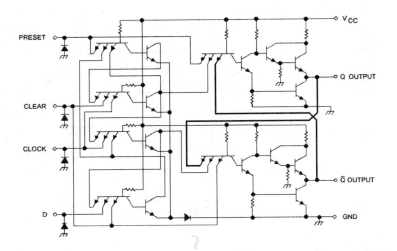

Figure 1-4   Schematic of a Typical CMOS D Flipflop Implementation

Even if you're the kind of person whose eyes glaze over when you see transistors on a schematic, you should still notice two things about Figure 1-4. The first thing is that this D flipflop is made with linear devices, i.e., transistors. If you can always keep the idea in the back of your head that all digital circuits are built from analog elements that have gain, impedance, offsets, leakages, and other analog nasties, then you are on the road to being an excellent digital designer. The second thing to notice is feedback (see highlighted signals) from the Q and /Q outputs back into the circuit. Feedback is what causes the flipflop to hold its state.

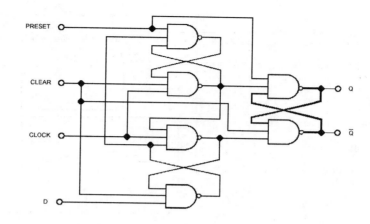

Figure 1-5   Schematic of a Typical CMOS D Flipflop Implementation (Gates)

If you are more comfortable with gates, a different view of the same D flipflop is shown in Figure 1-5. This is a higher level of abstraction; the transistors and resistors are hidden. Those pesky transistors are still there! Again, note highlighted feedback path.

Listing 1-11 shows a Verilog version of a latch, and Figure 1-6 shows the schematic extracted from this Verilog design. The underlying circuit that implements RS Latch (LATRS) is a circuit functionally similar to Figure 1-5. It's not a digital circuit!

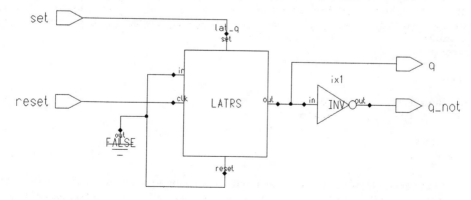

Figure 1-6   Schematic of Latch Flipflop Implementation

Listing 1-11 Latch Verilog Code

```
// Your Basic Latch.
// This is a bad coding style: do not create latches this way!

module latch(q, q_not, set, reset);
output      q, q_not;
input       set, reset;
reg         q;

wire        set, reset;

assign      q_not =      ~q;

    always @ (set or reset)
    begin
            if (set)
            q       =      1;
            else if (reset)
            q       =      0;
    end
endmodule
```

The latch uses feedback to hold a state: this feedback is implied in Listing 1-11 by not defining q for all combinations of input conditions. For undefined inputs, q will hold its previous state. The logic that determines a latch output state may include a clock signal but typically does not and is therefore a level-sensitive rather than an edge-triggered construct.

Listing 1-12 Verilog Code That Creates a Latch

```
module lev_lat(test_in1, enable_input, test_out1);
input       test_in1, enable_input;
output      test_out1;
reg         test_out1;

always @ (test_in1 or enable_input)
if (enable_input) begin
    test_out1      <=      test_in1;
    end
endmodule
```

In the example of Listing 1-12, test_out1 will change only while enable_input is high, then test_out1 will follow test_in1. This will synthesize to a combinational latch as illustrated in Figure 1-7. We'll discourage this type of coding style unless the latch is driven by a synchronous circuit and drives a synchronous circuit, resulting in a pseudosynchronous design.

Is a latch a good design construct? That depends on the designer's intent. If the designer intended to create a latch construct, then a synthesized latch is good. If the designer did not intend to create a latch construct (which Verilog is very inclined to create), then a latch is bad. In general, we will scrutinize all synthesized latches suspiciously, because they are, at best, pseudosynchronous constructs.

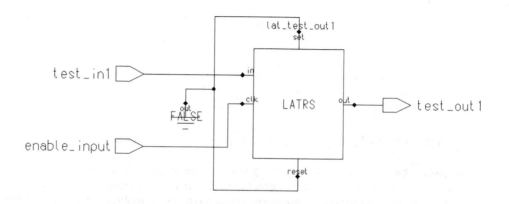

Figure 1-7 Latch Circuit Schematic (Reset-Set Latch)

A better design infers a clocked flipflop structure, as in Listing 1-13, with the respective schematic shown in Figure 1-8.

Listing 1-13 Cascaded Flipflops with Synchronous Reset

```
module edge_lat (clk, rst, test_in1, enable_input, test_out2);
input      clk, rst, test_in1, enable_input;
reg        test_out1, test_out2;
output     test_out2;

always @ (posedge clk or posedge rst)
begin
    if (rst) test_out1   <=    0;
    else if (enable_input) begin
            test_out2     <=    test_out1;
            test_out1     <=    test_in1;
    end
end
endmodule
```

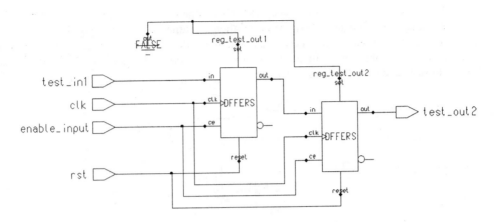

Figure 1-8   Schematic for Cascaded Flipflops with Synchronous Reset

Listing 1-13 demonstrates a flipflop with synchronous reset where the reset input is evaluated only on clock edges. If the target hardware does not support a synchronous reset, logic will be added to set the D input low when reset is asserted as shown in Figure 1-9. Listing 1-14 illustrates a flipflop with asynchronous reset where the **rst** signal is "evaluated" on a continuous basis. Notice that the dedicated global set/reset (GSR) resource of the flipflops are not used. It would be much more efficient to synthesize a synchronous reset signal and connect it to the GSR. This type of assignment is covered in Chapter 5.

Listing 1-14 Verilog Flipflop with Asynchronous Reset

```
module edgetrig (clk, rst, test_in1, enable_input, test_out2);
input       clk, rst, test_in1, enable_input;
reg         test_out1, test_out1;
output      test_out2;

always @ (posedge clk)
begin
    if (rst)
            test_out1      <=      0;
    else if (enable_input)          begin
            test_out2      <=       test_out1;
            test_out1      <=       test_in1;
    end
end
endmodule
```

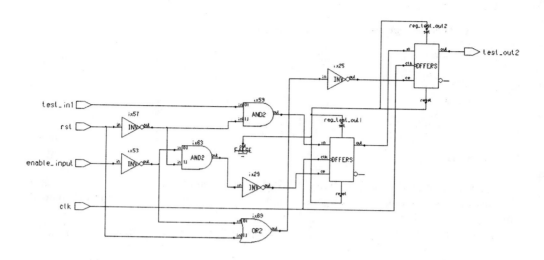

Figure 1-9   Schematic for Cascaded Flipflops with Synchronous Reset

BLOCKING AND NONBLOCKING ASSIGNMENTS

So far, we've used only nonblocking assignments (<=). A blocking assignment (=), when the variable is defined outside the **always** statement where it is used, holds off future assignments until the previous assignment is complete. How can synthesized hardware hold off an assignment? By storing an old value in a latch, that's how. This means that blocking assignments are order sensitive; they are executed in the begin/end sequential block in the order in which they are encountered by the compiler (top to bottom).

Listing 1-15 Blocking Statement Example 1

```
/* The blocking statement of the first blocking assignment must be
completed before any later assignments will be performed. In this
example, two sets of flipflops will be created (see Figure 1-10)
because an intermediate value is required to create data_out. */

module blocking(clock, reset, data_in, data_out);
input      clock, reset;
input      data_in;
reg        data_temp;
output     data_out;
```

```
reg            data_out;

    always @ (posedge clock or posedge reset)
    if (reset)
    begin
        data_out       =       0;
        data_temp      =       0;
    end
    else
    begin
        data_out       =    data_temp;
        data_temp      =    data_in;
    end
endmodule
```

The synthesized logic for Listing 1-15, shown in Figure 1-10, illustrates the blocking assignment of data_temp and data_out: a flipflop is synthesized to create the intermediate (pipelined) data_temp variable.

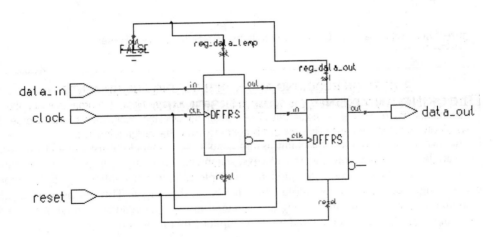

Figure 1-10 Blocking Statement Example 1

In Listing 1-16, the blocking statements are reversed. Notice how the resulting logic, as illustrated in Figure 1-11, is different from the logic of Figure 1-10.

Listing 1-16 Blocking Statement Example 2

```
/* The blocking statements are reversed, making the data_temp
variable redundant, so data_temp gets optimized out. One set of
flipflops is created (see Figure 1-11) because the intermediate
value is 'blocked' and not needed to create data_out. */

module block2(clock, reset, data_in, data_out);
    input  clock, reset, data_in;
    reg    data_temp;
    output data_out;
    reg    data_out;

    always @ (posedge clock or posedge reset)
    if (reset)    begin
        data_out      =      0;
        data_temp     =      0;
    end
    else
    begin
        data_temp     =  data_in;   // Switch order.
        data_out      =  data_temp;
    end
endmodule
```

A NOTE ON BLOCKING AND NONBLOCKING ASSIGNMENTS

In a set of blocking assignments that appear in the same **always** block, the order in which the statements are evaluated is significant. The use of nonblocking assignments avoids order sensitivity and tends to create flipflops: this is generally what the designer intends.

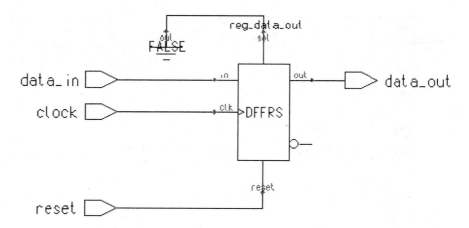

Figure 1-11   Blocking Assignment Example 2

If we replace the blocking assignments with nonblocking assignments, the order of the sequential instructions no longer matters. All right-hand values are evaluated at the positive edge of the clock, and all assignments are made at the same time. The synthesized logic for Listing 1-17, shown in Figure 1-12, illustrates the nonblocking assignments of data_temp and data_out and the resulting synthesized design which is equivalent to the logic of Listing 1-16.

Listing 1-17   Nonblocking Assignment Example

```
// Nonblocking Logic Example
// The order of the nonblocking assignments is not significant.

module nonblock(clock, reset, data_in, data_out);
input       clock, reset;
input       data_in;
reg         data_temp;
output      data_out;
reg         data_out;

    always @ (posedge clock or posedge reset)
    if (reset)
    begin
        data_out        <=      0;
        data_temp       <=      0;
    end
```

```
        else
        begin
            data_out          <=        data_temp;
            data_temp         <=        data_in;
        end
endmodule
```

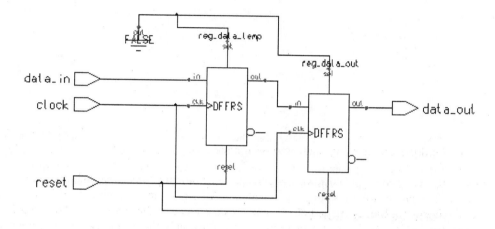

Figure 1-12 Nonblocking Assignment Example 3

MISCELLANEOUS VERILOG SYNTAX ITEMS

Numbers

Unless defined otherwise by the designer, a Verilog number is 32 bits wide. The format of a Verilog number is **size'base value**. The ' is the single quote (tick or closing quote), not to be confused with ' (accent grave, opening quote, or back tick) which is used to identify text substitution and compiler directives. Both tick and back tick are used in Verilog, which will frustrate a newbie. Underscores are legal in a number to aid in readability. All numbers are padded to the left with zeros, x's, or z's (if the leftmost defined value is x or z) as necessary. If the number is unsized, the assumed size is just large enough to hold the defined value when the value gets used for comparison or assignment. X or x is undefined, Z or z is high impedance. Verilog allows the use of ? in place of z. Numbers without an explicit base are assumed to be decimal. All nets are assumed to be Z unless driven.

Number examples:

```
1'b0          // A single bit, zero value.
'b0           // 32 bits, all zeros.
32'b0         // 32 bits, all zeros,
              //  0000_0000_0000_0000_0000_0000_0000_0000).
4'ha          // A 4-bit hex number (1010).
5'h5          // A 5-bit hex number (00101).
4'hz          // zzzz.
4'h?ZZ?       // zzzz, ? is an alternate form of z.
4'bx          // xxxx.
9             // A 32-bit number (it's padded to the left
              //  with 28 zeroes).
a             // An illegal number.
```

Verilog is a loosely typed language. For example, it accepts what looks like an 8-bit value like 4'hab without complaint (the number will be recognized as 1011 or b and the upper nibble will be ignored). The use of a Lint program like Verilint will flag problems like this. Otherwise, the Verilog designer must stay alert to guard against such errors.

Forms of Negation

! is logical negation; the result is a single bit value, true (1) or false (0). ~ (tilde) is bitwise negation. We can use a ! (sometimes called a bang) to invert a single bit value, and the result is the same as using a ~ (tilde), but this is a bad habit! As soon as someone comes in and changes the single bit to a multibit vector, the two operators are no longer equivalent, and this can be a difficult problem to track down (see Listing 1-18).

Listing 1-18 Negation example

```
module negation (clk, resetn);
input        clk, resetn;
reg [3:0]    c, d, e;

always @ (posedge clk or negedge resetn)
begin
        if (~resetn)     // Active low asynchronous reset.
        begin

        c       <=      5; // Bad form to async set a value like
                           //  this. This is called a magic
                           //  number and should be a parameter.
```

```
                d       <=      0;
                e       <=      0;
                end
                else    begin
                d       <=      !c;     // d gets assigned value of 0;
                e       <=      ~c;     // e gets assigned value of 1010.
                end
        end
        endmodule
```

Forms of AND/OR

& is the symbol for the AND operation. & is a bitwise AND, && is a logical (true/false) AND. As illustrated in Listing 1-19, these two forms are not functionally equivalent.

Listing 1-19 Logical and Bitwise AND Examples

```
a   =   4'b1000 &    4'b0001;     // a = 4'b0000;
b   =   4'b1000 &&   4'b0001;     // b = 1'b0.
```

| (pipe) is the symbol for the OR operation, where | is a bitwise OR and || is a logical OR. As illustrated in Listing 1-20, these two forms are not functionally equivalent.

Listing 1-20 Logical and Bitwise OR Examples

```
a   =   4'b1000 |    4'b0001;     // a = 4'b1001;
b   =   4'b1000 ||   4'b0001;     // b = 1'b1.
```

Listing 1-21 AND/OR Examples

```
module and_or (clk, resetn, and_test, or_test);
    input           clk, resetn, and_test, or_test;
    reg             a;
    reg [3:0]       b;
    reg [3:0]       c;
    reg [3:0]       d;
    reg [3:0]       e;
    reg [3:0]       g;

    always @ (posedge clk or negedge resetn)
    begin
```

```
        if (~resetn)  // Active low asynchronous reset.
        begin
        a        <=      0;
        b        <=      4'd4;  // Bad form to async set values
                               //  like this, should be a
                               //  parameter.
        c        <=      4'd5;
        d        <=      0;
        e        <=      0;
        g        <=      0;
        end

        else if (and_test)
        begin
d       <=      (c && !a);   // d gets assigned value of 0.
e       <=      (c & !a);    // e gets assigned value of
                             //  1010.
g       <=      (b & c);     // g gets assigned the value
                             //  0100.
        end
else if (or_test == 1)       // Equivalent to simply (or_test).
        begin
e       <=      (c | !a);    // e gets assigned value of all
                             //  1's (1111).
g       <=      (b | c);     // g gets assigned the value 0101.
        end
        else
        begin
d       <=      0;           // Assign default values to avoid
                             //  unwanted latches.
e       <=      0;
g       <=      0;
        end

end
endmodule
```

In Listing 1-21, the final **else** condition bears some comment. We did not cover all input conditions in the logic above the final **else** condition. For example, what output do we want if neither and_test or or_test is asserted? Without the final **else** defined, Verilog interprets a change from a defined condition to an undefined condition as a hold condition (if outputs are not commanded, the last value gets held). This causes latches to be created. Generally, this is not what the designer intends; thus, we need to make sure that all conditions are defined.

Equality Operators

== === are logical operators; the result is either true or false except that the == (called logical equality) version will have an unknown (x) result if any of the compared bits are x or z. The === (called case equality) version looks for exact match of bits including x's and z's and returns only a true or false. Prepending a ! (bang) means "is not equal." In the equality examples of Listing 1-22, there are several if statements that will evaluate to true. As the block is examined from top to bottom, only the first true condition will be accepted. The later ones will not be evaluated. This is called priority encoding, and, like instantiating latches, Verilog has a natural tendency to use this structure. It can result in many levels of cascaded logic! Pay close attention. The alternative option is more of a MUXstyle of structure where inputs are evaluated in parallel, which may be what you intend. We'll talk more about this later.

Listing 1-22 Equality Examples

```
module eq_test (clk, resetn, and_test, or_test);
input         clk, resetn, and_test, or_test;
reg           result;
reg [3:0]     b;
reg [3:0]     c;
reg [3:0]     d;
reg [3:0]     e;
reg [4:0]     g;
reg [3:0]     h, i, j;

always @ (posedge clk or negedge resetn)
begin
        if (~resetn) // Active low asynchronous reset.
        begin

        result <=     0;      // We'll use this register to
                              //  mirror the equality result.
        b       <=    4'b1x00; // Bad form to async set values
                              //  like this; should be a
                              //  parameter.
        c       <=    4'b1z00;
        d       <=    4'b1000;
        e       <=    4'b1001;
        g       <=    4'b01001;
        h       <=    4'b1z00;
        i       <=    4'b0110;
        j       <=    4'b011x;
        end

// The following test fails.
```

```
    else if ((b == d) == 1)
            result <=      1'bx;

    else if (b == d)      // This test is the same as previous
                          //  line. Fails.
            result <=      1'bx;

    else if ((b == d) == 0)   // This test fails because of the
                              //  x value in b.
            result <=      1'bx;

    else if ((b != d) == 1)   // This test is the same as in the
                              //  previous line. Fails.
            result <=      1'b0;

    else if ((b == d) == 1'bx) // This test passes because the
                               //  b value is x.
            result <=      1'b1;  // All following true conditions
                                  //  will be ignored.

    else if (c === d)          // This test fails.
            result <=      1'b0;

    else if (e == g)          // This test passes because e is
                              //  padded with 0's to become equal
                              //  in size to g.
            result <=      1'b0;  // Be careful when variables sizes
                                  //  don't match.

    else if (b == c)          // This test fails (returns false).
            result <=      1'b0;

    else if (b != c)          // This test passes (returns true).
            result <=      1'b1;

    else if ( d == e)         // This test fails (returns false).
            result <=      1'b0;

    else if (b !== c)         // This test passes (returns true).
            result <=      1'b1;

    else if (c == h)          // This test fails (returns x).
            result <=      1'bx;

    else if (c===h)           // This test passes (returns true).
            result <=      1'b1;

    else if (e == !i)     // This test passes (returns true).
            result <=      1'b1;

    else if (e != j)      // This test fails (returns x).
                          //  An inverted x (unknown) is
                          //  still an unknown.
```

```
        result <=      1'bx;

    end
    endmodule
```

The designer can choose between the following **if** statement forms:

if (~resetn) ...

if (resetn == 1`b0)

Both are equivalent. Which is easy to read and easier to understand? That's a matter of opinion. Note the use of an 'n' suffix to indicate an active low (asserted when low or low-true are other ways to describe this) signal. There are various ways of identifying active low signals—for example, reset_not, resetl, or reset*, or resetN. It helps to identify the assertion sense as part of the label; the main thing is to be consistent when selecting labels.

Other equalities are supported, including greater than (>), less than (<), greater than or equal to (>=), and less than or equal to (<=).

Shift Operators

>> n and << n identify right-shift (divide by 2n) and left-shift (multiply by 2n) operations. This operation will fill left and right values with zeros as necessary to fill the register. Operating on a value which contains an x or a z gives an x result in all bit positions. Some examples of using the shift operators are presented in Listing 1-23.

Listing 1-23 Shift Operator Examples

```
module shifter (clk, resetn, shift_right_test, shift_left_test);
input           clk, resetn;
input           shift_right_test;
input           shift_left_test;
reg [3:0]   a;
reg [3:0]   b;
reg [3:0]   c;
reg         d;
reg [3:0]   e, f;

    always @ (posedge clk or negedge resetn)
    begin
        if (~resetn) // Active low asynchronous reset.
        begin

        a       <=      'b1001;
        b       <=      0;      // It's bad form to async set
```

```
                                 //  values like this.
            c       <=      0;
            d       <=      0;
            e       <=      'bx000;
            end

            else if (shift_right_test)
            begin

            c       <=      a >> 2;       // c gets assigned value of
                                          //  0010.
            d       <=      a >> 5;       // Regardless of the value
                                          //  of a, d will always get
                                          //  assigned to 0.
                                          // Verilog will not complain
                                          //  about this; use caution.
            f       <=      e >> 1;       // Result is xxxx because of
                                          //  x in e.
            end

            else if (shift_left_test)
            begin

            c       <=      a << 2;       // c gets assigned value of
                                          //  0100.
            d       <=      a << 5;       // Regardless of the value
                                          //  of a, d will always get
                                          //  assigned to 0.
                                          // Verilog will not complain
                                          //  about this; use caution.
            f       <=      e << 1;       // Result is xxxx because of
                                          //  of x in e.
            end

            else
            begin
            d       <=      0;            // Assign values default to avoid
                                          //  unwanted latches.
            e       <=      0;
            f       <=      0;
            end

    end
    endmodule
```

Conditional Operator

A shorthand method of doing a conditional uses a ternary form (which means arranged in order by threes).

```
output_assignment <= expression ? true_assignment :
false_assignment;
```

This is a common way of defining a MUX. If the expression being evaluated resolves to x or z, the output_bus is evaluated bit-by-bit, and Verilog will try to resolve the output values. If both input bits are 1 (which means the input condition doesn't matter), then the output bit is a 1. Same for both input bits being 0. Any bits that can't be resolved are assigned an x value. If the true_assignment or the false_assignment register width is not wide enough to fill the output_assignment, the output_assignment bits are left-filled with zeros. See Listing 1-24.

Listing 1-24 Conditional Example

```verilog
    module cond_tst (clk, resetn, tristate_control, input_bus,
output_bus);
    input         clk, resetn;
    input         tristate_control;
    input  [7:0]  input_bus;
    output        output_bus;
    reg    [7:0]  output_bus;

    always @ (posedge clk or negedge resetn)
    begin
        if (~resetn) // Active low asynchronous reset.
        output_bus    <=    8'bz;

        else

// Assign output_bus = input_bus if tristate_control is
//   true and assign output_bus = high impedance if
//   tristate_control is false.
        output_bus    <=    tristate_control ? input_bus : 8'bz;

    end
    endmodule
```

Math Operators

Verilog supports a small set of math operators including addition (+), subtraction (-), multiplication (*), division (/), and modulus (%); however, the synthesis tool probably limits the usage of multiplication and division to constant powers of two (in other words, a left shifter or right shifter will be synthesized) and may not support modulus. The + and - math operators will instantiate preoptimized adders. Verilog assumes all reg and wire variables are unsigned.

Parameters

Parameters are a useful way of making constants more readable. Parameters are used only in the modules where they are defined, but they can be changed by higher-level modules. Parameters cannot be changed at run time, but they can be changed at compile time. This is useful in cases where a parameter changes the defined number of signals or the number of instances some construct is used. Not all parameters have to be assigned, but if there is a positional assignment list, parameters can't be skipped.

A parameter can also be defined in terms of other constants or parameters. To aid in reading the code, some people use upper-case characters for parameters.

Listings 1-25 and 1-26 demonstrate Verilog hierarchy, where a module list descends into the hierarchy, starting at the top, and with module names separated by periods.

Listing 1-25 Parameter Example, Top Module

```
module top;
reg         clk, resetn;
parameter   byte_width   = 8;
defparam
      u1.reg_width        = 16;  // This parameter will
                                 //  replace the first
                                 //  parameter found in
                                 //  the u1 instantiation
                                 //  of reg_width.

defparam
      u2.reg_width    =       byte_width * 2;
parm_tst u1 (clk, reset, output_bus);  // Create a version
                                       //  of parm_tst with
                                       //  reg_width = 16.
parm_tst u2 (clk, reset, output_bus);  // This version of
                                       //  parm_tst also has
                                       //  reg_width of 16.
parm_tst u3 (clk, reset, output_bus);  // This version of
                                       //  parm_tst has a
                                       //  reg_width of 8.

endmodule
```

Listing 1-26 Parameter Example, Lower Module

```
module      parm_tst (clk, resetn, output_bus);
input       clk, resetn;
parameter   reg_width   = 8;  // This constant can be
                              // overridden by a parameter
                              // value passed into the
                              // module.
parameter   byte_signal       = 8'd99;
parameter   byte_signal_true  = 8'hff;
```

```
parameter     byte_signal_false   = 8'h00;
output        [reg_width - 1 : 0] output_bus;
reg           [reg_width - 1 : 0] output_bus;
reg           [7:0] byte_count;

always @ (posedge clk or negedge resetn)
begin
        if (~resetn) // Active low asynchronous reset.
        begin
        output_bus     <=      8'b0;
        byte_count     <=      8'b0;
        end
        else if (byte_count == byte_signal)
        output_bus     <=      byte_signal_true;
        else
        begin
        output_bus     <=      byte_signal_false;
        byte_count     <=      byte_count + 1;
        end
end
endmodule
```

Concatenations

Concatenations are groupings of signals or values and are enclosed in curly brackets {} with commas separating the concatenated expressions, as shown in Listing 1-27. All concatenated values must be sized. Note the use of [ ] to identify the bit select or register index. It's legal to define a register like backwards_reg, but, regardless of the numbers used, the leftmost definition is always the most significant bit. Usually, you'll see the largest number occurring on the left side of the colon (:) unless a one-dimensional array of variables (like a RAM) is being created.

Listing 1-27 Concatenation Example

```verilog
module backward;
reg [0:2] backwards_reg;
reg [2:0] test;
/*   {1'b0, test, 8'h55} is the same as:

{1'b0, test[2], test[1], test[0], 1'b0, 1'b1, 1'b0, 1'b1, 1'b0,
1'b1, 1'b0, 1'b1} */

always @ (test)
    begin

    test        =       backwards_reg;
// The assignment above is equivalent to the assignments below:
    test[2]     =       backwards_reg[0];
    test[1]     =       backwards_reg[1];
    test[0]     =       backwards_reg[2];
    end
endmodule
```

Digital Design Strategies and Techniques

*F*rom a design entry point of view, the digital designer describes a design in as high a level of abstraction as possible. If it were possible to write one line of code that resulted in 25,000 gates of usable hardware (this day will come when a typical design is 2,500,000 gates), we'd agree that this is a very efficient way to do design work. We use sophisticated software tools to translate the abstract top-level design into a netlist that represents hardware and hardware interconnection.

The top-level design is processed in many steps before it is implemented in FPGA hardware. Each of these steps will be discussed in more detail later in this chapter.

DESIGN PROCESSING STEPS

- The design is parsed for syntax errors.
- The design is minimized and optimized for the target architecture.
- Recognized structure elements are replaced with selected library modules or cores.
- Timing and resource requirements are estimated.
- The design is converted to a netlist.
- The design elements and modules are linked together and 'black box' modules are replaced with library or core module netlists.
- Floorplanning and routing attempts are made until the timing and resource constraints are met.
- Timing and resource reports are extracted from the design. A timing annotated netlist is created to support post-route simulation.
- The device configuration files are created.

ANALOG BUILDING BLOCKS FOR DIGITAL PRIMITIVES

There will be many views of a design. The designer must be comfortable changing between different views of the same project as it evolves into a bitstream file formatted to configure an FPGA. It helps to keep in mind that all digital design elements are implemented with analog components. **There is no magic device that acts like a NAND gate.** We implement digital logic with analog devices like transistors, diodes, and resistors as shown in Figures 2-1, 2-2, and 2-3. Transistors can act as digital switches (on or off) or as analog transfer gates (pass mode). For the transistor impaired, N FETs are ON with a "one" on the gate, P FETs are ON with a "zero" on the gate.

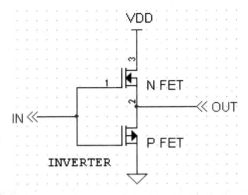

Figure 2-1 Discrete Logic: Simplified Inverter

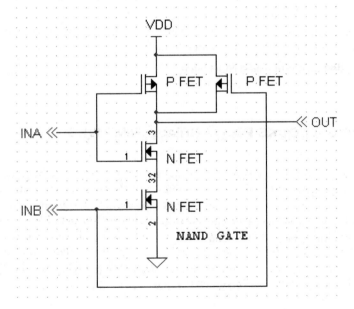

Figure 2-2 Discrete Logic: Simplified NAND Gate

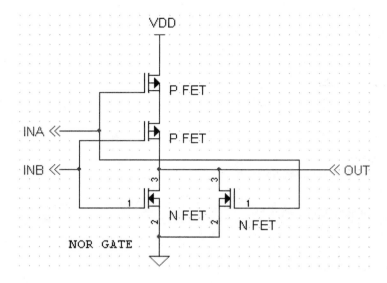

Figure 2-3 Discrete Logic: Simplified NOR Gate

USING A LUT TO IMPLEMENT LOGIC FUNCTIONS

Most FPGAs use a multiplexer (MUX) Look-Up Table (LUT) as a basic logic element. There are two reasons for doing this:

1. The LUT is versatile (any function of the inputs is possible)
2. The LUT is efficiently implemented in silicon.

The MUX control inputs are used as logic inputs, and the multiplex inputs are strapped to logic levels to implement the desired function. Figure 2-4 illustrates an inverter implemented using this method.

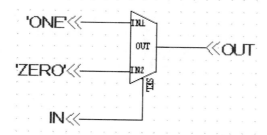

Figure 2-4   MUX Configured as an Inverter

A hidden advantage to using the MUX LUT as a logic element is provided by the capacitive loading and the "break-before-make" switching character of the MUX output. When the inputs change, the output is held and tends to change cleanly without glitching.

Synthesis Example

Changing back to the digital world, let's refer to the Overheat Detector design of Chapter 1, reprinted here as Listing 2-1.

Listing 2-1   Overheat Detection Source Code

```verilog
module overheat (clock, reset, overheat_in, pushbutton_in,
overheat_out);
input       clock, reset, overheat_in, pushbutton_in;
output      overheat_out;
reg         overheat_out;
reg         pushbutton_sync1, pushbutton_sync2;
reg         overheat_in_sync1, overheat_in_sync2;

// Always synchronize inputs that are not phase related to
//   the system clock.
// Use double-synchronizing flipflops for external signals
//   to minimize metastability problems.
// Even better would be some type of filtering and latching
//   for poorly behaving external signals that will bounce
//   and have slow rise/fall times.

always @ (posedge clock or posedge reset)
begin
    if (reset)
        begin
            pushbutton_sync1    <=      1'b0;
            pushbutton_sync2    <=      1'b0;
            overheat_in_sync1   <=      1'b0;
```

```
                    overheat_in_sync2     <=        1'b0;
                end
        else    begin
                pushbutton_sync1      <=        pushbutton_in;
                pushbutton_sync2      <=        pushbutton_sync1;
                overheat_in_sync1     <=        overheat_in;
                overheat_in_sync2     <=        overheat_in_sync1;
                end
    end

    // Latch the overheat output signal when overheat is
    //  asserted and the user presses the pushbutton.
    always @ (posedge clock or posedge reset)
    begin
        if (reset)
                overheat_out <=        1'b0;

    // Overheat_out is held forever (or until reset).
        else if (overheat_in_sync2 && pushbutton_sync2)
                overheat_out <=        1'b1;
    end

    endmodule
```

The synthesis tool converts our simple 40-line source code into an ugly EDIF netlist almost 300 lines long. This netlist holds all the design elements and information regarding the compiler version, target part, and all the design constraints the synthesizer knows about. This netlist is designed to be interpreted by other computer programs and doesn't contribute much usable information to the designer, so we won't look at an example.

A graphical version (a schematic) of the netlist as shown in Figure 2-5 is more useful to us in understanding what the synthesis tool created, particularly for the HDL impaired. Note the correct use of global resources for clock and reset. Because Verilog does not support direct assignment of hardware resources (the biggest problem for the Verilog FGPA designer), it is the designer's job to assure that these inferences are made correctly.

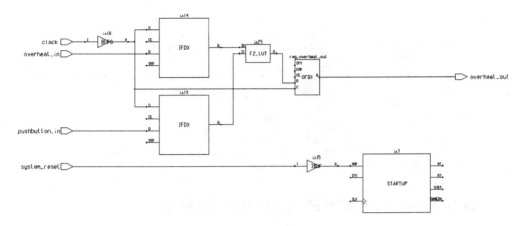

Figure 2-5   Schematic Extracted from the EDIF Netlist

The synthesis tool has some understanding of the target architecture and can provide estimates of the design timing and resource requirement, see Listing 2-2. This estimate will not include black-box modules that are later imported by the FPGA place-and-route tool.

Listing 2-2   Synthesis Resource Estimate

```
*******************************************************

Cell: overheat    View: INTERFACE    Library: work

*******************************************************

    Number of ports :                        5
    Number of nets :                         13
    Number of instances :                    10
    Number of references to this view :       0

Total accumulated area :
    Number of BUFG :                          1
    Number of CLB Flip Flops :                2
    Number of FG Function Generators :        1
    Number of IBUF :                          1
    Number of IOB Input Flip Flops :          2
    Number of IOB Output Flip Flops :         1
    Number of Packed CLBs :                   1
    Number of STARTUP :                       1

***************************************************
Device Utilization for 4010xlPQ100
***************************************************
Resource              Used     Avail    Utilization
---------------------------------------------------
```

IOs	5	77	6.49%
FG Function Generators	1	800	0.13%
H Function Generators	0	400	0.00%
CLB Flip Flops	2	800	0.25%

```
                    Clock Frequency Report
     Clock               : Frequency
     ---------------------------------------
     clock               : 118.8 MHz
```

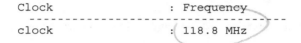

DISCUSSION OF DESIGN PROCESSING STEPS

Syntax Checking

The first step is to submit your code to a compiler, simulator, and/or Lint program that will identify syntax, typing, and other errors. Each program evaluates the code differently. If there is some confusion about what the syntax check says, it can be very helpful to try another interpreter. Listings 2-3 through 2-6 illustrate four ways that an error is reported for a simple problem inserted in the overheat.v code. A semicolon was appended on one of the **if** statements as so:

```
    if (overheat_in_sync & pushbutton_sync);
```

Listing 2-3   Error Reporting by Exemplar LeonardoSpectrum Synthesis Tool

```
35  always @ (posedge clock or posedge reset)
36      begin
37      if (reset)
38          overheat_out    <= 1'b0;
39
40  // Overheat_out is held forever (or until reset).
41      else if (overheat_in_sync2 && pushbutton_sync2);
42          overheat_out    <= 1'b1;
43      end
```

LeonardoSpectrum flagged "C:/Verilog/SourceCode/overheat.v", line 37: Error, more than one sequential statement (if statement) in asynchronous process not supported.

.**Listing 2-4** Error Reporting by Model Technology ModelSim

```
vlog C:/verilog/overheat.v
# - Compiling module overheat
# ERROR: C:/verilog/overheat.v[28]: near "else": expecting: END
# ERROR: C:/verilog/overheat.v[29]: near "end": expecting: ENDMODULE
```

ModelSim reported an error on the next line; at least in the right neighborhood of the error.

Listing 2-5 Error Reporting by Silos III

```
Reading "c:\verilog\verilog\overheat.v"
sim to 0
    Highest level modules (that have been auto-instantiated):
         (overheat overheat

c:\verilog\verilog\overheat.v (38) : error 3.229 : expecting
"end", or statement, not integer constant

error 2.188 : errors are too severe to simulate
```

Listing 2-6 Error Reporting by Verilint

```
Processing source file c:\verilog\verilog\overheat.v
  (E363)  c:\verilog\verilog\overheat.v, line  37: Syntax error:
 1 syntax error
End of interHDL inc. Verilint (R) Version 3.14, 1 errors, 0
warnings
```

The point of this exercise is to illustrate that different tools give different (and more or less useful) error messages, and it makes good sense to have several tools available for checking your code, particularly a Lint tool. Verilint (or a similar Verilog Lint tool) is useful because it's fast, easy to use, and catches many different types of errors. This type of tool can save many hours of frustration. Regardless, this example illustrates how much trouble a single misplaced semicolon can cause.

Design Minimization and Optimization

The end result of all of our work is a configuration of hardware. This hardware can be an FPGA, a semicustom FPGA conversion, or some sort of ASIC (standard cell, gate array, full custom). If the result is an FPGA, the hardware will have an underlying structure that varies depending on the design approach taken by the FPGA vendor. The logic structure of a Xilinx 4K family is illustrated in Figure 2-6. We'll take a closer look at this and other device architectures in Chapter 7.

The Xilinx 4K family Configurable Logic Block (CLB) is basically two 4-input LUTs feeding a pair of flipflops. The Verilog code we write gets mapped into this structure by the synthesis tool.

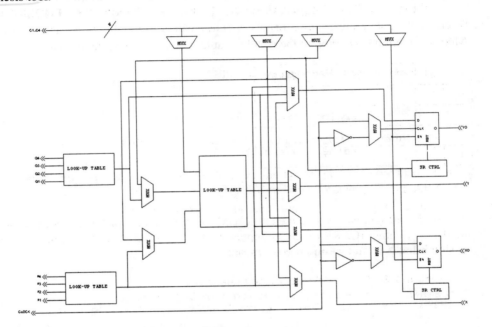

Figure 2-6   Typical Xilinx Configurable Logic Block Structure

The synthesizer translates the design to a form suitable for the target hardware by:

- Flattening the design into large Boolean equations with one equation for each module output, design section output, or register output. Redundant registers may be identified and optimized out. For example, the code fragment of Listing 2-7 might be flattened into the Boolean equation of Listing 2-8.

Listing 2-7   Simple Adder Code

```
// Simple adder (no carry input).
module adder(clock, reset, a, b, c);
input      clock, reset, a, b;
reg        [1:0]  c;
```

```
always @ (posedge clock or posedge reset)
    begin  if (reset)
              c      =      2'b0;
       else
              c      =      a + b; // Adder.
       end
endmodule
```

To create the gate representation of this circuit, create a truth table (see Table 2-1) which defines all the input and output conditions.

a	b	c[1] - CARRY	c[0] - SUM
0	0	0	0
0	1	0	1
1	0	0	1
1	1	1	0

Table 2-1   Simple Adder Truth Table

By inspection, we see that the c[0] (SUM) output can be represented by an XOR gate and the c[1] output (CARRY) can be represented by an AND gate. A flattened version of the simple adder circuit is illustrated in Figure 2-7.

Listing 2-8   Simple Adder Boolean Equations

```
c[0]     <=     a ^ b;// ^ is the Verilog Boolean XOR operator.
c[1]     <=     a & b;// & is the Verilog Boolean AND operator.
```

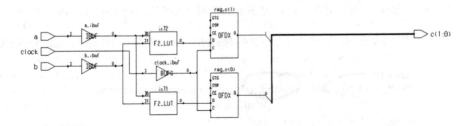

Figure 2-7   Flattened Schematic of Simple Adder Circuit

The logic mapped into the top F2_LUT to create c[1] (ix51) is (!I0 * I1) + (I0 * !I1), equivalent to the XOR function. The logic mapped into the lower F2_LUT to create c[0] (ix50) is (I0 * I1).

- Minimizing the Boolean equations. This is done by recognizing and removing redundant logic terms (even if, for controlling fanout or providing hazard coverage, we want them to remain in the design).

The synthesizer can't recognize redundant logic that crosses register boundaries (though it may recognize and delete redundant registers). If there is any chance for logic minimization, this must be part of the design input. The best opportunities for logic reduction are created and implemented by the designer.

- Recognized structure elements are replaced with selected modules. For example, the synthesizer might recognize a construct like a <= a – 1 as a down counter and replace the logic with a predefined circuit optimized for the target architecture for either area or speed.

- Timing and resource requirements are estimated. The compiler can only estimate the design timing and resource requirements. The manufacturer may have made changes to the timing parameters (the device manufacturer will always be ahead of other companies, who rely on the manufacturer for data). Another reason the timing estimate may not be accurate is that the library and black-box elements are not yet part of the design netlist. These elements are inserted when the design is linked and the final netlist is created and flattened.

- The design is converted to a netlist. There are various flavors of netlists, but the most common format at present is EDIF.

- The design elements and modules are linked together and 'black-box' modules are replaced with library module netlists. The netlist created by the compiler may be flattened (all the modules merged into one netlist) or the hierarchy may be maintained with the modules kept separate. With the hierarchy maintained, the design is easier for the designer to understand as it appears more like it was created.

- Floorplanning and routing attempts are made until the timing and resource constraints are met. Floorplanning assigns elements from the device logic to the designed circuitry. The place and route of the design is very much like the place and route of a printed circuit board. The efficiency of routing and the resulting speed of the routed design depend on the arrangement of the module elements, which affects the interconnect between modules. There are limited routing resources in an FPGA. When the routing gets dense (congested), long routing paths may be necessary to complete a signal path. This slows the design and causes routing problems for signals that must travel across or around the congested area. Some FPGA vendors advertise the capability of 100% routing of all logic, but others make densities of 65% (Altera) and 85% (Xilinx) more reasonable. Manual floorplanning can increase the usable logic density.

- Timing and resource reports are extracted from the design. A timing-annotated netlist may be created to support post-route simulation. A common format for a timing-annotated netlist is the SDF format as illustrated in Listing 2-9. SDF stands for Standard Delay Format. This file includes estimated gate delays based on the FPGA design rules.

Listing 2-9   Example of an SDF Netlist

```
(DELAYFILE
 (SDFVERSION "2.0")
 (DESIGN "adder")
 (DATE "08/31/99 09:21:34")
 (VENDOR "Exemplar Logic, Inc., Alameda")
 (PROGRAM "LeonardoSpectrum Level 3")
 (VERSION "v1999.1d")
 (DIVIDER /)
 (VOLTAGE)
 (PROCESS)
 (TEMPERATURE)
 (TIMESCALE 1 ns)
(CELL
 (CELLTYPE "F2_LUT")
 (INSTANCE ix72)
 (DELAY
  (ABSOLUTE
   (PORT I0 (::3.25) (::3.25))
   (PORT I1 (::3.25) (::3.25)))))
(CELL
 (CELLTYPE "F2_LUT")
 (INSTANCE ix71)
 (DELAY
  (ABSOLUTE
   (PORT I0 (::3.25) (::3.25))
   (PORT I1 (::3.25) (::3.25)))))
(CELL
 (CELLTYPE "BUFG")
 (INSTANCE clock_ibuf)
 (DELAY
  (ABSOLUTE
   (PORT I (::0.00) (::0.00)))))
(CELL
 (CELLTYPE "OFDX")
 (INSTANCE reg_c_1)
 (DELAY
  (ABSOLUTE
   (PORT C (::3.25) (::3.25))
   (PORT D (::2.77) (::2.77)))))
```

```
(CELL
 (CELLTYPE "OFDX")
 (INSTANCE reg_c_0)
 (DELAY
  (ABSOLUTE
   (PORT C (::3.25) (::3.25))
   (PORT D (::2.77) (::2.77)))))
(CELL
 (CELLTYPE "IBUF")
 (INSTANCE reset_ibuf)
 (DELAY
  (ABSOLUTE
   (PORT I (::2.77) (::2.77)))))
(CELL
 (CELLTYPE "IBUF")
 (INSTANCE a_ibuf)
 (DELAY
  (ABSOLUTE
   (PORT I (::2.77) (::2.77)))))
(CELL
 (CELLTYPE "IBUF")
 (INSTANCE b_ibuf)
 (DELAY
  (ABSOLUTE
   (PORT I (::2.77) (::2.77)))))
(CELL
 (CELLTYPE "STARTUP")
 (INSTANCE ix56)
 (DELAY
  (ABSOLUTE
   (PORT GSR (::2.77) (::2.77)))))
)
```

- The device configuration files are created. The download file can be programmed into a serial EPROM, downloaded through a serial or parallel cable, or stored in memory and written to the device by a microprocessor, or by a stand-alone EPROM with address and data control generated by the FPGA itself. The device might be ISP (In-System Programmable) or a reprogrammable type (plugged into a programmer, programmed, then installed in the destination design).

Shifty Logic Circuits

Many people, when asked to draw a two-input NOR Gate, will draw a circuit that looks like Figure 2-8. In my experience this circuit seems shifty or flaky. This is not just a sign of mental illness. The output **is** very likely to be glitchy when the inputs change. We're digital designers and we want the analog aspects of our design to be minimized.

Figure 2-9 shows a typical circuit where the simple OR gate might be used. The resistance and capacitance of Figure 2-9 do not have to be discrete devices on a circuit board, they could be parasitic values associated with signal routing and loading.

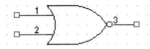

Figure 2-8   Combinational Two-Input NOR Gate

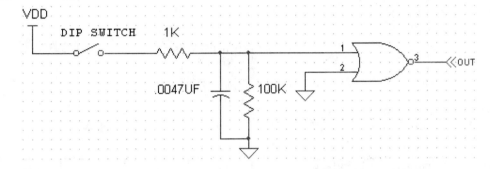

Figure 2-9   Simple Combinational Circuit

The oscilloscope trace shown in Figure 2-10 demonstrates one problem with the combinational circuit. One input is strapped low, so the output should just be the inverse of the other input, right? Where did those nasty glitches on the output come from? The input is a noisy signal that crosses the input threshold (where the input is between being recognized as one or zero by the gate input) very slowly. The RC network just exaggerates the problem and is exactly the kind of thing you see when some bonehead tries to filter out the switch contact bounce. The right way to filter switch bounce is to use feedback (hysteresis).

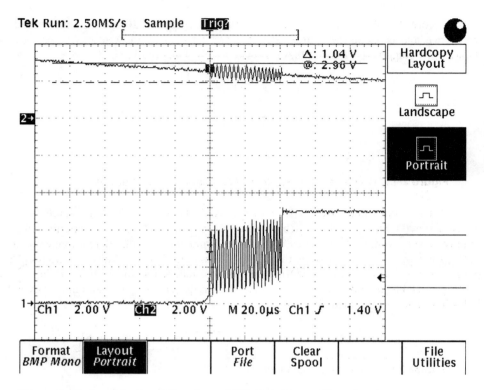

Tek Run: 2.50MS/s   Sample   **Trig?**

Δ: 1.04 V
@: 2.96 V

Hardcopy
Layout

Landscape

Portrait

2→

1→ Ch1   2.00 V   **Ch2**   2.00 V   M 20.0µs Ch1 ʃ   1.40 V

Format   Layout   Port   Clear   File
BMP Mono *Portrait*   File   Spool   Utilities

Figure 2-10 Combinational Two-Input NOR Gate Output Transients

Fine, you say. You'll make sure that the input always changes quickly to minimize glitches. So, you invent a circuit that switches infinitely fast (you can store this circuit on the same shelf as your perpetual motion machine). Anyway, that's still not good enough, because there is another cause of glitches. When the inputs are changing at nearly the same time, again the output can be indeterminate. The circuit of Figure 2-11 demonstrates this problem. A resistor-capacitor (RC) network is added to delay the input signal. Again, the output has nasty transients. So, your design won't use RC networks between inputs like this. Well, the RC time delay might be caused by mixed routing paths between inputs (signal skew) or by signal loading where each signal destination contributes a capacitive load. The R part of Figure 2-11 represents the sum of the source and routing impedance (proportional to route length) and the C part represents net loading (proportional to the number of loads on the net). The only control you have of this problem is making sure that signals have low fanout (a measure of the signal loading represented by destination logic elements where each gate load is counted as a fanout of 1). Most synthesis tools allow a fanout constraint to be defined to control loading (signals are split and driven by separate buffers).

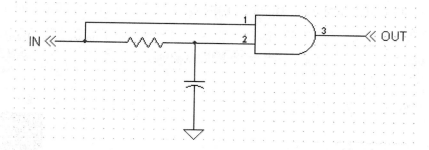

Figure 2-11 Combinational Two-Input AND Gate with RC Network

When I am asked to draw a two-input AND Gate, it looks like Figure 2-12. The difference is the addition of a synchronizing flipflop. The output of this circuit will not be glitchy if synchronous logic rules are followed and the setup/hold requirements for the flipflop are met (see the next section for a discussion of setup and hold times). This is particularly safe if the input signal is synchronous, too. If the signal at the D input of the flipflop is stable in time to meet the setup-time requirement and maintained beyond the hold-time requirement, then all is well.

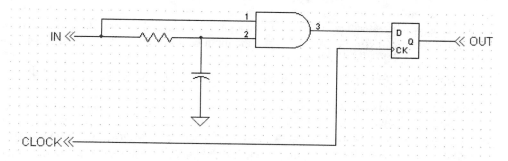

Figure 2-12 Synchronous AND Gate

SYNCHRONOUS LOGIC RULES

Metastability

Literally, metastability means beyond-settled? Something other than steady? If a signal is metastable, it is not stable, it is neither 1 nor 0, or it oscillates and will eventually resolve to a 1 or 0, but we don't know which. As a digital designer, I hope this idea keeps you up late at night.

Metastability occurs when a clock edge is random with respect to a change of an asynchronous input signal. If the relation of the clock and signal is truly random, then it is inevitable that an input change will occur so close to a clock edge that the output is unpredictable. This problem manifests itself as a flipflop output that takes a long time to resolve, often much longer than the typical clock-to-Q output delay listed in the flipflop datasheet.

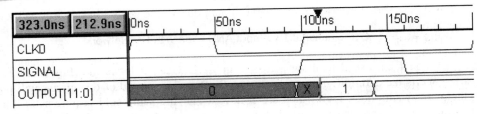

Figure 2-13 Metastable Output

Figure 2-13 illustrates the metastability problem; if **SIGNAL** changes within the setup/hold window of the flipflop, the output is unknown for a period. How long is this period? It depends on the characteristics of the flipflop and its environment: how fast is the flipflop, how much gain does it have, and how much noise is present in the system. How big is this problem? It depends on how often the input changes and how wide the setup/hold window is compared to the clock period.

We'll never get to zero metastability, but hopefully the statistical probability of metastability will be microscopic. I don't know about you, but if I can get the mean time between failures in my design to 100,000 years or so, that's good enough.

The closest we will get to a solution to the metastability problem is to use synchronous design techniques. This means a synchronizing clock is used to qualify, gate, or trigger a circuit. The time between clock edges is used to allow signals to propagate and settle. It's like a game; if you can get your signal to the next flipflop before the next clock setup time, then you win.

Setup and Hold Time

For the output of a flipflop to be predictable (not metastable), the inputs must meet the setup and hold time requirement of the flipflop.

- The setup time, often represented as T_{su}, is the time period, BEFORE the edge of the synchronizing clock, when the input is required to be stable. If the setup time is violated, the output value is indeterminate.

- The hold time, often represented as T_h, is the time period, AFTER the synchronizing clock edge, when the input is required to be stable. If the hold time is violated, again the output value is not guaranteed.

The setup and hold requirement comes from the analog nature of the flipflop design. The flipflop uses feedback implemented with cross-coupled gates to hold a state. It takes time for the gates to achieve their stable state. In a perfect world, an edge-triggered flipflop would change states exactly synchronous with the clock edge. The clock edge would be infinitely fast, and the flipflop would change states instantaneously. Real World clocks have rise/fall times, and flipflops require stable inputs during the setup/hold time to achieve a stable output state.

The flipflop metastability problem will never go away as long as a signal has a random phase relation to the flipflop clock. However, IC manufacturers have made great progress in closing the metastability window (this window is the setup plus hold time window). By increasing the speed of the flipflop, we make the metastability window narrower and less of a problem. The fact is, most problems that designers blame on metastability is related to asynchronous design technique. **Each FPGA input should drive one and exactly one flipflop.** The output of this single flipflop can be used to drive another flipflop for added security or can be used to drive the rest of your synchronous system. When an asynchronous input drives multiple flipflops, and the input changes near the clock edge, some flipflop outputs will change and some will not. This is not a metastability problem; this is an asynchronous input problem!

Figure 2-14 illustrates this. The RC delays represent signal delays due to routing and load inside the FPGA. We want all three flipflop outputs to be the same, but, depending on the phase of the input signal, sometimes the outputs will not be the same. If we synchronize the input with a single flipflop and do not violate its setup/hold time requirement, then all outputs are assured to be the same. That's what we want!

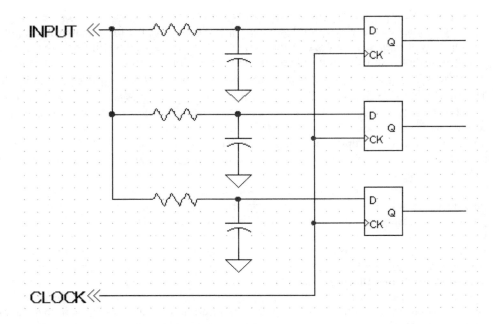

Figure 2-14 Asynchronous Input Problem

How can we absolutely assure that the inputs are not going to change during the setup and hold period of the flipflop? The answer is an important part of the solution for the question: "How can I create a nearly trouble-free design?"

> Always synchronize your inputs! This means an asynchronous input drives exactly one flipflop. The output of this flipflop can be safely used to drive the rest of your synchronous circuitry.

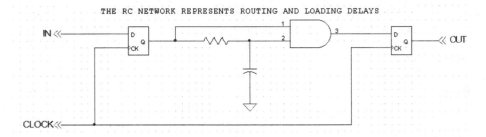

Figure 2-15 Synchronous AND Gate with Synchronous Inputs

Figure 2-15 shows a synchronous AND gate with synchronous inputs.

This goes a long way toward solving our problems, but the fussy among us might be asking why it works. It looks like the output of the synchronizing flipflops changes at a clock transition; isn't that a problem for the output flipflop? Before we look at that, let's consider a common circuit. If you were asked to design a divide-by-two circuit, you might draw something like Figure 2-16.

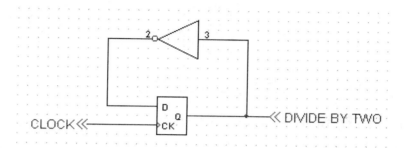

Figure 2-16 Divide-by-Two Circuit

This circuit could hardly be simpler; the inverting output is fed back to the D input, and the output changes state on every other clock edge. It is interesting to think about a situation where this circuit does not work. Let's assume that the device technology has some easy numbers to work with, so all delays are 1 nsec.

Flipflop Specification:	
Flipflop Minimum Input Setup Time:	1 nsec
Flipflop Minimum Input Hold Time:	1 nsec
Clock-to-Output Delay (Maximum):	1 nsec
Maximum Propagation Delay Time (Q output to D input)	1 nsec

For repeatable results, the D input must be stable 1 nsec before the clock edge and must remain stable after the clock edge for 1 nsec. The flipflop output is guaranteed to reach its final value less than 1 nsec after the clock edge. It takes less than 1 nsec for the signal to propagate from the Q output back to the D input. At what clock frequency does this circuit begin to fail?

Rising edges of the clock must not occur before setup time + output delay + routing delay, or 3 nsec. This means the input clock had better not have a frequency greater than 333.333 MHz. This is a high frequency, most likely achievable only with an ASIC using today's technology. An FPGA will have longer (possibly much longer) delays and will have correspondingly lower maximum clock frequencies.

The delays for the device elements are provided by the device vendor. The number of delays can be mind-boggling. An FPGA has a complicated mix of delays; clock to Q, routing delays through switch elements, delays through signal multiplexers (look-up tables), and delays proportional to signal loading, among others. For example, for a 4000XL device, Xilinx specifies 41 timing parameters in 4 speed grades, for a total of 164 individual timing numbers. Memorize them; there will be a test later. Fortunately, the compiler knows these published delays and will calculate the totals for your circuit design. Let's consider another simple circuit, two flipflops in series as shown in Figure 2-17.

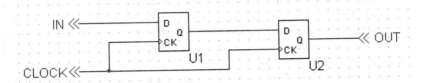

Figure 2-17 Two Flipflops Connected in Series

Again, this is deceptively simple. How can this circuit work reliably? What if the minimum clock-to-output delay (a value that is rarely specified, but often estimated as 25% of typical) for U1 is less than the hold-time requirement for U2? So, you tear up your data book looking for the hold-time requirement, and with a sigh of relief (if you're lucky) you see that it is specified as zero. The suspicious engineer will say, hold on a nanosecond, how can it be zero? All the logic circuitry we've ever looked at requires some hold time greater than zero. And that's correct. It has to be so, but the designer of the FPGA logic cell has done some work for us and has put in delays to guarantee that the logic path (the logic in series with the D input) has a shorter delay than the clock path. Essentially, this is done by adding the hold time to the setup time, then delaying the clock enough to satisfy this extended setup time. With reference to the clock edge, the input signal takes longer to arrive at the D input, but it also stays around longer. Even if the input signal changes coincident with the clock edge, the clock delay inside the logic cell will make sure it stays valid long enough to satisfy the buried hold-time requirement of the flipflop. This simplifies the analysis of the FPGA design and assures that a circuit like Figure 2-18 will function.

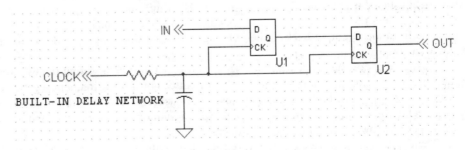

Figure 2-18 Two Flipflops Connected in Series with Internal Delays

In summary, the FPGA chip designer has created a logic cell that assures the circuit of Figure 2-17 will work. ASIC designers don't have this luxury and must account for delay and tolerance build-ups in their design. We do not have this luxury when dealing with signals from outside the FPGA. The signal characteristics of external signals must be examined and understood completely. If there is any sign of slow or glitchy signals, then we will implement circuits with hysteresis (like a Schmitt trigger) and will use a two-flipflop synchronizing circuit to minimize metastability.

Hysteresis is a circuit that adds positive feedback to the input. The idea is that when the output switches, it adds to the input to help prevent oscillation. The amount of feedback should be slightly greater than the noise on the input signal. Xilinx doesn't widely advertise this information, but all their FPGA inputs have a few hundred millivolts of hysteresis; this makes their inputs friendly to noisy environments.

To complete our analysis, we must consider clock-skew. In a perfect world, all flipflops in our design will receive clock edges that are exactly synchronous. The first thing to understand is the clock-skew problem is not related to the operating frequency of your design! Even a slow design can have clock-skew problems.

Let's expand the circuit of Figure 2-17 to show clock-skew, see Figure 2-19. Imagine that the flipflops are located far apart in the design and the second flipflop clock is delayed from the clock 'seen' by the first flipflop.

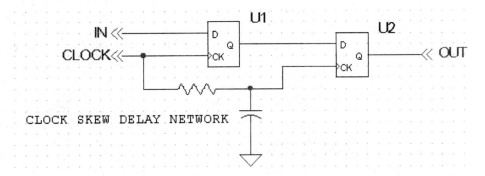

Figure 2-19 Two Flipflops Connected in Series with Clock Skew

What is the problem? Let's call t1 the clock-to-output delay period and t2 the propagation delay of the signal across the device to the D input of the second flipflop. We are hoping (and perhaps assuming) the value clocked into U2 is the old value of the Q output of U1. If the skew of the clock is too long, then we'll get the new value of U1-Q—or worse, we'll violate the setup time of U2 and get an unknown output from U2. We're digital engineers; we don't like unknowns. What is the solution? Fortunately, the FPGA designer provided low-skew clock networks carefully crafted to assure that the longest skew of the clock anywhere across the device is shorter than the shortest sum of clock-to-Q and signal routing propagation times. If you can use a global low-skew clock network, then there's no problem. If you create an asynchronous design by using a routed clock (one that travels through random logic in the design), a gated clock, a MUX'd clock, or are designing an ASIC (where the clock networks are all custom designed), then **you** are responsible for assuring that this requirement is met.

Handling External Signals

We must also carefully analyze the situation where the FPGA designer has no control of one or more of the signals. Consider the case where an input source, represented by the flipflop U1 in Figure 2-17, is off-chip and is connected to a flipflop clocked by the FPGA clock. If U1 is a fast device, it is very possible that a race condition, which means signals arrive at synchronizing flipflops at different times, will occur. The race problem occurs when signals are changing at the input of a gate at the same time. This results in an unknown output. We're digital designers; we like 1's and 0's. Unknown output states make us neurotic and twitchy.

This signal-race situation is much worse if there is no input-synchronizing flipflop in the input, because the race condition propagates across the design to all the circuits sensitive to the inputs. Very bad. At least, if there is an input-synchronizing flipflop, the only setup/hold time requirement is on that specific flipflop; once the timing is worked out for that device, the signal is well conditioned for operation inside the design. In a case like this, the easy solution is to make sure that the external device runs off the same clock as the logic synchronizing clock inside the design and is a slow device so the output can't change fast enough to cause a race condition. Proving this can be a problem, because chip manufacturers almost never provide a minimum clock-to-Q output time. This is good for the manufacturers because it allows them to improve the IC process (make the device smaller, faster, and cheaper to build) without changing the data sheet. It's bad for the designer using the parts who is diligently trying to do a worst-case timing analysis.

Using Alternate Clock Edges

A solution might be to clock external devices on the clock edge opposite to the one used inside the FPGA. Xilinx allows a flipflop to be clocked by either the rising or falling clock edge. Careful analysis must be done to assure that the timing works out. The clock-skew and setup time must be less than 1/2 a clock period compared to the full clock period allowed internal to the FPGA/ASIC design. A schematic of a circuit that uses the alternate clock edge is illustrated in Figures 2-20 with the resulting timing waveforms of Figure 2-21.

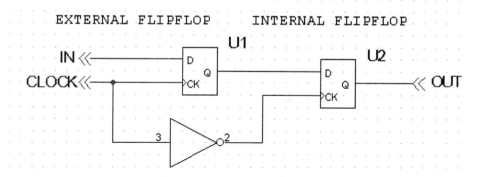

EXTERNAL FLIPFLOP   INTERNAL FLIPFLOP

Figure 2-20 Two Flipflops Connected in Series Using Alternate Clock Edges

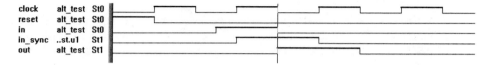

clock	alt_test	St0
reset	alt_test	St0
in	alt_test	St0
in_sync	..st.u1	St1
out	alt_test	St1

Figure 2-21 Two Flipflops Connected in Series Using Alternate Clock Edges, Timing Diagram

CLOCKING STRATEGIES

> **THE MOST IMPORTANT DECISION THE FPGA DESIGNER MAKES!**
> The single most important decision the designer makes about a design is the clocking strategy. This must be considered carefully. An error in clocking can doom a design. There is something worse than making a bad decision on the clocking strategy: not thinking about the clocks at all.

We've already decided that we want to create a synchronous design. This means there is at least one clock (preferably exactly one clock). Still, decisions remain about the clocking strategy used in the design. For the most trouble-free design, use one master clock. But what if the design has different clock domains it must interface with? What if using a single clock results in too much power consumption? There is no one answer to this problem; the answer depends on what you're trying to accomplish. Here are some suggested clock strategies:

1. When designing an ASIC, if power consumption is NOT an issue, it's best to use one master clock on all flipflops and replace lower-frequency clocks with

clock enables to qualify logic wherever it makes sense to run at a lower frequency. Otherwise, just run at the master clock rate and be happy. This is the ideal situation. The design has one clock, which results in the simplest timing analysis. This design will be the easiest on which to use automated analysis and test tools. ATPG (Automatic Test Procedure Generation) works best on this type of design.

2. When designing an ASIC and power IS an issue (for battery operation or where the package power dissipation is a problem, for example), running flipflops with lower-frequency clocks in selected parts of the design is okay. The power consumed by a circuit is proportional to the clock frequency and the number of gates switching at the clock frequency. To reduce power consumption, make the design smaller and/or reduce the clock frequency. Minimize the amount of circuitry running at high speed. You are forced to deal with the problem of synchronizing signals crossing clock domains in exchange for reduced power consumption.

3. When designing an ASIC, but using FPGAs as prototypes, the desire would be to run with one master clock. This ties you to FPGAs that are fast and ASIClike (Quicklogic, Gatefield, or some other antifuse One-Time Programmable type).

4. When designing an ASIC, and using FPGAs as prototypes, but using slow (that's slow compared to ASIC processes) SRAM-based devices (like Xilinx or Altera) it would be desirable to run all flipflops off a single master clock, but you will probably be forced to run modules at the lowest possible speed to get the design to work. Drive flipflops with multiple clocks (divided or from external lower-frequency clocks), partition the design intelligently by creating the clocks in a central clock-generator module and minimizing the interconnect between clock domains, and make sure signals that cross clock domains are properly synchronized. Logic qualified with lower-frequency clocks used as clock enables will also work.

5. When doing a fast (by FPGA terms) FPGA design (which may become an FPGA-to-ASIC conversion), the best method is to use up the global clock resources, partition the design to minimize signals crossing clock domains, and synchronize signals properly. The FPGA-conversion folks routinely deal with multiple clocks. Some attention must be paid, but it's a well-worn path.

6. When doing a slow FPGA design, thank your lucky stars and pick the method that works for you; either strategy is fine.

Clock Enable

Verilog HDL does not support dedicated clock-enable signals. The hardware (FPGA or ASIC) may have dedicated clock-enable resources, but Verilog does not give direct control of this signal assignment. In the meantime, synthesis vendors will provide this support through compiler directives. This means that code like Listing 2-9, depending on whether the target hardware has dedicated clock-enable support, might synthesize in different ways. One way a design might be interpreted by the synthesizer is illustrated in Figure 2-22 where a clock-enable feature is available in the FPGA logic block design.

Listing 2-10 Clock-Enable Example

```
module clock_en(out,in,clock,clock_enable1,clock_enable2,reset);

output     out;
input      in, clock, clock_enable1, clock_enable2, reset;
reg        out;

always @ (posedge clock or posedge reset)
    begin  if (reset)
            out   <=   0;
    else if (clock_enable1)
            out   <=    out;   // Hold output if not enabled.
    else    out   <=    (in & clock_enable2);
    end
endmodule
```

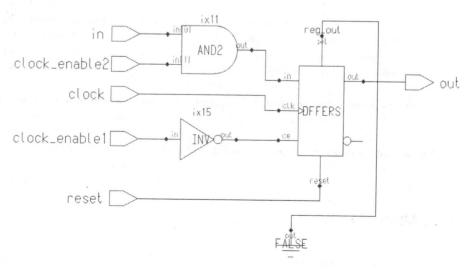

Figure 2-22 Synthesized Clock Enable

Some logic may get included in the logic that drives the clock enable, as shown in Figure 2-23. Note that the logic is not exactly the same; the point is that the synthesizer may insert added logic into the clock-enable path.

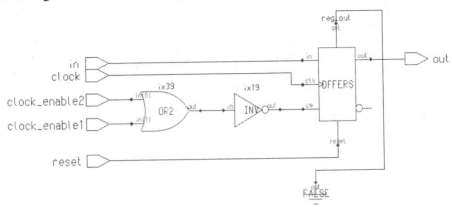

Figure 2-23 Synthesized Clock Enable (Mixed)

The next example, Figure 2-24, shows a clock-enable implemented in a technology that does not have a clock-enable feature in the logic block. The clock-enable is created with combinational feedback that holds the output when **clock_enable** is not asserted.

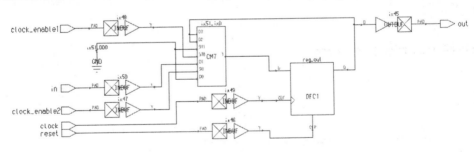

Figure 2-24 Synthesized Clock Enable (Routed)

LOGIC MINIMIZATION

A synthesizer can recognize and remove redundant logic. For example, the code fragments of Listings 2-11 and 2-12, are equivalent.

Listing 2-11 Redundant Logic Example 1 Code Fragment

```
input      test1, test2, test3;
output     sample;

sample =  ((test1 & test2 & test3) |  (test1 & !test2 & test3)
| (test1 & test2 & !test3));
```

Listing 2-12 Redundant Logic Example 2 Code Fragment

```
input      test1, test2, test3;
output     sample;

sample =  (test1 & (test2 | test3));
```

The logic is minimized even if the designer intentionally put in the redundant logic to provide hazard coverage. Hazard coverage is the addition of redundant logic to cover up race conditions. This text will never suggest using hazard coverage; always use synchronous design techniques to avoid hazards.

The compiler can also recognize equivalent logic equations. An alternate form of an equation might use less area or fewer levels of logic when implemented in an FPGA. The compiler will try alternate equation forms and use the equation that best meets the design requirements.

DeMorgan's Theorems

```
~(a & b)   =      (~a | ~b);
~(a | b)   =      (~a & ~b);
```

Schematically, DeMorgan's law looks like Figure 2-25.

Figure 2-25 Schematic Form of DeMorgan's Law

There is a corollary to the AND/OR form that can be applied to the exclusive-OR form:

```
 a ^ b      =      ~a ^ ~b;
~(a ^ b)    =      ~a ^ b       =      a ^ ~b;
```

AND/OR functions are duals of each other (like division is the dual of multiplication). DeMorgan's law defines the conversion between the AND/OR equation forms.

The compiler can also manipulate equations using the laws of Boolean algebra. These laws are:

Commutative Law

```
a | b      =      b | a;
```

Associative Law

```
a | (b | c) =      (a | b) | c;
```

Distributive Law

```
a & (b | c) =      (a & b) | (a & c);
```

Because the designer uses synchronous techniques and doesn't clog up the design with complicated structures between registers, the ability of the synthesis tool to extract redundant logic is limited. There may be simpler logic, but the synthesizer will not be able to extract it if the logic is spread across register boundaries. Examine Figure 2-26, which implements the logic of Listing 2-10 with synchronous techniques. The synthesizer will not find the redundancy! Except for some propagation delays, the two circuits shown in Figure 2-26 are equivalent.

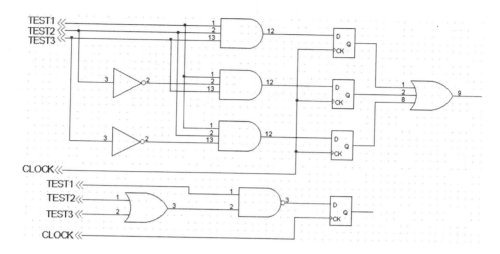

Figure 2-26 Redundant Logic Terms Spread across Register Boundaries

The best logic synthesizer is the one between your ears. A poorly planned design will always be poor regardless of how great the compilers become. When doing a design, a good designer keeps a model of the synthesized logic in her head and doesn't allow the logic to grow so complex that it becomes a problem for the synthesis tool. One way of taking advantage of the synthesis tool's capability to minimize and pack logic effectively is to never create purely combinational modules. None of the popular FPGA architectures have purely combinational logic elements. There is generally a register that goes wasted if a CLB is used only for combinational logic. Mix the combinational logic with the synchronous logic to allow the synthesis tool to merge the logic into the resources available in the device. The logic block architecture uses combinational logic or LUTs (Look-Up Tables) that feed into registers. Write your logic that way!

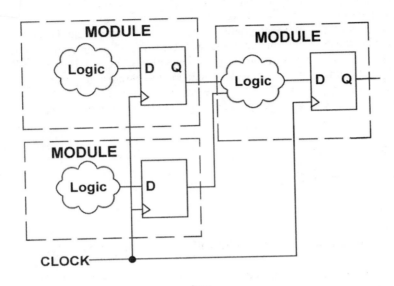

Figure 2-27 Combinational Logic Clouds Feeding Flipflops

Notice how the logic of Figure 2-27 is partitioned into modules.

WHAT DOES THE SYNTHESIZER DO?

It's helpful to think about what the synthesizer is doing. The synthesis tool takes Verilog HDL and maps it into hardware. First, the synthesizer will minimize logic equations by removing redundant logic terms. Then the design will be a huge set of Boolean equations. The remaining problem can be thought of as a simple division:

$$A/B$$

where **A** is the full design and **B** represents the hardware elements available in the target CPLD, FPGA, or ASIC. In general, for a CPLD the hardware structure will be multi-input Logic Elements (LE), for an FPGA the hardware structure will be a 3- or 4-input look-up tables (LUT), and for an ASIC the hardware structure will be a more freeform collection of library elements. Assuming the basic logic element is a 4-input LUT, the synthesis tool will partition our complicated denominator into many equations, each a function of 4 inputs.

There will be many sets of equations that will implement our design, and the synthesis tool will attempt to find ones that meet the design goals of size and speed.

A truth table lists all input combinations and defines an output condition for each. A truth table is a tabular equation form and works well for software manipulation of equations. The compiler will extract a sum-of-products (SOP) equation from your HDL code. The SOP is developed by collecting terms that give a 1 result and ORing them together.

Let's do a SOP representation of a 7-segment decoder. This decoder, similar to a CMOS 4513, will convert 4-bit binary-coded decimal (BCD) number to device pins that drive a 7-segment display.

Here is the truth table:

Input BCD b3 b2 b1 b0	Segment a b c d e f g
0 0 0 0	1 1 1 1 1 1 0
0 0 0 1	0 1 1 0 0 0 0
0 0 1 0	1 1 0 1 1 0 1
0 0 1 1	1 1 1 1 0 0 1
0 1 0 0	0 1 1 0 0 1 1
0 1 0 1	1 0 1 1 0 1 1
0 1 1 0	1 0 1 1 1 1 1
0 1 1 1	1 1 1 0 0 0 0
1 0 0 0	1 1 1 1 1 1 1
1 0 0 1	1 1 1 1 0 1 1

Let's collect the input terms that cause the 'a' segment to be asserted.

```
a = (((!b3 & !b2 & !b1 & !b0) | (!b3 & !b2 & b1 & !b0)
    | (!b3 & !b2 & b1 &  b0) | (!b3 &  b2 & !b1 &  b0)
    | (!b3 &  b2 &  b1 & !b0) | (!b3 &  b2 &  b1 &  b0)
    | ( b3 & !b2 & !b1 & !b0) |( b3 & !b2 & !b1 &  b0)));
```

We can get a hint about how the reduction algorithm works by extracting and examining two terms of the equation:

```
(!b3 & !b2 & !b1 & !b0)|(b3 & !b2 & !b1 & !b0)=(!b2 & !b1 & !b0);
```

The equation terms differ only in the b3 term, which is asserted low in the first term and asserted high in the second. Clearly the b3 term doesn't matter, is redundant, and can be removed without affecting the logic.

Next we'll convert the 'a' segment equations to standard decimal-sum form by replacing all negated terms with 0 and all true terms with 1. A term like (!b3 & !b2 & !b1 & !b0), which has all terms negated, becomes (0,0,0,0), and the whole term can be represented by a decimal 0. The next term, (!b3 & !b2 & b1 & !b0), (0,0,1,0) becomes 2, and so on, until we collect all the terms that lead to the 'a' segment being asserted:

```
a = (0,2,3,5,6,7,8,9)
```

This form of the Boolean equation is used in the Quine-McCluskey method of reducing logic equations. A DOS freeware version of a Quine-McCluskey logic reduction program is included on the CD-ROM and is called QM.exe.

The Quine-McCluskey algorithm arranges terms in order of the number of the (0) terms. Only terms whose total numbers of negated terms differ by 1 can possibly be combined. For example, when we combined (0,0,0,0) with (1,0,0,0), this combination was possible because the first term has 4 zeros and the second term has 3 zeros. The Quine-McCluskey algorithm exhaustively tests terms and combined terms against each other to determine the minimum logic expression.

Running QM with the logic terms for segment 'a' gives the reduced equation:

```
a =((!b3 & !b2 & !b0)|(b3 & ! b2 & !b1)|(!b3 & b2 & b0)|(!b3 &
b1));
```

Let's see if we can follow what the synthesizer does with this logic defined as a Verilog design in Listing 2-13.

Listing 2-13   Verilog Design for 7-Segment Display Decoder 'a' Term

```
module seven_seg (clk, reset, bcd_input, a_segment);

input            clk, reset;
input      [3:0] bcd_input;
output           a_segment;
reg              a_segment;

always @ (posedge clk or posedge reset)
    if (reset)
            a_segment    <=     0;
    else
    begin case (bcd_input)
{1'b0, 1'b0, 1'b0, 1'b0}: a_segment <= 1'b1;
{1'b0, 1'b0, 1'b0, 1'b1}: a_segment <= 1'b0;
{1'b0, 1'b0, 1'b1, 1'b0}: a_segment <= 1'b1;
{1'b0, 1'b0, 1'b1, 1'b1}: a_segment <= 1'b1;
{1'b0, 1'b1, 1'b0, 1'b0}: a_segment <= 1'b0;
{1'b0, 1'b1, 1'b0, 1'b1}: a_segment <= 1'b1;
{1'b0, 1'b1, 1'b1, 1'b0}: a_segment <= 1'b1;
{1'b0, 1'b1, 1'b1, 1'b1}: a_segment <= 1'b1;
{1'b1, 1'b0, 1'b0, 1'b0}: a_segment <= 1'b1;
{1'b1, 1'b0, 1'b0, 1'b1}: a_segment <= 1'b1;
```

```
default: a_segment <= 0;
    endcase
    end
endmodule
```

For Xilinx 4xxx logic, which uses a 4-input LUT feeding a flipflop as a primitive, the synthesizer arranges the logic to efficiently use the CLB resources and gives the circuit of Figure 2-28 for the 'a' logic.

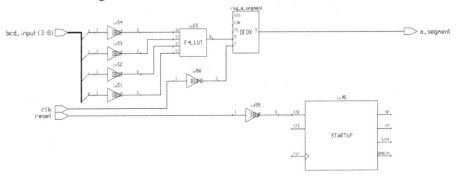

Figure 2-28 Synthesized Logic for 7-Segment Display Decoder 'a' Term Logic

AREA/DELAY OPTIMIZATION

When implementing a design, there are two fundamental properties: how big is it and how fast will it operate? Synthesizing a logic design is much like autorouting a circuit board. When routing a circuit-board trace, there are many options. Which path should the signal take? What is the signal priority compared to other signals? There is no one answer. The circuit-board trace can take a nearly unlimited set of paths to its destination. The right answer occurs when the routing has met the requirements of the design, even if it's possible to get better area/delay performance. This bears special emphasis. **The designer's work will not be judged by how perfect it is!** The designer's work will be judged by how well it meets the system requirements for product cost, development cost, performance, reliability, maintainability, and time to market. The quest for perfection will not be rewarded. **The goal of our quest is to achieve 'good enough.'** This does not mean we're going to deliver a bad design. Our design still must meet timing requirements and use good design practices.

The concept of design cost weighs area and speed (delay) against each other. In many cases, the fastest design is not the smallest. In many cases, the smallest design is not the fastest. The designer has successfully accomplished the design if it fits into the technology selected and runs fast enough to meet the needs of the system. How easy or difficult this problem is depends on many factors: the size of the selected device, the architecture of the device technology, the system speed requirement, and the skill and design approach of the designer.

The experienced designer always leaves a way out of a problem by insuring that a faster or denser device, if at all possible, is available in the same device footprint. This way, instead of redesigning a circuit board to accommodate a new device at great expense and loss of time, a faster and/or denser device can be easily substituted.

A Digital Circuit Toolbox

*T*his chapter presents some fundamental digital design concepts implemented in Verilog.

VERILOG HIERARCHY REVISITED

Verilog uses a powerful method of isolating and maintaining identifiers. A module which is not instantiated by other modules will be considered as a top module. The top module will generally instantiate other modules which will appear underneath it in the design hierarchy. This top module is called the root module. The design identifiers include module instances, tasks, functions, or named begin/end blocks.

Each design identifier creates a new branch of the hierarchy tree. Each node of the tree is unique and contains identifiers which will not conflict with other identifiers in other branches or elements of the hierarchy. A signal can be accessed anywhere in the design by referencing it by its hierarchical description with periods separating the hierarchical elements.

Listing 3-1 contains some example file names.

Listing 3-1   Examples of Hierarchical Naming

```
top.device_bus1[5:0]
top.device_bus2[3:0]
top.device_bus3[3:0]
top.s1[3:0]
top.s2[4:0]
top.s3[3:0]
top.s4[4:0]
top.s5[5:0]
top.msb1
top.msb2

top.u1.in1        // u1 is instantiated in the top module.

top.u2.in1        // u2 is instantiated in the top module.

top.u3.add1[4:0]
```

TRISTATE SIGNALS AND BUSSES

Tristate busses are allowed by most FPGA architectures on device output pins. Listing 3-2 provides an example. In addition, some FPGAs allow internal tristate signals. Internal tristates can save a lot of logic when selecting between different sets of control or data signals. In other words, different logic trees feed a tristate bus with one logic tree enabled at a time. With this method, an entire logic construct can be switched quickly. If internal tristates are not allowed, the synthesis tool may have a control to automatically substitute MUXes. This replacement will consume many more gates and is likely to be much slower than a tristate bus structure. If conversion to an ASIC is intended, check with the ASIC vendor. Internal tristates are an ASIC conversion issue; the vendor may not offer internal tristates and may or may not offer automatic expansion of tristate nets to logically controlled nets. Internal tristates can cause also problems during simulation.

Listing 3-2 Tristate Bus Example

```
     module tristate (input_bus, output_bus, tri_control);
     input   [7:0]  input_bus;
     input          tri_control; // Tristate control signal.
     output [7:0] output_bus;
// The first condition is the tri_control true condition,
//  the second is the false condition.

     assign output_bus =      tri_control ? input_bus : 8'bz;
     endmodule
```

In the conditional part of the assign statement, both input_bus and tri_control can be logic equations. For internal tristates, use the **tri** net type as illustrated in Listing 3-3.

Listing 3-3 Internal Tristate Example

```
     module tristat2 (input_bus1, input_bus2, input_bus3,
input_bus4, tri_control, output_bus, output_control);

input      [7:0]  input_bus1, input_bus2, input_bus3, input_bus4;
input      [1:0]  tri_control;
input             output_control;
tri        [7:0]  tri_bus;
output     [7:0]  output_bus;

     parameter zero     =      2'b00;
     parameter one =      2'b01;
     parameter two =      2'b10;
     parameter three    =      2'b11;

assign tri_bus = (tri_control == zero)  ? input_bus1 : 8'bz;
assign tri_bus = (tri_control == one)   ? input_bus2 : 8'bz;
assign tri_bus = (tri_control == two)   ? input_bus3 : 8'bz;
assign tri_bus = (tri_control == three)? input_bus4 : 8'bz;
assign output_bus =      output_control ? tri_bus : 8'b0;
     endmodule
```

It is the designer's responsibility to insure that the tristate buffer enables are mutually exclusive so that bus conflicts are avoided. Even transient tristate bus conflicts can cause excessive power consumption and, if allowed to occur to long or too often, can overheat and damage the device.

The schematic shown in Figure 3-1 has three levels of buffers. The ones on the left are input pin buffers, the ones in the middle are internal tristate buffers, and the ones on the right are output pin buffers.

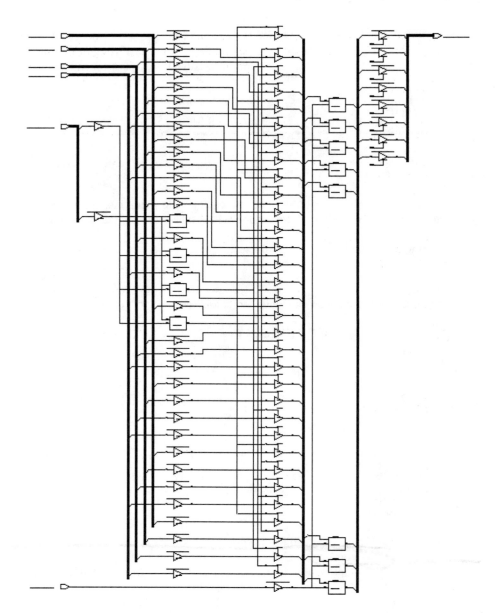

Figure 3-1   Schematic for Internal Tristate Buffer Design

In Figure 3-3, the logic is the same (same Verilog source file) but the internal tristates have been converted to MUXes. Note that one level of tristate buffering in Figure 3-1 has been converted to two levels of MUX LUTs in Figure 3-3. This will result in a slower operating speed. This type of conversion will occur if the design is converted to an ASIC technology. This change was caused by checking the 'Allow converting of internal tristates' in Exemplar Logic's LeonardoSpectrum Optimize, Advanced Options menu as illustrated in Figure 3-2.

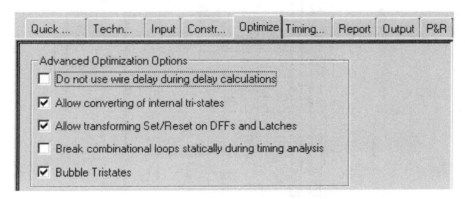

Figure 3-2   Tristate Buffers Converted to MUXes

The boxes in the middle of Figure 3-3 are the MUX LUTs that replaced the internal tristate buffers.

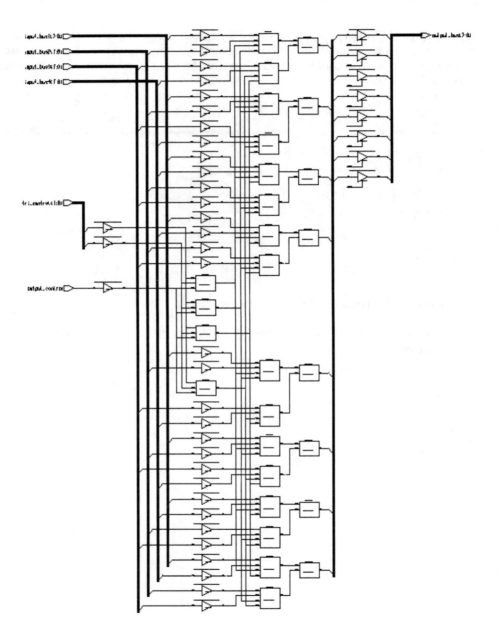

Figure 3-3   Schematic for MUX Version of Tristate Buffer Design

BIDIRECTIONAL BUSSES

Bidirectional busses, as shown in Listing 3-4 and Figure 3-4, are easy to define in Verilog. The signal is divided into two parts: the driver part, which is tristated, and the input part. The two parts are then wired together. The module port must be defined as **inout** in the port definition section.

Listing 3-4   Bidirectional Bus Example

```
module bidir (bidir_bus, direction_sig, use_bidir_sig);
inout          [7:0]  bidir_bus;
input                 direction_sig;
output         [7:0]  use_bidir_sig;
reg            [7:0]  output_bus;
wire           [7:0]  bidir_input;

// When direction_sig is true, output_bus drives the
//   bidir_bus port pins.

// The bidir_bus signals are accessible inside the design
//   on the bidir_input bus.

// Output part, MUX form.
assign bidir_bus = direction_sig ? output_bus : 8'bz;

// Input part.
assign bidir_input      =       bidir_bus;

// Assign so the input does not get optimized in synthesis.
assign use_bidir_sig    =       bidir_input;

  endmodule
```

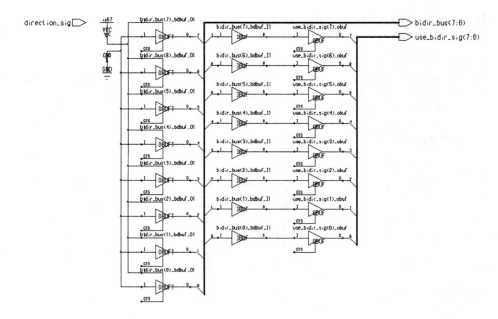

Figure 3-4   Schematic for Bidirectional Bus Design

PRIORITY ENCODERS

If/else Priority Encoder

if-else statements can have an implied priority with precedence assigned to the first instructions encountered in a **begin/end** block. Listing 3-5 illustrates a priority encoder with the extracted schematic shown in Figure 3-5. If signal **a** is asserted, it has priority, and none of the other signals matter. From a delay point of view, signal **x** passes through one level of logic and is faster than signal **z**, which passes through three layers of logic.

Listing 3-5   Priority Encoder Example

```
module priority (d, a, b, c, x, y, z);
input     a, b, c, x, y, z;
output    d;
reg  d;
```

```
always @ (a or b or c or x or y or z)
     begin
     if (a) d          =          x;
     else if (b)
               d        =          y;
     else if (c)
               d        =          z;
     else
               d        =          1'b0;
     end
endmodule
```

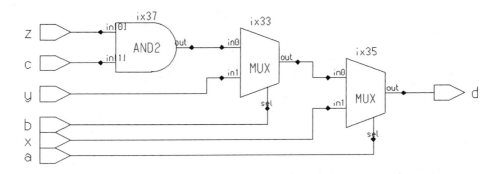

Figure 3-5   Priority Encoder Schematic

Priority in Case Statements

Like an **if/else** block, **case** blocks will create a priority encoder unless a **full case** compile option is available and selected or all input combinations have defined outputs states. Selection of **full case** informs the compiler that the cases are mutually exclusive and do not overlap. If one case is found true, then by definition no other case can be true. Since a conflict is not allowed in a parallel case design, the cases should not prioritized, but they will be if conflicting cases are defined. If it is possible for more than one case to be true (resulting in conflicting cases), then the first one encountered by the compiler will have priority over later cases which might be true (lower-priority cases are considered don't-care conditions when the higher-priority case is evaluated). This means the statement order has meaning. This may not be the behavior the designer wants. To avoid the priority encoding, make sure all cases are covered or use the compiler directive to define the design as a **full case** design, and avoid conflicting (or contradictory) cases.

When the case input condition list is not complete, a latch is created as shown in Listing 3-6 and Figure 3-7. For cases not defined, the previous output is held. This may not be what the designer intends. To prevent the creation of a latch, use a default case to cover all undefined cases as shown in Listing 3-7, or check the LeonardoSpectrum **full case** option box as shown in Figure 3-6. Using the **full case** option creates a MUX implementation, as shown in Figure 3-8.

The **parallel case** check box will still create a latch but forces undefined outputs to a known state, as shown in Figure 3-9.

Listing 3-6   Case Example, Latch Created

```
module case1 (d, a, x, y, z);
input       [2:0]  a;
input              x, y, z;
output             d;
reg                d;

always @ (a or x or y or z)
begin
    case (a)
    3'b001:     d     =     x;
    3'b010:     d     =     y;
    3'b100:     d     =     z;
    endcase
end
endmodule
```

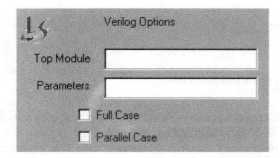

Figure 3-6   LeonardoSpectrum Verilog Case Options

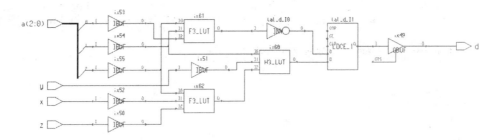

Figure 3-7 Case Schematic with Latch

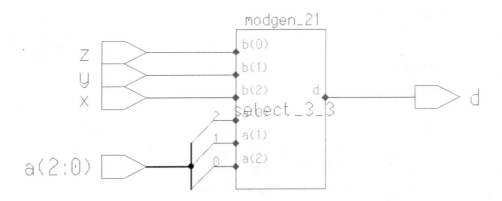

Figure 3-8 Case Schematic, Full Case Selected

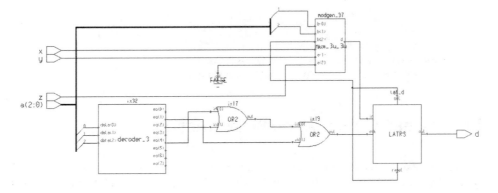

Figure 3-9 Case Schematic, Parallel Case Selected, Latch Created

The logic of Listing 3-7 is slightly different: as in Figure 3-8, all undefined cases are set by default to zeroes. Still, notice in Figure 3-10 that a MUX was inferred without a latch.

Listing 3-7 Case Example with Default Case

```
module case2 (d, a, x, y, z);
input      [2:0]  a;
input             x, y, z;
output            d;
reg               d;

always @ (a or x or y or z)
begin
    case (a)
    3'b001:      d     =     x;
    3'b010:      d     =     y;
    3'b100:      d     =     z;
    default:     d     =     1'b0;
    endcase
end
endmodule
```

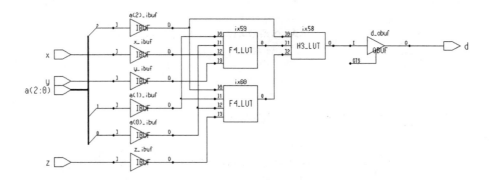

Figure 3-10 Case Schematic with Default Case

AREA/SPEED OPTIMIZATION IN SYNTHESIS

We've taken some preliminary looks at what the synthesizer does; let's explore this a little more. The optimization of synthesis for ASICs and FPGAs falls into two general categories, speed/delay or area. Obviously, the design must operate at a high enough speed to meet the design requirements. The faster the FPGA, the more expensive the device. The design must fit into the chosen device. Larger devices are also more expensive. The FPGA designer constantly struggles with the size (area) and speed of the synthesized logic. Size and speed are influenced by coding style, but we'll talk about that later.

The trade-off between speed (or delay) and area can be illustrated with an AND gate design as shown in Listing 3-8.

Listing 3-8 Duplicated Logic Example

```verilog
module optimize(a, b, c, d, e, f, g ,h , i, j, k, l, m, z);
output    a, b, c, d, z;
reg a, b, c, d, z;
input     e, f, g, h, i, j, k, l, m;

always @ (e or f or g or h or i or j or k or l)
    begin
        a    =    e & f & g & h & i & j & k & l;
        z    =    m & a;
    end

always @ (e or f or g or h or i or j or k or l)
    begin
        b    =    e & f & g & h & i & j & k & l;
    end

always @ (e or f or g or h or i or j or k or l)
    begin
        c    =    e & f & g & h & i & j & k & l;
    end

always @ (e or f or g or h or i or j or k or l)
    begin
        d    =    e & f & g & h & i & j & k & l;
    end

endmodule
```

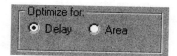

Figure 3-11 Area/Delay Optimization Selection in LeonardoSpectrum

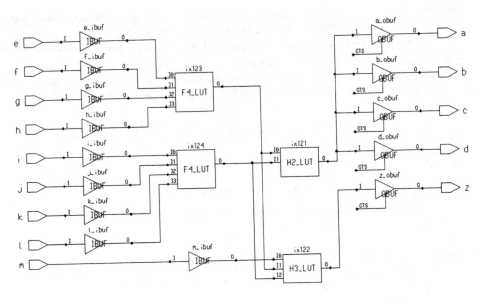

Figure 3-12 Illustration of Signals and Routing after Speed (Delay) Optimization

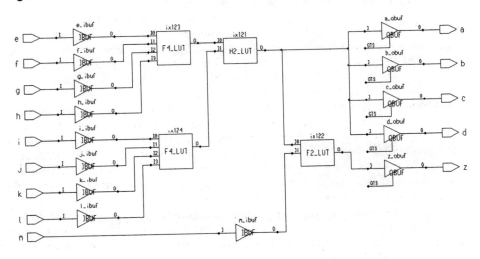

Figure 3-13 Illustration of Signals and Routing After Area Optimization

The difference between the circuits of Figures 3-12 and 3-13 is subtle; the logic is exactly the same. The difference between the two designs is the selection of area/delay optimization on the Quick Setup tab in LeonardoSpectrum (this selection can also be made in the

Optimize tab). However, you will notice that signal **z** in Figure 3-12 passes through 2 levels of logic, while it passes through 3 levels of logic in Figure 3-13. Signal **z** will be created faster in Figure 3-12 at the expense of increased FPGA real estate.

Another way to look at this design is to view the critical path. The critical path is the longest delay in the design, and LeonardoSpectrum will extract this path so it can be analyzed. The critical paths are illustrated in Figures 3-14 and 3-15.

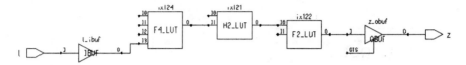

Figure 3-14 Design Optimized for Area, Critical Path

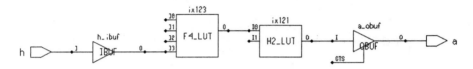

Figure 3-15 Design Optimized for Delay, Critical Path

Figure 3-15 shows the delay improvement, four layers of logic compared to five. For this design, the difference between critical paths is 22.78 nsec (delay optimization) and 24.57 nsec (area optimization), a 10% difference. The battle the FPGA designer faces is trying to fit the design into a small (cheap) and slow device and still achieve the necessary performance. This can be more an art than a science.

From this example, it should be begin to be clear how many options the synthesis tool has for implementing a logic function. Regarding coding style, this example illustrates that grouping together logic that shares inputs and/or outputs is helpful to the synthesis tool. The best partitioning would keep them inside the same always block, or at least in the same module as much as possible. The best design partitioner is the one between your ears! Don't make the synthesis tool work too hard to group functions of common inputs and outputs, group them yourself in block structures and modules.

The synthesizer is best at optimizing combinational logic within a module. It may find redundant logic in separate modules, but let's not make the synthesizer work harder than it has to. Try to keep combinational inputs and outputs of related signals grouped together in the same module.

Here's another design approach that will help. When working with a design team, there should be an agreement about where flipflops occur at module boundaries. Typically, the structure is per Figure 3-16. As long as all modules have this form, they will work well together. Without this agreement, you may have to use synchronizing flipflops on inputs because you don't know what you're interfacing to.

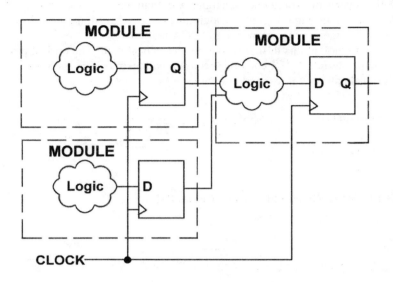

Figure 3-16 Suggested Module Boundary Selection and Register Assignment

It bears mentioning that area and delay are not always a trade-off, sometimes the more compact design is also the fastest. It has fewer gates, so it's certainly possible that there might be fewer levels of logic. It just depends on the design architecture and how well the synthesis tool optimizes this design.

TRADE-OFF BETWEEN OPERATING SPEED AND LATENCY

Another trade-off between area and speed is the one between latency and circuit operating speed. Latency is the time period between when a signal occurs at the input of a design element and when it finally propagates through the circuit to the output. Many times a design can tolerate latency as long as the design throughput is fast. For faster throughput, the designer splits up the logic so that fewer operations (layers of logic) appear between clocks. This is illustrated in Listings 3-9 and 3-10. Functionally, the designs are the same, but the design of Listing 3-10 will have greater latency (it will take three clock periods for the output to appear at the output pins) and will operate at a higher clock rate. The design of Listing 3-9 will use fewer flipflops, has less latency (the output will appear in one clock cycle), and will operate at a lower clock rate than that of Listing 3-10.

Listing 3-9 Logic with Low Latency and Low Operating Speed

```
module latency1 (clk, reset, a, b, c, d, e, f);
input             clk, reset;
input       [15:0] a, b, c , d, e;
output            f;
reg         [15:0] f;

always @ (posedge clk or posedge reset)
    begin
    if (reset)
            f       <=      0;
            else

// The next equation must resolve in one clock period.
            f       <=      ( a & b & c & d & e);
    end
    endmodule
```

Listing 3-10 Logic with High Latency and High Operating Speed

```
module latency2 (clk, reset, a, b, c, d, e, f);
input             clk, reset;
input       [15:0] a, b, c, d, e;
output            f;
reg         [15:0] ab, cd, f;

always @ (posedge clk or posedge reset)
    begin
    if (reset)
            begin
            ab      <=      0;
            cd      <=      0;
            f       <=      0;
            end
            else

// The remaining equations each must resolve in one clock
//   period.
    begin
            ab      <=      (a & b);
            cd      <=      (c & d);
            f       <=      (ab & cd & e);
    end
    end
endmodule
```

As a comparison, targeting a Xilinx 4010XL-3 device, the circuit of Listing 3-9 uses 16 packed CLBs and will operate at 78.9 MHz. The circuit of Listing 3-10 uses 24 packed CLBs and will operate at 87.1 MHz. We've added hardware resources to increase operating speed. Almost any circuit can be sped up by pipelining to reduce the amount of logic that must resolve in a clock cycle.

Synthesis tools do a great job of implementing your logic, but the designer must take responsibility for the overall design architecture. If a design must operate at high clock rates, then break up the logic so there is less logic being resolved between clock edges. It's a poor designer who blames the tools for the poor performance of his or her design. There is always a design approach that will improve timing. Yes, always!

Delays in FPGA Logic Elements

Timing Constraints

There are two strategies for improving the performance of a design. Method One: assist the synthesis tool in identifying critical logic by applying timing constraints. Timing constraints are discussed in Chapter 6. This gives priority to logic that must run fast at the expense of less critical areas of the design. Method Two: write the code to give the synthesis tool an easier problem to solve. Most problems can be resolved by reworking the source code. Pipeline the logic or use fast structural (schematiclike) elements to implement the logic.

Test points

Experienced designers make mistakes. Knowing this, the experienced designer makes the design easy to test and debug. A powerful technique for troubleshooting is to bring out test points connected to easily accessible connections. For example, the layout of an HP logic analyzer probe pod is shown in Figure 3-17. Put a double row of 0.1" header pins (either through-hole or SMT types, SMT is better because it has less impact on PCB routing channels and does not poke more holes in the power/ground planes) on the circuit board. Notice that ground is connected to pin 20 and the Logic Analyzer clocks are connected to pins 2 and 3. Pins are numbered, with odd pins 1 through 19 on one side and 2 through 20 on the other. Assign test[15:0] to device pins (which are tied to the test connector). Bring signals to be tested up through the hierarchy to the top-level module in the manner of Listing 3-11.

Listing 3-11 Test-Point Wiring Example

```
module top_lev(test, clk, reset);
output          test;
wire    [15:0] test;
wire    [15:0] cnt;
input          clk, reset;
```

```
assign test[15:0] =        cnt[15:0];

lower_level u1 (cnt, clk, reset);
endmodule

module low_lev (cnt, clk, reset);
input             clk, reset;
output            cnt;
reg        [15:0] cnt;

always @ (posedge clk or posedge reset)
begin
    if (reset)
        cnt                    <=      0;
    else   begin
        cnt                    <=      cnt + 1;
        end
end
endmodule
```

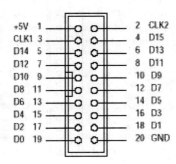

Figure 3-17 Logic Analyzer Header Layout, Top View of PCB

The 20-pin HP (p/n 1251-8106) logic analyzer pod has built-in termination networks (similar to Figure 3-18) and plugs into a dual-row tenth-inch center header as shown in Figure 3-17. To save money on pods and connect directly to the 40 pin logic analyzer pod, put a 40-pin dual-row tenth-inch center header on the board per Figure 3-19 and termination networks on the circuit board per Figure 3-18.

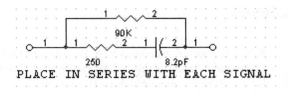

PLACE IN SERIES WITH EACH SIGNAL

Figure 3-18 Logic Analyzer Header Termination Network Schematic

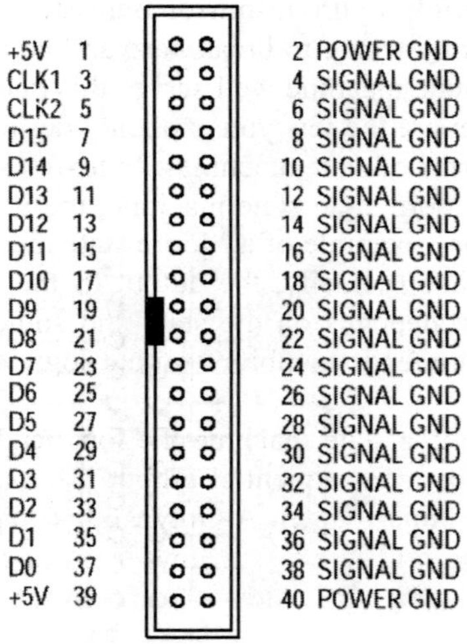

+5V	1	2 POWER GND
CLK1	3	4 SIGNAL GND
CLK2	5	6 SIGNAL GND
D15	7	8 SIGNAL GND
D14	9	10 SIGNAL GND
D13	11	12 SIGNAL GND
D12	13	14 SIGNAL GND
D11	15	16 SIGNAL GND
D10	17	18 SIGNAL GND
D9	19	20 SIGNAL GND
D8	21	22 SIGNAL GND
D7	23	24 SIGNAL GND
D6	25	26 SIGNAL GND
D5	27	28 SIGNAL GND
D4	29	30 SIGNAL GND
D3	31	32 SIGNAL GND
D2	33	34 SIGNAL GND
D1	35	36 SIGNAL GND
D0	37	38 SIGNAL GND
+5V	39	40 POWER GND

Figure 3-19 Logic Analyzer Header Layout, Top View of PCB

To expand the number of signals available for test, a MUX can used to select between sets of signals connected to the test points. Be aware: the designer can run into Heisenberg's Uncertainty theorem. This means that the method of taking a measurement can affect the thing being measured. Keep in mind that the signal that passes through the MUX is one or more logic levels removed from the internal signal, and the precise timing will be different. For low-speed signals, this may not be important. Adding logic and routing for test points can complicate the routing and result in slower timing. You didn't expect to get something for nothing, did you?

Study the test equipment in your lab. Design the circuit board to allow easy interface to that test equipment. Provide easy access to grounds to connect to your oscilloscope or voltmeter (we never seem to be able to find a ground or power connection where we need it). Leave room around parts to allow the use of sockets or test clips.

STATE MACHINES

It is very common to use sequential processes to solve a design problem. One event follows another and steers a sequential machine through its states. This is a great method of dividing and conquering a design. A Finite State Machine (FSM) uses a set of registers, called state registers, to identify the current machine state. The current state depends on the inputs and the history of inputs.

You can call me a nut, but I consider state machines (some people insist on calling them finite state machines or FSMs, but since I've never seen an infinite state machine, I don't feel any compulsion to keep the finite label) to be one of technology's wonders, as beautiful as an Escher print, a current-mirror transistor pair, or a toroidal transformer. As designers, we are constantly trying to break hard and complicated problems into pieces that are easier to solve. The state machine well serves this quest. Once you are in a certain state, the only inputs that matter are the few you explicitly define yourself.

There are many forms of state machines. In textbooks they are divided into the Mealy and Moore types. In a Moore style state machine, the output depends only on the state. A synchronous counter is one example of a Moore state machine; the output is dependent only on the state of the machine (actually, the output IS the state of the machine). In a Mealy state machine, the output depends on the state and some input conditions or signals. The style that this book recommends combines output logic and state assignments in the same always block.

It is helpful to create a state machine the longhand way. For a counter with outputs encoded using Gray code, each sequential output differs by exactly one bit. We'll discuss Gray coding again later in this chapter. A Gray Code counter is a simple state machine; let's design one with gates and registers to see how it is done. First, create a present-state/next-state chart as shown in Listing 3-12. After a clock edge, the present-state values are replaced with the next-state values.

Listing 3-12 State Machine Example, a 3-bit Gray Code Counter

Present State			Next State		
d2	d1	d0	n2	n1	n0
0	0	0	0	0	1
0	0	1	0	1	1
0	1	1	0	1	0
0	1	0	1	1	0
1	1	0	1	1	1
1	1	1	1	0	1
1	0	1	1	0	0
1	0	0	0	0	0

Collect all the terms that result in the next state bits being set to a 1 and OR them all together to create a sum-of-products (SOP) representation of the next-state decoder logic as shown in Listing 3-13.

Listing 3-13 State Machine Example, Next-State Logic

```
n2 <=  (~d2 &  d1 & ~d0) |  (d2 & d1 & ~d0) |  (d2 & d1 & d0)
       |  (d2 & ~d1 &  d0);

n1 <=  (~d2 & ~d1 &  d0) |  (~d2 & d1 & d0) |  (~d2 & d1 & ~d0)
       |  (d2 &  d1 & ~d0);

n0 <=  (~d2 & ~d1 & ~d0) |  (~d2 & ~d1 & d0) |  (d2 & d1 & ~d0)
       |  ( d2 &   d1 &   d0);
```

The logic of Figure 3-20 shows the next-state decoding logic on the left and the state register on the right. Let's implement the present/next-state logic with a Verilog state machine and see how it looks. I used a **case** structure in Listing 3-14 to create the next-state decoders, so the code looks different than the logic above, but it's the same, trust me.

Listing 3-14 Gray Code State Machine Verilog Example

```
module gray1 (clk, reset, cnt, flag_output);
input           clk, reset;
output          cnt;
wire      [2:0] cnt;    // cnt is the present-state logic.
reg       [2:0] next_state, flag_output;
output          flag_output;

assign cnt =    next_state;

always @ (posedge clk or posedge reset)
    if (reset)      begin
    next_state      <=      3'b0;
    flag_output     <=      1'b0;
    end

    else begin case (next_state)
    3'b000: begin
            next_state      <=      3'b001;
            flag_output     <=      1'b0;
            end

    3'b001: begin
            next_state      <=      3'b011;
            flag_output     <=      1'b0;
            end

    3'b011: begin
            next_state      <=      3'b010;
            flag_output     <=      1'b1;
            end

    3'b010: begin
            next_state      <=      3'b110;
```

```
                    flag_output    <=      1'b0;
                    end

          3'b110: begin
                    next_state     <=      3'b111;
                    flag_output    <=      1'b0;
                    end

          3'b111: begin
                    next_state     <=      3'b101;
                    flag_output    <=      1'b0;
                    end

          3'b101: begin
                    next_state     <=      3'b100;
                    flag_output    <=      1'b0;
                    end

          3'b100: begin
                    next_state     <=      3'b000;
                    flag_output    <=      1'b0;
                    end
          default: begin
                    next_state     <=      3'b0;
                    flag_output    <=      1'b0;
                    end
          endcase
          end
endmodule
```

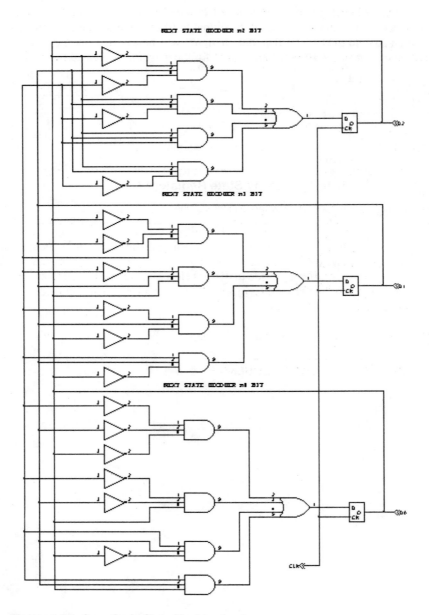

Figure 3-20 Gray Code State Machine Logic

An output, called flag_output, was added to the Gray code design. This shows how we add outputs to a state machine. I want the output to be asserted during the 010 state, so it is set in the prior state (011). The flag_output signal will be asserted on entry to state 010 and cleared on exit of state 010. See Figure 3-21 for the waveforms created by this logic.

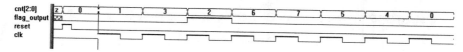

Figure 3-21 Gray Code State Machine Waveforms

How Many State Registers?

The number of available states = 2^n, where n is the number of state registers.

Using a state machine is a great way to partition a problem. When the state machine is in a given state, neglecting the clock and reset inputs, nothing else matters except the logic and the inputs explicitly referred to inside that state. How can we create a state machine that will synthesize effectively? At around eight state registers and inputs, I'd consider breaking up the state machine into smaller ones.

Let's talk about another way to create Gray Code logic.

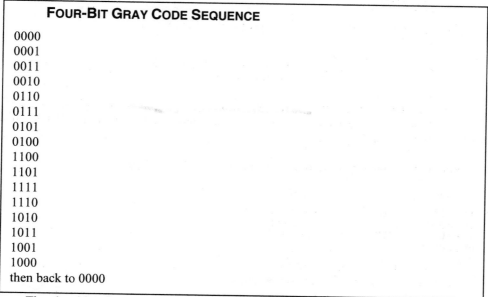

FOUR-BIT GRAY CODE SEQUENCE

0000
0001
0011
0010
0110
0111
0101
0100
1100
1101
1111
1110
1010
1011
1001
1000
then back to 0000

The algorithm for converting binary to Gray Code is:

```
gray MSB = binary MSB
next Gray bit = (corresponding binary bit XOR'd (added without
carry) with the next-highest-order binary bit)
```

Listing 3-15 illustrates the algorithm for converting from binary to Gray Code.

Listing 3-15 Verilog Code for Converting Binary to Gray Code

```verilog
module bin2gry (clk, reset, binary_input, gray_output);
   input              clk, reset;
   input       [3:0]  binary_input;
   output             gray_output;
   reg         [3:0]  gray_output;

   always @ (posedge clk or posedge reset)
       if (reset)
       begin
              gray_output   <=      4'b0;
       end

       else begin
       gray_output[3] <=    binary_input[3];
       gray_output[2] <=    binary_input[3] ^ binary_input[2];
       gray_output[1] <=    binary_input[2] ^ binary_input[1];
       gray_output[0] <=    binary_input[1] ^ binary_input[0];

       end
       endmodule
```

The algorithm for converting from Gray Code to binary:

```
binary MSB = gray MSB
next binary bit  = (previously determined binary bit XOR'd with
                        corresponding Gray bit).
```

A synchronous version of a Gray Code to binary converter is shown in Listing 3-16.
The conversion algorithm is modified slightly, so all bits are calculated in parallel and will
converge in a single clock period.

Listing 3-16 Verilog Code for Converting Binary to Gray Code

```verilog
module gry2bin (clk, reset, gray_in, binary_output);
   input              clk, reset;
   input       [3:0]  gray_in;
   output             binary_output;
   reg         [3:0]  binary_output;

   always @ (posedge clk or posedge reset)
       if (reset)
```

```
        begin
                binary_output <=      4'b0;
        end

        else begin
binary_output[3] <= gray_in[3];
binary_output[2] <= gray_in[3]^gray_in[2];
binary_output[1] <=(gray_in[3]^gray_in[2])^gray_in[1];
binary_output[0] <=((gray_in[3]^gray_in[2])^gray_in[1])^gray_in[0];

        end
        endmodule
```

State Assignments

The state assignments can make a big difference in how efficiently your logic will synthesize. We will use parameters and `ifdef statements to select between encoding assignments as shown in Listing 3-17. A binary count is the easiest to test and debug, but using Gray Code for state assignments that occur in sequence will synthesize the most efficiently. State machine state coding can also be used to directly generate output signals by using a flipflop for both a state register and an output register. Using this method, the clever designer can save some logic and create a faster design.

Listing 3-17 Example of Selecting Binary/Gray Code State Assignments

```
module ifdef_test (clk, reset, count_output);
input       clk, reset;
output      count_output;
reg  [2:0]  count_output;

//`define binary

`ifdef binary
parameter   state_zero   =    3'b000;
parameter   state_one    =    3'b001;
parameter   state_two    =    3'b010;
parameter   state_three  =    3'b011;
parameter   state_four   =    3'b100;
parameter   state_five   =    3'b101;
parameter   state_six    =    3'b110;
parameter   state_seven  =    3'b111;

`else
parameter   state_zero   =    3'b000;
parameter   state_one    =    3'b001;
parameter   state_two    =    3'b011;
parameter   state_three  =    3'b010;
parameter   state_four   =    3'b110;
parameter   state_five   =    3'b111;
parameter   state_six    =    3'b101;
```

```
parameter   state_seven   =        3'b100;

`endif

always @ (posedge clk or posedge reset)
      if (reset)
      begin
            count_output <=     state_zero;
      end

      else begin case (count_output)
      state_zero:   count_output <= state_one;
      state_one:    count_output <= state_two;
      state_two:    count_output <= state_three;
      state_three:  count_output <= state_four;
      state_four:   count_output <= state_five;
      state_five:   count_output <= state_six;
      state_six:    count_output <= state_seven;
      state_seven:  count_output <= state_zero;

      default:      count_output <= state_zero;

      endcase
      end
      endmodule
```

One-Hot State Assignments

Some designs benefit from one-hot state assignments. One-hot means that each state is assigned a single-state flipflop which is active only in the assigned state. This type of coding tends to spread out the FPGA logic and can make the logic easier to synthesize. Most FPGA architectures have a lot of registers, so it may not be a terrible penalty to consume some with the one-hot scheme: a one-hot state machine uses more flipflops than a Gray/binary-coded state machine, one flipflop per state. However, a one-hot design is not a cure-all. In some cases a one-hot design uses more logic than binary or gray coding. Definitely check to make sure you're really getting the benefit you expect when using one-hot coding.

One aspect of the one-hot assignment to consider is the many unused or default condition states which should be handled. By definition, the one-hot method uses one active flipflop at a time, but what if two registers get asserted by a noise hit or metastable input condition. Will the design recover? How will these cases be covered? This question is tough to answer, so I generally stick to binary- or Gray-coded state assignments.

Notice that eight registers are required in Listing 3-18 to support the same number of state assignments as Listing 3-17. Also note that a useful reset state (all state registers = zero) is not used.

Listing 3-18 One-hot State Assignment Code Fragment

```
parameter    state_zero    =    8'b00000001;
parameter    state_one     =    8'b00000010;
parameter    state_two     =    8'b00000100;
parameter    state_three   =    8'b00001000;
parameter    state_four    =    8'b00010000;
parameter    state_five    =    8'b00100000;
parameter    state_six     =    8'b01000000;
parameter    state_seven   =    8'b10000000;
```

An alternate version of one-hot state coding is one-cold, in which all state registers are set except one as shown in Listing 3-19.

Listing 3-19 One-cold State Assignment Code Fragment

```
parameter    state_zero    =    8'b11111110;
parameter    state_one     =    8'b11111101;
parameter    state_two     =    8'b11111011;
parameter    state_three   =    8'b11110111;
parameter    state_four    =    8'b11101111;
parameter    state_five    =    8'b11011111;
parameter    state_six     =    8'b10111111;
parameter    state_seven   =    8'b01111111;
```

ADDERS

Binary adders are supported by the Verilog synthesis. The synthesis tool will examine each instance of the + operator and will try to implement the logic with a preoptimized module. The optimization can be influenced by compilation settings and may be optimized for area or speed/delay. If the design is slow and small, then using adders may be trivial and may not result in any problems. However, the logic required to implement one line of code (a <= b + c;) can be huge if the input vectors are wide.

The designer should be aware that the synthesis tool is searching for adders. Don't make the job of identifying and extracting them too difficult. Make the adder standalone as much as possible; i.e., don't bury it too deeply in your logic.

Half-Adder Logic

A half-adder sums two inputs. The reason it is not a "complete" or full-adder is that it ignores carry input signals. Logic is added to sum in a carry input to create a full adder.

Figure 3-22 shows a half-adder truth table and the associated schematic is shown in Figure 3-23.

in a	inb	carry output	cum output
0	0	0	0
0	1	0	1
1	0	0	1
1	1	1	0

Figure 3-22 Half-Adder Truth Table

By inspection, we can see that the carry output is a **AND** b (a **&** b) and the sum output is a **XOR** b (a ^ b).

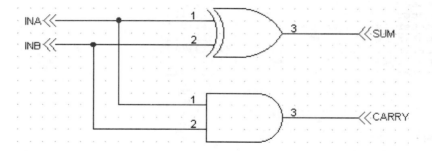

Figure 3-23 Half-Adder Schematic

We don't have to use the Verilog synthesizer's version of a half adder if we think we can do a better job than the synthesis tool; we can make our own. After we build a byte-wide adder, we'll compare our results with those of LeonardoSpectrum and admire how much smarter we are than the synthesis-tool vendor.

Listing 3-20 Verilog Version of Half Adder

```
module half_adder (ina, inb, sum_out, carry_out, reset, clk);
    input       ina, inb, reset, clk;
    output      sum_out, carry_out;
    reg         sum_out, carry_out;

    always @ (posedge clk or posedge reset)
    begin  if (reset)
```

```
      begin sum_out      <=     0;
            carry_out    <=     0;
      end
      else begin
            sum_out      <=     ina ^ inb;
            carry_out    <=     ina & inb;
      end
   end
   endmodule
```

Unfortunately, the half adder of Listing 3-20 only does half the job when adding multibit values. As designers, we aren't finding much job opportunity in designing single-bit adders. To turn the half adder into a full adder, we take the output of a half adder and connect it into another half adder. The carry input becomes the other input for the second stage as shown in the truth table of Figure 3-24 and the logic of Listing 3-21.

in a	inb	carry in	sum	carry out
0	0	0	0	0
0	0	1	1	0
0	1	0	1	0
0	1	1	0	1
1	0	0	1	0
1	0	1	0	1
1	1	0	0	1
1	1	1	1	1

Figure 3-24 Full-Adder Truth Table

To create the equations for the full adder, cascade two half adders as shown in Figure 3-25.

Listing 3-21 Verilog Code Fragment for Full Adder

```
// Cascaded half adder equations.
carry_out   <=      (ina & inb) | ((ina ^ inb) & carry_in));
sum_out     <=      (ina ^ inb) ^ carry_in;
```

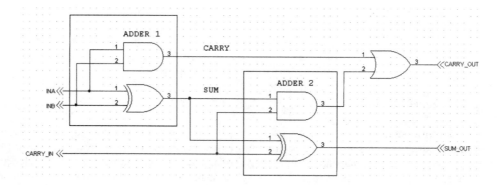

Figure 3-25 Full-Adder Schematic

Listing 3-22 Verilog Version of Full Adder


```
module full_adder (carry_out, sum_out, ina, inb, carry_in, clk,
reset);
        input        ina, inb, carry_in;
        input        clk, reset;
        output       carry_out, sum_out;
        reg          carry_out, sum_out;

        always @ (posedge clk or posedge reset)
              if (reset) begin
                    carry_out    <=    0;
                    sum_out      <=    0;
                    end
              else
// Cascaded half adder equations.
      begin
              carry_out <=  (ina & inb) + ((ina ^ inb) & carry_in);
              sum_out   <= ((ina ^ inb) ^ carry_in);
      end
      endmodule
```

You'll notice in Listing 3-22 and Figure 3-26 that by habit, I changed the combinational full-adder design to a synchronous version. In Figure 3-26, the modgen box is simply an OR gate.

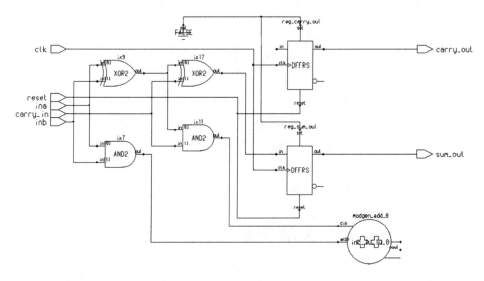

Figure 3-26 Full-Adder Schematic after Synthesis

To create wider adders, in a structural manner, we can cascade as many of these full adders as we wish. To create large adders, we should break the design into small modules no larger than four-bits wide, and stitch them together. This aids the synthesizer and will generally improve area and speed performance.

The carry output of one adder feeds the carry input of the higher-order bit. Note: the size of the output register must be one larger than that of the input registers in order to accept the carry output of the last stage. An exception to this occurs where the input set of data inputs is limited so that a carry is not possible. The carry input for the LSB adder is fixed at 0. An example of this type of adder is presented in Listing 3-23. To make this design work, the full_adder.v design must be included in the project. Listing 3-23 is also an example of a simple hierarchy.

Listing 3-23 Homebrew Structural Version of Byte-Wide Full Adder

```
module byte_adder (byte_a, byte_b, sum_output, clk, reset);
    input  [7:0]  byte_a, byte_b;
    input         clk, reset;
    output [8:0]  sum_output;
    wire   [7:0]  carry_output;

full_adder u1 (carry_output[0], sum_output[0], byte_a[0],
byte_b[0], 1'b0, clk, reset);
full_adder u2 (carry_output[1], sum_output[1], byte_a[1],
byte_b[1], carry_output[0], clk, reset);
full_adder u3 (carry_output[2], sum_output[2], byte_a[2],
byte_b[2], carry_output[1], clk, reset);
full_adder u4 (carry_output[3], sum_output[3], byte_a[3],
byte_b[3], carry_output[2], clk, reset);
full_adder u5 (carry_output[4], sum_output[4], byte_a[4],
byte_b[4], carry_output[3], clk, reset);
full_adder u6 (carry_output[5], sum_output[5], byte_a[5],
byte_b[5], carry_output[4], clk, reset);
full_adder u7 (carry_output[6], sum_output[6], byte_a[6],
byte_b[6], carry_output[5], clk, reset);
full_adder u8 (carry_output[7], sum_output[7], byte_a[7],
byte_b[7], carry_output[6], clk, reset);
assign sum_output[8]    =    carry_output[7];

endmodule
```

The synthesis summary for the byte_adder design is shown in Listing 3-24.

Listing 3-24 Homebrew Byte-Wide Full-Adder Synthesis Summary

```
Info, Instances dissolved by autodissolve in View
.work.byte_adder.INTERFACE
"C:/Verilog/SourceCode/byte_adder.v", line 7: u1 (full_adder)
"C:/Verilog/SourceCode/byte_adder.v", line 8: u2 (full_adder)
"C:/Verilog/SourceCode/byte_adder.v", line 9: u3 (full_adder)
"C:/Verilog/SourceCode/byte_adder.v", line 10: u4 (full_adder)
"C:/Verilog/SourceCode/byte_adder.v", line 11: u5 (full_adder)
"C:/Verilog/SourceCode/byte_adder.v", line 12: u6 (full_adder)
"C:/Verilog/SourceCode/byte_adder.v", line 13: u7 (full_adder)
"C:/Verilog/SourceCode/byte_adder.v", line 14: u8 (full_adder)
Using wire table: 4013xl-3_avg
Info, Inferred net 'reset' as GSR net.
-- Start optimization for design .work.byte_adder.INTERFACE
Using wire table: 4013xl-3_avg

      Pass    Area    Delay    DFFs  PIs   POs  --CPU--
              (FGs)   (ns)                      min:sec
       1       16      12       16    18    9   00:00
Info, Added global buffer BUFG for port clk
Using wire table: 4013xl-3_avg
-- Start timing optimization for design .work.byte_adder.INTERFACE
```

```
No critical paths to optimize at this level

**********************************************************

Cell: byte_adder    View: INTERFACE    Library: work

**********************************************************

Number of ports :                        27
Number of nets :                         68
Number of instances :                    51
Number of references to this view :       0

Total accumulated area :
Number of BUFG :                          1
Number of CLB Flip Flops :                7
Number of FG Function Generators :       16
Number of IBUF :                         17
Number of IOB Output Flip Flops :         9
Number of Packed CLBs :                   8
Number of STARTUP :                       1

***************************************************
Device Utilization for 4010xlPQ100
***************************************************
Resource               Used    Avail   Utilization
---------------------------------------------------
IOs                     27      77       35.06%
FG Function Generators  16      800       2.00%
H Function Generators    0      400       0.00%
CLB Flip Flops           7      800       0.88%


-------------------------------------------------
                          Clock Frequency Report
        Clock           : Frequency
        ---------------------------------
        clk             : 77.6 MHz
```

Listing 3-25 is an example of letting the synthesizer do all the work. We just use the Verilog addition operator (+) to create the sum of two bytes. Listing 3-26 presents the statistics for the synthesized design.

Listing 3-25 Synthesis-Tool Version of Byte-Wide Full Adder

```
module byte_adder2 (byte_a, byte_b, sum_output, clk, reset);
    input  [7:0] byte_a, byte_b;
    input        clk, reset;
    output       sum_output;
    reg    [8:0] sum_output;

    always @ (posedge clk or posedge reset)
    begin
    if (reset)   sum_output   <=    0;
```

```
        else        sum_output    <=      byte_a + byte_b;
        end
endmodule
```

Listing 3-26 Synthesis-Tool Version of Byte-Wide Full Adder, Synthesis Summary

```
Info, Inferred net 'reset' as GSR net.
-- Start optimization for design .work.byte_adder2.INTERFACE
Using wire table: 4013xl-3_avg

        Pass      Area    Delay     DFFs   PIs    POs --CPU--
                  (FGs)   (ns)                         min:sec
         1         8       7         9     18      9   00:00
Info, Added global buffer BUFG for port clk
Using wire table: 4013xl-3_avg
-- Start timing optimization for design
.work.byte_adder2.INTERFACE
No critical paths to optimize at this level

**********************************************************

Cell: byte_adder2   View: INTERFACE    Library: work

**********************************************************

  Number of ports :                       27
  Number of nets :                        103
  Number of instances :                    48
  Number of references to this view :       0

Total accumulated area :
  Number of BUFG :                          1
  Number of CY4 :                           5
  Number of FG Function Generators :        8
  Number of IBUF :                         17
  Number of IOB Output Flip Flops :         9
  Number of STARTUP :                       1

**************************************************
Device Utilization for 4010xlPQ100
**************************************************
Resource               Used    Avail   Utilization
-------------------------------------------------------
IOs                     27      77      35.06%
FG Function Generators  8       800     1.00%
H Function Generators   0       400     0.00%
CLB Flip Flops          0       800     0.00%


-------------------------------------------------
                     Clock Frequency Report

     Clock                  : Frequency
        ---------------------------------------
```

```
clk                    : 135.1 MHz
```

Compare our homebrew bytewide adder with the LeonardoSpectrum version. We didn't do very well, did we? Our version was twice as large and twice as slow.

We can improve our adder design by looking at some of the problems with our approach. The adder we created is a Ripple Carry Adder (RCA). It is small in area, but slow. The problem with the RCA is easy to illustrate. Imagine I give you 2 binary numbers to add:

```
10101
11001
```

Suppose I ask you what is the result of adding only the highest-order bits (1 + 1)? You say that you can't answer my question without figuring out if a carry is generated by the addition of all the lower-order bits. There you go! The carry must be calculated for all the lower-order bits before the highest-order bits can be added. The output is not available until the carry from each adder "ripples" through all stages to the summation and final carry outputs. This adder would be faster if only we could "look ahead" and generate the carry outputs in parallel instead of in series. We evaluate the inputs to create carry signals which are added with partial sums. Oddly enough, others have thought of this idea and have created an adder architecture call Carry Look Ahead (CLA Adder).

The CLA Adder is described in terms of Generate (carry terms) and Propagate (sum terms) a shown in Listing 3-27.

Listing 3-27 Carry Generate and Carry Propagate Logic Code Fragment

```
// Definition of propagate/generate terms (not Verilog!)
    generate[i]  =      (a[i] & b[i]);
    propagate[i] =      (a[i] ^ b[i]);
```

To describe a cascade-able (expandable) adder in terms of generate/propagate signals, we need to add the carry from the previous stage(s); the propagate will be a single-bit adder (OR gate) as shown in Listing 3-28.

Listing 3-28 Carry Generate and Carry Propagate Logic, Expandable Adder

```
// Cascade-able propagate/generate terms (not Verilog!)
carry[i]     =    generate[i] | (propagate[i] & carry[i-1]);
propagate[i] =    (a[i] | b[i]);
```

The sum is still formed by cascading half-adders, adding in the propagate (sum) term and the carry term that is calculated in parallel. To make the blocks generic, the s[0] stage, even though a carry-in at this stage is not allowed, will still use a carry input wired to 0.

Carry Select Adder

Another strategy for speeding up an adder adds even more hardware. Redundant hardware is added to calculate the sum assuming a carry input and assuming no carry input. The output is selected via multiplexer based on whether carry is required or not.

Carry Skip Adder

Another strategy for speeding up the adder allows the use of an inverter for cases where the inputs are not equal. The addition uses the XOR function and creates an output when the inputs are different, the sum is the inverse of the carry bit and the carry bit just passes through. This type of adder is usually implemented in groups, probably groups of 4. This version uses less real estate than a CLA and is about as fast.

There are other adder strategies which area for speed. The main thing is: get an appreciation for the logic that is synthesized when the Verilog addition operator is used. The best synthesis strategy: cheat! Keep the adder input lengths short and fight the system engineer to reduce resolution to the point of diminishing returns. Don't implement a 16-bit adder if a 14-bit adder will do. Also, run the adder at the lowest possible clock frequency.

SUBTRACTORS

The subtractor is similar to the adder and there are corresponding versions of subtractors for the adders described above (Ripple Borrow Subtractor, Borrow Save Subtractor, Borrow Select Subtractor, and so on). We will discuss the Ripple Borrow Adder to illustrate the similarity to Adder circuits. Figure 3-27 illustrates ina - inb in a half-borrow circuit.

in a	inb	borrow output	diff output
0	0	0	0
0	1	1	0
1	0	0	1
1	1	0	0

Figure 3-27 Half-Adder Truth Table

Listing 3-29 Subtractor Logic Code Fragment

```
Bout = ~ina & inb;     // Note similarity to adder: carry =
                       //   ina & inb.
Diff =  ina & ~inb;    // Note similarity to adder
                       // xor: sum = (ina &
                       // ~inb) | (~ina & inb).
```

Let's expand the half-borrow logic for the full subtractor, again ina – inb as shown in Figure 3-28.

borrow input	ina	inb	borrow output	diff
0	0	0	0	0
0	0	1	1	1
0	1	0	0	0
0	1	1	0	0
1	0	0	1	1
1	0	1	1	0
1	1	0	0	1
1	1	1	1	1

Figure 3-28 Full-Subtractor Truth Table

MULTIPLIERS

The Verilog language supports unsigned multiplication and division by powers of two. This in not a big challenge; these are simply shift-left (a multiply by two for each binary shift left) and shift-right (a divide by two for each binary shift right) operations. This doesn't mean we give up. FPGAs are capable of performing sophisticated math functions at high speed; we need to use library modules (which limits portability) or create the logic ourselves. Again, the best strategy for dealing with advanced math is to cheat. Work with the system engineer to reduce the numbers of bits to be multiplied. Don't use eight bits when seven will do. Do a model in C to manipulate test data and examine the results. Use the lowest resolution possible to achieve acceptable results. Implementing a multiplier is easier if the variable inputs are multiplied by constants. If the input range is limited, this might save some logic (suppose, for example, a variable is eight bits wide, but the range of legal inputs is 0—160? Every bit helps simplify logic and can increase operating speed).

The result of multiplication requires n + m bits of width, where n and m are the sizes of the input variables. For example, when multiplying two four-bit values, a register eight bits wide is required to hold the maximum result.

Hard-Wired Multipliers

The best way to illustrate the multiplication algorithm is by example. Let's assume we want to multiply an integer nibble n by a constant integer nibble with a value of D(16).

2^3	2^2	2^1	2^0	Bit weight
n3	n2	n1	n0	Variable nibble to be multiplied
1	1	0	1	Constant nibble to multiply variable by D(16)

The multiplication process shifts and adds. The leftmost digit means add n0. The n1 digit can be ignored, it does not affect the result (an example of simplification due to multiplying by a constant). The n2 digit means: multiply n by 4 (shift n left twice) and add. The n3 digit means: multiply n by 8 (shift n left three times) and add.

Here's what we get:

Result = (n * 8) + (n * 4) + (n * 1)

Let's assume the variable is B(16) or 1011(2) and plug the numbers in.

Result = (1011 * 8) + (1011 * 4) + (1011 * 1)
Result = 1011000 + 101100 + 1011
Result = 10001111 = 8F(16)

This is cool: multiplication turns into a bunch of shift and adds. We already know how to shift and we already know how to add, so we're in good shape. To turn this into a generic multiplier, we have to be prepared to add a shifted value (or zero) for each bit.

Let's see what a Verilog version of this multiplier might look like (see Listing 3-30). This is just one way to do the logic! I could have used the shift operator. I could have used structural adders. To speed the design up, I could have pipelined the intermediate sums to reduce the considerable amount of combinational logic between flipflops.

Listing 3-30 Hard-Wired Multiplier Example

```
module byte_mult (nibble_in, byte_out, clk, reset);
    input   [3:0]  nibble_in;
    input          clk, reset;
    output         byte_out;
    reg     [7:0]  byte_out;

    always @ (posedge clk or posedge reset)
    if (reset)
          byte_out    <=     0;
    else
    begin
// Shift nibble by padding with zeroes. MSB must be zero to make
//   the size of the left-hand side match the set size of the
//   right-hand side.
          byte_out    <=     {1'b0, nibble_in[3:0], 3'b0}
                      +      {2'b0, nibble_in[3:0], 2'b0}
                      +      {4'b0, nibble_in[3:0]};
    end

endmodule
```

Hard-wired multipliers are fully custom and not at all generic. If you're trying to convince the system designer that a hard-wired multiplier is the right answer, be careful what you promise. Changing the constant you multiply by requires changing the code. If you are having resource problems in the FPGA, there may not be enough room to squeeze in a new set of coefficients (count the number of 1's in the desired constant; there will be a shift/add for each 1 present in the constant). Adding resolution to the input or the constant can increase the logic considerably.

Generic Multipliers

To change the hard-wired multiplier to a generic 4-by-4 multiplier, we must create logic which allows all the shift and adds to be used (whether they are used or not depends on the data values). Again, there are many ways to do this, the example of Listing 3-31 is just one way.

Listing 3-31 Generic 4 x 4 Multiplier Example

```
module byte_mult2 (nibble1, nibble2, byte_out, clk, reset);
     input  [3:0]  nibble1, nibble2;
     input         clk, reset;
     output        byte_out;
     reg    [7:0]  byte_out, stored3, stored2, stored1, stored0;

     always @ (posedge clk or posedge reset)
     if (reset)
     begin
             byte_out      <=      0;
             stored3       <=      0;
             stored2       <=      0;
             stored1       <=      0;
             stored0       <=      0;
     end
     else
     begin
// Shift nibble by padding with zeroes. MSB must be zero to make
//   the size of the left-hand side match the set size of the
//   right-hand side.
stored3   <=    nibble1[3] ? {1'b0, nibble2[3:0], 3'b0} : 8'b0;
stored2   <=    nibble1[2] ? {2'b0, nibble2[3:0], 2'b0} : 8'b0;
stored1   <=    nibble1[1] ? {3'b0, nibble2[3:0], 3'b0} : 8'b0;
stored0   <=    nibble1[0] ? {4'b0, nibble2[3:0]}       : 8'b0;
byte_out  <=    stored3 + stored2 + stored1 + stored0;
     end
endmodule
```

One thing about Listing 3-31 should be mentioned. Verilog will let you do dumb things; there are no checks to make sure registers are wide enough to accept the data you are calculating. Normally, you'd expect all sum registers to be one bit larger than the largest width of number to be added. However, because I know the nature of the numbers stored in the store registers (i.e., that the MSB is guaranteed to be zero), I can get away with the stored width being the same as the byte_out width. We know that 8 bits are all that are required to store the value of two nibbles multiplied together. Use caution when making assumptions like this!

Multiplying by Fractional Values

Often, the constant coefficients are fractional values. These are easily handled by scaling the coefficients into integer values, then scaling the result back again. You will want to reduce the resolution and values to the minimum easiest numbers to deal with. Let's say the system engineer asks for a coefficient of 0.80. Won't an easier number like 0.75 (2^{-1} (or ½) + 2^{-2} (or ¼)) work with acceptable results? If so, the job is easier. If not, then so be it.

To multiply a nibble n by 0.75, realize that 0.75 x 4 = 2 (a number we like a lot) and that (n x 4) / 4 = n. So, multiply the coefficient by 4, then divide the result by 4 later and you're even.

If the system engineer absolutely insists on a coefficient like 0.8, ask for the required accuracy (10%?, 5%?, 1%?), then factor 0.8 into binary (0.8 = ½ + ¼ + 1/32 ...) and do more scaling shifts as required.

More Digital Circuits: Counters, ROMs, and RAMs

This chapter presents an assortment of digital designs implemented with Verilog.

RIPPLE COUNTERS

The most common (generic) counter is a ripple counter, so described because the output ripples from stage to stage. If we create a Verilog counter like Listing 4-1, using the binary-counter option in Exemplar Logic LeonardoSpectrum's Input File menu as shown in Figure 4-1, we'll find the result is a ripple counter.

Listing 4-1   Verilog Code for Simple Counter

```
module ripple1 (count_out, clk, reset);
    input              clk, reset;
    output             count_out;
    reg          [3:0] count_out;

    always @ (posedge clk or posedge reset)
    if (reset)
          count_out     <=      0;
    else
          count_out     <=      count_out + 1;

endmodule
```

Figure 4-1   Counter Style Selection

The problem with the ripple counter is that, because more than one output is changing at once, using combinational logic to decode output states results in glitchy signals. To avoid this problem, use counters like Gray Code or Johnson counters.

JOHNSON COUNTERS

The Johnson counter is a type of shift counter. A shift counter uses little combinational logic to create the count logic and therefore can operate at high speed (the operating speed is limited only by how fast a flipflop can switch states and by the propagation delay of the simple count logic). The Johnson counter wraps an inverted version of the highest-order bit back to the lowest-order bit. Like the Gray Code counter, it has one output that changes at each clock. This results in a glitch-free output when decoded with combinational logic. Disadvantages include the requirement of more registers to store the count variable (around n/2 registers are required, where n is the number of registers) and lack of error recovery. If a bad count pattern gets loaded, it will recirculate until the registers are reinitialized (if this ever happens!). The schematic for a Johnson counter is shown in Figure 4-2 with corresponding Verilog code in Listing 4-2 and count sequence in Listing 4-3.

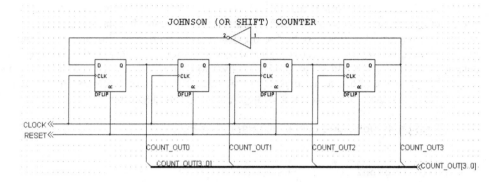

Figure 4-2 Johnson Counter Schematic

Listing 4-2 Johnson Counter Verilog Code

```verilog
module johnson1(clock, reset, count_out);
    input               clock, reset;
    output              count_out;
    reg         [3:0]   count_out;

    always @ (clock or reset)
    if (reset)
        count_out           <=      0;
    else begin
        count_out[3:1]      <=      count_out[2:0];
        count_out[0]        <=      ~count_out[3];
    end
    endmodule
```

Listing 4-3 Johnson Counter Output Sequence

0000
1000
1100
1110
1111
0111
0011
0001
0000
Repeat...

The alert designer notices that not all states are used in the count cycle. We have eight count states that are not used. Wasted counter states indicate that the design does not use registers efficiently, but this may not be important. However, if an illegal count occurs due to noise, there is no way to recover. Illegal states without recovery will make the careful designer nervous. Let's add some logic, as shown in Listing 4-4, to detect and recover from those illegal states. This logic makes the counter a lot more complex, but it may be worthwhile to create a robust counter with glitchless output decoding.

Listing 4-4   Johnson Counter with Error Recovery

```verilog
module johnson2(clock, reset, count_out);
    input                 clock, reset;
    output                count_out;
    reg         [3:0]     count_out;

    always @ (posedge clock or posedge reset)
    if (reset)
            count_out     <=      0;

    // Add fault recovery.
    else    if (count_out == 4'h2)     count_out     <=     0;
    else    if (count_out == 4'h4)     count_out     <=     0;
    else    if (count_out == 4'h5)     count_out     <=     0;
    else    if (count_out == 4'h6)     count_out     <=     0;
    else    if (count_out == 4'h9)     count_out     <=     0;
    else    if (count_out == 4'ha)     count_out     <=     0;
    else    if (count_out == 4'hb)     count_out     <=     0;
    else    if (count_out == 4'hd)     count_out     <=     0;
    else    begin
                count_out[3:1]    <=      count_out[2:0];
                count_out[0]      <=      ~count_out[3];
    end
endmodule
```

Another method of error recovery to consider is allowing an external device (like a microcontroller) to reinitialize the counter if an error occurs. Generally, software designers complain if the hardware staff creates logic that can't be written to (or read from after a write occurs) by the software. Ability to read and write registers adds to the testability of the hardware, which is generally a good thing. This adds logic, which increases the design size and reduces the operating speed—bad things.

LINEAR FEEDBACK SHIFT REGISTERS

A type of counter that is quite interesting is a Linear Feedback Shift Register or LFSR counter. It is similar to the Johnson counter except that instead of an inverter from the last stage back to the first stage, a small number of taps are recycled. The counter next-state logic is very simple (a few XOR or XNOR gates). With maximal-length logic (taps selected to give the maximal count), a small number of registers can create counts of up to 2^{n-1} (compared to a binary-counter count length of 2^n). The one state that is missing from a maximal-length LSFR count sequence is the no-recovery state (all zeros for an XOR version or all ones for an XNOR version). An LFSR counter can operate at high speed compared to a binary counter because the feedback logic is very simple. For cases where the count value is arbitrary (the LFSR count sequence is pseudorandom) the LFSR counter can be a good solution.

How these can counters work can be illustrated by example. A maximal-length 4-bit LFSR counter can use the taps [3,0] (maximal length might be achieved with other taps, too). The taps are the register outputs that are fed back. Figure 4-3 has four flipflops and a single XNOR gate.

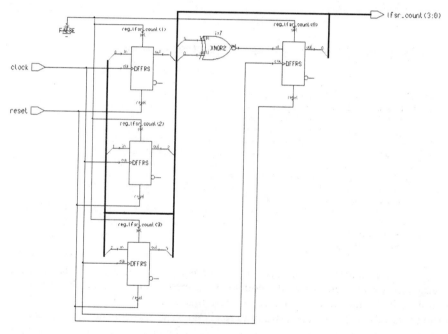

Figure 4-3   4-Bit LFSR Counter Schematic

This version is sometimes called 'many-to-one'; notice how taps are derived from many outputs, then XOR'd back to the input. There is also a variation called 'one-to-many' where all the feedback terms are combined before being fed back.

This counter of Listing 4-5 is an XNOR version. I use this generally use this version because the illegal state is all ones; I prefer to reset all registers on power-up (rather than preset some or all of the registers, which is necessary with the XOR version). Listing 4-6 presents a simple test fixture for testing the Verilog design of Listing 4-5.

Listing 4-5   Verilog Version of a 4-bit LFSR Counter

```
module lfsr4 (clock, reset, lfsr_count);
    input           clock, reset;
    output          lfsr_count;
    reg    [3:0]    lfsr_count;

    always @ (posedge clock or posedge reset)
    if (reset)
    lfsr_count              <=    0;
    else
    begin
    lfsr_count[3:1]         <=    lfsr_count[2:0];
    lfsr_count[0] <=    lfsr_count[3] ~^ lfsr_count[0];
    end endmodule
```

Listing 4-6   Simple Test Fixture for 4-bit LFSR Counter

```
module lfsr4_tf(clock, reset, lfsr_count);
`timescale 1ns / 1ns
output          clock, reset;
reg             clock, reset;
input      [3:0] lfsr_count;
parameter clk_period        =     20;

lfsr4 u1 (clock, reset, lfsr_count);

always begin
    #(clk_period / 2) clock = ~clock;
    end
initial begin
            clock       =     0;
            reset       =     1; // Assert the system reset.
    #75     reset       =     0;
end
endmodule
```

Figure 4-4 shows the count sequence for the 4-bit LFSR counter.

```
//    binary hex
//    0000        0
//    0001        1
//    0010        2
//    0101        5
//    1010        a
//    0100        4
//    1001        9
//    0011        3
//    0110        6
//    1101        d
```

```
//    1011          b
//    0111          7
//    1110          e
//    1100          c
//    1000          8

//    0000          0           Repeat sequence...
```

Figure 4-4   4-Bit LFSR Count Sequence

Looks like a big mess, doesn't it? That's part of the LSFR counter's charm. Sequential values are loosely correlated, or pseudorandom. This can be useful for reducing clock harmonic noise. For example, in a binary counter, the lowest-order bit toggles on every clock; this results in noise that is highly correlated to the system clock and adds energy at subharmonics of the system clock. This harmonic energy is a large source of system noise. An LFSR counter generates more wideband noise with lower peak energy content, because the counter bits are changing in a more random manner.

Table 4-1 lists taps for maximal-length LFSR counters. Other tap selections are possible for some of the counter lengths.

Number of Bits	Length of Loop	Taps
2 *	3	[1,0]
3 *	7	[2,0]
4	15	[3,0]
5 *	31	[4,1]
6	63	[5,0]
7 *	127	[6,0]
8	255	[7,3,2,1]
9	511	[8,3]
10	1,023	[9,2]
11	2,047	[10,1]
12	4,095	[11,5,3,0]
13 *	8,191	[12,3,2,0]
14	16,383	[13,4,2,0]
15	32,767	[14,0]
16	65,535	[15,4,2,1]
17 *	131,071	[16,2]
18	262,143	[17,6]

Number of Bits	Length of Loop	Taps
19 *	524,287	[18,4,1,0]
20	1,048,575	[19,2]
21	2,097,151	[20,1]
22	4,194,303	[21,0]
23	8,388,607	[22,4]
24	16,777,215	[23,3,2,0]
25	33,554,431	[24,2]
26	67,108,863	[25,5,1,0]
27	134,217,727	[26,4,1,0]
28	268,435,455	[27,2]
29	536,870,911	[28,1]
30	1,073,741,823	[29,5,3,0]
31 *	2,147,483,647	[30,2]
32	4,294,967,295	[31,6,5,1]

* indicates sequences whose length is a prime number
Sequences 2, 3, 5, 7, 13, 17, 19, 31 have lengths that are prime numbers.
This table is from *Designus Maximus Unleashed* by Clive Maxfield; it is copyrighted by Butterworth-Heinemann, 1998, and is used by permission.

Table 4-1   Maximal-Length LFSR Taps

From Table 4-1, you can see we can create a 31-bit counter with 31 registers and a single XOR gate. Imagine the ripple-carry logic required to create a 31-bit binary counter!

An example of the use of a LFSR counter is to create simple logic for a divide-by-N circuit. In this design, a terminal count is provided as an input to be compared to. Listing 4-7 illustrates an 8-bit divide-by-N counter, Listing 4-8 shows a test fixture, Listing 4-9 is the output list of the pseudorandom count sequence, and Figure 4-5 shows the waveforms at the count rollover.

Listing 4-7   Verilog Version of a 8-bit Divide-by-N LFSR Counter

```
// 8-bit Divide-by-N LSFR Counter.
module lfsr8 (clock, reset, lfsr_count, terminal_cnt, rollover);
    input           clock, reset;
    input   [7:0]   terminal_cnt;
    output          lfsr_count;
    reg     [7:0]   lfsr_count;
    output          rollover;
```

```
    reg             rollover;

    always @ (posedge clock or posedge reset)
    if (reset)
    begin
            lfsr_count    <=    0;
            rollover      <=    0;
    end
    else
      if (lfsr_count == terminal_cnt)// Test for terminal count.
    begin
            rollover      <=    1;
            lfsr_count    <=    0;
    end
    else begin
    rollover              <=    0;
    lfsr_count[7:1]       <=    lfsr_count[6:0];
    lfsr_count[0] <=    lfsr_count[7] ~^ (lfsr_count[3]
                            ~^ (lfsr_count[2] ~^ lfsr_count[1]));
    end
endmodule
```

Listing 4-8   Verilog Version of a 8-bit Divide-by-N LFSR Counter Test Fixture

```
// 8-bit Divide-by-N LSFR Counter Test Fixture.
module lfsr8_tf(clock, reset, lfsr_count, terminal_cnt);
`timescale 1ns / 1ns
output          clock, reset;
reg             clock, reset;
input    [7:0]  lfsr_count;
output   [7:0]  terminal_cnt;
reg             terminal_cnt;
wire            rollover;

parameter clk_period        =       20;

lfsr8 u1 (clock, reset, lfsr_count, terminal_cnt, rollover);

always
    begin
    #(clk_period / 2) clock    = ~clock;
    end

initial
begin
    clock           =    0;
    reset           =    1;      // Assert the system reset.
    terminal_cnt =    8'd66; // Test assignment.
    #75 reset       =    0;
end
endmodule
```

Listing 4-9   8-bit Divide-by-N LFSR Counter Count Sequence

```
lfsr_count = 00, rollover = 0 lfsr_count = 00, rollover = 0
lfsr_count = 00, rollover = 0 lfsr_count = 00, rollover = 0
lfsr_count = 01, rollover = 0 lfsr_count = 03, rollover = 0
lfsr_count = 06, rollover = 0 lfsr_count = 0d, rollover = 0
lfsr_count = 1b, rollover = 0 lfsr_count = 37, rollover = 0
lfsr_count = 6f, rollover = 0 lfsr_count = de, rollover = 0
lfsr_count = bd, rollover = 0 lfsr_count = 7a, rollover = 0
lfsr_count = f5, rollover = 0 lfsr_count = eb, rollover = 0
lfsr_count = d6, rollover = 0 lfsr_count = ac, rollover = 0
lfsr_count = 58, rollover = 0 lfsr_count = b0, rollover = 0
lfsr_count = 60, rollover = 0 lfsr_count = c1, rollover = 0
lfsr_count = 82, rollover = 0 lfsr_count = 05, rollover = 0
lfsr_count = 0a, rollover = 0 lfsr_count = 15, rollover = 0
lfsr_count = 2a, rollover = 0 lfsr_count = 55, rollover = 0
lfsr_count = aa, rollover = 0 lfsr_count = 54, rollover = 0
lfsr_count = a8, rollover = 0 lfsr_count = 51, rollover = 0
lfsr_count = a3, rollover = 0 lfsr_count = 47, rollover = 0
lfsr_count = 8f, rollover = 0 lfsr_count = 1f, rollover = 0
lfsr_count = 3e, rollover = 0 lfsr_count = 7c, rollover = 0
lfsr_count = f9, rollover = 0 lfsr_count = f3, rollover = 0
lfsr_count = e7, rollover = 0 lfsr_count = ce, rollover = 0
lfsr_count = 9d, rollover = 0 lfsr_count = 3a, rollover = 0
lfsr_count = 75, rollover = 0 lfsr_count = ea, rollover = 0
lfsr_count = d4, rollover = 0 lfsr_count = a9, rollover = 0
lfsr_count = 53, rollover = 0 lfsr_count = a6, rollover = 0
lfsr_count = 4c, rollover = 0 lfsr_count = 99, rollover = 0
lfsr_count = 33, rollover = 0 lfsr_count = 66, rollover = 0
lfsr_count = cd, rollover = 0 lfsr_count = 9a, rollover = 0
lfsr_count = 34, rollover = 0 lfsr_count = 68, rollover = 0
lfsr_count = d0, rollover = 0 lfsr_count = a0, rollover = 0
lfsr_count = 40, rollover = 0 lfsr_count = 81, rollover = 0
lfsr_count = 02, rollover = 0 lfsr_count = 04, rollover = 0
lfsr_count = 08, rollover = 0 lfsr_count = 10, rollover = 0
lfsr_count = 21, rollover = 0 lfsr_count = 43, rollover = 0
lfsr_count = 86, rollover = 0 lfsr_count = 0c, rollover = 0
lfsr_count = 19, rollover = 0 lfsr_count = 32, rollover = 0
lfsr_count = 64, rollover = 0 lfsr_count = c8, rollover = 0
lfsr_count = 91, rollover = 0 lfsr_count = 22, rollover = 0
lfsr_count = 44, rollover = 0 lfsr_count = 88, rollover = 0
lfsr_count = 11, rollover = 0 lfsr_count = 23, rollover = 0
lfsr_count = 46, rollover = 0 lfsr_count = 8d, rollover = 0
lfsr_count = 1a, rollover = 0 lfsr_count = 35, rollover = 0
lfsr_count = 6a, rollover = 0 lfsr_count = d5, rollover = 0
lfsr_count = ab, rollover = 0 lfsr_count = 56, rollover = 0
lfsr_count = ad, rollover = 0 lfsr_count = 5a, rollover = 0
lfsr_count = b5, rollover = 0 lfsr_count = 6b, rollover = 0
lfsr_count = d7, rollover = 0 lfsr_count = ae, rollover = 0
lfsr_count = 5d, rollover = 0 lfsr_count = bb, rollover = 0
lfsr_count = 76, rollover = 0 lfsr_count = ed, rollover = 0
lfsr_count = da, rollover = 0 lfsr_count = b4, rollover = 0
lfsr_count = 69, rollover = 0 lfsr_count = d2, rollover = 0
lfsr_count = a5, rollover = 0 lfsr_count = 4b, rollover = 0
lfsr_count = 97, rollover = 0 lfsr_count = 2e, rollover = 0
```

```
lfsr_count = 5c, rollover = 0 lfsr_count = b9, rollover = 0
lfsr_count = 73, rollover = 0 lfsr_count = e6, rollover = 0
lfsr_count = cc, rollover = 0 lfsr_count = 98, rollover = 0
lfsr_count = 31, rollover = 0 lfsr_count = 63, rollover = 0
lfsr_count = c6, rollover = 0 lfsr_count = 8c, rollover = 0
lfsr_count = 18, rollover = 0 lfsr_count = 30, rollover = 0
lfsr_count = 61, rollover = 0 lfsr_count = c3, rollover = 0
lfsr_count = 87, rollover = 0 lfsr_count = 0e, rollover = 0
lfsr_count = 1c, rollover = 0 lfsr_count = 39, rollover = 0
lfsr_count = 72, rollover = 0 lfsr_count = e4, rollover = 0
lfsr_count = c9, rollover = 0 lfsr_count = 93, rollover = 0
lfsr_count = 27, rollover = 0 lfsr_count = 4f, rollover = 0
lfsr_count = 9e, rollover = 0 lfsr_count = 3d, rollover = 0
lfsr_count = 7b, rollover = 0 lfsr_count = f7, rollover = 0
lfsr_count = ee, rollover = 0 lfsr_count = dd, rollover = 0
lfsr_count = ba, rollover = 0 lfsr_count = 74, rollover = 0
lfsr_count = e8, rollover = 0 lfsr_count = d1, rollover = 0
lfsr_count = a2, rollover = 0 lfsr_count = 45, rollover = 0
lfsr_count = 8a, rollover = 0 lfsr_count = 14, rollover = 0
lfsr_count = 28, rollover = 0 lfsr_count = 50, rollover = 0
lfsr_count = a1, rollover = 0 lfsr_count = 42, rollover = 0
lfsr_count = 00, rollover = 1 lfsr_count = 01, rollover = 0
```

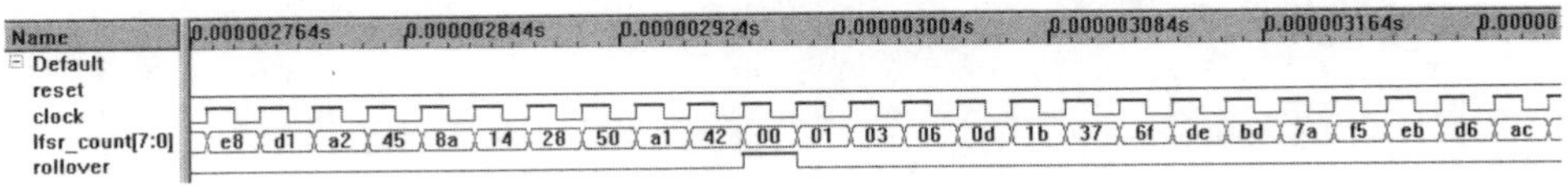

Figure 4-5 8-Bit Divide-by-N LFSR Count Simulation at Rollover

The one-to-many variation as shown in Listing 4-10 splits the XOR (or XNORs) into 2-input gates and distributes them throughout the register array. Note: The same taps are used, simply in a different form. In words, the 4-bit counter taps [3,0] means: XOR (or XNOR) the output of register 0 and register 3 and connect that result to the input of register 1. The last register is wrapped back to register 0. This will still result in a maximal-length sequence, but the count sequence (and terminal count value for a given count) will be different. The schematic extracted from Listing 4-10 is shown in Figure 4-6. The output waveform is shown in Figure 4-7.

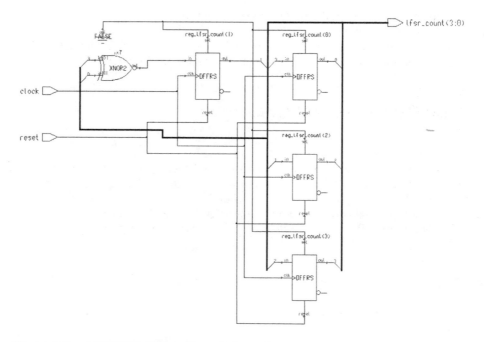

Figure 4-6   4-Bit LFSR One-to-Many Schematic

Listing 4-10 4-Bit LFSR One-to-Many Code

```
module lfsr4v2 (clock, reset, lfsr_count);
    input           clock, reset;
    output          lfsr_count;
    reg     [3:0]   lfsr_count;

    always @ (posedge clock or posedge reset)
    if (reset)
    lfsr_count              <=      0;
    else    begin
    lfsr_count[0] <=        lfsr_count[3];
    lfsr_count[1] <=        lfsr_count[3] ~^ lfsr_count[0];
    lfsr_count[3:2]         <=      lfsr_count[2:1];
    end
endmodule
```

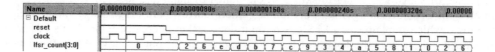

Figure 4-7   4-Bit LFSR One-to-Many Output Waveforms

For a more detailed explanation of LFSR counters, see Max Maxfield's *Designus Maximus Unleashed* (details on this book can be found in the Bibliography).

CYCLIC REDUNDANCY CHECKSUMS

Logic similar to the LFSR is used to create Cyclic Redundancy Checksums, or CRCs. Checksums are used to test a data packet to try to determine if an error has occurred. An ordinary checksum simply adds up the data bytes or words and discards any carry beyond a predetermined resolution. For example, an 8-bit checksum would use modulo-256 addition and discard all carries that result in numbers greater than 255 (FF in hex).

Let's assume a data packet consists of the following 8 bytes :

hex data
99
D0
AA
01
09
83
AF
BE

We can use our hex calculator to find that the sum of these numbers is 40D(16). We discard all but the lower 8 bits and get a checksum of 0D. The receiving logic can do the same addition and see if the received data gives a checksum of 0D. This gives us some small confidence that the data was received correctly. What if we want more confidence? We could send a 16-bit checksum instead; this would give a 10-byte packet and a checksum of 40D. Now, for multiple errors, the chance of detecting an error is 1 in 65,536 instead of 1 in 256. If an error causes a number greater than expected in one byte and a later error causes a corresponding number the same amount less than expected, the checksum will match and we'll think a bad packet is good. What if this is not good enough? A more random sequence of numbers would give us better error detection.

The idea behind a CRC is to do division instead of addition. The data packet is looked at as a huge binary number. We select a polynomial to divide this binary data with, and the remainder becomes our checksum. The sequence of remainders is more random than a sequence of sums. I'm going to skip a whole bunch of math and just tell you that logic to implement CRC division with a polynomial (where borrows are discarded) looks a lot like the logic which implements a LFSR. An input data packet is created with N bits of zeroes appended, where N is the length of the CRC, and is shifted out serially. While the data is transmitted, the CRC is calculated and then appended in place of the zeroes. This becomes the transmitted data packet.

At the receiver, the same CRC calculation is performed on the incoming data packet (including the CRC bits), and the remainder will be zero if no error is detected. Let's illustrate this with a simple example. Xilinx uses a 16-bit CRC to validate the serial data used for FPGA configuration. The schematic for this logic is shown in Figure 4-8. Xilinx uses XOR logic, one-to-many configuration, and [15,14,1,0] feedback taps.

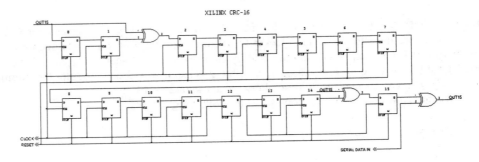

Figure 4-8   CRC-16 Schematic

Notice how similar this logic is to the LFSR with the addition of a data input as a modulation source. Listing 4-11 implements CRC-16 logic.

Listing 4-11 Verilog Version of CRC-16 Logic

```
module crc16 (clock, reset, serial_data_in, serial_data_out);
input              clock, reset, serial_data_in;
output             serial_data_out;
reg        [15:0] crc_output;
assign serial_data_out = serial_data_in ^ crc_output[15];
    always @ (posedge clock or posedge reset)
    if (reset) crc_output <=    0;
    else begin
    crc_output[14:3]      <=     crc_output[13:2];
    crc_output[1] <=    crc_output[0];
    crc_output[2] <=    crc_output[1]   ^ serial_data_out;
    crc_output[15]        <=     crc_output[14] ^ serial_data_out;
    crc_output[0] <=    crc_output[15] ^ serial_data_out;
end
endmodule
```

ROM

ROM stands for Read-Only Memory. This memory is initialized when the FPGA is configured and cannot be changed after configuration (if it could be changed, then it would be RAM). As an example, we can implement the four-bit LFSR counter with a ROM if we want (we won't want to if we have any sense, but we'll do it anyway for the purpose of illustration); see Listing 4-12 and Figure 4-9.

Listing 4-12 ROM Version of LFSR Counter

```
module lfsr_rom (binary_in, lfsr_out, clk, reset);
input       [3:0]  binary_in;
input              clk, reset;
output      [3:0]  lfsr_out;
reg         [3:0]  lfsr_out;

always @ (posedge clk or posedge reset)
begin
    if (reset)
            lfsr_out      <=      4'b0000;
    else case (binary_in)
4'b0000:    lfsr_out      <=      4'b0000;
4'b0001:    lfsr_out      <=      4'b0001;
4'b0010:    lfsr_out      <=      4'b0010;
4'b0011:    lfsr_out      <=      4'b0101;
4'b0100:    lfsr_out      <=      4'b1010;
4'b0101:    lfsr_out      <=      4'b0100;
4'b0110:    lfsr_out      <=      4'b1001;
4'b0111:    lfsr_out      <=      4'b0011;
4'b1000:    lfsr_out      <=      4'b0110;
4'b1001:    lfsr_out      <=      4'b1101;
4'b1010:    lfsr_out      <=      4'b1011;
4'b1011:    lfsr_out      <=      4'b0111;
4'b1100:    lfsr_out      <=      4'b1110;
4'b1101:    lfsr_out      <=      4'b1100;
4'b1110:    lfsr_out      <=      4'b1000;
4'b1111:    lfsr_out      <=      4'b0000; // Unused combination.
//default:lfsr_out <= 4'b0; Not needed, all combinations covered.
    endcase
    end
    endmodule
```

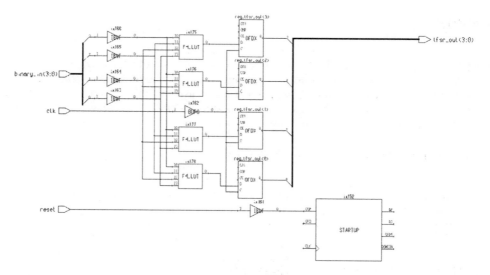

Figure 4-9   ROM Version of LFSR Counter Schematic

Because Xilinx implements combinations of four inputs very effectively, this function is efficient (not as efficient as the LFSR algorithm: the ROM version uses 2 packed CLBs, whereas our earlier design used 1 packed CLB). However, since the logic goes up by the square of the number of inputs, the ROM implemented in CLBs can get quite large. Another name for a ROM design like this is a Look-Up Table (LUT).

Many of the Xilinx CLBs have a RAM mode where a 16-by-1 memory element can be used in place of a CLB. This can be a very effective way to create RAM and ROM modules. We'll explore the use of LogiBLOX and memory modules in Chapter 8. Something else to keep in mind is that many ASIC technologies do not have RAM capability. During ASIC conversion, ROM/RAM elements will be replaced with random logic, and this can result in a quite large ASIC design.

RAM

RAM stands for Random Access Memory, but that is not too helpful. A RAM is an array of memory (or storage) cells, addressable in groups N elements wide (data width, like x4, x8, x16, or x32) and M elements deep (number of N-width elements). We can synthesize a RAM out of CLBs, so let's do a simple 16x1 block (a very tiny RAM block) and see how it looks. This design assumes that internal three-state drivers are available.

Note: One useful thing about the CLB RAM in an FPGA is the ability to initialize the RAM register cells on reset.

RAM

137

16x1 RAM block

There are 16 memory cells, so we need $2^n = 16$ address lines, or four address lines as shown in Listing 4-13.

Listing 4-13 Verilog 16x1 RAM Example Using CLBs

```
module ram16x1(ram_data, ram_addr, ram_rwn, clock, reset);
inout              ram_data;
input      [3:0]   ram_addr;
input              ram_rwn, clock, reset;      // Active low write.
reg        [15:0]  ram_data_reg;
wire               ram_data_in;

assign ram_data = ram_rwn ? ram_data_reg[ram_data_reg[ram_addr]] :
1'bz;
assign ram_data_in       =        ram_data;

always @ (posedge clock or posedge reset)
if (reset) ram_data_reg <=     0;
else case ({ram_addr, ram_rwn})
{4'h0, 1'b0} : ram_data_reg[0]          <=      ram_data_in;
{4'h1, 1'b0} : ram_data_reg[1]          <=      ram_data_in;
{4'h2, 1'b0} : ram_data_reg[2]          <=      ram_data_in;
{4'h3, 1'b0} : ram_data_reg[3]          <=      ram_data_in;
{4'h4, 1'b0} : ram_data_reg[4]          <=      ram_data_in;
{4'h5, 1'b0} : ram_data_reg[5]          <=      ram_data_in;
{4'h6, 1'b0} : ram_data_reg[6]          <=      ram_data_in;
{4'h7, 1'b0} : ram_data_reg[7]          <=      ram_data_in;
{4'h8, 1'b0} : ram_data_reg[8]          <=      ram_data_in;
{4'h9, 1'b0} : ram_data_reg[9]          <=      ram_data_in;
{4'ha, 1'b0} : ram_data_reg[10] <=      ram_data_in;
{4'hb, 1'b0} : ram_data_reg[11] <=      ram_data_in;
{4'hc, 1'b0} : ram_data_reg[12] <=      ram_data_in;
{4'hd, 1'b0} : ram_data_reg[13] <=      ram_data_in;
{4'he, 1'b0} : ram_data_reg[14] <=      ram_data_in;
{4'hf, 1'b0} : ram_data_reg[15] <=      ram_data_in;
default:       ram_data_reg              <=      ram_data_reg;
endcase
endmodule
```

Figure 4-10 shows the schematic of the logic synthesized from Listing 4-13. Listing 4-14 summarizes the resources used by this design.

Listing 4-14 Design Summary for Verilog 16x1 RAM Example Using CLBs

```
Total accumulated area :
Number of BUFG :                        1
Number of CLB Flip Flops :             16
Number of FG Function Generators :     29
```

```
Number of H Function Generators :      3
Number of IBUF :                       7
Number of OBUFT :                      1
Number of Packed CLBs :                15
Number of STARTUP :                    1
*************************************************
Device Utilization for 4010xlPQ100
Resource                 Used    Avail    Utilization
----------------------------------------------------
IOs                       8       77        10.39%
FG Function Generators    29      800        3.62%
H Function Generators     3       400        0.75%
CLB Flip Flops            16      800        2.00%
----------------------------------------------------
     Clock Frequency Report
     Clock        : Frequency
     clock        : 41.1 MHz
```

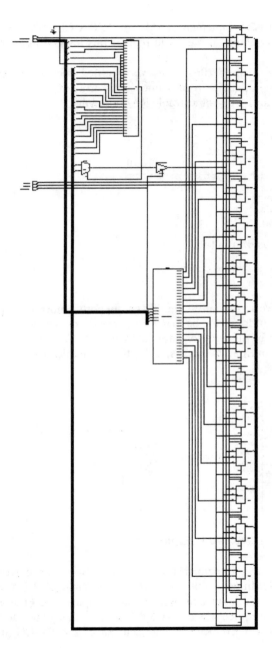

Figure 4-10 Schematic for Verilog 16x1 RAM Example Using CLBs

This illustrates how inefficient it is to implement RAM with FPGA CLBs. CLBs are designed to implement random logic functions. If we could replace this logic with a RAM cell, it would consume one CLB!

RAM elements are easy to create with Verilog. However, Verilog does not support two-dimensional arrays, so the RAM is modeled as a one-dimensional array of vectors.

Listing 4-15 is an example of a 256-by-8 synthesizable RAM module.

Listing 4-15 Verilog RAM Example

```
module ram_mod1(rwn, addr, data_port);
input       rwn;
input       [7:0] addr;
inout       [7:0] data_port;
reg         [7:0] ramdata [0:255];

assign data_port = (rwn) ? ramdata[addr]  : 8'hz;
always @ (rwn or addr)
    if (~rwn) ramdata[addr] = data_port;
endmodule
```

The RAM of Listing 4-15 will work, but unless the FPGA supports embedded RAM blocks, it will consume a huge amount of logic and be many times more expensive than any SRAM device you could buy. It might be all right for a tiny amount of RAM (on the order of 8 bytes), otherwise another solution must be found. Using flipflops to implement RAM is very inefficient.

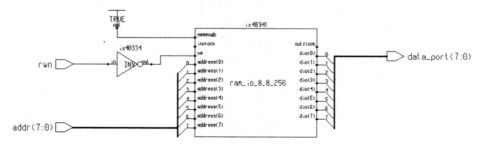

Figure 4-11 Schematic for Verilog 256x8 RAM Example

From Figure 4-11, you can see that Exemplar Logic LeonardoSpectrum correctly inferred a RAM from the Verilog code. In the Xilinx 4000XL family, embedded RAM is supported; see Figure 4-12. This schematic looks complicated, but compare it to Figure 4-13. The design in Figure 4-13 was compiled for an XC3000 device; this older device architecture does not have distributed CLB RAM. The schematic for the XC3000 implementation has 39 sheets!

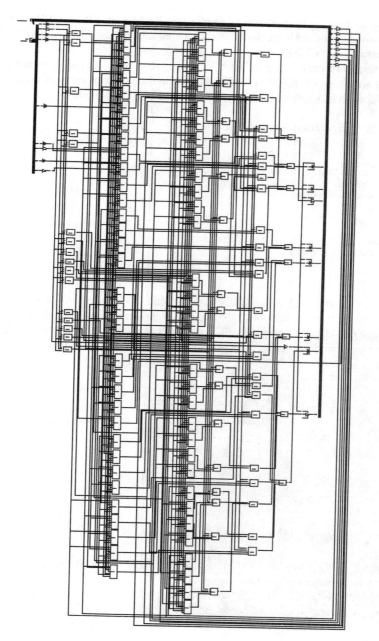

Figure 4-12 256x8 RAM Implemented in the 4000XL Device Family, Sheet 1 of 1

Figure 4-13 256x8 RAM Implemented in the XC3000 Device Family, Sheet 1 of 39

The designer often needs to implement RAM blocks to store an array of input or output data, configuration information, tables, or parameters. Many modern FPGA/CPLD architectures include RAM available as blocks (typical of Altera devices) or distributed across the device design so that a CLB can be configured as a LUT or as a RAM element (typical of Xilinx devices). You can see that using a single CLB as a 16-by-1 RAM cell is a good deal for the designer; it's fast and doesn't consume much of the FPGA resources.

What do you do if you need more than a trivial amount of RAM? There are two solutions. One is to pick an FPGA architecture that has enough built-in RAM to solve the problem (remember to leave yourself some wiggle room—if you need 1K of RAM, pick a device and architecture that has at least 2K available); the other is to put a real SRAM in the design. Though RAM blocks or distributed RAM cells are available in modern FPGAs, it is probably more expensive to use FPGA silicon for RAM than to use a real RAM IC. An additional consideration is the issue RAM raises during conversion to an ASIC.

Trade-offs Between Internal and External RAM

Internal RAM Features

- Speed. Not only are the RAM cells fast (in general), but we avoid the speed penalty of driving signals on and off the device.
- Timing. By staying on the chip, the clock/data relationship is known to the place-and-route tool. This eases our timing analysis. Internal FPGA signals are tweaked so the register hold time is zero. The external RAM may or may not have a zero hold time. Regardless, the delays associated with device I/O must be considered and will result in some sort of minimum hold time that must be accounted for in the design.
- Initialization. A nice feature of the FPGA RAM is the ability to initialize the RAM content on power-up. This initialization can be to write all zeros or to take RAM values from a file and store them in the RAM array. This can avoid requiring other means of initializing RAM (like having a microprocessor write to every location on power-up, for example).

Internal RAM Problems

- Cost. The silicon expended on internal RAM cells is probably more expensive than an external RAM device. The cost advantage is offset slightly by the cost associated with stuffing an extra device on the board and consuming extra FPGA pins.

Instantiating RAM

How do we instantiate RAM modules? Xilinx offers a tool called LogiBLOX for creating RAM modules, an example of a LogiBLOX module is shown in Listing 4-16. More detail on the procedure of creating a Xilinx LogiBLOX module is provided in Chapter 8.

Listing 4-16 Xilinx Synchronous Dualport RAM

```
module x_ram1 (clk, ram_data, ram_a_addr, ram_b_addr, ram_a_data,
ram_b_data, wr_strobe);
// Dualport RAM using Xilinx LogiBLOX.

input       [15:0] ram_data;
input       [4:1]  ram_a_addr;
input       [4:1]  ram_b_addr;
input              wr_strobe;
input              clk;
output      [15:0] ram_a_data;
output      [15:0] ram_b_data;

//-------------------------------------------------------
// LogiBLOX DP_RAM Module "r16x16dp"
// Created by LogiBLOX version M1.3.7
//     on Thu Feb 12 15:27:46 1998
// Attributes
//     MODTYPE = DP_RAM
//     BUS_WIDTH = 16
//     DEPTH = 16
//-------------------------------------------------------
r16x16dp  ramblk1
(.A({ram_a_addr[4],ram_a_addr[3],ram_a_addr[2],ram_a_addr[1]}),
.SPO(ram_a_data),
.DI(ram_data),
.WR_EN(wr_strobe),
.WR_CLK(clk),
.DPO(ram_b_data),
.DPRA({ram_b_addr[4],ram_b_addr[3],ram_b_addr[2],ram_b_addr[1]}));

endmodule
```

The r16x16dp.vei module, shown in Listing 4-17, is simply a placeholder for the presynthesized netlist (r16x16dp.ngo) that will be inserted during the place-and-route process. It defines the module ports, but that is all. The interface part of this automatically generated file was cut and pasted into the module that instantiates the placeholder module. This .vei file must be included in Exemplar Logic LeonardoSpectrum's input file list shown in Listing 4-16.

Listing 4-17 RAM Placeholder Module (r16x16dp.vei)

```
//------------------------------------------------------
// LogiBLOX DP_RAM Module "r16x16dp"
// Created by LogiBLOX version M1.5.19
//     on Sun May 30 14:19:03 1999
// Attributes
//     MODTYPE = DP_RAM
//     BUS_WIDTH = 4
//     DEPTH = 16
//     STYLE = MAX_SPEED
//     USE_RPM = FALSE
//------------------------------------------------------

module r16x16dp(A, SPO, DI, WR_EN, WR_CLK, DPO, DPRA);
input      [3:0]  A;
output     [3:0]  SPO;
input      [3:0]  DI;
input             WR_EN;
input             WR_CLK;
output     [3:0]  DPO;
input      [3:0]  DPRA;
endmodule
```

It's easy to imagine using an external RAM in place of the LogiBLOX RAM; the difference is that module port pins must actually connect to device pins. An interesting expansion of the RAM interface occurs when multiple modules need RAM access. In this case an arbitration scheme can prioritize and negotiate access to the RAM. An example of external RAM interface with a simple arbiter (which allows multiple sources to access the RAM) is shown in Listing 4-18. There are probably better ways to implement this design, but this is a *Real World* example that was used in a commercial design.

Listing 4-18 RAM Access Interface and Arbitration Design

```
// arbit1.v © 1998 Advanced Technology Video, Inc.
// Reproduced with permission.
module arbit1 (clk, reset, chan0_ramaddr, chan0_dat_from_ram,
chan0_dat_to_ram, chan1_ramaddr, chan1_dat_from_ram,
chan1_dat_to_ram, address_preset, ram_rwn, ram_addr,
ram_data_pins, data_rd, data_wr, up_data_to_ram, up_data_from_ram,
sram_addr_strobe, rd_ack, wr_ack, ram_data_oe);

// System inputs.
input             clk, reset;   // System clock and reset.

// Control signals.
output     [2:0]  rd_ack;       // Acknowledge: read complete.
reg        [2:0]  rd_ack;
output     [2:0]  wr_ack;       // Acknowledge: write complete.
reg        [2:0]  wr_ack;
```

```
// RAM interface.
input       [12:1] chan0_ramaddr;// Channel 0 RAM address pointer.
wire        [12:1] chan0_ramaddr;
input       [12:1] chan1_ramaddr;// Channel 1 RAM address pointer.
wire        [12:1] chan1_ramaddr;
output      [15:0] chan0_dat_from_ram;// Channel 0 RAM read data.
reg         [15:0] chan0_dat_from_ram;
output      [15:0] chan1_dat_from_ram;// Channel 0 RAM read data.
reg         [15:0] chan1_dat_from_ram;
input       [15:0] chan0_dat_to_ram;   // Channel 0 RAM write data.
wire        [15:0] chan0_dat_to_ram;
output      [15:0] chan1_dat_to_ram;   // Channel 1 RAM write data.
wire        [15:0] chan1_dat_to_ram;
input       [2:0]  data_rd;            // RAM read request.
wire        [2:0]  data_rd;
input       [2:0]  data_wr;            // RAM write request.
wire        [2:0]  data_wr;
input              sram_addr_strobe;   // Preloads address counter.
input       [15:0] up_data_to_ram;     // Data written into RAM.
output      [15:0] up_data_from_ram;   // Data read from RAM.
reg         [15:0] up_data_from_ram;
input       [12:0] address_preset;     // Microprocessor address
                                       // counter preset input.

// RAM I/O ports.
output             ram_rwn;            // SRAM read/write, high = read.
output      [12:0] ram_addr;           // SRAM address pins.
reg         [12:0] ram_addr;
inout       [7:0]  ram_data_pins;// RAM data to be written.
wire        [7:0]  ram_data_in;
reg         [7:0]  ram_data_out;
output             ram_data_oe;        // RAM output enable.
reg                ram_data_oe;

// Local variables.
reg         [3:0]  ram_state;
reg                ram_rdn;
reg         [11:0] ram_addr_ctr;// Register: store auto-incremented
                                // addresses. Counts words.

parameter ram_state_idle    =       0;
parameter ram_state1        =       1;
parameter ram_state2        =       2;
parameter ram_state3        =       3;
parameter ram_state4        =       4;
parameter ram_state5        =       5;
parameter ram_state6        =       6;
parameter ram_state7        =       7;
parameter ram_state8        =       8;
parameter ram_state9        =       9;
parameter ram_state10       =      10;
parameter ram_state11       =      11;
parameter ram_state12       =      12;
parameter ram_state13       =      13;
parameter ram_state14       =      14;
parameter ram_state15       =      15;
assign ram_rwn = ~ram_rdn;     // Active high local signal.
```

```
// Control of SRAM data pins.
assign ram_data_pins      = ram_data_oe ? ram_data_out : 8'bz;
assign ram_data_in        = ram_data_pins;

    always @ (posedge clk or posedge reset) begin
        if (reset)
        begin
            ram_state        <=      ram_state_idle;
            ram_rdn          <=      0;
            ram_addr         <=      0;
            ram_data_out     <=      0;
            rd_ack           <=      0;
            wr_ack           <=      0;
            ram_data_oe      <=      0;
        end else begin

        case (ram_state)
        ram_state_idle: begin
            begin
            ram_rdn          <=      0;
            ram_addr         <=      0;
            ram_data_out     <=      0;
            ram_data_oe      <=      0;
            end

            if (data_rd[0]) begin
            ram_rdn          <=      0;
            ram_addr         <=      {chan0_ramaddr, 1'b0};
            ram_state        <=      ram_state1;
            end

            else if (data_rd[1]) begin
            ram_rdn          <=      0;
            ram_addr         <=      {chan1_ramaddr, 1'b0};
            ram_state        <=      ram_state3;
            end

            else if (data_wr[0]) begin
            ram_rdn          <=      1;
            ram_addr         <=      {chan0_ramaddr, 1'b0};
            ram_data_out     <=      chan0_dat_to_ram[7:0];
            ram_data_oe      <=      1;
            ram_state        <=      ram_state5;
            end

            else if (data_wr[1]) begin
            ram_rdn          <=      1;
            ram_addr         <=      {chan1_ramaddr, 1'b0};
            ram_data_out     <=      chan1_dat_to_ram[7:0];
            ram_data_oe      <=      1;
            ram_state        <=      ram_state8;
            end

            else if (data_rd[2])// Processor read request.
            begin
            ram_rdn          <=      0;
            ram_addr         <=      {ram_addr_ctr, 1'b0};
```

```
                  ram_state     <=      ram_state11;
                  end

                  else if (data_wr[2])// Processor write request.
                  begin
                  ram_rdn       <=      1;
                  ram_addr      <=      {ram_addr_ctr, 1'b0};
                  ram_data_out  <=      up_data_from_ram[7:0];
                  ram_data_oe   <=      1;
                  ram_state     <=      ram_state13;
                  end

                  else                  // Default.
                  ram_state     <=      ram_state_idle;
        end

// Read channel 0.
        ram_state1: begin
                  ram_rdn       <=      0;
                  ram_addr      <=      {chan0_ramaddr, 1'b1};
                  chan0_dat_from_ram[7:0] <= ram_data_in;
                  rd_ack[0]      <=     1;       // Issue early.
                  ram_state     <=      ram_state2;
                  end

        ram_state2: begin
                  ram_rdn       <=      0;
                  ram_addr      <=      {chan0_ramaddr, 1'b1};
                  chan0_dat_from_ram[15:8] <= ram_data_in;
                  rd_ack[0]      <=     1;       // Hold ack until
                                                 //  read is released.

                  if (data_rd[0])
                  ram_state     <=      ram_state2;  // Hold until
                                                     //  rd released.

                  else begin
                  rd_ack[0]      <=     0;       // Release ack.
                  ram_state     <=      ram_state_idle;
                  end
                  end

// Read channel 1.
        ram_state3: begin
                  ram_rdn       <=      0;
                  ram_addr      <=      {chan1_ramaddr, 1'b1};
                  chan1_dat_from_ram[7:0] <= ram_data_in;
                  rd_ack[1]      <=     1;       // Issue early.
                  ram_state     <=      ram_state4;
                  end

        ram_state4: begin
                  ram_rdn       <=      0;
                  ram_addr      <=      {chan1_ramaddr, 1'b1};
                  chan1_dat_from_ram[15:8] <= ram_data_in;
                  rd_ack[1]      <=     1;       // Hold ack until
                                                 //  read is released.

                  if (data_rd[1]) // Hold until rd released.
                  ram_state     <=      ram_state4;
```

```
                    else begin
                    rd_ack[1]        <=      0;      // Release ack.
                    ram_state        <=      ram_state_idle;
                    end
                    end
// Write channel 0.
            ram_state5: begin
                    ram_rdn          <=      0;
                    ram_addr         <=      {chan0_ramaddr, 1'b0};
                    ram_data_out     <=      chan1_dat_to_ram[7:0];
                    ram_data_oe      <=      1;
                    ram_state        <=      ram_state6;
                    end

            ram_state6: begin
                    ram_rdn          <=      1;
                    ram_addr         <=      {chan0_ramaddr, 1'b1};
                    ram_data_out     <=      chan1_dat_to_ram[15:8];
                    ram_data_oe      <=      1;
                    wr_ack[0]        <=      1;      // Release early.
                    ram_state        <=      ram_state7;
                    end

            ram_state7: begin
                    ram_rdn          <=      0;
                    ram_addr         <=      {chan1_ramaddr, 1'b1};
                    ram_data_out     <=      chan1_dat_to_ram[15:8];
                    ram_data_oe      <=      1;
                    wr_ack[0]        <=      1;      // Hold until write is
                                                     //  released.
                    if (data_wr[0]) // Hold until wr released.
                    ram_state        <=      ram_state7;
                    else begin
                    wr_ack[0]        <=      0;      // Release ack.
                    ram_state        <=      ram_state_idle;
                    end
                    end
// Write channel 1.
            ram_state8: begin
                    ram_rdn          <=      0;
                    ram_addr         <=      {chan1_ramaddr, 1'b0};
                    ram_data_out     <=      chan1_dat_to_ram[7:0];
                    ram_data_oe      <=      1;
                    ram_state        <=      ram_state9;
                    end

            ram_state9: begin
                    ram_rdn          <=      1;
                    ram_addr         <=      {chan1_ramaddr, 1'b1};
                    ram_data_out     <=      chan1_dat_to_ram[15:8];
                    ram_data_oe      <=      1;
                    wr_ack[1]        <=      1;      // Release early.
                    ram_state        <=      ram_state10;
                    end
            ram_state10: begin
```

```
                ram_rdn          <=       0;
                ram_addr         <=       {chan1_ramaddr, 1'b1};
                ram_data_out     <=       chan1_dat_to_ram[15:8];
                ram_data_oe      <=       1;
                wr_ack[1]        <=       1; // Hold ack until
                                          //   write is released.
                if (data_wr[1]) // Hold until wr released.
                ram_state        <=       ram_state10;
                else begin
                wr_ack[1]        <=       0;      // Release ack.
                ram_state        <=       ram_state_idle;
                end
                end

// Microprocessor initiated read.
        ram_state11: begin
                ram_rdn          <=       0;
                ram_addr         <=       {ram_addr_ctr, 1'b1};
                up_data_from_ram[7:0]      <=       ram_data_in;
                ram_state        <=       ram_state12;
                end

        ram_state12: // Address counter incremented
                begin  //  in this state.
                ram_rdn          <=       0;
                ram_addr         <=       {ram_addr_ctr, 1'b1};
                rd_ack[2]                  <=       1;
                up_data_from_ram[15:8]     <=       ram_data_in;
                ram_state        <=       ram_state_idle;
                end

// Microprocessor initiated write.
        ram_state13: begin
                ram_rdn          <=       0;
                ram_addr         <=       {ram_addr_ctr, 1'b0};
                ram_data_out     <=       up_data_to_ram[7:0];
                ram_data_oe      <=       1;
                ram_state        <=       ram_state14;
                end

        ram_state14: begin
                ram_rdn          <=       1;
                ram_addr         <=       {ram_addr_ctr, 1'b1};
                ram_data_out     <=       up_data_to_ram[15:8];
                ram_data_oe      <=       1;
                wr_ack[2]        <=       1; // Release early.
                ram_state        <=       ram_state15;
                end

        ram_state15: // Address counter incremented
        begin           //  in this state.
        ram_rdn          <=       0;
        ram_addr         <=       {ram_addr_ctr, 1'b1};
        ram_data_out     <=       up_data_to_ram[15:8];
        ram_data_oe      <=       1;
        wr_ack[2]        <=       0;
        ram_state        <=       ram_state_idle;
```

```
              end
              default: ram_state    <=         ram_state_idle;
              endcase
              end
              end

// Increment address counter when microprocessor reads or writes.
     always @ (posedge clk or posedge reset)
     begin
              if (reset)    ram_addr_ctr  <=       0;
              else if (sram_addr_strobe)
                            ram_addr_ctr  <=         address_preset;
              else if ((ram_state == ram_state12) |
                      (ram_state == ram_state15))
                            ram_addr_ctr  <=       ram_addr_ctr + 1;
     end
endmodule
```

Modern synthesis tools can extract RAM from logic structures as long as we don't bury them so deep that they are hard for the compiler to find. This means a random logic design is parsed and the compiler will try to extract modules that are more efficiently implemented as RAM blocks.

FIFO NOTES

FIFOs (First-In First-Out memories) are used to change data rates between systems. Data is written at one rate and read out at a different (same or faster) rate. When you take your first look at a FIFO, it appears like a register file that expands and contracts like an accordion. However, it is really designed as a RAM block with an independent write address counter and an independent read address counter. For each FIFO write, the write counter (usually a Gray Code counter) gets incremented; for each FIFO read, the read counter gets incremented. The minimum set of flags includes an empty flag (set when the read and write pointers have caught up to each other and are equal) and a full flag (again set when the read and write flags are equal, but equal this time because the write address has wrapped around). The major goal of a FIFO system design is to prevent an overrun which results in data loss either due to new data not being written or old data being written over. The factors that influence overrun are the depth of the FIFO and the read and write frequencies.

One of the challenges of designing a FIFO is the flag design. The full flag, for example, is set in the write clock domain, but must be read and cleared in the read clock domain. This requires synchronization between the two domains, always a tricky task.

Like a RAM, a FIFO can be built out of registers. However, unless the FIFO is very small, you're not going to want to build a FIFO out of registers (use RAM instead), because the design is inefficient.

Verilog Test Fixtures

SRAM-based FPGA designers don't simulate their designs enough. It is easy to burn a part and try it, so that is our tendency. We can argue some advantage to this method; after all, the end result is a part that works, right? Still, any tool that improves the quality of our design must be used. ASIC designers and designers using antifuse technology don't have the luxury (or crutch, depending on your point of view) of trying a part that is not virtually guaranteed to work. Instead of downloading a configuration file, these designers either program an expensive device (which is thrown away if it doesn't work) or go through a full ASIC fabrication turn (which can cost tens and hundreds of thousands of dollars). This is why ASICs (and ASIClike devices) have long simulation processes that drive management nuts. The designers are fooling around with their computers all day instead of delivering product!

Verilog was designed as a simulation and test language. It has excellent features and has been thoroughly thought out and developed. Except for the cost of the simulator software and the danger of falling into the endless 'paralysis of analysis' loop, there is no reason the FPGA designer shouldn't regularly use a simulator. There are some excellent books that cover Verilog simulation in detail (see the bibliography at the end of this book); we'll just do a quick and dirty overview in this chapter.

Most simulators have a waveform viewer, and a lot of effort is put into making this viewer attractive to the eye. The problem is that a human brain is required to analyze and interpret the waveforms. Waveforms are great and we've used them throughout this text to show input and output signals. However, Verilog supports automated testing. This is a great way to test and validate a design and later design changes. You can make a design change and carefully evaluate the effect on the area of interest, but how do you know you didn't break something in another part of the design that used to work?

This doesn't mean the automated test fixtures are a panacea. They are often a pain in the rear. You'll spend a lot of time revising the test fixture to 'fix' tests where signals that don't matter were improperly or too strictly tested.

BUILT-IN SELF-TEST (BIST)

During manufacturing, an FPGA can be programmed to perform both internal and external self-tests, then later programmed to support the embedded (shippable) application. External hardware like DRAM, SRAM, FIFOs, etc. can be thoroughly tested, with the test results indicated via LED or serial port (which might exist for test only).

COMPILER DIRECTIVES

Many powerful compiler directives are available in Verilog. Note the use of the ` (back tick or accent grave) as part of these compiler directives.

`define, `ifdef, `else, `endif, `undef   Verilog supports conditional compilation and execution. Code may support simulation and not be synthesizable, or may be conditionally synthesized to support optional features. A macro variable can be defined to control compilation and might have a form like that shown in Listing 5-1.

Listing 5-1   `ifdef Example

```
// Conditional Compilation Example.
// Comment out the next line for synthesis.
`define test_mode;        // Define test_mode macro.

...

`ifdef test_mode
```

```
// Insert test_mode code here. Could be a test module
//   definition or simulation directives, not just inline
//   code.

     data_bus        <=        test_points;
`else
// Insert non-test_mode code here.
// The `else portion is optional.
     data_bus        <=        internal_data;

`endif
// Continue with unconditional code here.
```

A macro definition can be 'undefined' by an `**undef** occurring later in the code.

`**include** filename   The directive is similar to the C language #include directive. The file pointed to by filename (which may be a file in the current path or a full path description) will be inserted in the Verilog code during compile time. Includes can be nested; in other words an included file may also have an included file.

`**timescale** unit/precision   The time unit used by the simulator is programmable. For example, in the code of Listing 5-3, there is a line that reads:

```
     #75 reset     =        0;
```

The number 75 represents a delay in units of the timescale unit, in this case 75 nsec. The delay tells the simulator to wait until simulation time has advanced by the delay value before executing the next directive.

DELAYS IN SYNTHESIS

Delays have meaning only for simulation, never for synthesis.

There is no magic hardware construct that will create a delay for you. The default, if no timescale directive is executed, is 1 nsec. The precision determines how delay values are rounded off and determine the simulation resolution. The precision must be equal to or less than the timescale unit. The timescale argument units are in s (seconds), ms (milliseconds), us (microseconds), ns (nanoseconds), ps (picoseconds), or fs (femtoseconds). Mostly, you'll see 1 ns / 1 ns, for delay units of 1 nsec with rounding of delay values to the nearest nsec. There can only be one timescale in a design.

System Tasks

Verilog system tasks start with a $.

$finish;**   When encountered in the code, **$finish ends the simulation. Without some termination point, the simulation will continue forever (or until your PC runs out of memory and crashes). **$finish** returns control of the computer back to the operating system.

$stop;   This system task halts simulation but does not return control to the operating system. Simulation can be continued from the stopping point, or other system commands can be executed at the current simulation time.

$display**(list element 1, list element 2);   This system task is similar to C's printf command. Verilog runs just fine in a nonwaveform output mode. If there are no waveforms, how can we tell what our design is doing? Stick some **$display commands in your design to view variables and other information (such as simulation time) as illustrated in Listings 5-2 and 5-3.

Listing 5-2   Simple $display Example

```
module display1 (clock, reset);
input           clock, reset;
reg        [7:0]  count_val;
always @ (posedge clock or posedge reset)
    if (reset)
    count_val     <=     0;
    else  begin
    count_val     <=     count_val + 1;
    $display (count_val);
    end
endmodule
```

Listing 5-3   Simple $display Example Test Fixture

```
// Display Test.
module displ_tf;
`timescale 1ns / 1ns
reg clock, reset;

parameter clk_period    =      20;
display1 u1 (clock, reset);
always     begin
    #(clk_period / 2) clock = ~clock;
    end
initial begin
    clock       =     0;
    reset       =     1; // Assert the system reset.
    #75 reset   =     0;
    #1000 $finish;
end
```

```
endmodule
```

Listing 5-4 shows the result of a Silos III simulation run. The first few zeros are the count_val register content during the reset period. The **$display** defaults to a decimal number format and includes a carriage return (newline) after each execution. If the newline is not desired, the $write system task can be used instead.

Listing 5-4   Simple $display Example Output Listing

```
           S I L O S   I I I    Version 99.100
          DEMO COPY LIMITED TO 100 to 200 DEVICES
      Copyright (c) 1999 by SIMUCAD Inc. All rights reserved.
      No part of this program may be reproduced, transmitted,
      transcribed, or stored in a retrieval system, in any
      form or by any means without the prior written consent of
        SIMUCAD Inc., 32970 Alvarado-Niles Road, Union City,
                  California, 94587, U.S.A.
             (510)-487-9700  Fax: (510)-487-9721
         Electronic Mail Address:   "silos@simucad.com"
!file .sav="display1"
!control .sav=3
!control .savcell=0
!control .disk=1000M

Reading "c:\verilog\sourcecode\displ_tf.v"
Reading "c:\verilog\sourcecode\display1.v"
sim to 0
      Highest level modules (that have been auto-instantiated):
            (displ_tf displ_tf
      3 total devices.
      Linking ...

      3 nets total: 11 saved and 0 monitored.
      74 registers total: 74 saved.
      Done.

      0 State changes on observable nets.

      Simulation stopped at the end of time 0.000000000s.
Ready: sim
   0
   1
   2
   3
   4
   5
   6
   7
   8
   9
```

```
10
11
12
13
14
15
16
17
18
19
20
21
22
23
24
25
26
27
28
29
30
31
32
33
34
35
36
37
38
39
40
41
42
43
44
45
46
47
48
49
   313 State changes on observable nets in 0.33 seconds.
   948 Events/second.

   Simulation stopped at the end of time 0.000001075s.
Ready:
```

Text and numbers can be formatted with escape string. An escape string is a string following a backslash (\) or %. Here are a few examples:

%h   Display numbers in hex format

%d   Display numbers in decimal (the default) format

%o   Display numbers in octal format

%b	Display numbers in binary format
%c	Display numbers as ASCII characters
%t	Display in current time format
"string"	Display text string
\n	newline
\t	tab
\literal	Literal could be another \ (to print a '\'), a " (quote), or % (print %).

To get some experience with this formatting, take a look at Listings 5-5, 5-6, and 5-7.

Listing 5-5   Simple $display Example Output Listing with Formatting

```
// Display Test with formatting.
module time_setup;
initial
    begin
// This timeformat is nsec (-9), 2 digits after decimal
//   place (2), ns text, and a minimum of 3 spaces for
//   time to be displayed in.
    $timeformat (-9, 2, " ns", 3);
    end
endmodule

module disp2_tf;
`timescale 1ns / 1ns
reg        clock, reset;
parameter  clk_period   =     20;

display2 u1 (clock, reset);
always begin
    #(clk_period / 2) clock = ~clock;
    end

initial
begin
    clock          =     0;
    reset          =     1; // Assert the system reset.
    #75 reset      =     0;
    #1000 $finish;
end
endmodule
```

Listing 5-6   Simple $display Example Output Listing with Formatting

```
module display2 (clock, reset);
input             clock, reset;
reg        [7:0]  count_val;
// Comment out the next line for terse printout.
`define verbose
always @ (posedge clock or posedge reset)
begin
    if (reset)    count_val    <=     0;
    else   begin
                  count_val    <=     count_val + 1;
        `ifdef verbose
        $write ("count_val = %h", count_val);
        $display (" Current time = %t", $time);
        `else
        $write (":", count_val);
        `endif
        end
end
endmodule
```

Listing 5-7   Simple $display Example Output Listing with Formatting

```
              S I L O S   I I I    Version 99.100
              DEMO COPY LIMITED TO 100 to 200 DEVICES
        Copyright (c) 1999 by SIMUCAD Inc. All rights reserved.
        No part of this program may be reproduced, transmitted,
        transcribed,   or stored in a retrieval system, in any
        form or by any means without the prior written consent of
          SIMUCAD Inc., 32970 Alvarado-Niles Road, Union City,
                    California, 94587, U.S.A.
              (510)-487-9700  Fax: (510)-487-9721
          Electronic Mail Address:   "silos@simucad.com"

!file .sav="display2"
!control .sav=3
!control .savcell=0
!control .disk=1000M

Reading "c:\verilog\sourcecode\time_setup.v"
Reading "c:\verilog\sourcecode\display2.v"
sim to 0
    Highest level modules (that have been auto-instantiated):
          (time_setup time_setup
          (disp2_tf disp2_tf
    4 total devices.
    Linking ...
    3 nets total: 11 saved and 0 monitored.
    74 registers total: 74 saved.
```

```
     Done.

     0 State changes on observable nets.
     Simulation stopped at the end of time 0.000000000s.
Ready: sim
count_val = 00 Current time = 90.00 ns
count_val = 01 Current time = 110.00 ns
count_val = 02 Current time = 130.00 ns
count_val = 03 Current time = 150.00 ns
count_val = 04 Current time = 170.00 ns
count_val = 05 Current time = 190.00 ns
count_val = 06 Current time = 210.00 ns
count_val = 07 Current time = 230.00 ns
count_val = 08 Current time = 250.00 ns
count_val = 09 Current time = 270.00 ns
count_val = 0a Current time = 290.00 ns
count_val = 0b Current time = 310.00 ns
count_val = 0c Current time = 330.00 ns
count_val = 0d Current time = 350.00 ns
count_val = 0e Current time = 370.00 ns
count_val = 0f Current time = 390.00 ns
count_val = 10 Current time = 410.00 ns
count_val = 11 Current time = 430.00 ns
count_val = 12 Current time = 450.00 ns
count_val = 13 Current time = 470.00 ns
count_val = 14 Current time = 490.00 ns
count_val = 15 Current time = 510.00 ns
count_val = 16 Current time = 530.00 ns
count_val = 17 Current time = 550.00 ns
count_val = 18 Current time = 570.00 ns
count_val = 19 Current time = 590.00 ns
count_val = 1a Current time = 610.00 ns
count_val = 1b Current time = 630.00 ns
count_val = 1c Current time = 650.00 ns
count_val = 1d Current time = 670.00 ns
count_val = 1e Current time = 690.00 ns
count_val = 1f Current time = 710.00 ns
count_val = 20 Current time = 730.00 ns
count_val = 21 Current time = 750.00 ns
count_val = 22 Current time = 770.00 ns
count_val = 23 Current time = 790.00 ns
count_val = 24 Current time = 810.00 ns
count_val = 25 Current time = 830.00 ns
count_val = 26 Current time = 850.00 ns
count_val = 27 Current time = 870.00 ns
count_val = 28 Current time = 890.00 ns
count_val = 29 Current time = 910.00 ns
count_val = 2a Current time = 930.00 ns
count_val = 2b Current time = 950.00 ns
count_val = 2c Current time = 970.00 ns
count_val = 2d Current time = 990.00 ns
count_val = 2e Current time = 1010.00 ns
count_val = 2f Current time = 1030.00 ns
count_val = 30 Current time = 1050.00 ns
count_val = 31 Current time = 1070.00 ns
```

```
313 State changes on observable nets in 0.76 seconds.
411 Events/second.

Simulation stopped at the end of time 0.000001075s.
Ready:
```

A list of variables can be displayed when they change by using the **$monitor** directive. The syntax of the **$monitor** signal list and formatting controls is very similar to those used for the **$display** directive. Some examples of the using the $monitor directive are presented in Listing 5-8 and Listing 5-9 with the corresponding output shown in Listing 5-10.

$monitor (signal list and formatting);

$monitoron/$monitoroff;

Listing 5-8 $monitor Example display3.v

```
module display3 (clock, reset);
input           clock, reset;
reg        [7:0] count_val;
always @ (posedge clock or posedge reset)
begin
      if (reset)    count_val    <=    0;
      else
      begin         count_val    <=    count_val + 1;
      end
end
endmodule
```

Listing 5-9 $monitor Example Test Fixture disp3_tf.v

```
// $monitor used in a test fixture.

module time_setup2;
initial
    begin
    `timescale 1ns / 1ns
    $timeformat (-9, 2, " ns", 3);
    end
endmodule

module disp3_tf;

    reg                clock, reset;
    wire         [7:0] count_val;
    parameter clk_period    =    20;
```

```
display3 u1 (clock, reset);

always
    begin
    #(clk_period / 2) clock = ~clock;
    end

initial
begin
    $monitor ($time, " Counter value: %h", u1.count_val);
    clock          =        0;
    reset          =        1;        // Assert the system reset.
    #75 reset      =        0;
    #1000 $finish;
end
endmodule
```

Listing 5-10 $monitor Example Output Listing

```
90000000000.00 ns Counter value: 01
110000000000.00 ns Counter value: 02
130000000000.00 ns Counter value: 03
150000000000.00 ns Counter value: 04
170000000000.00 ns Counter value: 05
190000000000.00 ns Counter value: 06
210000000000.00 ns Counter value: 07
230000000000.00 ns Counter value: 08
250000000000.00 ns Counter value: 09
270000000000.00 ns Counter value: 0a
290000000000.00 ns Counter value: 0b
310000000000.00 ns Counter value: 0c
330000000000.00 ns Counter value: 0d
350000000000.00 ns Counter value: 0e
370000000000.00 ns Counter value: 0f
390000000000.00 ns Counter value: 10
410000000000.00 ns Counter value: 11
430000000000.00 ns Counter value: 12
450000000000.00 ns Counter value: 13
470000000000.00 ns Counter value: 14
490000000000.00 ns Counter value: 15
510000000000.00 ns Counter value: 16
530000000000.00 ns Counter value: 17
550000000000.00 ns Counter value: 18
570000000000.00 ns Counter value: 19
590000000000.00 ns Counter value: 1a
610000000000.00 ns Counter value: 1b
630000000000.00 ns Counter value: 1c
650000000000.00 ns Counter value: 1d
670000000000.00 ns Counter value: 1e
690000000000.00 ns Counter value: 1f
710000000000.00 ns Counter value: 20
```

```
730000000000.00  ns  Counter  value:  21
750000000000.00  ns  Counter  value:  22
770000000000.00  ns  Counter  value:  23
790000000000.00  ns  Counter  value:  24
810000000000.00  ns  Counter  value:  25
830000000000.00  ns  Counter  value:  26
850000000000.00  ns  Counter  value:  27
870000000000.00  ns  Counter  value:  28
890000000000.00  ns  Counter  value:  29
910000000000.00  ns  Counter  value:  2a
930000000000.00  ns  Counter  value:  2b
950000000000.00  ns  Counter  value:  2c
970000000000.00  ns  Counter  value:  2d
990000000000.00  ns  Counter  value:  2e
1010000000000.00  ns  Counter  value:  2f
1030000000000.00  ns  Counter  value:  30
1050000000000.00  ns  Counter  value:  31
1070000000000.00  ns  Counter  value:  32
```

There are many file commands, we'll touch on the highlights.

$dumpfile ("filename");

$dumpvars(levels of hierarchy, module variables extracted from);

$dumpvars(0, module the variables extracted from);

$dumpvars

$dumpon;

$dumpoff;

$dumpall;

$dumplimit(filesize in bytes);

Verilog can save simulation results in an ASCII file. The format of this file is called Value Change Dump or VCD. An entry in the file occurs only when a variable value changes. The **$dumpvars** directive without an argument list will dump all the variables in the design. The **$dumpvars** (0, module name) directive will dump variables from the listed module and all modules instantiated by the listed module. Variables can be identified hierarchically in the file list (module1.module2.variable_name).

The VCD file can get very large. Setting a **$dumplimit** will stop the dump when the VCD file reaches the specified limit. Some examples of the $dump directive is shown in Listing 5-11 and Listing 5-12, with a partial output listing shown in Listing 5-13.

Listing 5-11 $dump Options

```
#100 $dumpon;      // Dump all variables after 100 time units.
#100 $dumpoff;     // Stop dump after 100 time units.
#100 $dumpall;     // Dump a snapshot of all variables.
```

Listing 5-12 $dumpvars Example Listing

```
// Value Change Dump Example.
module time_setup3;
initial begin
    `timescale 10ns / 1ns
    $timeformat (-9, 2, " ns", 3);
    $dumpfile ("bigdump.dmp"); // Open file.
    end
endmodule

module disp4_tf;
    reg          clock, reset;
    wire    [7:0] count_val;
    parameter    clk_period  =     20;

display4 u1 (clock, reset);
always begin
    #(clk_period / 2) clock = ~clock;
    end
initial begin
        $timeformat (-9, 2, " ns", 3);
        $dumpvars;
        clock      =      0;
        reset      =      1;     // Assert the system reset.
    #75 reset      =      0;
    #1000 $finish;
end
endmodule

module display4 (clock, reset);
input clock, reset;

reg [7:0] count_val;

always @ (posedge clock or posedge reset)
begin
    if (reset)
    count_val    <=     0;
    else
    begin
    count_val    <=     count_val + 1;
```

```
        end
    end
    endmodule
```

Listing 5-13 $dumpvars Output Listing Extract

```
$scope module disp4_tf $end
$var reg   1 !     reset $end
$var reg   1 "     clock $end

$scope module u1 $end
$var wire  1 #     clock $end
$var wire  1 $     reset $end
$var reg   8 %     count_val [7:0] $end
$upscope $end

$upscope $end

$enddefinitions $end
#0
$dumpvars
1!
0"
0#
1$
b00000000 %
$end
```

Listing 5-13 is a small part of the bigdump.dmp. Note that each signal in the scope of **$dumpvars** (because **$dumpvars** was not limited in scope, all signals in the design are dumped) is assigned a key character (! = reset, for example) and this shorthand is used in the dumpfile. The VCD is not human-friendly, but is a format that can be read by other tools.

   $readmemh ("filename", memory_name);   Read hex values from a file.

   $readmemb ("filename", memory_name);   Read binary values from a file.

   Optional starting and ending addresses can be added to place limits on the data pulled from the file. The address is an index into the array, the nth data element. It is acceptable to have a start address, but no end address, in which case the file is read to the end of the memory array.

   $readmemh ("filename", memory_name, start_addr, end_address);

AUTOMATED TESTING

The only way to assure thorough testing of a design is to automate the task. A check-off list can be created. When a new revision of code is being released, all the automated tests should be run again. The process is maddening, because most of the effort to resolve problems will be in test-fixture errors, not design errors. Still, there is no better way to test a design.

As an example, let's design and test a simple digital filter as shown in Listing 5-14. The source code for this design is shown in Listing 5-15. The output values are shown in Figure 5-1. This design implements a one-dimensional low-pass pyramidal filter uses five samples with coefficients of 0.0625, 0.125, 0.625, 0.125, and 0.625 (note the sum of these coefficients is 1). This filter is crude and suffers from truncation errors but will serve as an example of automated testing.

Listing 5-14 Pyramidal Filter Test Fixture

```
// Pyramidal Filter Example.

module time_setup4;
initial
    begin
    `timescale 1ns / 1ns
    $timeformat (-9, 2, " ns", 3);
    end
endmodule

module pf1_tf;

    reg            clock, reset;
    reg      [7:0] tap_unfilt;

// Define array where test values will come from.
    reg      [7:0] test_pattern[0:31];

// Define array for testing filter output.
    reg      [7:0] verify_pattern[0:31];
    reg      [4:0] mem_index;
    wire     [7:0] tap_filt;
    reg      [7:0] tap_test, filt_test;
    reg            flag;

    parameter clk_period   =      20;

pfilt1 u1 (clock, reset, tap_unfilt, tap_filt);

always begin
    #(clk_period / 2)
```

```
        clock              =        ~clock;
        tap_unfilt         =        test_pattern [mem_index];
//      filt_test          =        tap_filt [mem_index];
        tap_test           =        verify_pattern [mem_index];
        mem_index          =        mem_index + 1;
        if (mem_index == 0) $finish;
        end

    always begin
        #(clk_period)
        if (!reset & (tap_filt != tap_test))
             begin
$display ($time, " ERROR! tap_filt = %h tap_test = %h", tap_filt,
tap_test);
             flag    <=    1;
             end
//      else $display ("All is okay.");
        end

    initial
    begin
    clock              =        0;
    mem_index          =        0;
    tap_test           =        0;
    filt_test          =        0;
    tap_unfilt         =        0;
    flag               =        0;
    reset              =        1;      // Assert the system reset.

    // Read test pattern data from file into
    //   test_pattern array.
    $readmemh ("pfilt1.tst", test_pattern);
    $readmemh ("verify1.tst", verify_pattern);

    #(clk_period * 2)          reset         =        0;
    end
    endmodule
```

Listing 5-15 Pyramidal Filter Verilog Code

```
// Pyramidal Filter Example.
// This implements a low-pass filter with coefficients:
//   .0625   .125   .625   .125   .0625
// Gain = 1.
module pfilt1 (clock, reset, tap4, tap_out[8:1]);
input              clock, reset;
input       [7:0]  tap4;
output             tap_out;
reg         [8:0]  tap_out;
reg         [7:0]  tap0, tap1, tap2, tap3;

// Intermediate summation (pipeline) registers.
```

```verilog
reg [4:0] sum1;
reg [5:0] sum2;
reg [7:0] sum3;

always @ (posedge clock or posedge reset)
begin
    if (reset)
    begin
    tap0            <=      0;
    tap1            <=      0;
    tap2            <=      0;
    tap3            <=      0;
    tap_out         <=      0;
    sum1            <=      0;
    sum2            <=      0;
    sum3            <=      0;
    end
    else    begin
    tap0            <=      tap1;
    tap1            <=      tap2;
    tap2            <=      tap3;
    tap3            <=      tap4;

// To multiply by 0.0625 (same as division by 16):
//   shift left 2 places.
// Result register must be 1 larger than input
//   registers to hold carry.
    sum1    <=      tap0[7:4] + tap4[7:4];

// To multiply by 0.125 (same as division by 8):
    sum2    <=      tap1[7:3] + tap3[7:3];

// To multiply by 0.625 (5/8) is the same as:
// (division by 2) + (division by 8).
    sum3    <=      tap2[7:1] + {2'b0, tap2[7:3]};

// Final sum adds sum1 + sum2 + sum3.
// If the design needs to be faster, it can be
//   further pipelined to spread out the summing logic.
// The LSB is truncated to give an 8-bit result. Logic
//   can be added, if necessary, to round-off to 8 bits
//   instead.
    tap_out[8:0] <=      {3'b0, sum1} + {2'b0, sum2} + sum3;
    end
end
endmodule
```

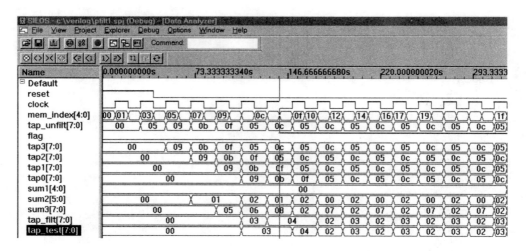

Figure 5-1   Pyramidal Filter Waveforms

The pyramidal filter design reads data from two external files. Data used to stimulate the filter is extracted from pfilt1.tst (shown in Listing 5-16) and identical data (except for an intentional error put in for test) used to test the filter output extracted from the file verify1.tst shown in Listing 5-17. The error is displayed as so:

```
140000000000.00 ns ERROR! tap_filt = 04 tap_test = 03
```

Three types of entries are allowed in files read by Verilog: numbers (either hex or binary), white space, and comments.

Listing 5-16 Pyramidal Filter Input Data List (pfilt1.tst)

```
0 // Each data value is entered twice because the
0 //   value is loaded on each clock edge; two values
5 //   are required to sustain a value through
5 //   a complete clock period.
9
9
b
b
f
f
5
5
c
c
5
```

```
5
c
c
5
5
c
c
5
5
c
c
5
5
c
c
5
5
```

Listing 5-17 Pyramidal Filter Test Data List (verify1.tst)

```
0
0
0
0
0
0
0
0
0
3
3
3   // Error added. Should be 4.
3   // Error added. Should be 4.
4
4
2
2
3
3
2
2
3
3
2
2
3
3
2
2
```

CHAPTER **6**

Real World Design: Tools, Techniques, and Trade-offs

*T*he *Real World* is specific, not generic. It is theoretically possible to write portable code that will run on any vendor's hardware (including ASIC processes), but the required compromises in performance and efficiency are generally not worth the trade-off. We, as over-worked FPGA designers, will find ourselves using vendor-specific libraries and techniques to achieve tight (fast and small) designs.

Now we have to choose an FPGA vendor. Eighty percent of the FPGA market is split between two powerhouses that dominate: Xilinx and Altera. Both are good companies with great technology. This book focuses on Xilinx FPGAs. We'll look at specific architecture differences between competing companies in Chapter 7. For compilers, at this writing, the market leaders are Exemplar Logic and Synplicity. Both are excellent products. In addition, Synopsis' FPGA Express is close enough to usable that it bears watching, and not just because, when bundled with Xilinx Design Manager, it's the cheapest package available. We are using Exemplar Logic's LeonardoSpectrum for this book.

The design flow and tools we will use are as follows:

- Specify the design. It doesn't make sense to start coding until the job is defined. In the *Real World* we often have to start a job before marketing has fully defined the requirements, but we'll try to get the job scoped out as much as possible first.

- Partition the design. Divide the job into sections. Reuse old designs as much as possible. We want our modules to be 5,000 to 10,000 gates. My estimate is approximately 20 gates per line (which can vary wildly), so this is 250 to 500 lines of code (semicolons) per module.

- Write the code. Use a color-coded editor to help avoid syntax errors (the color coding acts as an on-the-fly syntax checker and is remarkably useful). Implement area, timing, clock/reset resource-assignment, and pin-assignment constraints.

- To help locate syntax problems, try compiling your design with every tool you can find, including different simulators. You'll find that each vendor provides differing error messages with differing levels of helpfulness.

- If possible, use a lint program like Verilint. There are several errors that a Verilog compiler will accept, like mismatched vectors and the creation of unwanted latches, that Verilint will catch. Pay close attention to warnings that may indicate problems with synthesis.

- Simulate the design. Write test fixtures and use automated testing and waveforms to verify the design. In this book, this means use Simucad's Silos III to simulate the design at as high a level as possible.

- Compile the code. In this book, this means use Exemplar Logic's LeonardoSpectrum to create a netlist. Watch the gate counts and speed estimates. Use the schematic viewer to assure that your code is being implemented in the manner you expect. Examine how clocks and resets are implemented. Make sure global signals are detected and handled in the manner you expect.

- Place and route the netlist. In this book, this means use Xilinx Design Manager to create a downloadable configuration file. Manipulate the place/route controls and perform as many place/route passes as necessary to achieve the design requirements.

- Download the design and test it in the target hardware. FPGA designers tend to jump to this step too soon, owing either to not having the right tools or to impatience. The designer should be very sure the design is good before testing in circuit.

COMPILING WITH LEONARDOSPECTRUM

LeonardoSpectrum has a graphical user interface and a wizard that leads the designer through the design requirements. Very quickly, however, the designer will find the use of scripts to be a faster and more efficient method of creating a netlist. The design script created by the Wizard can be captured and run. Listing 6-1 is an example script created by the design wizard.

Listing 6-1 Example LeonardoSpectrum Script

```
set register2register 50
set input2register 50
set input2output 50
set register2output 50
set output_file "C:/verilog/latch.edf"
set novendor_constraint_file FALSE
_gc_read_init
_gc_run_init
set input_file_list { "C:/verilog/latch.v" }
set part 4013xlPQ160
set process 3
set wire_table 4013xl-3_avg
set nowrite_eqn FALSE
set chip TRUE
set area TRUE
set report brief
set global_sr reset
set output_file "C:/verilog/latch.edf"
set target xi4xl
_gc_read
set register2register 50
set input2register 50
set input2output 50
set register2output 50
set output_file ""
```

Let's look at this script line-by-line.

set register2register 50 In the design wizard, I selected an overall constraint of 20 MHz, which gives a clock period of 50 nsec. This constraint means that all signals between registers (from a register output to a register input) must resolve in 50 nsec.

set input2register 50 Based on the overall design requirement of running with a 20 MHz clock, all signals between the device input and a register must resolve in 50 nsec. The designer must consider the problem of insuring this requirement is met in the logic outside the device. It may be that a much tighter constraint must be applied to these nodes, depending on the timing of the external circuitry. Devices that have I/O registers make this problem much easier to solve.

set input2output 50 Based on the overall clock requirement of 20 MHz, all signals between logic and a device pin this logic drives must be resolved in 50 nsec. This constraint may need to be much tighter to satisfy the circuitry outside the device.

set register2output 50 Based on the overall clock requirement of 20 MHz, all signals between a register and a device output pin must be resolved in 50 nsec. This constraint may need to be much tighter to satisfy the circuitry outside the device. Devices that have I/O registers make this problem much easier to solve.

set global_sr reset Connect the global set/reset resource to the reset signal. Xilinx supports the connection of a user-defined global reset, which can be used by any register in the device. The signal still has to be identified and used in every always block where the reset is desired.

lut_max_fanout 4 To control the output loading (which affects the area and speed of the design), LeonardoSpectrum allows the designer to control the maximum number of loads that will be connected to a CLB. In this case, a light load of 4 is used. This will result in many buffers being used to reduce loading.

set output_file "C:/verilog/latch.edf" The netlist created by the compiler will be in the form of an EDIF (.edf) file and will be saved in the indicated path. Note usage of UNIX-style forward slashes in the path! Options for file output include: .edf (edif), .edif (edif), .eds(edif), .sdf (standard delay format), .v (verilog), .verilog (verilog), .vhd (vhdl), .vhdl (vhdl), .xdb (binary dump), .xnf (Xilinx netlist format).

set novendor_constraint_file FALSE This double negative means that we will create a FPGA vendor (in this case: Xilinx) constraint file and use that to guide the place and route of our logic.

set input_file_list { "C:/verilog/latch.v" } This is the list of input files to be linked together. In this case just one file is used to create the design. Note usage of UNIX-style forward slashes in the path. Options for file output include: .edf (edif), .edif (edif), .eds(edif), .sdf (standard delay format), .v (verilog), .verilog (verilog), .vhd (vhdl), .vhdl (vhdl), .xdb (binary dump), .xnf (Xilinx netlist format).

set part 4013xlPQ160 The device we will implement this design in is a Xilinx 4013XL (roughly 13,000 gates) in a PQ160 (160-pin surface-mount) package.

set process 3 We are using the LeonardoSpectrum Level 3 design flow. Levels 1 and 2 are subsets of level 3, level one is a single-vendor FPGA design flow; level 2 is multi-vendor FPGA flow; level 3 is multivendor and includes ASIC flows.

set wire_table 4013xl-3_avg The delays will be based on average (as compared to worst-case) loading for a -3 speed grade device.

set nowrite_eqn FALSE Here's another double negative that means we will write device equations into the schematic when the schematic is extracted from the netlist.

set chip TRUE The netlist will be compiled to a device and will include I/O pins for pins at the top level.

set area TRUE The design will be compiled for area optimization. The option is to compile for speed. LeonardoSpectrum Level 3 allows individual modules to be compiled for either area or speed—a great feature.

set report brief The report will be concise.

hierarchy_preserve TRUE LeonardoSpectrum will combine modules in an attempt to reduce logic by maintaining the hierarchy. This reduction is not allowed. Setting this TRUE during debugging is useful because it is more likely that your signal names will be preserved.

set target xi4xl Implement the design using primitives from the Xilinx 4000XL library.

To refresh our memory, Listing 6-2 is the design we're working with. This design has a problem: an inadvertent latch is created. LeonardoSpectrum is polite enough to point this out to us in the message log of Listing 6-3 (see bold-highlighted text).

Listing 6-2 Verilog Latch

```
// Your Basic Latch.
module latch2(q, q_not, set, reset);
    output      q, q_not;
    reg         q;
    input       set, reset;

    wire        set, reset;

    assign q_not =      ~q;
```

```
    always @ (set or reset)
    begin
            if (set)
            q       =       1;
            else if (reset)
            q       =       0;
    end
endmodule
```

Listing 6-3   LeonardoSpectrum Message Log for Verilog Latch

```
-- Reading target technology xi4xl
Reading library file
`C:\EXEMPLAR\LEOSPEC\V19991D\lib\xi4xl.syn`...
Library version = 1.8
Delays assume: Process=3
-- read -tech xi4xl { "C:/Verilog/SourceCode/latch2.v" }
-- Reading file 'C:/Verilog/SourceCode/latch2.v'...
-- Loading module latch2
-- Compiling root module 'latch2'
"C:/Verilog/SourceCode/latch2.v",line 4: Warning, q is not always
assigned. latches could be needed.
-- Pre Optimizing Design .work.latch2.INTERFACE
Info: Finished reading design
->_gc_run
-- Run Started On Mon Sep 06 10:42:20 Pacific Daylight Time 1999
--
-- optimize -target xi4xl -effort quick -chip -area -
hierarchy=auto
Using wire table: 4013xl-3_avg
Info, Inferred net 'set' as GSR net.
-- Start optimization for design .work.latch2.INTERFACE
Using wire table: 4013xl-3_avg

        Pass    Area    Delay    DFFs   PIs   POs  --CPU--
                (FGs)   (ns)                         min:sec
        1        0        7         0     2     2   00:00
Info, Added global buffer BUFG for port reset
Using wire table: 4013xl-3_avg
-- Start timing optimization for design .work.latch2.INTERFACE
No critical paths to optimize at this level

***********************************************************

Cell: latch2    View: INTERFACE    Library: work

***********************************************************

Number of ports :                          4
Number of nets :                          10
Number of instances :                      9
Number of references to this view :        0
```

```
Total accumulated area :
 Number of BUFG :                                        1
 Number of CLB Latches :                                 1
 Number of IBUF :                                        1
 Number of OBUF :                                        2
 Number of STARTUP :                                     1

* * * * * * * * * * * * * * * * * * * * * * * * * * * * * * * * * * * * * * * * * * * *
Device Utilization for 4010xlPQ100
* * * * * * * * * * * * * * * * * * * * * * * * * * * * * * * * * * * * * * * * * * * *
Resource                     Used     Avail    Utilization
---------------------------------------------------------
IOs                            4        77        5.19%
FG Function Generators         0       800        0.00%
H Function Generators          0       400        0.00%
CLB Flip Flops                 0       800        0.00%


---------------------------------------------------------
                             Clock Frequency Report

       Clock               : Frequency
       ---------------------------------------------------

       reset               : 3333.3 MHz
```

Some items in the message log bear comment.

- Reading library file `C:\EXEMPLAR\LEOSPEC\V19991D\lib\xi4xl.syn`...

The library that LeonardoSpectrum uses to implement the latch design is the xi4xl library for the Xilinx 4xxxXL family.

- "C:/verilog/latch.v",line 6: Warning, q is not always assigned. latches could be needed.

LeonardoSpectrum has very politely warned that a latch has been created. Generally, this is an error in the code caused by not defining all output conditions completely.

- optimize -target xi4xl -effort quick -chip -area -flatten=TRUE

We have selected a Xilinx 4010XL as a target device. We have selected a quick optimization as compared to an extended (multipass) compilation where multiple trials are evaluated. We have selected the chip mode, so device pins will be assigned at the top level. We have selected area optimization instead of optimization for speed. The netlist is flattened into one merged netlist; the hierarchy (where each module has a different section of the netlist) is dissolved.

- Info, Inferred net 'set' as GSR net.

LeonardoSpectrum has selected the set signal to be used as a global set (GSR stands for Global Set-Reset) resource. Xilinx has a globally routed signal that can be used for a set or reset without consuming the generic routing of the device; generally this network is used for a global reset.

Pass	Area (FGs)	Delay (ns)	DFFs	PIs	POs	--CPU-- min:sec
1	0	7	0	2	2	00:00

We selected a 1-pass optimization; this pass resulted in a delay of 7 nsec. This design uses no D flipflops, uses two input ports and two output ports, and took zero seconds to compile. All right, not 0 seconds, but it compiled fast.

• Info, Added global buffer BUFG for port reset

In addition to the Global SR resource, the 4xxxXL family has eight global signals available (BUFG). Generally they are used for clocks, but LeonardoSpectrum has automatically extracted the reset signal and assigned it to a Global Buffer.

• Info, setting outputs in top level view 'INTERFACE' to fast.

The output pins assigned in this module use fast buffers. Generally, the designer should use slow buffers where possible to reduce power consumption and noise.

• Using wire table: 4013xl-3_avg

Use average loading during analysis. The alternative is to use worst-case loading that includes the worst-case effects of temperature and power-supply voltage. The -default mode is for quick and dirty lab testing. The -default mode can also be used when the speed effects are not pertinent—for example, if the FPGA is being used to emulate a design that will be implemented in a faster technology (an ASIC).

• IOs   4   77   5.19%

We've used a very small part of the 4010XL device.

• Writing file C:/verilog/latch.edf

The output of the LeonardoSpectrum tool is an EDIF netlist which will be used by the Xilinx place-and-route tool to create a device configuration file (.bit file).

To get control of LeonardoSpectrums' configuration settings, look under the Tools toolbar. There you'll find a tab called Variable Editor; this pulls down a list of all the LeonardoSpectrum settings, some of which (like xlx_fast_slew, which sets the pin default drive to fast slew rate unless otherwise constrained) are not available in the GUI.

Running LeonardoSpectrum in the Batch Mode

Once you're familiar with LeonardoSpectrum and want to get things done faster and in a more repeatable and controlled manner compared to using the GUI, you can run in in the batch mode with the spectrum executable (this program was called elsyn in previous versions of LeonardoSpectrum). Make sure the DOS PATH environment setting in autoexec.bat points to the spectrum program. For example, in my environment, this path is c:\exemplar\LeoSpec\v1999.1d\bin\win32.

For example, an elementary command mode which will compile our basic latch design might look like:

```
spectrum -source basiclatch.v  -edif_file basiclatch.edf -ta xi4e
```

Another way is to cut and paste from the GUI filtered command window and create a file like basiclatch.run as shown in Listing 6-4.

Listing 6-4   Sample LeonardoSpectrum Executable Script File

```
restore_project_script C:/Verilog/verilog/basiclatch.scr
_gc_read_init
_gc_run_init
set input_file_list { "C:/Verilog/verilog/basiclatch.v" }
set part 4013xlPQ160
set process 3
set wire_table 4000xl-default
set pack_clbs FALSE
set timespec_generate FALSE
set nowrite_eqn FALSE
set chip TRUE
set macro FALSE
set area TRUE
set delay FALSE
set report brief
set hierarchy_preserve FALSE
set output_file "C:/Verilog/verilog/basiclatch.edf"
set novendor_constraint_file FALSE
set target xi4xl
_gc_read
_gc_run
```

This file was invoked with the command line: spectrum –file basiclatch.scr. Type "spectrum -batchhelp" to list all the command-line options (similar to Listing 6-5).

Listing 6-5   LeonardoSpectrum Batch Mode Commands

```
-nomap_global_bufs
```
Don't use global buffers for clocks and other global signals (Xilinx/Actel).

`-use_qclk_bufs`
Use quadrant clocks for Actel 3200dx architecture.

`-insert_global_bufs`
Use global buffers for clocks and other global signals (Xilinx/Actel).

`-max_cap_load <float>`
Override default max_cap_load if specified in the library.

`-max_fanout_load <float>`
Override default max_fanout_load if specified in the library.

`-lut_max_fanout <integer>`
Specify net fanout for LUT technologies (Xilinx, Altera Flex, and Lucent ORCA).

`-noenable_dff_map`
Disable clock-enable detection from HDLs.

`-enable_dff_map_optimize`
Enable use of flipflop clock-enable extracted from random logic.

`-exclude <list>`
Don't use listed gate in mapping.

`-include <list>`
Map to specified synchronous DFFs and DLATCHes.

`-pal_device`
Disable map to complex IOs for Actel.

`-wire_tree <string>`
Interconnect wire tree : best|balanced|worst = default.

`-wire_table <string>`
Wire load model to use for interconnect delays.

`-nowire_table`
Ignore interconnect delays during delay analysis.

`-nobreak_loops_in_delay`
Don't break combinational loops statically for timing analysis.

`-crit_path_analysis_mode <string>`
maximum(report setup violations) | minimum(report hold violations) | both = default.

`-num_crit_paths <integer>`
Report <integer> number of critical paths.

`-crit_path_slack <float>`
Slack threshold in nanoseconds.

`-crit_path_arrival <float>`
Arrival threshold in nanoseconds.

`-crit_path_longest`
Show longest paths rather than critical paths.

`-crit_path_detail <string>`
full(detailed point-to-point)(default) | short(startpoint-endpoint)

`-crit_path_no_io_terminals`
Don't report paths terminating in primary outputs.

`-crit_path_no_int_terminals`
Don't report paths terminating in internal endpoints.

`-crit_paths_from <list>`
Report only paths starting at this <list> port, port_inst or instance.

`-crit_paths_to <list>`
Report only paths ending at this <list> port, port_inst or instance.

`-crit_paths_thru <list>`
Report only critical paths through the <list> net.

`-crit_paths_not_thru <list>`
Report only critical paths that do not go through <list> net.

`-crit_path_report_input_pins`
Report input pins of gates. Default = off.

`-crit_path_report_nets`
Report net names. Default = off.

`-nocounter_extract`
Disable automatic extraction of counters.

`-noram_extract`
Disable automatic extraction of rams.

`-nodecoder_extract`
Disable automatic extraction of decoders.

`-optimize_cpu_limit <integer>`

Set a CPU limit for optimization.

`-notimespec_generate`
Don't create TIMESPEC info from user constraints; Xilinx only.

`-nopack_clbs`
Don't pack look-up tables (LUTs) into CLBs; for Xilinx 4K families only.

`-write_clb_packing`
Print CLB packing (HBLKNM) info, if available, in XNF/EDIF.

`-crit_path_rpt <string>`
Write critical path reporting in this file.

`-nocrit_path_rpt`
Don't create a critical path reporting file.

`-report_brief| -report_full`
Generate a concise design summary or a detailed one. Default = full.

`-map_area_weight <float>`
A number between 0 and 1.0. The larger this number, the more mapping will try to minimize area.

`-map_delay_weight <float>`
A number between 0 and 1.0. The larger this number, the more mapping will try to minimize delay.

`-simple_port_names`
Create simple names for vector ports: %s%d instead of %s(%d).

`-bus_name_style <string>`
Naming style for vector ports and nets: default %s(%d)| simple %s%d| old_galileo %s_%d

`-nobus`
Write busses in expanded form. This may be required for the Xilinx EDIF reader.

`-nowrite_eqn`
Don't write equations in output; use technology primitives instead.

`-nopld_xor_decomp`
Don't do XOR decomposition for Altera MAX and Xilinx CPLD technologies.

`-noglobal_symbol`
Delete startup (GSR) block.

`-notime_opt`
Don't run timing optimization.

`-max_frequency <float>`
Desired maximum operating frequency in MHz.

```
-edifin_ground_net_names <list>
```
Specify that net(s) with <list> name(s) are ground nets.

```
-edifin_power_net_names <list>
```
Specify that net(s) with <list> name(s) are power nets.

```
-edifin_ground_port_names <list>
```
Specify that port(s) with <list> name(s) are ground ports.

```
-edifin_power_port_names <list>
```
Specify that port(s) with <list> name(s) are power ports.

```
-edifin_ignore_port_names <list>
```
Specify that port(s) with <list> name(s) are ignored ports.

```
-edifout_power_ground_style_is_net
```
Write out power and ground as undriven nets with an extracted or inferred net name.

```
-edifout_power_net_name <string>
```
Use <string> name for power nets when 'edifout_power_ground_style_is_net' is TRUE; default = 'VCC'.

```
-edifout_ground_net_name <string>
```
Use <string> name for ground nets when 'edifout_power_ground_style_is_net' is TRUE; default = 'GND'.

COMPLETE DESIGN FLOW, 8-BIT EQUALITY COMPARATOR

So far, we've done only half the design work: the design entry and synthesis. To finish the job, we need to run the Xilinx place-and-route tool, the Design Manager. To illustrate how this is tool is used, we'll take an example design all the way through the process. This design is similar to an HC688, an 8-bit equality comparator. This design compares two bytes and generates a signal called **equal** if they are equivalent. A **cascade** input is also provided to expand the inputs that are compared; if **cascade** is not asserted, the **equal** output is inhibited. Because of personal preference, I've made a couple of design changes; all signals are active high, and I made the **equal** output synchronous. See Listing 6-6 for the Verilog code for this design.

Listing 6-6   8-Bit Equality Comparator

```
// Synchronous 8-bit equality comparator.
// All signals changed to be active high.
// Output made synchronous.

module hc688s (equal, clock, reset, cascade, a, b);
```

```
output                  equal;
input                   clock, reset;
input                   cascade;
input         [7:0]     a, b;
reg                     equal;

always @ (posedge clock or posedge reset)
    begin
    if (reset)
    equal  <=       0;
    else if (~cascade)
    equal  <=       0;
    else if (a == b)
    equal  <=       1;
    else
    equal  <=       0;        // Make sure all input cases are covered.
    end
endmodule
```

The Verilog code is simple enough; **equal** can go high only if cascade is high and the **a** and **b** input bytes are equal. Let's see what LeonardoSpectrum makes of this design by looking at the extracted schematic of Figure 6-1

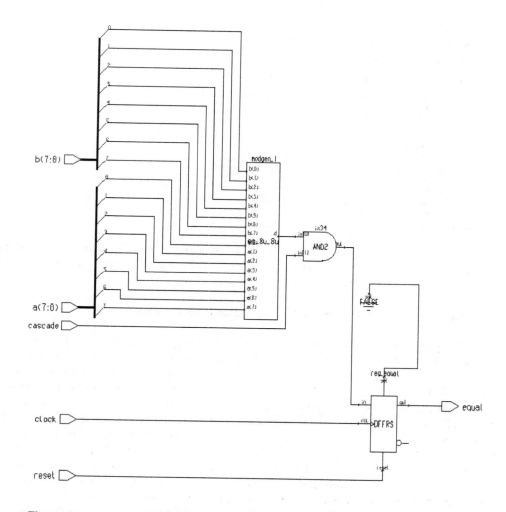

Figure 6-1 HC688s LeonardoSpectrum RTL Schematic

From Figure 6-1 we can see that the **equal** output is created by a flipflop and that the clock and reset were implemented as intended. LeonardoSpectrum has instantiated a library function from their module generator (modgen) to do the equality-test logic. For greater detail, LeonardoSpectrum has another schematic view option, the gate-level schematic, shown in Figure 6-2.

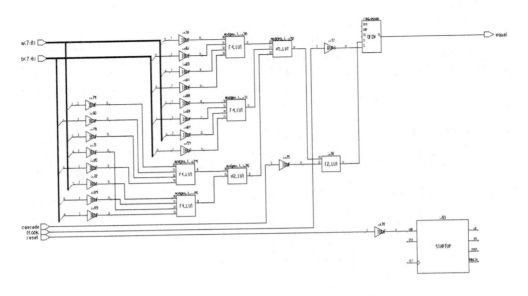

Figure 6-2   HC688s LeonardoSpectrum Gate-Level Schematic

The gate-level schematic shows the logic as it is mapped into Xilinx hardware. The Xilinx Configurable Logic Block (CLB) will be explored in more detail in Chapter 7; for now we can note the assignment of our logic to 2- and 4-input look-up tables (LUTs), the use of global buffers for clock and reset, and the flipflop that drives the **equal** output signal.

A couple of things should be noted about these schematic views. First of all, they are graphical representations of the netlist that LeonardoSpectrum synthesized. There is still some processing to be done on the design by the Xilinx Design Manager (the place-and-route tool). The use of this schematic is as a sanity check; if the design is not being synthesized effectively, the designer can try different compilation options or design in a more structural way. For example, the designer can replace the high-level equality operator (==) with structural gates to assert more control of how the design is synthesized.

LeonardoSpectrum provides one last view of the schematic, the critical path as shown in Figure 6-3.

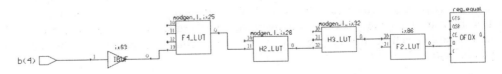

Figure 6-3   HC688s LeonardoSpectrum Critical-Path Schematic

The critical path is the longest delay path through the design. If the design needs to be optimized for greater speed, the designer should focus on redesigning this path to remove layers of logic. From this schematic, we can see that the longest delay path is from the **b[4]** input to the **equal** output, and there are four layers of logic in this path. Like the adders we studied earlier, there is probably a way to add extra logic to "look ahead" and streamline this logic, if necessary.

For this design, compiling to optimize for delay didn't change anything, but for most designs there will be a change in interpreting the design, hopefully a change for the better.

There is one more view that has some value. The output of the synthesizer is a netlist, in this case an EDIF (.edf) file, but this type of file is not intended to be read by humans. LeonardoSpectrum can also generate a structural version of the netlist in a Verilog format. In fact, one great feature of LeonardoSpectrum is the ability to translate between netlists of various types. Anyway, we're learning Verilog, so let's look at the Verilog version of the netlist as shown in Listing 6-7.

Listing 6-7 8-Bit Equality Comparator Structural Netlist

```verilog
//
// Verilog description for cell hc688s,
// 09/06/99 11:00:40
//

module hc688s ( equal, clock, reset, cascade, a, b ) ;

    output equal ;
    input clock ;
    input reset ;
    input cascade ;
    input [7:0]a ;
    input [7:0]b ;

    wire nx12, modgen_eq_2_nx21, modgen_eq_2_nx22,
modgen_eq_2_nx23, modgen_eq_2_nx28, modgen_eq_2_nx29, clock_int,
reset_int, cascade_int, a_7__int, a_6__int, a_5__int, a_4__int,
a_3__int, a_2__int, a_1__int, a_0__int, b_7__int, b_6__int,
b_5__int, b_4__int, b_3__int, b_2__int, b_1__int, b_0__int, nx15;
    wire [8:0] \$dummy ;

    assign modgen_eq_2_nx22 = ( ~a_7__int &&   ~b_7__int &&
~a_6__int &&   ~b_6__int) || ( ~a_7__int && ~ b_7__int && a_6__int
&& b_6__int) || (a_7__int && b_7__int && ~ a_6__int &&
~b_6__int) || (a_7__int && b_7__int && a_6__int && b_6__int) ;

    assign modgen_eq_2_nx23 = ( ~a_5__int &&   ~b_5__int &&
~a_4__int &&   ~b_4__int) || ( ~a_5__int && ~ b_5__int && a_4__int
&& b_4__int) || (a_5__int && b_5__int && ~ a_4__int &&
~b_4__int) || (a_5__int && b_5__int && a_4__int && b_4__int) ;

    assign modgen_eq_2_nx21 = (modgen_eq_2_nx22 &&
modgen_eq_2_nx23) ;
```

```
    assign modgen_eq_2_nx28 = ( ~a_3__int &&  ~b_3__int &&
~a_2__int &&  ~b_2__int) || ( ~a_3__int && ~ b_3__int && a_2__int
&& b_2__int) || (a_3__int && b_3__int && ~ a_2__int &&
~b_2__int) || (a_3__int && b_3__int && a_2__int && b_2__int) ;

    assign modgen_eq_2_nx29 = ( ~a_1__int &&  ~b_1__int &&
~a_0__int &&  ~b_0__int) || ( ~a_1__int && ~ b_1__int && a_0__int
&& b_0__int) || (a_1__int && b_1__int && ~ a_0__int &&
~b_0__int) || (a_1__int && b_1__int && a_0__int && b_0__int) ;

    assign nx12 = (modgen_eq_2_nx28 && modgen_eq_2_nx29 &&
modgen_eq_2_nx21);

    STARTUP ix63 (.Q2 (\$dummy [0]), .Q3 (\$dummy [1]), .Q1Q4
(\$dummy [2]), .DONEIN (\$dummy [3]), .GSR (reset_int), .GTS
(\$dummy [4]), .CLK (
        \$dummy [5])) ;

    IBUF b_0__ibuf (.O (b_0__int), .I (b[0])) ;
    IBUF b_1__ibuf (.O (b_1__int), .I (b[1])) ;
    IBUF b_2__ibuf (.O (b_2__int), .I (b[2])) ;
    IBUF b_3__ibuf (.O (b_3__int), .I (b[3])) ;
    IBUF b_4__ibuf (.O (b_4__int), .I (b[4])) ;
    IBUF b_5__ibuf (.O (b_5__int), .I (b[5])) ;
    IBUF b_6__ibuf (.O (b_6__int), .I (b[6])) ;
    IBUF b_7__ibuf (.O (b_7__int), .I (b[7])) ;
    IBUF a_0__ibuf (.O (a_0__int), .I (a[0])) ;
    IBUF a_1__ibuf (.O (a_1__int), .I (a[1])) ;
    IBUF a_2__ibuf (.O (a_2__int), .I (a[2])) ;
    IBUF a_3__ibuf (.O (a_3__int), .I (a[3])) ;
    IBUF a_4__ibuf (.O (a_4__int), .I (a[4])) ;
    IBUF a_5__ibuf (.O (a_5__int), .I (a[5])) ;
    IBUF a_6__ibuf (.O (a_6__int), .I (a[6])) ;
    IBUF a_7__ibuf (.O (a_7__int), .I (a[7])) ;
    IBUF cascade_ibuf (.O (cascade_int), .I (cascade)) ;
    IBUF reset_ibuf (.O (reset_int), .I (reset)) ;
    OFDX reg_equal (.Q (equal), .C (clock_int), .D (nx15), .CE
(\$dummy [6]), .GSR (\$dummy [7]), .GTS (\$dummy [8])) ;

    BUFG clock_ibuf (.O (clock_int), .I (clock)) ;

    assign nx15 = (nx12 && cascade_int) ;
endmodule
```

This is a bit of an ugly mess, but there are a few things we can extract from it. Note the _int attached to the internal signals. This is very polite; some synthesizers convert a useful signal name like clock into a signal name like ifght_2746 instead of clock_int which makes it very difficult to search netlists. We want the synthesizer to do whatever is necessary to isolate a signal as it gets routed, but keep some part of the signal name we assigned in there somewhere. The equality module is modgen_2, and it gets wired up to the input buffers (ibufs). The **equal** register is an OFDX (output D flipflop); note the assignments for Q output, clock/data/clock enable. The GTS is a global tristate control and the GSR is the global set/reset control.

The place-and-route tool works on the netlist that is extracted from the input design and influenced by the design constraints and synthesis controls. If there is a problem with synthesized logic, it may help to look at the netlist and make sure things are being synthesized in a reasonable manner.

Another netlist form is the .xnf (Xilinx Netlist Format) which is very readable. Sadly though, Xilinx is moving to standardize on the much-less-readable EDIF format.

8-BIT EQUALITY COMPARATOR WITH HIERARCHY

Let's hook up a few of our equality comparators and see what effect a hierarchical design has on the resulting netlist. The hier688 design, shown in Listing 6-8, instantiates three of our hc688s designs to create a 24-bit address decoder.

Listing 6-8   8-Bit Equality Comparator Hierarchical Example

```
module hier688(chip_select, output_enable, addr, rwn, clock,
reset);
output          chip_select, output_enable;
input     [23:0] addr;
input          rwn, clock, reset;
wire           low, middle, high;
reg            chip_select, output_enable;
parameter  low_range   =    8'h80;
parameter  mid_range   =    8'ha0;
parameter  high_range  =    8'hff;

// Tie off cascade input for low address comparator.
hc688s u1 (low,    clock, reset, 1'b1,   addr[7:0],   low_range);
hc688s u2 (middle, clock, reset, low,    addr[15:8],  mid_range);
hc688s u3 (high,   clock, reset, middle, addr[23:16], high_range);

// Synchronize the module outputs.
always @ (posedge clock or posedge reset)
    begin
          if (reset)
                begin
                chip_select        <=      0;
                output_enable <=    0;
                end
          else
                begin
                chip_select        <=      high;
                output_enable <=    (high & ~rwn);
                end
    end
```

```
endmodule
```

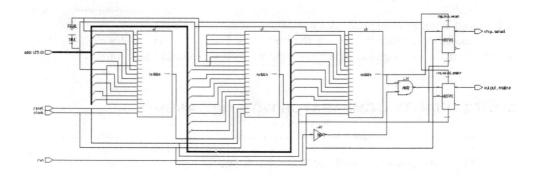

Figure 6-4   Hierarchical HC688s Gate-Level Schematic

The schematic of Figure 6-4 is not very legible, but you can see that our structural use of the HC688 decoders results in cascaded logic. This design is not going to be very fast, but is easy to put together as it reuses predesigned HC688 modules. Although we're not going to analyze the critical path, clearly it will be from a low-order address input to the **output_enable** output signal.

Let's carry this design into the a real device. We do this by placing and routing the design and creating a configuration file for the Xilinx device where our design will live. We will open the Design Manager, create a new project, and browse (see Figure 6-5) until we find the hier688.edf netlist. The Design Manager has a one-button operation (the idea is: if the designer falls over dead, his or her head will hit the keyboard, and a place-and-route will still take place). We'll play dumb and just run the default Design Manager flow and see what we get.

A convenient way to execute the Design Manager is to create a shortcut icon on your Windows desktop. For example, in my environment the command line is: C:\Xilinx\bin\nt\dsgnmgr.exe.

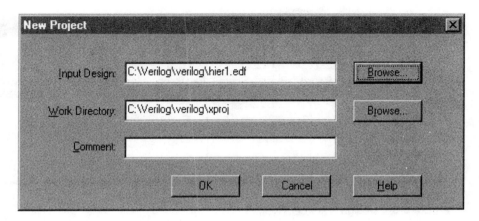

Figure 6-5   Opening a Design With Xilinx Design Manager

Listing 6-9   8-Bit Equality Comparator Hierarchical Example, Xilinx Translation Report


```
ngdbuild:   version M1.5.19
Copyright (c) 1995-1998 Xilinx, Inc.  All rights reserved.

Command Line: ngdbuild -p xc4010xl-3-pq100 -dd ..
C:\Verilog\SourceCode\hier688.edf hier688.ngd

Launcher: Executing edif2ngd "C:\Verilog\SourceCode\hier688.edf"
"C:\Verilog\SourceCode\xproj\ver1\hier688.ngo"
Reading NGO file "C:/Verilog/SourceCode/xproj/ver1/hier688.ngo"
...
Reading component libraries for design expansion...

Checking timing specifications ...

Checking expanded design ...

NGDBUILD Design Results Summary:
  Number of errors:      0
  Number of warnings:    0

Writing NGD file "hier688.ngd" ...

Writing NGDBUILD log file "hier688.bld"...
```

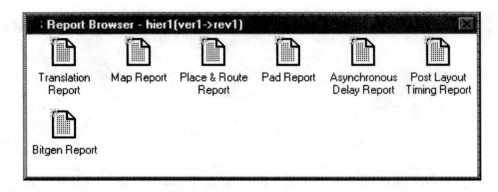

Figure 6-6   Design Manager Reports

Figure 6-6 shows the Report Browser window. If we click on the Translation Report, we will see the report of Listing 6-9, and we can see that the input design was read without error. The EDIF netlist is converted to a Xilinx binary netlist file: a .ngo file.

Listing 6-10 8-Bit Equality Comparator Hierarchical Example, Xilinx Place and Route
          Report

```
Starting Constructive Placer.  REAL time: 7 secs
Placer score = 13350
Placer score = 9810
Placer score = 6780
Placer score = 5730
Placer score = 5190
Placer score = 4440
Placer score = 3720
Placer score = 3570
Placer score = 3480
Placer score = 3270
Placer score = 3090
Finished Constructive Placer.  REAL time: 7 secs
```

Listing 6-10 is a clip from the Xilinx place-and-route report. Like a printed circuit board autorouter, the place-and-route tool tries different placements and selects the ones with the better results. At this point an estimate of the timing can be extracted.

Listing 6-11 Equality Comparator Hierarchical Example, Xilinx Average Delay Report

```
The Number of signals not completely routed for this design is: 0

    The Average Connection Delay for this design is:        1.929 ns
    The Average Connection Delay on critical nets is:       0.000 ns
    The Average Clock Skew for this design is:              0.098 ns
    The Maximum Pin Delay is:                               5.937 ns
    The Average Connection Delay on the 10 Worst Nets is:   2.983 ns

    Listing Pin Delays by value: (ns)

d <= 10   < d <= 20   < d <= 30   < d <= 40   < d <= 50   d > 50
-------   ---------   ---------   ---------   ---------   -------
   37             0           0           0           0         0
```

The signal delays are binned per Listing 6-11. This is a moderately fast design (looks like it would run at 100 MHz to me) but only because very little of the device is used! As the device gets fuller and more logic competes with routing resources, the design will get slower.

Listing 6-12 8-Bit Equality Comparator Hierarchical Example, Xilinx Pad Report

```
# Pinout constraints listing
# These constraints are in PCF grammar format
# and may be cut and pasted into the PCF file
# after the "SCHEMATIC END ;" statement to
# preserve this pinout for future design iterations.
#
COMP "addr(0)"  LOCATE = SITE "P90" ;
COMP "addr(1)"  LOCATE = SITE "P89" ;
COMP "addr(10)" LOCATE = SITE "P36" ;
COMP "addr(11)" LOCATE = SITE "P35" ;
COMP "addr(12)" LOCATE = SITE "P37" ;
COMP "addr(13)" LOCATE = SITE "P39" ;
COMP "addr(14)" LOCATE = SITE "P44" ;
COMP "addr(15)" LOCATE = SITE "P42" ;
COMP "addr(16)" LOCATE = SITE "P32" ;
COMP "addr(17)" LOCATE = SITE "P22" ;
COMP "addr(18)" LOCATE = SITE "P30" ;
COMP "addr(19)" LOCATE = SITE "P31" ;
COMP "addr(2)"  LOCATE = SITE "P93" ;
COMP "addr(20)" LOCATE = SITE "P23" ;
COMP "addr(21)" LOCATE = SITE "P21" ;
COMP "addr(22)" LOCATE = SITE "P24" ;
COMP "addr(23)" LOCATE = SITE "P33" ;
COMP "addr(3)"  LOCATE = SITE "P95" ;
COMP "addr(4)"  LOCATE = SITE "P97" ;
COMP "addr(5)"  LOCATE = SITE "P94" ;
COMP "addr(6)"  LOCATE = SITE "P88" ;
```

```
COMP "addr(7)" LOCATE = SITE "P96" ;
COMP "addr(8)" LOCATE = SITE "P38" ;
COMP "addr(9)" LOCATE = SITE "P43" ;
COMP "chip_select" LOCATE = SITE "P20" ;
COMP "clock" LOCATE = SITE "P5" ;
COMP "output_enable" LOCATE = SITE "P18" ;
COMP "reset" LOCATE = SITE "P56" ;
COMP "rwn" LOCATE = SITE "P17" ;
```

We did not assign pin locations in the input design. The first time through it is not a bad idea to let the place-and-route tool assign the pins (particularly with Altera devices). The FPGA design tries to allow pins to be assigned in a universal manner (i.e., not be sensitive to pin usage by the designer; allow any I/O pin to be used with logic anywhere on the chip), but there is some assumption made, for example, that data flow is horizontal (with relation to the Pin 1 location on the device) and control is vertical. On the other hand, for the PWB design, you may want to control the pin locations and keep addresses together and that sort of thing. Once the circuit board has been designed, we don't want the compiler reassigning pins, so we are going to constrain the pin locations. The pins assigned by the Xilinx place-and-route tool can be located in the Pad Report as shown in Listing 6-12. This file can be cut, pasted, and edited into the LeonardoSpectrum Constraint file to lock down pin assignments as shown in Listing 6-13. This can also be done in Xilinx Design Manager, but I prefer to lock these pins in the design capture environment.

Listing 6-13 8-Bit Equality Comparator, Xilinx Pin Assignments

```
addr(0)       INPUT      P90
addr(1)       INPUT      P89
addr(10)      INPUT      P36
addr(11)      INPUT      P35
addr(12)      INPUT      P37
addr(13)      INPUT      P39
addr(14)      INPUT      P44
addr(15)      INPUT      P42
addr(16)      INPUT      P32
addr(17)      INPUT      P22
addr(18)      INPUT      P30
addr(19)      INPUT      P31
addr(2)       INPUT      P93
addr(20)      INPUT      P23
addr(21)      INPUT      P21
addr(22)      INPUT      P24
addr(23)      INPUT      P33
addr(3)       INPUT      P95
addr(4)       INPUT      P97
addr(5)       INPUT      P94
addr(6)       INPUT      P88
addr(7)       INPUT      P96
addr(8)       INPUT      P38
```

```
addr(9)             INPUT       P43
chip_select         OUTPUT      P20
clock               INPUT       P5
output_enable       OUTPUT      P18
reset               INPUT       P56
rwn                 INPUT       P17
```

These pins can be assigned in the LeonardoSpectrum environment by going to the **Constraints** Tab, finding the **Input** or **Output** tab, and filling in the entry box for Pin Location. Make sure to hit the **Apply** button once all the pin assignments are filled in (see Figure 6-7). They can also be assigned in the batch mode as so:

```
set_attribute -port {<hierarchical net name>} -name PIN_NUMBER -
value PXX
```

Note: replace XX with the desired pin number.

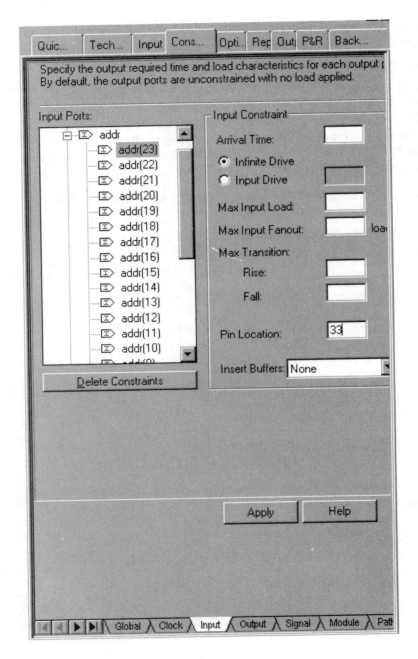

Figure 6-7   LeonardoSpectrum Pin Assignment using the GUI

These are not the only required pin assignments on the circuit board. We must hook up the dedicated signals including power, ground, and configuration signals on the board-level schematic.

Listing 6-14 8-Bit Equality Comparator Hierarchical Example, Xilinx Asynchronous Delay Report

```
The 20 Worst Net Delays are:
-------------------------------
| Max Delay (ns)  | Netname    |
-------------------------------
      5.937          low
      4.154          middle
      3.314          high
      2.751          clock_int
      2.508          reset_int
      2.490          addr(23)_int
      2.228          addr(17)_int
      2.187          addr(21)_int
      2.179          addr(4)_int
      2.097          addr(1)_int
      2.085          addr(7)_int
      1.823          addr(14)_int
      1.823          addr(10)_int
      1.767          addr(9)_int
      1.754          addr(22)_int
      1.739          addr(0)_int
      1.705          addr(15)_int
      1.693          addr(11)_int
      1.637          addr(6)_int
      1.557          addr(16)_int
```

The top 20 delays can be viewed in the Asynchronous Delay Report as shown in Listing 6-14. From this, we can guess that this design would run at 168 MHz, not bad for a slow −3 speed grade part. Again, we're using only a tiny percentage of the device. Still, this is not the full story, this is just the delays between individual nodes; to get the full delay we have to run full timing analysis with this result:

```
Timing constraint: Default period analysis
  34 items analyzed, 0 timing errors detected.
  Minimum period is   9.967ns.

Delay:      9.967ns low to middle (8.027ns delay plus 1.940ns
setup)
```

```
Path low to middle contains 2 levels of logic:
Path starting from Comp: CLB_R1C10.K (from clock_int)
To          Delay type          Delay(ns)       Physical
Logical Resources                                Resource
---------------------------------------------------  --------
CLB_R1C10.XQ       Tcko                2.090R      low
                                                   u1_reg_equal
CLB_R20C10.C2      net (fanout=1)      5.937R      low
CLB_R20C10.K       Thh1ck              1.940R      middle
modgen_eq_3_ix18                                   u2_reg_equal
---------------------------------------------------
Total (4.030ns logic, 5.937ns route)      9.967ns (to clock_int)
      (40.4% logic, 59.6% route)
```

This tells us that the worst-case delay from flipflop to flipflop is 9.967 nsec, so we can really only run our clock at 100 MHz, not nearly so impressive.

OPTIMIZATION OPTIONS IN THE XILINX ENVIRONMENT

The Xilinx place-and-route tool, called the Design Manager, converts the EDIF netlist into a configuration file that can be loaded into a target device. Some of the place-and-route tool optimization parameters are configurable by the designer. To get into the **options** menu, select options from the implementation menu as shown in Figure 6-8.

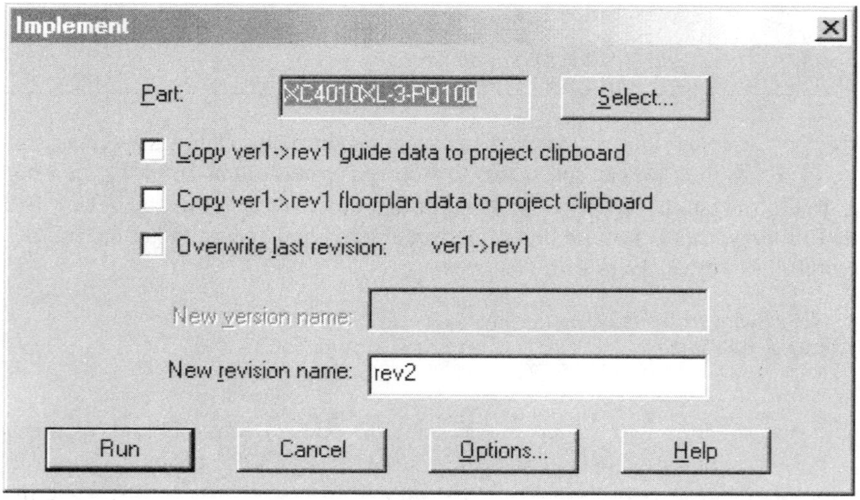

Figure 6-8   Xilinx Design Manager Options Selection

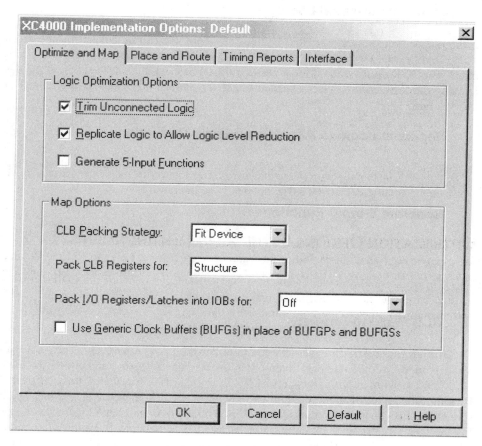

Figure 6-9   Xilinx Design Manager Implementation Options

MAPPING OPTIONS

The synthesized netlist has some placeholders for precompiled library elements. The mapper finds the library elements (.ngo files, a binary netlist format) and merges them in. The mapper then converts the merged netlist into a physical netlist with specific hardware elements assigned to all the netlist logic elements. The mapper output is an .ncf (physical netlist format) file. The user can configure the mapping process with the following options from the Implementation Options window shown in Figure 6-9.

Trim Unconnected Logic

If the mapper encounters logic that is not used, this logic can be deleted from the design. This simplifies the logic and speeds up the place-and-route process. However, the designer might want to keep the unused logic because it will be used in a later version of the design. Leaving the logic in may give a better estimate of the resources and timing related to the final design.

Replicate Logic to Allow Logic Level Reduction

Redundant logic can be added to the design to reduce driver loading and speed up the design (the basic area/speed trade-off).

Generate 5-Input Functions

Generally, the basic Xilinx logic element is a 4-input look-up table. However, the CLB logic can be configured to combine CLBs and to create 5-input LUTs to be used. Again, this is a speed/area trade-off. The 5-input CLB configuration can use more CLBs but allow a higher operating speed.

CLB Packing Strategy

The mapper uses a set of rules to attempt to utilize the CLBs effectively. The CLB Packing Strategy modifies the logic partitioning to allow less signal sharing and allows the use of a CLB flipflop without the associated LUT. Again, this is a speed/area trade-off; the CLB Packing Strategy can use more logic but may allow the design to run at a higher operating speed. The **Fit Device** option packs the CLBs with possibly unrelated logic until the design fits into the target device or until no more packing is possible. Turning this option **Off** allows only related logic (logic with shared inputs) to be packed into a CLB.

Pack CLB Registers for Minimum Area or Structure

This option controls register ordering but analyzing bussed signal names. The **Minimum Area** option will result in a denser design with registers mapped in a more random order. The **Structure** option enables register-ordering analysis.

Pack I/O Registers/Latches into IOBs for Inputs Only, Outputs Only, Inputs and Outputs, and Off

Normally, the synthesis tool assigns logic to I/O buffers (IOBs). However, this option allows the mapper to assign IOBs and can result in better CLB packing. Use the **Off** option to allow the synthesis tool to control IOB assignment.

Use Generic Clock Buffers (BUFGs) in Place of BUFGPs and BUFGSs

Older Xilinx devices used primary (BUFGP) and secondary (BUFGS) global buffers for global signals, so some synthesis tools may make these assignments. Newer Xilinx devices use a pool of generic global buffers (BUFGs). Enabling this option will allow the replacement of BUFGSs and BUFGPs with BUFGs.

Place-and-Route Options

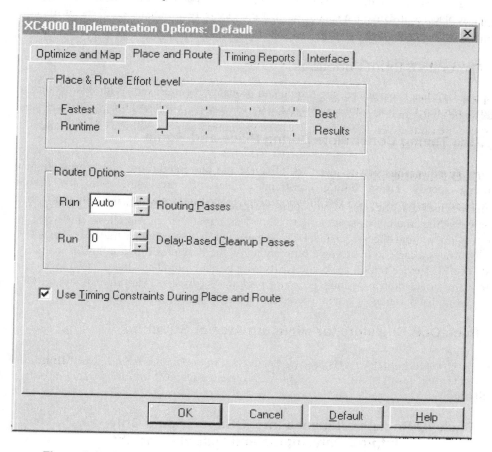

Figure 6-10 Xilinx Design Manager Place-and-Route Options

Place & Route Effort Level

Another trade-off is the amount of time spent optimizing a design versus the optimization results as shown in the Place and Route menu in Figure 6-10. If the place-and-route tool tries longer, it will have more options to select from, and the area/speed results will probably be better. Higher effort levels will increase the run time.

Router Option, Run Routing Passes

The designer can select the number of routing passes. Each routing pass is a complete attempt at placement. Once the router has met the design requirements (the design fits into the device with all timing constraints met), the router exits.

Run Delay-Based Cleanup Passes

Once a design has been placed, the timing can probably be improved. With this option the designer can run 1 to 5 additional cleanup passes to attempt to improve the operating speed.

Use Timing Constraints During Place-and-Route

The timing constraints can be used to influence the place-and-route and achieve higher operating speeds. Using timing constraints trades off processing time for design performance. Turn this option **Off** to ignore timing constraints and speed up the place-and-route process.

LOGIC LEVEL TIMING REPORT/POST LAYOUT TIMING REPORT

XC4000 Implementation Options: Default   ☒

| Optimize and Map | Place and Route | Timing Reports | Interface |

┌─ Logic Level Timing Report ────────────────────────────────────┐

☐ Produce Logic Level Timing Report

Limit Report to ☐ 1 ☐ Paths per Timing Constraint

○ Report Paths Using Advanced Design Analysis (No Timing Constraints)

◉ Report Paths in Timing Constraints

○ Report Paths Failing Timing Constraints

┌─ Post Layout Timing Report ────────────────────────────────────┐

☑ Produce Post Layout Timing Report

Limit Report to ☐ 3 ☐ Paths per Timing Constraint

○ Report Paths Using Advanced Design Analysis (No Timing Constraints)

○ Report Paths in Timing Constraints

◉ Report Paths Failing Timing Constraints

[OK]   [Cancel]   [Default]   [Help]

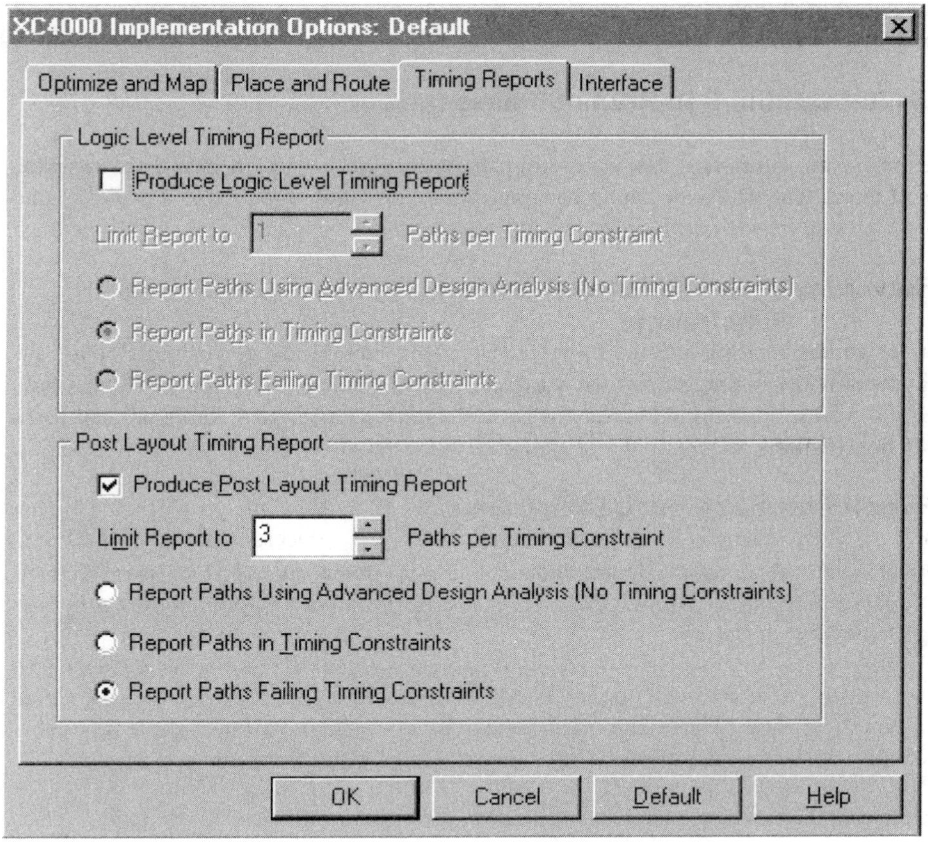

Figure 6-11 Xilinx Design Manager Implementation Options

Produce Logic Level Timing Report

For a quick view of the timing performance of the design, a logic level timing report can be produced by selecting the check box shown in Figure 6-11. These estimated results can be reviewed without going through the complete (and often very time-consuming) place-and-route process.

Produce Post Layout Timing Report

A top-level report of the device timing can be reviewed with this brief timing report. The maximum clock speed is reported. For error and path reports the entries are sorted by constraint and delay value. Negative slack-time values indicate a constraint that was not met.

Limit Report to n Paths per Timing Constraint

This setting, either Summary, No Limit, or s number from one to ten, limits the reported number of worst-case paths per timing constraint.

Report Paths Using Advanced Design Analysis (No Timing Constraints)

This option provides a timing analysis when no user constraints are present. The analysis includes all clocks, the required offset for each clock, and a listing of combinational paths sorted by delay value.

Report Paths in Timing Constraints

This option generates a timing report based on timing constraints. The number of paths reported per constraint is per the selection made in the **Limit Report to n Paths per Timing Constraint** dialog box.

Listing 6-15 is an example of a timing report for a signal in the hier688.v design. All the delay paths between rwn and output_enable are listed, along with the positive slack time (good!). Note that 80% of the delay is in logic. This percentage will get smaller (possibly much smaller) as the design gets more dense and the logic fights for routing resources.

Listing 6-15 Example, Xilinx Timing Report

```
==================================================================
Timing constraint: TS01 = MAXDELAY FROM TIMEGRP "PADS" TO TIMEGRP
"FFS" 50nS;
 30 items analyzed, 0 timing errors detected.
 Maximum delay is  13.354ns.
------------------------------------------------------------------
Slack:     36.646ns path rwn to output_enable relative to
           50.000ns delay constraint

Path rwn to output_enable contains 3 levels of logic:
Path starting from Comp: P102.PAD
```

```
To                      Delay type          Delay(ns)  Physical
Resource
                                                       Logical
Resource(s)
----------------------------------------------------   --------
P102.I1                 Tpid                   3.000R  rwn
                                                       IPAD_rwn
                                                       ix46
CLB_R7C14.F2            net (fanout=1)         1.215R  rwn_int
CLB_R7C14.X            Tilo                    2.700R  D
                                                       ix79
P99.O                   net (fanout=1)         1.439R  D
P99.OK                  Took                   5.000R  output_enable

reg_output_enable
------------------------------------------------------
Total (10.700ns logic, 2.654ns route)     13.354ns  (to clock_int)
      (80.1% logic, 19.9% route)
```

Report Paths Failing Timing Constraints

This option generates a report of signals and paths that fail the timing constraints, listed from worst to best. The logic and routing delays are identified and the failing path delays are broken out to show all the delays that build up to cause the problem. A close examination of the delays will provide clues to areas that can be pipelined or simplified to make the design run faster or identify areas where the constraint is over-specified.

The number of paths reported per constraint is per the selection made in the **Limit Report to n Paths per Timing Constraint** dialog box.

Interface Options

Macro Search Path

When the netlist is merged and .ngo files are inserted, the compiler searches for the proper file to insert. The user can add other search paths. Multiple search paths can be entered, a semicolon being used as path separator.

Rules File

To be merged in the ncf netlist, the filetype must be an ngo. The **rules file** path can point to a utility for converting other netlist file formats to an .ngo filetype.

Create I/O Pads from Ports

Some design tools convert PAD symbols into module port symbols. This checkbox option will convert top-level module ports into PADs (device pins).

Simulation Options

Simulation Data Options

Xilinx can create a timing-annotated netlist in three flavors: EDIF, VHDL, and Verilog. We'll want to use the Verilog option to support Verilog simulation, of course. Vendors supported for this version of the Xilinx place-and-route tool include generic EDIF, generic Verilog, generic VHDL, ActiveVHDL, Concept NC-Verilog, Concept Verilog-XL, Foundation EDIF, ModelSim Verilog (for the purposes of this book, this is the option we will use), ModelSim VHDL, NC-Verilog, Quicksim, Verilog-XL, Viewsim-XL, Viewsim-EDIF, VSS, and Default.

Correlate Simulation Data to Input Design

To use your logic gate and signal names instead of the names assigned by the place-and-route tool in the optimized netlist, check this checkbox.

Simulation Netlist Name

Define the filename for the simulation output file. If you want to keep multiple versions of the simulation file, enter the filenames here, otherwise the new file will overwrite the previous one.

VHDL/VERILOG SIMULATION OPTIONS

Bring Out Global Set/Reset Net as a Port

For simulation purposes, it can be handy to have the internal Set/Reset node available as a port at the toplevel of the design. The signal name that drives the Global Set/Reset (GSR) resource can be entered in the dialog box to match the HDL design.

Bring Out Global Tristate Net as a Port

For simulation purposes, it can be handy to have the internal tristate control node available as a port at the toplevel of the design. The signal name that drives the Global Tristate (GTS) resource can be entered in the dialog box to match the HDL design. This tristate controls all device outputs and is useful for isolating a device from a circuit board being tested (stimulated) with external equipment.

Generate Test Fixture/Testbench File

Check this checkbox to create a Verilog test fixture (.tv) template file.

Include `uselib Directive in Verilog File

Xilinx provides a set of timing-annotated SIMPRIM (SIMulation PRIMitive) files. The path to these files can be automatically inserted in the Verilog test-fixture file by checking this checkbox.

Generate Pin File

Check this checkbox to create signal-to-pin (.pin) mapping file.

Retain Hierarchy in Netlist

The Verilog test-fixture file can maintain the input design hierarchy or flatten the netlist into one big file. Check this checkbox to maintain the input design hierarchy.

Configuration Options

Xilinx devices are SRAM based and must have their configuration loaded after each power-on. There are many configuration modes, including serial PROM, parallel master, parallel slave, download cable, etc.

Configuration Rate

Slow (1 MHz) or Fast (8 MHz) internal configuration clock (master modes). These are approximate speeds.

Threshold Levels (XC4000E and XC4000EX Only)

Select between a TTL-compatible input threshold (nominally 30% of the power-supply value) or CMOS threshold (nominally 50% of the power-supply value) and output drive. Select **Read from Design** to use the TTL/CMOS input level defined in the physical constraints (PCF) file.

Configuration Pins

Various pull-up and pull-down options are available for the TDO, Mode, and Done configuration pins, including a tristate mode.

Perform CRC During Configuration

The internal Xilinx configuration logic can perform a four-bit partial CRC check of configuration data frames or just do a simple check of the 0110 pattern at the end of each frame.

Produce ASCII Configuration File

The normal configuration file is a binary .bit file. An ASCII version (.rbt) of this configuration bitstream file can also be created.

5V Tolerant I/Os (XC4000XLA and XC4000XV Only)

I/O pins on a low-voltage device can be configured to withstand higher drive voltages for mixed-power-supply operation.

Start-Up Options

Start-up Clock

Configuration can be started based on an internal (CCLK) or external clock (User Clock) source.

Synchronize Start-up to DONE Input Pin

When multiple devices are configured in a daisy-chain fashion, they are configured one at a time. Once an earlier device is DONE being configured, it can enable the next device to be configured.

Output Events

Control signals can be asserted or released with different timing. These status signals include Done, Enable Outputs, and Release Set/Reset.

Readback

The device configuration can be read when readback is enabled (readback can be disabled for design security reasons). This tab includes options for the readback clock source (internal or external) and termination of the readback process.

Tie Unused Interconnect

Unused pins can be tied high or low to reduce noise and power consumption.

Advanced Options

In the master parallel configuration mode, where the FPGA generates address lines to control a parallel memory device, the configuration address lines can be configured for 18 or 22 lines.

OTHER DESIGN MANAGER TOOLS

Design Manager tools include the Flow Engine (which we used to perform the place-and-route process), Timing Analyzer, Floor Planner, PROM File Formatter, Hardware Debugger (which includes the FPGA download utility), and the EPIC Design Editor.

Timing Analyzer

The Timing Analyzer will provide a report of selected paths in the design. For example, it is possible to examine all clocks in the design. Specific paths can be excluded.

```
================================================================
Timing constraint: Default period analysis
 12 items analyzed, 0 timing errors detected.
 Maximum delay is  11.647ns.
----------------------------------------------------------------
Delay:     11.647ns device_bus2(0) to device_bus1(2)

Path device_bus2(0) to device_bus1(2) contains 3 levels of logic:
Path starting from Comp: P46.PAD
```

To Resource Resource(s)	Delay type	Delay(ns)	Physical Logical
P46.I2	Tpid	1.560R	device_bus2(0)
IPAD_device_bus2(0)			ix57
CLB_R24C1.G2 device_bus2(0)_int	net (fanout=3)	2.016R	
CLB_R24C1.Y device_bus1_dup0(3)	Tilo	1.590R	ix66
P44.O device_bus1_dup0(2)	net (fanout=1)	2.441R	
P44.PAD	Topf	4.040R	device_bus1(2) ix50
OPAD_device_bus1(2)			
Total (7.190ns logic, 4.457ns route) (61.7% logic, 38.3% route)		11.647ns	

Listing 6-16 Example, Xilinx Timing Report

List 6-16 shows a generic timing report for the worst path (critical path) in the hier688 design. The maximum delay for this path is 11.647 nsec. Note the division of time between logic and routes listed at the bottom. As the design gets denser, the routing will be a higher percentage of the delay.

Floor Planner

Floor planning is a procedure where the arrangement and location of logic inside the FPGA is manipulated and optimized. Figure 6-12 illustrates a typical device floorplan. Some aspects of the design are obvious to the designer and may or may not be recognized by the automated place-and-route tools. Which parts of the design are critical and should be located adjacent to other logic elements? Can things be switched around to get a more faster and more efficient design? Humans are better at these types of tasks than computers.

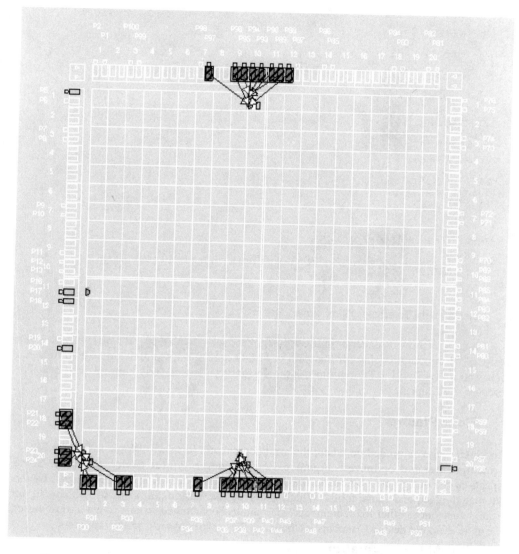

Figure 6-12 Xilinx Design Manager Floor Planner Tool

Figure 6-13 shows a zoom view of the hier688 logic, the pin assignments, the CLBs, and a rats-nest view of the signal routing.

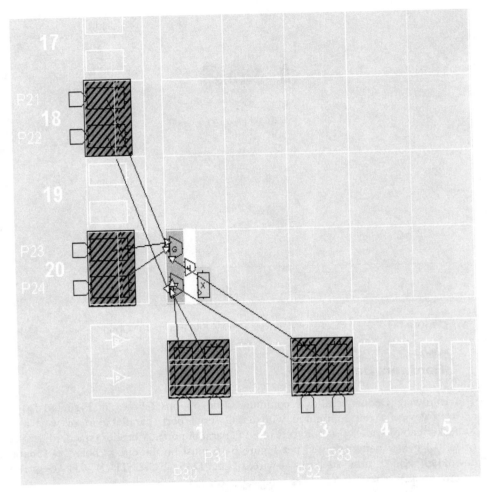

Figure 6-13 Xilinx Design Manager Floor Planner Tool, hier688 Design Zoom View

PROM File Formatter

Xilinx supports serial and parallel configuration PROM versions. A file can also be created and linked into a microcontroller PROM. Large devices may require multiple PROMs. The PROM File Formatter allows the design to be split into multiple configuration devices as shown in Figure 6-14.

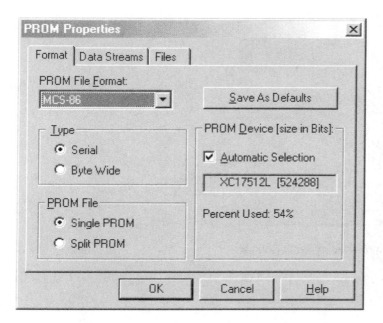

Figure 6-14 Xilinx Design Manager PROM File Formatter Options

Hardware Debugger

The Hardware Debugger allows communication options (shown in Figure 6-15) which allow a device to be configured with a PC serial port, parallel port or with a Xilinx Xchecker cable (which also connects to a PC parallel port). A header (standard 0.25 square posts, 0.1 center pattern) wired per Figure 6-16 must on the circuit board to support this download. Xilinx also supports 4-wire (TDI, TMS, TCK, TDO) JTAG serial-port programming.

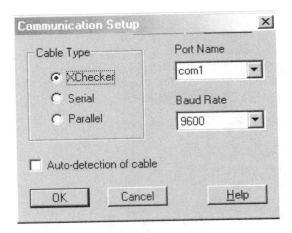

Figure 6-15 Communication Setup Options

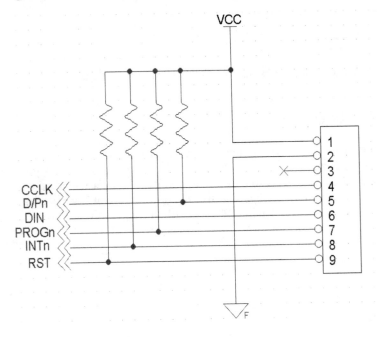

Figure 6-16 Xilinx Xchecker Cable Header Wiring

EPIC Design Editor

This tool provides a graphical representation of the design as if you were looking down at the physical device itself (see Figure 6-17). Pins, pin buffers and registers, global signals, signal routing, and CLBs are all visible. Some routing can be done at this level. For example, it is possible to hook up test-points without resynthesizing and recompiling.

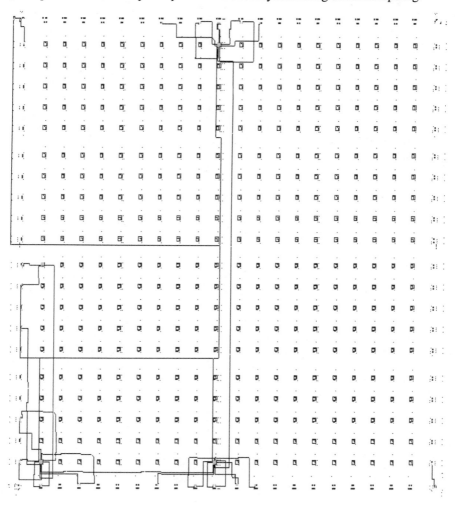

Figure 6-17 EPIC Representation of the hier688 Design

A Look at Competing Architectures

I used to think of FPGA vendors as all-knowing and mysterious entities, magically creating products which sell in copious quantities. The reality is that these companies are in business and are made up of people, good and bad, just like you and me. The FPGA manufacturers, which include Xilinx, Altera, Lucent, Actel, Lattice/Vantis, Quicklogic, Atmel, and others buy their packages from the same sources and pay nearly the same prices for them. Most (Lucent and Atmel are exceptions) contract their manufacturing to foundries that all have similar business models.

FACTORS THAT DETERMINE INTEGRATED CIRCUIT PRICING

- The package. A high proportion of the cost of an integrated circuit is in the packaging (just like the cost of potato chips).

- The silicon. This includes the "square footage" and the complexity in number of layers and lithography. This is similar to a warehouse, where the price is correlated to how big it is and how many floors it has. Other factors can contribute, like whether the IC fab process is "mainstream" or not. Some programmable devices use EEPROM technology or specialized materials, such as the tungsten plugs that Actel uses for layer interconnect vias.

- The volume, or the economy of scale. If you want a cheap IC, you have to either buy a lot of them or leverage mass quantities consumed by industry (in other words, if you want a cheap device, buy an IC that many other companies are buying). To turn this around, in order for a foundry to sell an IC cheaply, it must produce a lot of them; it doesn't much matter if one customer or many customers buy the product. FPGAs are flexible and are used by many designers in many industries. ASICs are specific and targeted toward specific customers (though these foundry customers may resell the device to a wide market; from Intel's point of view, the microprocessor is a type of an ASIC, for example).

These factors hold up only when a competitive situation exists. Where sources are limited by specialized processes, proprietary technology, and small markets, the economic situation is different and prices go up.

The FPGA market is dynamic and exciting but is also a bewildering mess of TLAs (Three Letter Acronyms) and hyperbole. Each FPGA vendor has a design strategy to solve a problem for the users of its products. The vendors have individual niches, strategies, and technologies. The main idea to keep in mind is that no ultimate design approach is ideal for each design target; each FPGA design has strengths and weaknesses. A Xilinx FPGA may be the best solution for one design problem (like random arrays of mixed functions); an Altera CPLD may be the best design solution for the next design (like datapath functions including digital filters); an Actel device might be the best for designs that require ASIClike performance.

FPGA DEVICE DESIGN

Other factors influence the design of an FPGA device, including the patent minefield. It can be quite galling to use a patented architecture and make your competitor rich with royalties. Can you design around a patent? Can you devise another way of solving a problem? Is it better to just license the patent? What features does your target market need? Are there gaps in a competitor's product line?

Figure 7-1   A Day in the Life of an FPGA Silicon Designer

The Verilog FPGA designer must be very aware of the target FPGA architecture. Keep in mind that your design will be implemented in look-up tables with significant routing propagation delays. Verilog can be a portable language, but the highest-performance designs are tailored for the target FPGA. How granular are the FPGA design elements? A Xilinx 4000XL FPGA can be thought of as an array of four input LUTs, any of which can be a 16-by-1 RAM. An Altera Flex 8K device is an array of Logic Array Blocks (LABs) which have four-input LUTs in groups of eight with dedicated RAM blocks spread around the die. How rich is the routing resource? Let's say you notice that the die inside an FPGA that Altera rates at 20,000 gates is about two-thirds the size of a similarly rated Xilinx device. Does this mean Altera more cleverly packs LUTs on a die, or that Xilinx believes much more routing resource is necessary to adequately support the use of the CLBs? Are internal tristate signals supported? How many global low-skew clock networks are available? Leaving vested interests and emotion aside, which architecture is better? Is it better use of silicon to provide more gates or more routing? There are no universal answers to these questions.

FPGA TECHNOLOGY SELECTION CHECKLIST

Just about any FPGA can serve about any job, given that the device has enough pins and gates. Often a device is selected for nonscientific reasons, such as what devices are in the company stockroom or which device the designer feels a need to put on her resume. This list will allow an objective comparison of FPGA technologies. We're not going to ask about gate count: each vendor counts gates in a different manner, so this number is nearly useless. These questions are more important than the device overview, because the technology is constantly changing.

- How many logic blocks and flipflops does the device contain?

- How much RAM does the device have (if any)? Dual port or single port? Distributed or in blocks? How big are the blocks? In what organization can they be used (X1, X2, X4, X8, X16, X32, etc.)?

- How many usable I/O pins does the device have?

Keep in mind that each device has power/ground and other dedicated pins that are not available for use as signals by the Verilog designer.

- How many low-skew global clock/reset/preset networks are available?

It is possible to route a clock or other global signal through signal routing channels, but the risk of design problems goes up due to clock skew.

- Are internal tristate busses supported?

Tristate busses can speedup a decoder considerably compared to a MUX structure.

- Are denser devices available in the same package and compatible pinout?

If the design grows, will the circuit board need to be redesigned to accommodate a denser device?

- Does the device pinout have to be locked before the FPGA design is complete?

A requirement to finish a PWB design early can favor an FPGA device (which has more capability of routing device pins to random logic elements) over a CPLD device.

- Can the FPGA be reloaded at power-up or must it be available instantly at power-up?

Imagine an FPGA that includes memory decoding for a microprocessor. If the microprocessor initializes the FPGA and the FPGA does not decode memory so that the microprocessor accesses memory properly, this might be a power-up issue. Often you'll see a fast PLD for memory decoding and clock generation along with the FPGA.

- Does the FPGA support in-circuit configuration for field upgrade or board customization?

- Does the FPGA have flipflops available for input pins?

Having flipflops available on the outside of the device near input pins allows fast and predictable latching of input signals.

- Does the FPGA have flipflops available for output pins?

Having flipflops available on the outside of the device near output pins creates fast and predictable clock-to-output times.

- Is a conversion to ASIC required?

If so, an antifuse device, with an ASIClike architecture and speed, should be considered.

- Is a socket required?

For one-time programmable parts, until the design is solid, a socket will be necessary to ease the changing of devices. This is not a trivial matter; fine-pitch packages can be a real challenge to socket.

Two vendors have about 80% of the FPGA market: Xilinx and Altera. Which one is larger is subject to debate at this writing and depends on how the numbers are counted. You can't be an FPGA designer without acknowledging these two companies (you need both on your resume to be most marketable). Other companies have great products and software! None yet comes close to achieving Altera and Xilinx's market share, and I think none ever will. Check the resources section at the end of this book for device-manufacturer website addresses and visit those sites for the latest data.

XILINX FPGA ARCHITECTURES

Configurable Logic Block

XC3000/XC3100 Series FPGAs

This is an older SRAM-based architecture. The CLBs have five logic inputs, two flipflops, a common clock, direct reset, and a clock enable. It's interesting to look at the clock-enable implementation (see Figure 7-3). A clock-enable MUX selects between the output of the look-up table and the latch. In the clock disabled mode, the output of the latch is fed back to the input.

As shown in Figure 7-2, XC3000 IOBs have input and output flipflops, programmable tristate, and pull-up resistor output control. This architecture does not have more modern features like SRAM and fast carry in/out.

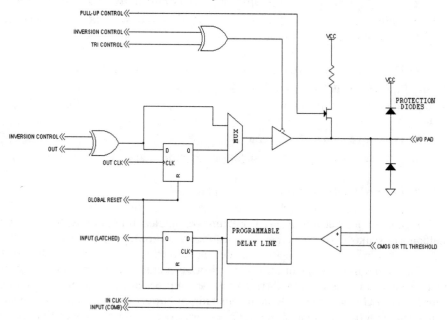

Figure 7-2   Xilinx 3K Family I/O Architecture

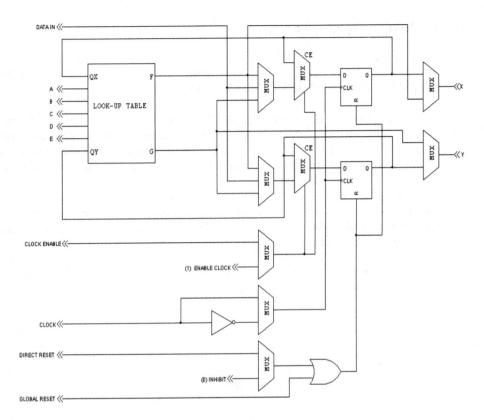

Figure 7-3 Xilinx 3K Family CLB Architecture

Signal routing on the FPGA is performed by pass transistors called Programmable Interconnect Points (PIPs). The pass transistors are controlled by RAM-based configuration bits. The routing between CLBs includes nondirectional connections, drivers between horizontal and vertical long lines, drivers between vertical and horizontal long lines, and other specialized types. Long lines bypass the PIPs and carry signals that travel long distances across the die. The 3K family includes a buffer which can be used to support an oscillator circuit (using a crystal, RC network, or resonator to set the operating frequency).

The Xilinx 3K family is an SRAM-based architecture. After power-up, device configuration is loaded into the device via serial EPROM, serial download cable, via parallel load from a microprocessor (slave mode) or byte or word-wide EPROM, or other means. When the power is removed from an SRAM-based device, the configuration is lost. On power-up, the Xilinx device automatically loads configuration data in the manner defined by programming mode pins.

XC4000 Series FPGAs

The Xilinx 4K family, compared to the 3K family, has greater densities, improved speed, and other added features. In particular, the addition of distributed RAM (the ability to configure a CLB as a 16-by-1 RAM cell) in the 4000E and 4000X families is a great feature for the designer.

The Xilinx CLB, as illustrated in Figure 7-4, contains two four-input LUTs, two D-type flipflops with dedicated clock enable, set or reset, a clock with configurable polarity, and fast carry-in and carry-out signal paths. Each CLB in a 4000E/XL device can be used as two 16X1 single-port RAMs, a single 16X1 dual-port RAM, or as a single-port 32X1 RAM. The dual-port RAM configuration is synchronous; the other modes can be non-synchronous (level-sensitive).

Other blocks provided by Xilinx include Input/Output blocks (IOBs) which include I/O registers and configurable terminations (pull-up or pull-down) and pin buffers (fast or slow). The 4000 family includes wide decoder blocks which are useful for fast decoders for up to nine inputs. The 4000 family includes an on-chip oscillator and dedicated low-skew networks that can be used for clocks and other fast global signals. The 4000 family supports internal tristate signals and busses.

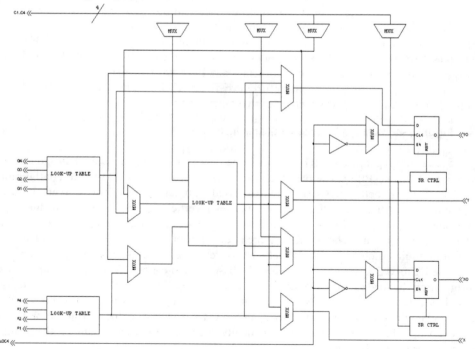

Figure 7-4   Xilinx 4K Family CLB Architecture

HardWire Devices

Xilinx offers a hardwired version of its FPGAs, which can save some cost for applications where the volume does not justify a conversion to a full custom ASIC. In this technology, Xilinx uses the same CLB architecture but replaces the SRAM routing and switching arrays with metal layers. The result is less silicon (smaller die) and equal-to or better-than timing compared to the FPGA. An advantage to conversion to HardWire is the low stress on the FPGA designer; Xilinx guarantees that the timing and function of the custom device will match the FPGA device. Conversion to a HardWire device is a test-vectorless process; Xilinx develops automated test coverage and guarantees the device will work in your application. This does not let the designer off the hook for doing a synchronous design and doing thorough testing. For example, all asynchronous logic needs to be reviewed for race conditions, because the HardWire device will most likely be faster than the FPGA design.

Virtex Series FPGAs

The latest devices from Xilinx are built with 0.22-micron lithography (with a roadmap to 0.18 micron) and five-layer metal technology. The million-gate device has 75,000,000 transistors. Interesting new features, as shown in Figure 7-5 and Figure 7-6, include mixed-voltage I/O (including low-voltage differential inputs to support busses like GTL), dedicated 4096-bit dual-port SRAM blocks, distributed RAM cells, multiple DLLs (Delay-Locked Loops) to provide controlled-delay clock networks, and vector-based routing (allowing flexible routing up/down/ left/right between CLBs). These are 2.5-volt devices, but the I/Os are tolerant of higher interface voltages.

Xilinx advertises that its million-gate device has 27,648 logic cells, 131,072 block RAM bits, and 660 user I/O pins. Consider that an 8031 microcontroller core is less than 600 gates (less than 100 CLBs), contains 256 bits of RAM, and has 32 user I/O pins. Welcome to the new millennium.

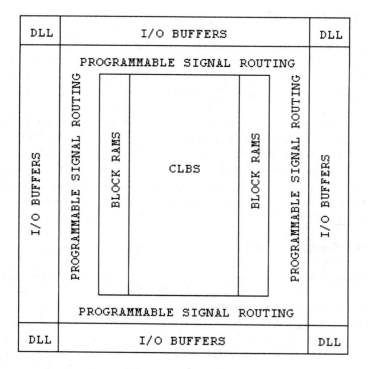

Figure 7-5   Xilinx Virtex Family Architecture

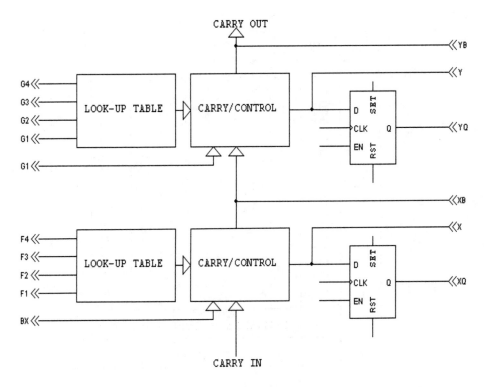

Figure 7-6 Xilinx Virtex Family CLB Architecture (one of two slices per cell shown)

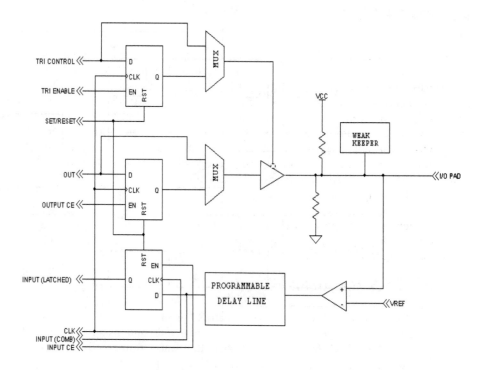

Figure 7-7   Xilinx Virtex Family Input/Output Block

Virtex I/O blocks, as shown in Figure 7-7, include programmable pull-up and pull-down resistors, a weak keeper circuit (this holds a signal value when a driver is removed), tristate control, I/O latches, and inputs with programmable delay (for shifting an input signal with respect to the clock edge).

Configuration Devices

During development, a download cable connected to a PC is the most convenient method for configuring an FPGA. Once the design is complete, a serial configuration device (serial PROM) can be used. One-Time Programmable (OTP) devices (from Altera, Xilinx, and Lucent) and reprogrammable versions (from Atmel) are available. To save the cost of the serial device, the parallel download mode from a microprocessor can be performed. This means the processor must be initialized and running before the FPGA can be configured. Also, Xilinx devices can be programmed via a JTAG serial port.

ALTERA CPLD ARCHITECTURES

Altera uses the phrase Complex Programmable Logic Devices (CPLD) to describe their design approach. Altera uses less routing resource than Xilinx. Their LABs (Logic Array Blocks) are more complex than Xilinx's CLBs and fewer of them are available on an Altera die. Is this approach better than Xilinx's? It depends on what you're trying to do. One thing in Altera's favor is that its place-and-route software has a much easier job than Xilinx's Design Manager because there is much less routing resource. This means the Altera software is fast and very deterministic; the same design, compiled with the same compilation settings, gives the same result every time. On one of the Usenet groups a designer said, "I love Altera's software and I love Xilinx's silicon." There is a lot of wisdom in that simple statement.

Because of the limited routing, it can be more difficult to route a design. The designer must not lock down the pins too early in the design cycle. As the design grows, it may not be possible to "reach" all the pins that were previously assigned. This is much less of an issue with Xilinx/Lucent/Actel architectures.

Altera FLEX8K Architecture

The FLEX8K (Flexible Logic Element matriX) is a SRAM-based, coarsely grained architecture (based on large blocks of logic elements) and contains an array of Logic Array Blocks (LABs). Each LAB has eight LEs (Logic Elements), four control input signals (used as clock, set/reset, carry in, and cascade in), 24 global logic inputs, eight local feedback inputs, and eight outputs. Compared to Xilinx, there is much less interconnect between LABs. For example, the LAB fast carry and cascade outputs are connected only to the LAB on the right, and the fast carry and cascade inputs come only from the LAB on the left. The FLEX8000 family does not support internal tristate busses (the compiler automatically replaces internal tristates with MUXs). Each LE has a four-input LUT and a flipflop.

In Figure 7-8, the IOE's are Input/Output Elements (pin buffers and registers). The structure of the IOEs are shown in Figure 7-9.

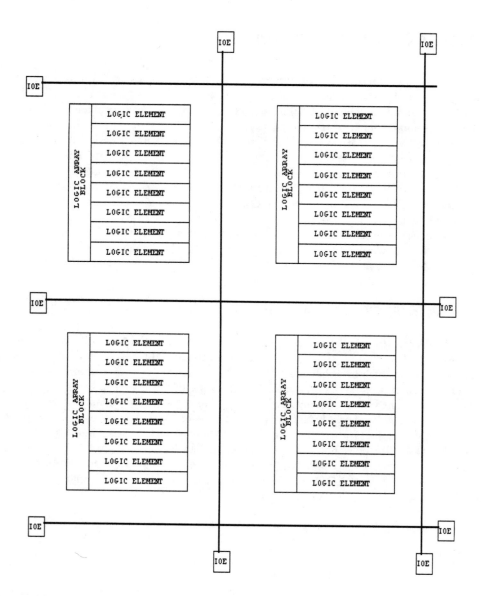

Figure 7-8   FLEX8000 Logic Structure

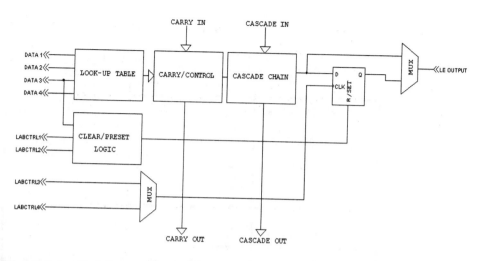

Figure 7-9   FLEX8000 Logic Element

Configuration modes include JTAG, JAM (a serial configuration standard that Altera is promoting), active/passive serial modes, active/passive parallel synchronous modes, and asynchronous modes.

Altera FLEX10K Architecture

Altera upgraded the FLEX8K family to create the FLEX10K family. FLEX10K includes embedded 2048-bit dual-port RAM blocks (Embedded Array Blocks or EABs) which are spread around the die. The 2048-bit EABs can be used as 2048-by-1, 1024-by-2, 512-by-4, or 256-by-8 arrays. They can also be combined with other EABs to create larger or deeper memory elements. The EABs can also be used for logic functions where they act as large LUTs. The EABs include input and output registers.

FLEX10K LEs are similar to the FLEX8K with the addition of an output connected to their fast routing channel (called FastTrack). In addition, a clock enable is added to the LE flipflop.

Altera APEX 20K Architecture

Building on the structure of the 8K/10K architectures, Altera has designed the APEX 20K family with a logic structure as shown in Figure 7-10. This family has much denser devices and advanced features like Clock PLL (for clock lock, multiplication and phase shift), a mix of logic structures (including RAM and wide PLD-type logic for decoders), a variety of input/output modes (to interface with single-ended and differential busses like Low Voltage Differential, Stub-Series Terminated, and Gunning Transceiver Logic). The number of Logic Elements in a LAB is expanded from 8 in the FLEX 8K/10K families to 10. The

Logic Elements are similar to the FLEX10K with added synchronous Load and Clear logic and more clock options.

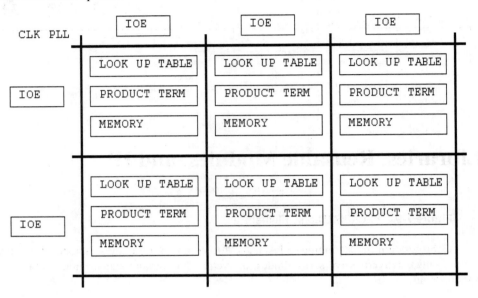

Figure 7-10 APEX 20K Logic Structure

Libraries, Reusable Modules, and IP

*I*ncreasing electronic design density is a trend that has continued over the last 40 years. The consumer's hunger for increasingly sophisticated gadgets, whether GPS, cellular telephones, games, home automation, networking, Internet commerce, audio/video entertainment, or computing, seems endless. We get more free time each year, and we are filling this time by playing with our electronic toys, all of which continue to get smaller, use less power, and grow more complicated. While the demand grows, the ability for industry to provide transistors and gates also seems endless. For the FPGA designer, this means designs will contain more gates.

Suppose an Engineer can design at a rate of 100 or so gates a day. Let's call this about 10 lines of Verilog code (this includes the overhead of test and documentation). Soon, the average FPGA design will be 200,000 gates. This means, unless the design methodology changes, that a two-person team will take 1,000 days to complete a design, almost three years! Each year the design task gets more complex, but the schedule remains about the same. The company expects an average project to be complete in a year and a complex project to be complete in a year and a half. Clearly, something has to give. There are several options.

KEYS TO INCREASED PRODUCTIVITY

- **The size of the design team must increase.**

The most productive team is composed of one to three expert designers. If the company can afford to wait for the product, this will be the cheapest way to get it. However, most companies (in spite of what they say) are not interested in efficiency and productivity. Instead, they are interested in getting the product on the market as soon as possible. So, large teams are created upon the theory that if one woman can bear a child in nine months, then they'll just have to get nine women to finish this job in one month.

The problem with large teams is that the complexity of the communication between team members increases exponentially as the number of team members increases linearly. If there are two team members, Jack and Jill, then Jack and Jill have to coordinate their work and there are two communication channels (Jack to Jill and Jill to Jack). If there are three team members, then Jack has to coordinate with Jill and Jerry, and Jill has to coordinate with Jack and Jerry, and so on, you get the idea. As confusing as this silly example is, real-life communication on a design team is worse.

It takes extraordinary effort to keep the team jelled and working in the same direction. Eventually, the design work of each team member must work with the design work of the other team members. This will not happen by accident. There will be more meetings (which reduces productivity), activity reports (which reduces productivity), more specifications to assure that design elements work together (which reduces productivity), and more chances of team conflict (which definitely reduces productivity).

Managing large teams is an art more than a science. Though the number of gates in a typical design is increasing exponentially, the ability for people to work together is not increasing much, if at all.

COFFMAN'S LAW

The average measure of intelligence of a room is inversely proportional to the number of people in the room.

All is not lost; there is an alternative to creating large design teams.

- **The individual designer must produce more code.**

In the hardware design world, an electrical designer of the 40s designed with a handful of vacuum tubes. In the 50s, the tubes were replaced with transistors. In the 60s, the transistors were replaced with integrated circuits (100s of transistors). Today, ICs with millions of transistors are common. So, we hardware designers became comfortable with creating designs by mixing and matching circuit elements we didn't design. There are two ways this can happen.

Each line of code can represent larger amounts of circuitry

As synthesis tools get smarter and FPGA designs get denser (so the number of gates required to implement a design becomes less important and we can afford to waste gates in order to produce a design more quickly), higher-level constructs become feasible. One day, we will implement a 1024-bit adder that runs at 100 MHz by writing a line of code like:

```
a    =    b + c;
```

Instead of handcrafting a look-ahead carry adder, the synthesis tool will infer an efficient adder based on your design constraints.

Designs will be reused

Modules will be included in your code from previous designs (the most common reuse method) or will be purchased or licensed from someone else. A lot of energy in our industry is focused on selling Intellectual Property (IP) designs to ASIC designers, and vendors would love to supply IP to the FPGA market, too. Frankly, the heavy-breathers in the ASIC and Design Automation areas think they will make large amounts of money selling designs to companies trying to reduce their product's time-to-market.

If only there were a tried-and-true market model for using IP! Well, there is, and it's related to the use of integrated circuits. This model has been used successfully for over 30 years, so it must work well. From a designer's point of view, specifications, pricing, and delivery of various IP offerings are evaluated and the right product is selected for the design at hand. The financial model for the device manufacturer is interesting to consider. The device is designed at great expense and placed on the market. The up-front cost to produce this design (which can be millions of dollars) is paid back slowly over time as the devices are purchased by electronics manufacturers. This strategy can be quite profitable if the design becomes popular, but it takes deep pockets to play this game. Can IP vendors play this way?

The IP provider must provide complete data which characterizes performance including throughput, latency, signal I/O requirements, module size, and power consumption. This assures that the design is appropriate to the application and allows comparison to other products. The successful IP offering will be a stand-alone module that performs specific functions that designers are comfortable with, like FIFOs and other types of memory-based modules, microcontrollers, filters, compression/decompression functions, and communication ports (UARTs, Ethernet, USB, etc.). For even wilder speculation about the type of IP that might be feasible, see the Afterword: A Look into the Future, Millions and Millions and Millions of Gates.

Before we get too excited about off-the-shelf IP, lets take a look at the simplest method of increasing design productivity, the use of built-in library elements.

LIBRARY ELEMENTS

Each FPGA vendor supplies a set of primitive library elements. The Verilog design is mapped to the hardware using primitives similar to these. The primitives are implemented in an efficient manner by the underlying hardware. They get more capable every year as the FPGA vendor adds elements to, and increases the utility of, the libraries. The FPGA vendor has a vested interest in providing design aids and shortcuts that increase the efficiency and ease of use of their products.

The expert designer keeps in mind various levels of abstraction for a design, including the types of library elements that will be used to implement the design. The following is an example of what sort of elements we might see in a vendor's primitive library:

1. AND   AND Gates
2. BPAD   Bidirectional Pad
3. CKBUF   Clock Buffer
4. FF   D Flipflop with Async Set, Reset, and Clock Enable
5. INV   Inverter
6. IPAD   Input pad
7. KEEPER   Weak State Keeper (holds last value if driver is removed)
8. LATCH   D Latch with Asynchronous Set and Reset
9. LATCHE   D Latch with Asynchronous Set, Reset, and Gate Enable
10. LUT   Look-up Table
11. MUX   Multiplexer
12. ONE   Logic "1" Generator
13. OPAD   Output Pad
14. OR   OR Gates
15. PD   Pull-down Resistor
16. PU   Pull-up Resistor
17. RAM   Read/Write Memory (can be used as Read-only)
18. SFF   D Flipflop with Asynchronous/Synchronous Set/Reset

19. SRL16E	Shift Register LUT
20. TRI	Tristate Buffer
21. UPAD	Unbonded Pad
22. XOR	Exclusive-OR Gates
23. ZERO	Logic "0" Generator

There will be various flavors of these primitives. For example, the following versions of the AND gate might be available:

1. AND2	2-Input AND with Noninverted Inputs
2. AND3	3-Input AND with Noninverted Inputs
3. AND4	4-Input AND with Noninverted Inputs
4. AND5	5-Input AND with Noninverted Inputs
5. AND6	6-Input AND with Noninverted Inputs
6. AND7	7-Input AND with Noninverted Inputs
7. AND8	8-Input AND with Noninverted Inputs
8. AND16	16-Input AND with Noninverted Inputs
9. AND32	32-Input AND with Noninverted Inputs

The Verilog compiler also uses a set of primitives. We see much similarity with the FPGA vendor primitive library.

1. FALSE
2. TRUE
3. INV
4. BUF
5. AND2
6. OR2
7. XOR2
8. NAND2
9. NOR2
10. MUX
11. DFFRS
12. DFFERS
13. LATRS

14. RSLAT
15. TRI
16. PULLUP
17. PULLDN
18. TRSTMEM
19. DON'T_CARE

The following device-specific library list is from Exemplar and is for the Xilinx 4000XL family. There is a similar library for generic primitives.

1. IBUF   Input Buffer
2. OBUF   Output Buffer
3. OBUF_NG   Inverting Output Buffer
4. OBUFT   Tristate Output Buffer
5. OBUFT_NG   Inverting Tristate Output Buffer
6. OUTFF   Output Flipflop
7. OFDX   Output D Flipflop with Active High OC
8. OFDXI   Output D Flipflop with Active Low OC
9. OFDTX   Output Flipflop with Tristate Output
10. OFDTXI   Tristate Output D Flipflop with Active Low OC
11. OFD   Output D Flipflop
12. OFD_NG   Output D Flipflop with Inverted Output
13. OFDX_NG   Output D Flipflop with Inverted Tristate Output
14. OFDI
15. OFDI_NG
16. OFDXI_NG
17. OFDT
18. OFDT_NG
19. OFDTX_NG
20. OUTFFT
21. OFDTI
22. OFDTI_NG
23. OFDTXI_NG
24. IFD   Input D Flipflop
25. IFDX

26. INFF	Input Flipflop	
27. IFD_NG		
28. IFDX_NG		
29. IFDI		
30. IFDXI		
31. IFDI_NG		
32. IFDXI_NG		
33. INLAT	Input Latch	
34. ILD_1		
35. ILDX_1		
36. ILD_1_NG		
37. ILDX_1_NG		
38. ILD		
39. ILDX		
40. ILDI		
41. ILDXI		
42. ILDI_1		
43. ILDXI_1		
44. ILDI_1_NG		
45. ILDXI_1_NG		
46. INREG	Input Register	
47. DFF	D Flipflop	
48. FDPE		
49. FDCE		
50. FD		
51. FD_GP		
52. FDP		
53. FD_NGP		
54. FD_NG		
55. FDC		
56. FDC_NG		
57. FDCE_NG		
58. FDE		
59. FDE_GP		
60. FDE_NGP		

61. FDE_NG
62. FDP_NG
63. FDPE_NG
64. OUTFFT_IBUF   Output Flipflop with Tristate and Input Buffer
65. OUTFFTX_IBUF
66. OBUFT_INFF_1   Output Tristate Buffer with Input Flipflop
67. OBUFT_INFFX_1
68. OBUFT_INLAT_1   Output Tristate Buffer with Input Latch
69. OUTFFT_INFF_1   Output Tristate Buffer with Input Flipflop
70. OUTFFTX_INFF_1
71. OUTFFT_INFFX_1
72. OUTFFTX_INFFX_1
73. OUTFFT_INLAT_1   Output Tristate Flipflop with Input Latch
74. OUTFFTX_INLAT_1
75. DLAT   D Latch
76. LDCE_1
77. LDPE_1
78. LD
79. LD_NG
80. LD_1
81. LDC
82. LDC_NG
83. LDCE
84. LDPE
85. LDP
86. LDP_NG
87. LD_NGP
88. BUFGLS
89. BUFGE   Global Buffer with Enable
90. BUFFCLK   Clock Buffer
91. BUFGS   Buffer to Global Resource (secondary)
92. BUFGP   Buffer to Global Resource (primary)
93. BUFG   Buffer to Global Network
94. BDBUF   Bidirectional Buffer

STRUCTURAL CODING STYLE

If you follow the digital design newsgroups (see the resources section), you will periodically see the schematic zealots presenting a case that efficient designs can generally be implemented only with schematics. This may be true, so, to the Verilog purist, it may make sense to do a schematic with text by wiring primitives together. Done properly, this will result in very compact and fast logic. However, it can get unwieldy very fast, so we'll want to use this approach only where necessary.

One drawback of a schematic design can't be argued: it's not very portable. Using IP in a design requires some portability if the IP is to be offered for sale to the design world. IP and HDL need each other.

Listing 8-1 is an example of the structural use of a library primitive, Figure 8-1 shows the corresponding synthesized circuit, and Figure 8-2 shows the Xilinx structural resource assignment.

Listing 8-1   Verilog Structural Design with Library Primitive

```verilog
// Structural Instantiation of Library Primitive.
module global_buffer (clock_out, data_out, chipsel, strobe,
data_in);

input      chipsel, strobe, data_in;
output     data_out;
reg        data_out;
wire       clock_in;
output     clock_out;

assign     clock_in = chipsel & strobe;

BUFG buf1 ( .I(clock_in), .O(clock_out) );

endmodule

// Create black box for buffer.
module BUFG (I, O);
input I;
output O;
endmodule
```

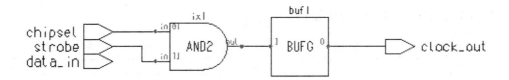

Figure 8-1   BUFG Structural Resource Assignment

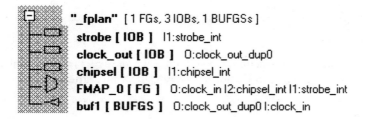

Figure 8-2   BUFG Structural Resource Assignment (information from Xilinx
                 Floorplanning Tool)

Figure 8-2, a list of resources used in the global_buffer design, shows that BUF1 was implemented as a BUFGS (the only type of global buffer available in the Xilinx 4000XL family).

A SMALL DIVERSION TO COMPARE A SCHEMATIC TO A VERILOG DESIGN

Figure 8-3 shows a schematic for a simple RAM implementation. It is interesting to compare this schematic with the Verilog structural version of this design as shown in Listing 8-2. More information on the LogiBLOX tool is presented in the next section.

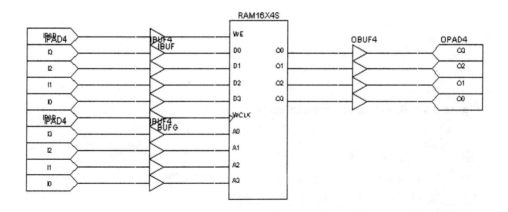

Figure 8-3   Schematic Using Library Primitives

Listing 8-2   Verilog Structural Schematic Example

```
// Structural Schematic Design Example.
module schematic(out_data, in_data, in_addr, clock, write_enable);
input      [3:0]   in_data, in_addr;
input              clock, write_enable;
output     [3:0]   out_data;
// Define the interface to the black box ram_module.
// This empty box will be filled with a predefined netlist
representing
//   a RAM block created by the Xilinx LogiBLOX tool.
//-------------------------------------------------------
// LogiBLOX SYNC_RAM Module "ram_module"
// Created by LogiBLOX version M1.5.19
//    on Mon Dec 28 17:21:11 1998
// Attributes
//    MODTYPE = SYNC_RAM
//    BUS_WIDTH = 4
//    DEPTH = 16
//    STYLE = MAX_SPEED
//    USE_RPM = FALSE
//-------------------------------------------------------
ram_module u1 ( .A(in_addr), .DO(out_data), .DI(in_data),
.WR_EN(write_enable),   .WR_CLK(clock) );
endmodule

module ram_module(A, DO, DI, WR_EN, WR_CLK);
input [3:0] A;
```

```
output [3:0] DO;
input [3:0] DI;
input WR_EN, WR_CLK;
endmodule
```

Figure 8-4 shows the LogiBLOX main menu.

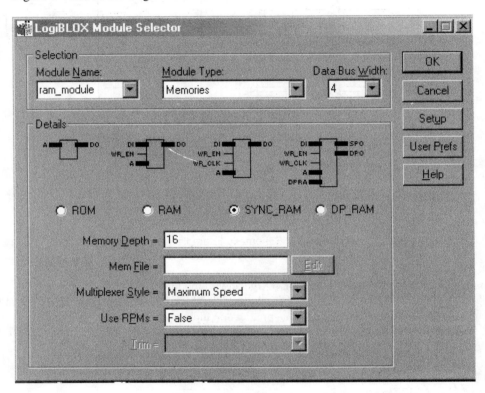

Figure 8-4   Creating a RAM Module with LogiBLOX

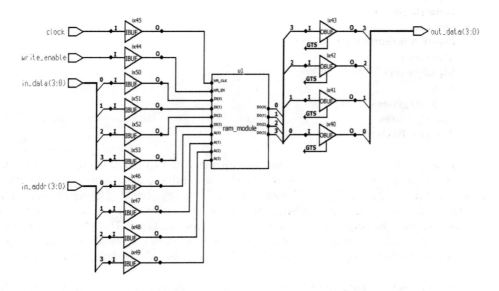

Figure 8-5 Structural Schematic using LogiBLOX RAM Module

Figure 8-5 shows the use of a LogiBLOX-generated module.

Which is better, the HDL or the schematic? Which is faster to create, more portable, and easier to understand? Which is prettier? Which is more portable? Notice that the compiler inferred buffers as required to implement the design. These buffers must be instantiated by the designer in the schematic.

USING LOGIBLOX MODULE GENERATOR

How was the RAM module an example of increasing design speed? We didn't invent a RAM module from scratch; we used a design tool to help create it. In this case, we used the Xilinx LogiBLOX tool to create it. Other modules can be created and parameterized, these include:

Accumulators
Adders/Subtractors
Clock Dividers
Comparators

> **Constants**
> **Counters**
> **Data Registers**
> **Decoders**
> **Inputs/Outputs**
> **Memories**
> **Multiplexers**
> **Pads**
> **Shift Registers**
> **Simple Gates**
> **Tristate Buffers**

Employing these types of schematiclike elements in a structural design can allow the HDL designer to use hardware-specific hardware configurations options. For example, under the Tristate Buffer block definition, there are three options for pull-up resistor: none, pull-up, and double pull-up. Options like double pull-up are not directly supported by Verilog but may be required for some design implementations. The use of a structural design, where HDL is employed in a structural (schematic) fashion, or where Verilog modules are stitched together with schematics, may be required in some cases. Use whatever works!

So, one way to increase the number of gates we design in a day is to use a tool that automates the creation of certain types of modules.

Another Module Generator, the CORE Generator Tool

Xilinx (with the MEMEC company) provides a core generator with a wider variety of more complex modules compared to LogiBLOX. Examples of the functions include:

- FPGA Development Tools (DSP and FPGA development platforms for evaluation and benchmarking of DSP and FPGA designs).
- Processor peripherals including C2910A Bit Slice Processor core, DRAM controller, M8237 DMA Controller, M8254 Programmable Timer, M8255 Programmable Peripheral Interface, M8259 Programmable Interrupt Controller, XF8256 Multifunction Microprocessor Support Controller, and XF8279 Programmable Keyboard Display Interface.
- Processor products including Intellicore™ Prototyping System, RISC CPU Core Demo, Scalable Development Platform, TX400 Series RISC CPU cores, and V8 uRISC Microprocessor.
- UARTS, including M16450, M16550A, and XF8250.
- Communication and Networking Cores, including ATM Cell Assembler, ATM Cell Delineation, ATM CRC10 Generator and Verifier, ATM CRC32 Generator and

Verifier, ATM Utopia Slave (CC-141), Forward Error Correction Reed-Solomon Decoder/Encoder and Viterbi Decoder, Telecommunications HDLC Protocol Core, and Telecommunications MT1FT1 Framer.

- XF9128 Video Terminal Logic Controller.

- Standard Bus Interface Cores, including IEEE 1394 Firewire Link Layer Core, Firewire SuperLINK core evaluation board, 2 Wire Serial Interface, PCMCIA cores, USB cores.

- And others.

These cores are a mix of Xilinx-supplied modules (which are available for free) and third-party-supplied modules (which must be licensed). An example of the use of these cores is a design called sincos8 based on the 8X8 Sin/Cos LUT core model. The CORE Generator tool created a file called sincos8.vei, a Verilog interface file. This file defines the ports used by the core and provides an example of the module instantiation for use by the designer. The sincos8.vei file looks like Listing 8-3.

Listing 8-3   sincos8.vei File

```
module sincos8 (
    ctrl,
    theta,
    c,
    dout);

input ctrl;
input [7:0] theta;
input c;
output [7:0] dout;
endmodule

// The following is an example of an instantiation:

sincos8 YourInstanceName (
    .ctrl(ctrl),
    .theta(theta),
    .c(c),
    .dout(dout));
```

The CORE Generator file also created a Verilog simulation file called sincos8.v. This file is 5,287 lines of code. Assuming we could write 100 lines of debugged code a day, we could write this module in a couple of months. It took the CORE Generator about five seconds. Assuming the module meets the needs of the design, that's not a bad leverage of productivity. If it doesn't work, we don't have any source code, so the core doesn't help. The file we link into our design is the compiled EDIF netlist called sincos8.edf. Out of curiosity, let's implement this design in a 4000XL device and see what it looks like. There are always some tricks to making the tools work; in this case, we need the bus delimiter to be parentheses B() (use B<> as delimiters for the XNF netlist format) in order for the Xilinx Design Manager to suck in the EDIF file properly. This is done by unchecking the Verilog Instantiation Template and Verilog Behavioral Simulation Model boxes (even though we want these files to be generated) in order to get the Netlist Bus Format we want as shown in Figure 3-6. In addition, in the Exemplar Leonardo EDIF output tab, we want to deselect the Allow Writing Busses checkbox, because Xilinx does not process EDIF busses properly.

Note that the Verilog compiler doesn't "know" anything about the black box (which is inserted during the downstream mapping process, as illustrated in Figure 8-6). Any estimate by the synthesis tool regarding speed and design size will not include the black-box modules.

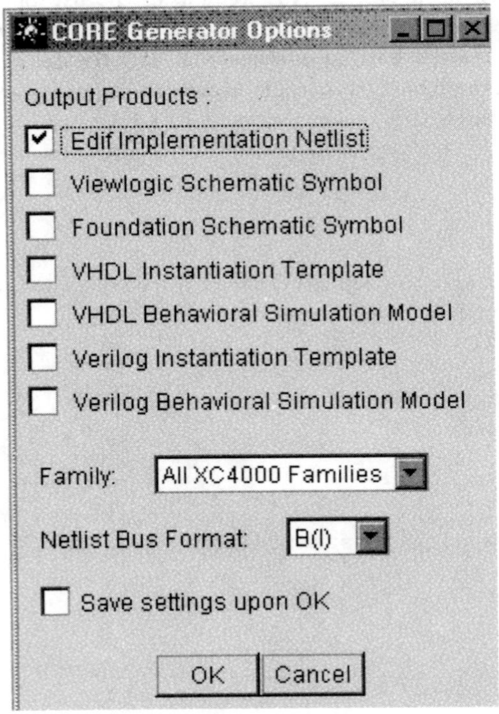

Figure 8-6   CORE Generator Options for Netlist Bus Format

Without really trying, this design runs at 61 MHz in the slowest 4005XL (-3) device. Listing 8-4 is a report on the resources used by this design.

Listing 8-4   sincos8 Design Example Resource Utilization

```
Loading device database for application par from file "map.ncd".
sincos8_example is NCD, device xc4005xl, package pc84, speed -3
Loading device from file '4005xl.nph' in environment C:/Xilinx.
Device speed data version:  xl_0.37 1.22 FINAL.

Device utilization summary:

      Number of External IOBs      18 out of 61          29%
         Flops:      0
         Latches:    0

      Number of CLBs:              25 out of 196 12%
         Total Latches:            0 out of 392          0%
         Total CLB Flops:          25 out of 392  6%
         4 input LUTs:             43 out of 392         10%
         3 input LUTs:             4 out of 196          2%

      Number of TBUFs:             28 out of 448          6%
```

Another example is an eight-wide and 16-deep FIFO called fifo8x16. The Verilog simulation file is 293 lines of code. Listing 8-5 shows the interface file.

Listing 8-5   fifo8x16.vei File

```verilog
module fifo8x16 (
    d,
    we,
    re,
    reset,
    c,
    full,
    empty,
    bufctr_ce,
    bufctr_updn,
    q);

input [7:0] d;
input  we, re, reset, c;
output full;
output empty;
output bufctr_ce;
output bufctr_updn;
output [7:0] q;
endmodule

// The following is an example of an instantiation:
```

```
fifo8x16 YourInstanceName (
    .d(d),
    .we(we),
    .re(re),
    .reset(reset),
    .c(c),
    .full(full),
    .empty(empty),
    .bufctr_ce(bufctr_ce),
    .bufctr_updn(bufctr_updn),
    .q(q));
```

We can see that using a CORE generator is an effective way to create complex modules and increase design efficiency. This is a hit-or-miss process, because, if a module does not meet the needs of the design after trying all available compiler options, without source code there is no way to make modifications, so another approach will be required (like taking the time to design an optimized module from scratch).

DESIGN REUSE, REUSING YOUR OWN CODE

As you get some designs under your belt, you will find that you'll reuse some of your design approaches and even certain modules. If you designed it, then you certainly understand its features and limitations and can make an almost instinctive judgment whether to reuse something or write it from scratch. What can you do to help make a design suitable for later use in other designs?

Designing Your Code for Reuse

- **Document your work.**

    Use a header that describes the design from a toplevel. The header should describe input and output requirements and any tricks or quirks that are embedded in the design. Put in lots of comments, not just describing each line of code, but explaining the overall intent and strategy for problem solving.

- **Use a version-control database product like SourceSafe or VCS.**

    Having a good database of old designs and following the discipline of using detailed comments for revisions can enhance the reusability of Verilog code. These products allow revisions to be "undone" and assure that a working version can be recovered. This feature alone can help you maintain your sanity when crunch time comes. These tools are even more critical when working with other designers.

- **Partition logic into small modules.**

Smaller modules, with dedicated specific functions, are more likely to be reusable than large, complex, and specialized modules.

- **Use synchronous design techniques.**

A synchronous design is more reliable and portable. For modules that must be asynchronous, put them in separate and well-documented modules; don't mix them in with the synchronous areas of your code.

- **Take a typing class.**

You should either be infinitely patient or a good typist to create long and descriptive labels. If you're a slow typist, you'll never use easy-to-read and informative labels like video_output_enable_active_low. Your code will benefit from liberal use of real English. Try to use fewer acronyms and abbreviations.

- **Don't do odd things with the clock.**

For example, try not to use gated clocks or both edges of a clock.

- **Don't use magic numbers.**

Magic numbers are constants embedded in the code as so:

```
(test_pattern == 4'he; // Example of magic number (4'he).)
```

and they should generally be parameters so they can be changed at a top level or in an include file.

- **Minimize Ports.**

Module partitions should be selected to minimize interconnects between modules, particularly where clock domains are crossed. Like an orange, designs have natural boundaries for isolation and cohesion. Use these natural boundaries to partition the design. Split up complex modules into smaller and simpler parts.

- **Don't fix something unless it's really broken.**

If you see something in a working module that you don't like, leave it alone. The possibility of inadvertently breaking something is so great that you must be absolutely sure there really is a problem before changing anything. Pretty code is not necessarily better code.

- **Get some help with sticky problems.**

If you have a problem and you're not sure what to do, or you're trying to select between competing options, talk to your peers about it. Get input from the newsgroups, Field Applications Engineers, or your neighbors—anywhere you can find it. Even if your cohorts have bad ideas, they may lead you to think about the problem in a different manner and may inspire a better approach. If you really can't find help among your coworkers, then find a better bunch of people to work with.

- **Archive Everything.**

   Keep scripts, make files, design notes, libraries, old versions, and all software used to compile and implement a design.

BUYING IP DESIGNS

What does an IP block look like? From a user's perspective, the interface must be defined, including clock signals [polarity (uses of rising or falling edges or both), maximum and minimum frequencies, duty cycle, and loading], reset/preset signals (polarity, synchronous or asynchronous, required duration, and loading), and requirements for other ports.

   The biggest issues with purchasing IP for an FPGA (I call this Revenue IP, some call it Silicon IP) are not technical but are related to negotiating a license. How much should the up-front payment be? How much for recurring payments (royalties)? What is the cost model for unexpected usage when product volumes are higher or lower than expected? How can usage be audited? How can the IP provider protect its investment and still provide enough data assure a successful implementation? These questions all must be addressed to make IP viable for a design.

   Will Revenue IP (RIP) ever be a significant part of the FPGA designer's life? As hardware designers, we are comfortable using hardware IP in the form of integrated circuits out of necessity. We are not ASIC designers, so we do not have to use expensive design tools and we don't have direct access to the foundries. We could create a functionally equivalent design, but it would take more board space, take longer to design, and cost more to implement. Two of these three drawbacks are not present when our design ends up in an FPGA. We can argue with management that the last drawback, the time to do the design, will be balanced by the avoiding up-front costs or royalties. So, RIP is the right acronym for Revenue IP. We will use all the free (vendor-provided) and cheap (vendor-subsidized) IP we can get our hands on, but we will resist paying for other types of IP. Still, we need to take a look at the current IP strategies. For FPGAs, they come in two flavors: firm/hard and soft.

Hard or Firm IP

In the ASIC business, Hard IP is like a Standard Cell, a core that is predesigned and characterized for a specific foundry process. This option does not really exist for FPGAs; the closest we get is with Hard/Firm IP—prerouted and preplaced modules that can be linked with our other modules. Hard/Firm IP is most like using an integrated circuit in our design. It is a black box from a user's point of view. The user can't change it; it can only be plunked into a design and used as-is, with all other circuitry and routing forced around it. These modules are provided with a behavioral model that allows the design to be evaluated and tested. From a vendor's point of view, this is the safest IP, as it is very difficult to reverse-engineer or to modify and present as a new design. From a user's point of view, hard IP is not very friendly; it is a one-size-fits-all solution and allows no flexibility other than built-in configuration options. It's not portable to new processes or technology without recompiling by the IP vendor.

The advantage is that the design can be fully characterized and the timing performance is completely predictable; the user can't screw it up.

Soft IP

From a user's point of view, having source code that can be tweaked, hacked, and synthesized is much more desirable. But how then, can the IP vendor be assured of being paid? Get all the money up front? That's not very likely. If a design ends up being 47% IP and 53% hacked by the user, what's the right compensation? What keeps the designer from creating timing problems when the design (which can be very complex) is modified? Who is responsible in this situation?

To protect the IP vendor, Soft IP might be encrypted or obfuscated (comments removed, informative labels replaced with truncated and useless ones, and the code compressed to be unreadable) so that it can be synthesized and integrated into other parts of the design but not easily reverse-engineered.

SUMMING UP

The most common form of design reuse for FPGA designers will be reusing your own modules. We have covered some ways to design your code that will improve reusability. The next most common reuse method will be using modules designed by other engineers at your company; this avoids extra cost and legal issues. The most common tools for increasing productivity will be vendor-supplied libraries and core generation tools. Third-party IP will be a small part of the FPGA designer's reuse strategy.

Designing for ASIC Conversion

There are some advantages to converting an FPGA design to an ASIC, including merging multiple FPGAs into one ASIC and creating a device that consumes less power and operates at higher speeds. However, the main advantage is reducing cost. The cost of an ASIC (even with non-recurring charges factored in) can be less than a third of that of an FPGA. What drives the decision to convert your FPGA design to an ASIC? Consider conversion if:

- The yearly usage is greater than 1,000.
- The design is unlikely to require modification.
- Additional protection from reverse engineering is desirable.
- Improved speed or reduced power consumption (compared to an FPGA) is necessary.

For ease of conversion and lower up-front costs, there are three options for converting an FPGA to a custom device: a hard-wired FPGA, an FPGA conversion using laser-programmed or custom-routed devices, and a full ASIC design. Using Verilog as a design and simulation tool greatly enhances ease of the converting to an ASIC, because all ASIC companies use and are comfortable with Verilog.

An FPGA is not a very good ASIC prototyping device, but they get more 'ASIClike' every year. Increasingly, designs will remain implemented in FPGAs because of their increasing densities and future cost reductions. Still, many of our designs will convert to ASICs. While FPGAs are getting cheaper and denser, so ASIC technology improves, too.

Why Is an FPGA a Poor ASIC Prototype?

- The FPGA vendor has designed-in "training wheels" which improve the chances of success for a designer using poor design methodology. Particularly, the clock network has delay designed in to create a zero-hold-time requirement for flipflops. The FPGA designer concentrates on meeting the setup-time requirement; the ASIC designer must meet both setup- and hold-time requirement window.

- The FPGA provides low-skew global networks for clock and reset/preset; these networks must be created in the ASIC design.

- The experimental FPGA design mindset (Unsure about something? Try it and see what happens) is dead wrong for designing ASICs. There is a huge cost to making an error in an ASIC in terms of foundry charges and leadtime. This requires a careful (some might say anal-retentive), cautious, and conservative design approach with extensive testing.

- It can be difficult to cram logic into an FPGA, then make it run at high-speed. The ASIC will have only the resources demanded by the design (routing and logic resources in the FPGA are present whether they are used or not); thus will it be smaller, use less power, and operate at higher speed. Therefore, a lot of wasted time may be spent optimizing a design to run in an FPGA.

In spite of these caveats, successful FPGA-to-ASIC conversions are done every day. Using some common-sense design strategies will make the process go smoothly. First, let's look at the technologies into which the FPGA might be converted.

HardWire Devices

In a Xilinx FPGA, about half the silicon is used to create the programmable routing network. Xilinx offers custom hard-wired versions where the CLBs are the same as a regular FPGA (though packed closer together), but the routing is replaced with custom metal runs. The design change is minimal (the device uses the same placement and signal routing as the FPGA), and the time span for conversion can be as low as a month or so. Minimum order quantities can be as low as 1,000 pieces. Packages and pinouts, including power and ground, can be identical to the original FPGA. Configuration signal emulation can be used. For example, the configuration DONE pin might be used to control a processor reset signal on the circuit board. Though the HardWire device does not require configuration, having the configuration pins act the same might be required. The HardWire devices are built on the same fab lines as the FPGA, so the process technology (lithography), the pin drive capability, the pin voltage tolerance, and the CLB layout are the same.

Because the HardWire silicon is so similar to the FPGA, the HardWire design can be captured just from the configuration (.bit) file. Still, the conversion engineers will request source design information, which can be informative during the conversion process.

One drawback to the HardWire device is encountered during production testing. The configurable devices can be programmed with a test pattern and checked out; the HardWire devices must have special test support designed-in (added). Xilinx offers ATPG (Automated Test Pattern Generation) and boundary scan test capability.

Altera (with their MPLDs or Masked PLDs) and Lucent (with their MACO, or Masked Array Conversion for ORCA) offer similar devices for their technologies.

Conversion Issues

Conversion to HardWire technology is the least demanding conversion for the FPGA designer. Xilinx guarantees that the HardWire design will act the same as the FPGA device. Still, an FPGA can mask race conditions that can create glitches, because signal routing transistors with capacitive loading act as a low-pass (RC) filter; this effect will be much reduced in the HardWire device. Race-condition glitches caused by asynchronous signals, which are "filtered out" in the FPGA design, can be uncovered. Asynchronous signals will be flagged by Xilinx during the conversion process, but it's up to the designer to take responsibility to insure no hazards exist.

SEMICUSTOM DEVICES

Various technologies exist for arrays where logic is placed on a die, then custom routing is created with laser programming, where routing segments are removed. Chip Express is a company that offers fast prototypes with laser-programmed routing (LPGA, or Laser Personalized Gate Arrays), which can be converted later to devices with one or two metal routing layers. Clear Logic also offers these types of devices (LPLD, or Laser-Processed

Logic Device). The trade-offs and design considerations are very similar to HardWire conversion issues.

Semicustom ASIC Conversion

Vendors like AMI (American Microsystems) and Orbit offer FPGA conversions to their Gate Array designs. These processes offer short lead times (4 to 6 weeks) and low NRE charges ($5K to $50K). These companies have a lot of experience with doing FPGA conversions and can smooth the conversion process considerably.

Full Custom ASIC Conversion

In an FPGA design, what the designer can do is limited because the FPGA has a predefined structure in which the design is implemented. An ASIC is more freeform. There are no training wheels to keep the designer out of trouble. All the features we take for granted, like programmable buffers, termination resistors, built-in oscillator buffers, and power-on reset/preset, are not present unless we specify them in the ASIC. The ASIC has some advantages because the routing is fully customized and only gates that are actually used get placed. Also, much greater densities are offered, so designs that live in multiple FPGAs can be combined into one.

List of Conversion Requirements

The designer must provide information to feed the conversion process. This information will be present on a checklist provided by the ASIC vendor and will include items like:

- The design netlist.
- Test fixtures and simulation results. The vendor will be comfortable with Verilog test fixtures, the more of these provided, the lower the risk of problems during conversion.
- Package, number of pins, pin format, and pin pitch.
- A list of clocks and clock frequencies.
- Gate-count estimate.
- Temperature range and special environmental requirements (like military specs, etc.).
- Pin list: pin names and pin locations. This includes power, ground, configuration, and unused pins.
- Special features, like pull-up or pull-down resistors, critical timing paths, pin driver requirements, RAM and ROM, FIFO's, and other special logic modules.

DESIGN RULES FOR ASIC CONVERSION

Conversion to an ASIC process can be stressful; there are hungry gators swimming in those waters! Some hazards to watch for include delay networks, race conditions, combinational feedback, pulse generators, floating internal busses, clock skew, and gated or divided clocks.

Most vendors offer a "turn-key" conversion process. In this design flow, the ASIC vendor takes complete responsibility for the conversion and provides all test vectors. This takes longer and is more expensive than a "joint-design" conversion, where the FPGA designer provides all or part of the test vectors and takes responsibility for the conversion.

Figure 9-1   Watch for those alligators!

AMI (American Microsystems, Inc.) offers a no-vector conversion; this is the most painless conversion for the FPGA designer who hates simulation. However, the designer must obey the following rules, which is nearly impossible:

- Altera, Xilinx, and Actel devices only.
- Single external master clock.
- No combinational feedback loops.

- No delay dependencies or pulse generators.
- Single external master set/reset signal.

SYNCHRONOUS DESIGN RULES

The first rule is to do a synchronous design. This is not always an easy rule to follow, but each clock added to a design should be carefully considered. Every clock domain, every signal that crosses a clock-domain boundary, and every asynchronous signal is a hazard unless dealt with exhaustively. If the purpose of a design is to convert from one clock domain to another (like a FIFO does), then, obviously, you have no choice. If you need to save power, but some of the design needs to run at high speed, then again you have no choice. My personal preference is to run a design at the possible lowest speed, because this reduces RFI emissions and makes the design more tolerant of the inefficiencies of a generic HDL implementation. If a section of the design must be asynchronous, put it in quarantine. Keep it segregated from the synchronous parts of the design and document it well so that the design intent and hazards are clear.

It's not hard to handle asynchronous signals, but it is easy to forget to do this handling. The result is a design that works, but does not work reliably.

SYNCHRONOUS DESIGNS

Synchronous designs do not contain gated clocks or multiplexed clocks. The number of clocks can be counted on one hand, preferably with four fingers left over.
John McGibbon
Memec Design Services

ASIC conversion vendors sometimes offer "vectorless" conversions if the design is 100% synchronous. This will reduce the span time for conversion and reduce cost. It also reduces stress on the FPGA designer because the test burden is removed. The ASIC vendor likes this, because the design is relatively trouble-free and the test vectors can be automatically generated. For the FPGA designer, creating a 100% synchronous design is almost impossible but is a very worthwhile goal.

Use Generic Logic Constructs

ASIC vendors who do FPGA conversions routinely replace RAM and other modules (like adders and counters) with parameterized modules selected from their library. However, each substitution contributes a new block to the design, and each change adds to the risk that something will go wrong. LogiBLOX or cores should be evaluated for ease of conversion or substitution before being used in the FPGA design. The netlist should be "untouched" as much as possible during the conversion process. If your design has nothing but NAND gates in it, it will convert painlessly, because no module substitution will occur.

In a gate array, your RAM and ROM modules will be replaced with registers. This results in an explosion of the gate count. For a 512-by-8 RAM module, 4,096 flipflops will be instantiated. The cell decoding logic adds to that number (decoding-logic complexity squares for each added address line).

One feature that is particularly troublesome during ASIC conversion is RAM initialization (or ROM contents, the same thing). The FPGA can write data into RAM cells during the power-up configuration process. There is no corresponding magic configuration mode in the ASIC; all RAM cells must be written to via the RAM data bus.

Power-On Conditions

Part of the training wheels for an FPGA design is the power-up initialization of all I/O pins via the use of GSR (Global Set/Reset) resources and the device configuration process. An ASIC will not have these features unless the designer specifically puts them in. The ASIC vendor tends not to want to use many global networks (like reset and/or preset networks) because they must be custom routed and they consume routing channels.

Internal Busses

Xilinx and other FPGA vendors allow the use of internal tristate busses and buskeepers to prevent problems due to floating buffer inputs. Some ASIC vendors do not have this capability or prefer not to use the technology because it complicates testing. Exemplar Leonardo has a feature where internal tristate busses can be automatically converted to MUXes for technologies that don't support internal tristate busses.

Configuration Pins

Often the FPGA configuration pins are used in external logic (for example, using the configuration DONE pin in a Power-On Reset logic). Special logic will have to be designed into the ASIC to provide configuration-pin emulation. The FPGA designer needs to define which signals are used and how the pins are expected to act. For common FPGA signals and architectures, the ASIC vendor will have some experience with these signals and will be able to assist.

Pin I/O Buffers

The input signal thresholds must be defined by the FPGA designer. Input threshold options include TTL (where the threshold voltage is about 30% of the supply rail), CMOS (where the voltage threshold is about 50% of the supply rail), or custom.

The output pin drive requirement must also be defined by the FPGA designer. The use of low-impedance (high-current) buffers should be minimized to reduce power consumption and RFI noise generated by the design. The ASIC process probably has more options for drive capacity than the FPGA. Always use the slowest and lowest-power pin buffer that will do the job.

OSCILLATORS

Oscillators are analog circuits, but sometimes oscillator buffers are available in FPGA technology. These are inverting buffers with low gain to help assure that the oscillator stays in the linear mode, the inverter provides 180 degrees of phase lag, and the RC (cheapest, sloppiest), ceramic resonator (cheap, but not too sloppy), or crystal (best performance, but more expensive) provides the remaining 180 degrees of phase lag to meet the requirement for oscillation (a closed loop with 360 degrees of phase shift and an overall gain of one). A typical gate oscillator is shown in Figure 9-2.

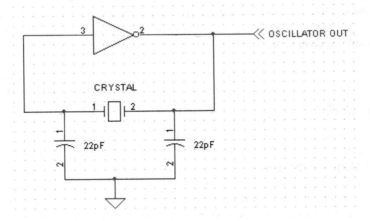

Figure 9-2   Typical Gate Oscillator Circuit

These circuits will need to be identified to the ASIC vendor to assure a compatible conversion. It's likely that the oscillator will end up being gated or multiplexed (this is much different than having a gated clock as part of the normal operating mode) so that the test equipment can drive the clock output with a clock of known frequency and phase. This circuitry will be added as part of the ASIC design process and probably will not be part of the FPGA design.

Never strap an oscillator enable pin high or low; put a resistor in so that an external source can enable or disable the oscillator as shown in Figure 9-3.

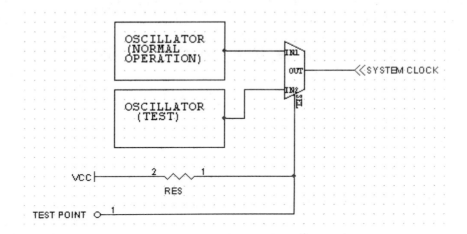

Figure 9-3   ASIC Oscillator Disable Circuit

For best performance, clock circuits should be isolated from other noise sources by physical distance or by guard rings, and the wiring should be kept tight to reduce loop areas. Note: the oscillator inverter is run in the linear mode, and the output should approximate a sinewave as much as possible to reduce EMI.

DELAY LINES

The FPGA designer sometimes uses a delay line to create time-delayed signals, particularly when interfacing with external SRAM or DRAM components. This delay is another analog circuit, so use caution! The delay line might be a string of buffers. This method of creating a delay is not recommended, because it depends on typical buffer delays which are not controlled and which change with temperature and process/technology changes.

During ASIC conversion, delay-line buffers will be replaced with buffers with different propagation delays (usually shorter, because ASIC buffers are typically faster than FPGA buffers) or will be completely removed because they represent redundant logic from a digital point of view. These delays must be documented and verified to insure they get implemented properly.

An option might be to use an external circuit to create the delay as shown in Figure 9-4. This circuit might be an RC delay with buffers to minimize the effect of changing the pin driver and pin loading during ASIC conversion. This delay is not precise and depends on the propagation delay of the pin drivers, the buffer propagation delays, the buffer threshold voltages, the tolerances of the RC components, operating temperature, and the ether-flux of the moon's gravitational field.

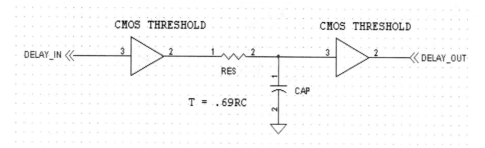

Figure 9-4   Typical External Buffer RC Delay Circuit

Even better, a delay can be created from a serpentine circuit board trace with about 175 picoseconds of delay per inch as shown in Figure 9-5. Remember to include the buffer delays, the pad delays, and the circuit-board trace delays. There are many assumption in this delay, and your mileage will vary. The reader is urged to read Johnson and Graham's *High Speed Digital Design, a Handbook of Black Magic* (see bibliography) before implementing a circuit like this.

Assumptions include the use of FR-4 circuit-board material, 20-mil traces, 0.6 inches per segment, 50-mil segment pitch, and that you have a valid exemption from Murphy's Law.

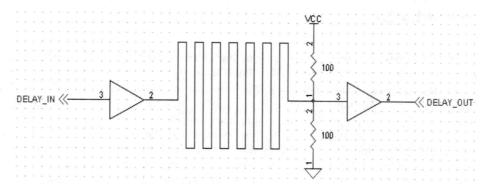

Figure 9-5   Typical External Trace Delay Line Circuit

Even better yet, think about spending some money and using a digital delay circuit like those available from Dallas Semiconductor and others.

THE LANGUAGE OF TEST

We're not going to cover test topics in depth, but we can learn a few buzzwords.

- **At-speed testing.** Testing performed at the actual operating speed of the design. Most testing is performed at slower clock speeds that are comfortable for the test equipment. These frequencies might be on the order of 1 to 5 MHz.

- **Boundary scan.** A test scheme where MUXes and latches are added to the design to support shifting serial data in and out. This allows test patterns to be applied and internal logic states to be read out.

- **BIST.** Built-In Self-Test, where hardware is added to the design to allow it to test itself.

- **Fault grading.** A measure of the how well the design hardware is tested. It is the ratio of the number of test vectors and the fault coverage.

- **Functional test.** Testing a device by applying user-provided test inputs and checking outputs. These tests are generally not very thorough. These are not parametric tests for AC performance.

- **I_{DDQ}** Tests of power-supply current when all internal nodes are quiet. The only inputs are terminations to prevent oscillation and to keep gates from going linear. This is a quick test to reject devices that were manufactured improperly.

- **JTAG.** Joint Test Action Group that created the IEEE 1149.1 boundary scan register and test access port (TAP) standard.

- **Observability.** The ability for test equipment to access an internal node. All output pins are observable.

- **Parametric testing.** Testing for gate input thresholds and output drive capability. These are analog tests which verify the ASIC processes.

- **Partial scan.** A scan test that covers only selected parts of the design.

- **Test coverage.** A figure of merit for a test suite; it's the ratio of all detected faults to the total number of possible faults.

- **Stuck-at faults.** A failure caused by a node staying in a zero or one state when it should be driven to a different state.

Boundary Scan

Because SRAM-based FPGA devices can reprogrammed, the FPGA manufacturer can load a test configuration and do a thorough production test. Custom devices, like your ASIC, must have test support designed in. A common method of providing test support is to insert boundary scan logic (BST), which creates a serial chain that runs near the outside of the device under test. This chain can include other devices. The serial chain can be four or five signals (TDI, Test Data Input, TDO, Test Data Output, TCLK, Test Clock, TMS, Test Mode Select, and an optional Test Reset, TRSTn). Inside the ASIC, MUXes are inserted which allow selected signals to be connected to a long shift register; this allows signals to be shifted in and out of the device being tested.

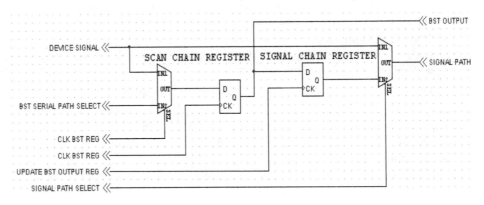

Figure 9-6   Boundary Scan Hardware Overhead

BST adds hardware to the ASIC as shown in Figure 9-6, the added hardware increases the ASIC design by 15 to 25%. It also adds delays to signal paths on the order of 1-2 nsec for each BST MUX. Insertion of the BST hardware and generation of scan vectors are automated processes. Note that the device signal always flows through a MUX. This architecture allows the serial chain to read device signals, or to shift (pass-through) other test signals in the chain, or to pass test signals into the signal chain.

There are other test methods. A complete discussion of them is beyond the scope of this book, but we can at least list them and say a few words about them. Tests can be divided into production tests (where the design is validated and process problems are tested for), design conversion tests (insuring that the design was converted properly; this is usually done mostly with designer-supplied functional test vectors), and static timing tests (to assure that the ASIC's different gate delays and clock skews don't cause problems).

IDDQ Test This is a quick test for production problems; if the current drain of the device is much higher than expected, then a manufacturing defect has probably occurred and the device can be quickly rejected.

Functional Test This type of test uses test vectors provided by the designer which emulate typical operating modes and look for predicted outputs. This type of test is generally not very thorough, because the designer doesn't think of all the various combinations of input modes and logic sequences.

ATPG (Automatic Test Vector Generation) These test vectors can include serial vectors (the ones that are clocked into the BST scan chain, if present) and parallel vectors (the ones presented in parallel to the device inputs).

PRINT-ON-CHANGE TEST VECTORS

The ASIC vendor will request print-on-change (POC) test vectors; this is an ASCII-formatted list of input sequences and expected output test patterns. Fortunately, it's not difficult to extract these vectors from the Verilog test fixture using **$display** and **$monitor** directives.

Listing 9-1   Simple POC Vector Example, OR Gate

```
            II      O
            NN      U
            12      T
TIME
0           00      0
50          01      0
53          01      1
100         00      1
103         00      0
150         10      0
153         10      1
```

From Listing 9-1, you can see that the delay through the gate is 3 nsec (the output changes in the period between 50 and 53 nsec).

Afterword: A Look into the Future, Millions and Millions and Millions of Gates

*P*ress Release: Xilinx Inc, July 7, **2005, San Jose, California.** Xilinx announces the latest member of the XZ-200 family, the XZ202XXL. The XZ202 supports 16 phase- and delay-locked clocks at speeds to 10 GHz with a 0.75 V power supply. Integrated analog features include octant power control (power can be switched on and off the device in eight sections), 10-bit A/D and D/A conversion with programmable top and bottom voltages, Sample/Track-and-Hold, SVGA monitor output, Delta-Modulation Converter, Voltage-to-Frequency Converter, PWM, high-speed data capture, switched-capacitor power supplies (to support RS-232 and other high-voltage I/O, and CCD/CMOS imagers), and operational/instrumentation amplifiers. Self- and on-the-fly reconfiguration is supported on an octant-by-octant basis. The XZ202 includes programmable thresholds for single-ended and differential I/Os, and up to 1500 I/O pins. 64-MB of high-speed DRAM is available on the core in 8-MB blocks. Each of the 32,768 CLBs can be configured as single-port or dual-port RAMs, each with a synchronous FIFO mode.

Each device is shipped with a factory-assigned 128-bit IPv6 address. Test support includes an integrated telephone modem, so that configuration read-out and test can be performed remotely by the Xilinx support staff. Twenty-four-hour worldwide support is provided from Xilinx support facilities in Silicon Valley and India. A free license for a built-in oscilloscope and logic analyzer core is provided with each device. A JTAG emulator and background debugger is included. A free Verilog design system (with Xilinx object-oriented extensions) is available.

A wide variety of IP cores are available for inexpensive licensing, including:

- Microprocessor, RISC, and DSP cores, 4 to 64 bit, 10 MHz to 1 GHz.
- Direct digital conversion for 2.4 GHz, GSM, PCS, and other radio frequencies and formats.
- JPEG, MJPEG, and MPEG encoding and decoding.
- Cable-ready and antenna-ready TV and AM/FM radio tuners.
- PGP and other encryption/decryption cores.
- DCT, FFT, wavelet, and other transforms.
- Games and educational cores, including Flight Simulator, Riven IV and Quake 2005.

Price and availability: $25.00 in 10,000 quantities, samples available in Q3 2005, with production in Q1 2006.

Xilinx is an equal-opportunity employer, and all Xilinx devices are Y3K compliant.

Resources

For updates and errata for *Real World FPGA Design with Verilog*, surf over to
www.bytechservices.com

To report errors or to compliment/complain about something, email to
kcoffman@sos.net

The World Wide Web is an excellent tool for research. The Usenet newsgroups are an excellent source of unfiltered information, opinions, and gossip.

Usenet Newsgroups
comp.lang.verilog
comp.lang.vhdl
comp.arch.fpga
comp.cad.synthesis

Verilog FAQ
http://www.siliconlogic.com/verilog/verilog/verilog-faq.html

FPGA and CPLD Manufacturers
www.actel.com
www.altera.com
www.latticesemi.com
www.lucent.com/micro/fpga/
www.manuflex.com
www.xilinx.com

Software Suppliers
www.bluepc.com
www.cadence.com
www.exemplar.com
www.model.com
www.simucad.com
www.synopsys.com
www.synplicity.com
www.veritools-web.com

Glossary

AHDL   Altera Hardware Description Language, a proprietary HDL.

algorithm   A step-by-step method of solving a problem.

antifuse   A connection link that turns into a low impedance when stressed.

ASIC   Application-Specific Integrated Circuit, an integrated circuit designed to perform a specific job, though the job might be generic (a microprocessor is an ASIC, for example).

ATPG   Automatic Test Pattern Generator.

asynchronous   Logic that operates without a reference clock. 90% of the problems the logic designer will face are related to asynchronous signal timing.

autorouting   A computerized method of determining signal or element interconnection.

behaviorial   A procedural coding style that describes logic without a direct link to the synthesized hardware. This is a more abstract form of logic definition compared with structural gates and continuous assignment statements.

bidirectional   A port that acts as both input and output (inout). This port will have output drivers connected to an input port. It is up to the designer to assure that only one output driver is active at a given time.

binary   A system with two states, either one or zero.

BIST   Built-In Self Test.

bit   A contraction for binary digit.

bitstream   FPGA/CPLD configuration information that is formatted for serial communication.

bitwise   Describes an operation where a bit in one vector acts on or is acted on by the corresponding bit in another vector.

blocking   A blocking assignment will complete before later statements get executed (i.e., statements that follow the blocking assignment are postponed until the blocking assignment is complete). In a sequential construct, the order of blocking assignments is significant and unwanted latches can be inferred.

Boolean   A system of symbolic logic based on the manipulation of symbols and numbers.

Buskeeper   A low-current driver circuit that maintains a logic state on a node when the bus is tristated.

buffer   A signal driver used to isolate signals or provide power gain for driving low impedance loads.

capacitance   The measure of how a circuit or circuit element stores or couples charges.

case   A multi-input decision statement. The test cases are prioritized, the earliest case that matches the input will be executed. The case decision is either true or false. The input is tested for an exact match to 0, 1, X, and Z conditions.

casex   A case decision that treats Z and X conditions as "don't care" (X) conditions.

casez   A case decision that treats Z conditions as a "don't care" (X) condition.

checksum   A modulo-n result of adding data values. A checksum is used to validate a data packet.

CLB   Configurable Logic Block, a basic Xilinx FPGA element consisting of a 3-5 input LUT.

CMOS   Complementary symmetry (i.e., uses both P- and N-style transistors) Metal Oxide Semiconductor.

combinational   An asynchronous operation that makes a direct and immediate assignment to the output.

concatenation   Items linked together in a continuous and related chain. In Verilog, items enclosed in { }, are linked together and operated on as a single entity.

configuration   The process of loading the FPGA with the user's design file(s).

constraints   Conditions and requirements added to a design to provide optimized performance. Constraints include signal path timing requirements, device pin assignments, and logic block relative locations, etc.

core   An intellectual property element, a pre-designed function block.

CPLD   Complex Programmable Logic Devices. Compared to an FPGA, a CPLD has more complex logic elements and more regimented routing tracks that lead to more deterministic, but less flexible, circuit performance.

CPU   Central Processing Unit.

CRC   Cyclic Redundancy Checksum. A pseudorandom number correlated to a data stream.

DeMorgan's Theorems   Two Boolean Logic theorems that convert between OR and AND forms. In Verilog form, here are the two theorems:

```
~(A | B)      =      (~A & ~B);
~(A & B)      =      (~A | ~B);
```

DFF   D-Type (edge-triggered) FlipFlop.

dissipation   Waste created during the performance of some useful task. In the context of FPGAs, this is power wasted when signals switch. This causes heating of the FPGA device. The dissipation (heating) is proportional to the signal loading and the switching frequency.

DLL   Delay-Locked Loop. A method of controlling clock skew across a device by delaying clocks paths a variable amount until all edges are nearly simultaneous.

DRAM   Dynamic Read-Only Memory.

EAB   Embedded Array Block. This is Altera's basic RAM block in their CPLDs.

edge-triggered   A signal that is evaluated only at the rising and/or falling edge of a reference clock.

EDIF   Electronic Design Interchange Format. This standard is administered by the Electronic Industries Association (EIA).

EEPROM   Electrically Erasable Programmable Read-Only Memory.

EMI   Electro Magnetic Interference. Some of the energy that is wasted during signal switching is radiated into space. If this energy, if not managed, can cause problems for other electronic circuits.

EPROM   Electrically Programmable Read-Only Memory.

fanout   A measure of the unit-loading of a driver.

feedback   A signal wrapped from an output back to the input.

FET   Field Effect Transistor.

FG   Function Generator. A 3-, 4-, or 5- input look-up table, a basic Xilinx logic element.

FIFO   First-In First-Out register set.

flatten   The process of merging modules and library parts to create a single homogenous netlist.

flipflop   A bistable multivibrator, a circuit where the output is either true or false. The output depends on the input and the input history (memory).

floorplan   The arrangement of logic elements in the physical structure of the device.

footprint   The arrangement and style of the physical pins and package of a device.

FPGA   Field Programmable Gate Array. Compared to a CPLD, the FPGA has more segmented routing and less complex logic elements. This leads to more flexible, but less deterministic, circuit performance.

FSM   Finite State Machine.

GAL   Generic Array Logic. Early PLDs had active-low or active-high polarity outputs, the GAL allowed programming the polarity of the output.

GIGO   Garbage-In, Garbage-Out. A maxim that the quality of the output is directly related to the quality of the input.

glitch   A short and unwanted signal transition.

GSR   Global Set/Reset. A dedicated and device-wide signal routing and buffering resource.

GTL   Gunning Transistor Logic.

GTS   Global TriState.

GUI   Graphical User Interface.

hazard   An overlap or dropout of input signals that cause a glitch.

HDL   Hardware Description Language. A text-based method of capturing a design.

hex   Short for hexadecimal, a numbering system with 16 values where each power is represented by the single digit 0-9 and A-F.

hierarchy   A pyramidal arrangement of modules.

hold time   The period of time after a clock edge that an input signal must be stable to assure the flipflop or latch output follows the input correctly.

hysteresis   A condition similar to friction where feedback is used to slow an output's response to an input signal change. Often used to help prevent glitches.

impedance   The opposition to a change of signal direction or strength. Impedance is the sum of resistance and reactance.

inout   A bidirectional module port.

input   A module port that is driven by an external signal or signals.

instance   An occurence of a signal, library part, or module.

instantiate   To create an occurence of a signal, library part, or module.

integer   A whole number (no fractional or decimal part). Verilog defines an integer to be at least 32 bits wide.

IP   Intellectual Property.

LAB   Logic Array Block. This is Altera's basic logic block in their CPLDs.

latch   A level-sensitive storage element. This circuit has feedback which allows it to "remember" its history and maintain a condition based on that history.

latency   The time it takes to process inputs to create the output. In a synchronous system this time can be measured in the number of clock cycles required to complete an operation.

LE   Logic Element. Altera's LABs are built of structured groups of these look-up tables.

Lint   A computer language syntax-checker.

LSB   Least Significant Bit.

LUT   Look-Up Table.

management   The person who provides guidance and direction for a team. The manager of a team sets the limit for team achievement.

metastability   When the setup- or hold-time for a flipflop is violated, the output becomes indeterminate, this characteristic of a flipflop is called metastability.

MSB   Most Significant Bit.

MUX   A multiplexer. A circuit where the output is switched or selected by a control or set of controls.

NAND   Not-AND, an AND gate with the output inverted.

net   A connection point similar to a trace on a circuit board.

netlist   A textual version of a design which includes all elements and their interconnections.

newbie   Someone who is new to a technology and therefore clueless.

nonblocking   An assignment that can be scheduled without blocking the procedural flow. Nonblocking assignments occur simultaneously and do not interfere with each other, their order in a sequential block is not significant.

nsec   Nanosecond (10^{-9}).

oscillator   A device that produces an alternating or pulsating output. These circuits are often used to create reference clocks for synchronous circuits. The basic requirements for an oscillator are: 360 degrees of feedback and an overall loop gain of 1. There is an old saying: if you're trying to design an oscillator, you will get an amplifier, if you're trying to design an amplifier, you will get an oscillator.

output   A module port that drives external signal or signals.

pad   A net that connects the FPGA logic to the outside world.

parameter   An operating value for a module. This is generally a value that can be changed during compilation.

PCB   Printed Circuit Board.

pipeline   A method of reducing logic that must be resolved between clock edges. Pipelining increases operating speed at the expense of latency.

PIP   Programmable Interconnect Point. Altera's method of making signal connections.

PLD   Programmable Logic Device.

PLL   Phase-Locked Loop. A method of synchronizing to a reference frequency.

portability   A measure of the ability to transfer a design from one target device to another.

POST   Power-On Self Test.

primitive   The most basic elements of a design. Verilog primitives are and, nand, nor, or, xor, and xnor. Primitives may also describe the elements of an FPGA/CPLD architecture (pin buffers, clock drivers, LUT's, etc.).

propagation   Signals are represented by charges. It takes time for charges to be distributed across and through circuitry, this time is called propagation.

pull-down   A termination resistor, unless the wire is otherwise driven, the resistor pulls the node to a logic low.

pull-up   A termination resistor, unless the wire is otherwise driven, the resistor pulls the node to a logic high.

PWB   Printed Wiring Board.

RAM   Random Access Memory.

reg   A data storage element which can be a latch, a flipflop, or a memory cell or cells. The default state of a Verilog reg is X.

RFI   Radio Frequency Interference.

route   The physical path a signal follows to get to its destination.

RTL   Register Transfer Level. RTL assumes a set of hardware constructs are defined in FPGA hardware and library elements. HDL code is mapped to these constructs. RTL constructs include circuit blocks like flipflops, latches, MUXs, etc., all connected together with the FPGA routing resources.

schematic   A graphical circuit diagram.

SDF   Standard Delay Format, a netlist that includes signal delay information.

sensitivity list   Also called an event list or event sensitivity list. This is an index of signals used in a block. This list drives the simulator: the simulator can evaluate signals that change and determine if the signal is used in a block. If the signal is not used, the block does not have to be processed.

setup time   The period of time before a clock edge that an input signal must be stable to assure the flipflop or latch output follows the input correctly.

skew   The time difference between when a signal is generated in one part of an FPGA and when it arrives at destination(s) at other parts of the FPGA.

slack time   The extra time available to allow logic to resolve before a timing violation occurs. Positive slack time is good, negative slack time is bad.

SMT   Surface Mount.

SRAM   Static Read-Only Memory.

structural   A form of HDL coding style where circuit elements are connected together like a schematic.

stuck   A form of logic fault. A signal can be stuck at a certain value (like a stuck-at-1 fault) when it should change based on some input change.

synchronous   A form of circuitry that uses a clock reference.

synthesis   The process of mapping HDL to the available hardware.

ternary   Arranged in a group of three.

threshold   The voltage level where a signal is resolved into a zero or one value. For TTL, this voltage is approximately 1.4V, for CMOS the voltage is approximately ½ the supply voltage.

tick   The accent grave or open quote symbol (` ) used by Verilog to identify compiler directives (`define for example). Not to be confused with the close quote symbol (') used in defining numbers (1'b0 for example).

timescale   The basic unit of time used during simulation. The default time unit in Verilog is nsec.

TLA   Three Letter Acronym.

toggle   To change state.

tri   A Verilog net that can be driven by only multiple sources.

tristate   Three levels of output drive, 0, 1, or Z (open or no drive).

uA   Microamp (10^{-6} Amps).

UART   Universal Asynchronous Receiver-Transmitter.

vector   Multibit net or register variable. Verilog only supports one-dimensional vectors. This can also be shorthand for test vectors, a set of input and output values used for test.

vendor   A supplier of goods or services.

VHDL   Very high-speed integrated circuit Hardware Description Language. This language has its roots in the Ada programming language and is the main competitor to Verilog.

Verilog   A HDL simulation language designed by Phil Moorby et al in 1983-1984 for Automated Integrated Design Systems (later called Gateway Design Automation). Gateway was acquired by Cadence in 1989. Cadence place Verilog into the public domain managed by the Open Verilog International (OVI) in 1990. IEEE Std 1364-1995 Standard Hardware Description Language Based on the Verilog® Hardware description Language was approved in 1995.

wire   A Verilog net that can be driven by only one source.

X   An unknown value.

XNOR   Exclusive NOR, the output is an inverted version of the XOR function.

XOR   Exclusive OR, the output is true only when the inputs are different.

Z   A high impedance value (open or not driven).

Bibliography

Bhasker, J., *A Verilog HDL Primer*, Star Galaxy Press, Allentown, PA, 1997.

Bhasker, J., *Verilog HDL Synthesis, A Practical Primer*, Star Galaxy Publishing, Allentown, PA, 1998.

Ciletti, Michael D., *Modeling, Synthesis and Rapid Prototyping with the Verilog HDL*, Prentice Hall, Upper Saddle River, NJ, 1999.

Johnson, Howard W., and Graham, Martin, *High-Speed Digital Design: A Handbook of Black Magic*, Prentice Hall, Upper Saddle River, NJ, 1992.

Keating, Michael, and Bricaud, Pierre, *Reuse Methodology Manual for System-on-a-Chip Designs*, Kluwer Academic Publishers, Norwell, MA, 1998.

Kurup, Pran, Abbasi, Taher, and Bedi, Ricky, *It's the Methodology, Stupid*, Bytek Designs, Palo Alto CA, 1998.

Lee, James M., *Verilog Quickstart*, Kluwer Academic Publishers, Norwell, MA, 1997.

Malvino, Albert Paul, and Leach, Donald P., *Digital Principles and Applications*, 2nd ed., McGraw-Hill Book Company, New York, NY, 1975

Maxfield, Clive "Max", *Designus Maximus Unleashed!*, Butterworth-Heinemann, Woburn, MA, 1998.

Palnitkar, Samir, *Verilog HDL, A Guide to Digital Design and Synthesis*, Prentice Hall, Upper Saddle River, NJ, 1996.

Sagdeo, Vivek, *The Complete Verilog Book*, Kluwer Academic Publishers, Norwell, MA, 1998.

Smith, Douglas J., *HDL Chip Design*, Doone Publications, Madison AL, 1997.

Smith, Michael J. S., *Application-Specific Integrated Circuits*, Addison-Wesley, Reading, MA, 1997.

Sternheim, Eli, Singh, Rajvir, Madhaven, Rajeev, and Trivedi, Yatin, *Digital Design and Synthesis with Verilog HDL*, Automata, San Jose, CA, 1993.

Zeidman, Bob, *Verilog Designer's Library*, Prentice Hall, Upper Saddle River, NJ, 1999.

Index

Photograph by Dwight Freeman

Ken Coffman has held a variety of jobs, including strawberry picker, dishwasher, laborer in a cat food factory, Air Force Sergeant, rock'n'roll bass player, college lecturer, electronics technician, injection-molding machine operator, electrical designer, engineering manager, and small business owner. He reserves the right to go back to washing dishes if electrical engineering doesn't pan out.

In 1995, Ken wrote a novel called *Alligator Alley* with his partner, Mark Bothum. He also wrote a screenplay based on the novel.

Ken is the task leader of the semantics section of the IEEE 1364.1 working group, the Verilog RTL synthesis specification. He holds a BSEET degree from Cogswell College North (now Henry Cogswell College).

He lives in the hills northeast of Seattle with his wife Judy and a dog named Bear.

LICENSE AGREEMENT AND LIMITED WARRANTY

READ THE FOLLOWING TERMS AND CONDITIONS CAREFULLY BEFORE OPENING THIS SOFTWARE MEDIA PACKAGE. THIS LEGAL DOCUMENT IS AN AGREEMENT BETWEEN YOU AND PRENTICE-HALL, INC. (THE "COMPANY"). BY OPENING THIS SEALED SOFTWARE MEDIA PACKAGE, YOU ARE AGREEING TO BE BOUND BY THESE TERMS AND CONDITIONS. IF YOU DO NOT AGREE WITH THESE TERMS AND CONDITIONS, DO NOT OPEN THE SOFTWARE MEDIA PACKAGE. PROMPTLY RETURN THE UNOPENED SOFTWARE MEDIA PACKAGE AND ALL ACCOMPANYING ITEMS TO THE PLACE YOU OBTAINED THEM FOR A FULL REFUND OF ANY SUMS YOU HAVE PAID.

1.   **GRANT OF LICENSE:** In consideration of your payment of the license fee, which is part of the price you paid for this product, and your agreement to abide by the terms and conditions of this Agreement, the Company grants to you a nonexclusive right to use and display the copy of the enclosed software program (hereinafter the "SOFTWARE") on a single computer (i.e., with a single CPU) at a single location so long as you comply with the terms of this Agreement. The Company reserves all rights not expressly granted to you under this Agreement.

2.   **OWNERSHIP OF SOFTWARE:** You own only the magnetic or physical media (the enclosed software media) on which the SOFTWARE is recorded or fixed, but the Company retains all the rights, title, and ownership to the SOFTWARE recorded on the original software media copy(ies) and all subsequent copies of the SOFTWARE, regardless of the form or media on which the original or other copies may exist. This license is not a sale of the original SOFTWARE or any copy to you.

3.   **COPY RESTRICTIONS:** This SOFTWARE and the accompanying printed materials and user manual (the "Documentation") are the subject of copyright. You may not copy the Documentation or the SOFTWARE, except that you may make a single copy of the SOFTWARE for backup or archival purposes only. You may be held legally responsible for any copying or copyright infringement which is caused or encouraged by your failure to abide by the terms of this restriction.

4.   **USE RESTRICTIONS:** You may not network the SOFTWARE or otherwise use it on more than one computer or computer terminal at the same time. You may physically transfer the SOFTWARE from one computer to another provided that the SOFTWARE is used on only one computer at a time. You may not distribute copies of the SOFTWARE or Documentation to others. You may not reverse engineer, disassemble, decompile, modify, adapt, translate, or create derivative works based on the SOFTWARE or the Documentation without the prior written consent of the Company.

5.   **TRANSFER RESTRICTIONS:** The enclosed SOFTWARE is licensed only to you and may not be transferred to any one else without the prior written consent of the Company. Any unauthorized transfer of the SOFTWARE shall result in the immediate termination of this Agreement.

6.   **TERMINATION:** This license is effective until terminated. This license will terminate automatically without notice from the Company and become null and void if you fail to comply with any provisions or limitations of this license. Upon termination, you shall destroy the Documentation and all copies of the SOFTWARE. All provisions of this Agreement as to warranties, limitation of liability, remedies or damages, and our ownership rights shall survive termination.

7.   **MISCELLANEOUS:** This Agreement shall be construed in accordance with the laws of the United States of America and the State of New York and shall benefit the Company, its affiliates, and assignees.

8.   **LIMITED WARRANTY AND DISCLAIMER OF WARRANTY:** The Company warrants that the SOFTWARE, when properly used in accordance with the Documentation, will operate in substantial conformity with the description of the SOFTWARE set forth in the Documentation. The Company does not warrant that the SOFTWARE will meet your requirements or that the operation of the SOFTWARE will be uninterrupted or error-free. The Company warrants that the media on which the SOFTWARE is delivered shall be free from defects in materials and workmanship under normal use for a period of thirty (30) days from the date of your purchase. Your only remedy and the Company's only obligation under these limited warranties is, at the Company's option, return of the warranted item for a refund of any amounts paid by you or replacement of the item. Any replacement of SOFTWARE or media under the warranties shall not extend the original warranty period. The limited warranty set forth above shall not apply to any SOFTWARE which the Company determines in good faith has been subject to misuse, neglect, improper installation, repair, alteration, or dam-

age by you. EXCEPT FOR THE EXPRESSED WARRANTIES SET FORTH ABOVE, THE COMPANY DISCLAIMS ALL WARRANTIES, EXPRESS OR IMPLIED, INCLUDING WITHOUT LIMITATION, THE IMPLIED WARRANTIES OF MERCHANTABILITY AND FITNESS FOR A PARTICULAR PURPOSE. EXCEPT FOR THE EXPRESS WARRANTY SET FORTH ABOVE, THE COMPANY DOES NOT WARRANT, GUARANTEE, OR MAKE ANY REPRESENTATION REGARDING THE USE OR THE RESULTS OF THE USE OF THE SOFTWARE IN TERMS OF ITS CORRECTNESS, ACCURACY, RELIABILITY, CURRENTNESS, OR OTHERWISE.

IN NO EVENT, SHALL THE COMPANY OR ITS EMPLOYEES, AGENTS, SUPPLIERS, OR CONTRACTORS BE LIABLE FOR ANY INCIDENTAL, INDIRECT, SPECIAL, OR CONSEQUENTIAL DAMAGES ARISING OUT OF OR IN CONNECTION WITH THE LICENSE GRANTED UNDER THIS AGREEMENT, OR FOR LOSS OF USE, LOSS OF DATA, LOSS OF INCOME OR PROFIT, OR OTHER LOSSES, SUSTAINED AS A RESULT OF INJURY TO ANY PERSON, OR LOSS OF OR DAMAGE TO PROPERTY, OR CLAIMS OF THIRD PARTIES, EVEN IF THE COMPANY OR AN AUTHORIZED REPRESENTATIVE OF THE COMPANY HAS BEEN ADVISED OF THE POSSIBILITY OF SUCH DAMAGES. IN NO EVENT SHALL LIABILITY OF THE COMPANY FOR DAMAGES WITH RESPECT TO THE SOFTWARE EXCEED THE AMOUNTS ACTUALLY PAID BY YOU, IF ANY, FOR THE SOFTWARE.

SOME JURISDICTIONS DO NOT ALLOW THE LIMITATION OF IMPLIED WARRANTIES OR LIABILITY FOR INCIDENTAL, INDIRECT, SPECIAL, OR CONSEQUENTIAL DAMAGES, SO THE ABOVE LIMITATIONS MAY NOT ALWAYS APPLY. THE WARRANTIES IN THIS AGREEMENT GIVE YOU SPECIFIC LEGAL RIGHTS AND YOU MAY ALSO HAVE OTHER RIGHTS WHICH VARY IN ACCORDANCE WITH LOCAL LAW.

ACKNOWLEDGMENT

YOU ACKNOWLEDGE THAT YOU HAVE READ THIS AGREEMENT, UNDERSTAND IT, AND AGREE TO BE BOUND BY ITS TERMS AND CONDITIONS. YOU ALSO AGREE THAT THIS AGREEMENT IS THE COMPLETE AND EXCLUSIVE STATEMENT OF THE AGREEMENT BETWEEN YOU AND THE COMPANY AND SUPERSEDES ALL PROPOSALS OR PRIOR AGREEMENTS, ORAL, OR WRITTEN, AND ANY OTHER COMMUNICATIONS BETWEEN YOU AND THE COMPANY OR ANY REPRESENTATIVE OF THE COMPANY RELATING TO THE SUBJECT MATTER OF THIS AGREEMENT.

Should you have any questions concerning this Agreement or if you wish to contact the Company for any reason, please contact in writing at the address below.

Robin Short
Prentice Hall PTR
One Lake Street
Upper Saddle River, New Jersey 07458

ABOUT THE CD-ROM

The CD-ROM contains all Verilog source code from the book, all project files, some useful utilities, an evaluation copy of Simucad's Silos III Verilog simulator, a demonstration version of David Murray's Prism Editor, and an evaluation version of Bytech Services' Emath-Pro for Windows.

About Silos III

Silos III, a Verilog HDL-based Logic Simulation Environment is one of the only logic simulation tools that includes a complete graphical debugging system. It has been engineered to handle large complex ASIC and FPGA designs with speed, ease of use, and simplicity.

The setup (setup.exe) utility for Silos III is in the SilosIII folder on the CD-ROM. Double-click on the setup icon or browse to find setup.exe in the Windows Run dialog box. Refer to www.simucad.com for application and technical support.

About Prism Editor

Prism editor is an 'environmentally friendly' editor designed for Windows NT/95/98. No matter what type of files you edit on a daily basis, the editor can incorporate them into a productive system. It has all the features of a fully functional text editor but it has a lot more too! Many people use it as a text viewer rather than just an editor. An ordinary text report can instantaneously be color coordinated and have it's own macros to assist with further analysis.

The setup (setup.exe) utility for the Prism Editor is in the PrismEditor folder on the CD-ROM. Double-click on the setup icon or browse to find setup.exe in the Windows Run dialog box. Registration procedures, updates, and support is accessed through the editor. The evaluation version of the Prism Editor is fully functional for 30 days. After 30 days, selected features are disabled. A special price was negotiated for purchasers of this book who provide the following book registration code: 130998516.

About Emath-Pro for Windows

Emath-Pro is a sophisticated formula calculator for electrical and electronic engineering applications. It contains formulas from basic electronics to advanced topics, such as Transmission Line formulas and Magnetics design formulas. Most formulas can be entered with any known variables and can be solved for the unknown variable. Emath-Pro is the essential formula solving software tool for Engineers, Technicians, and Students.

The setup (setup.exe) utility for the Emath-Pro for Windows is in the Emath folder on the CD-ROM. This demonstration version is fully functional, users who choose to register can do so at www.bytechservices.com

Technical Support

Prentice Hall does not offer support for this software. If there is a problem with the media, however, you may obtain a replacement CD-ROM by emailing a description of the problem to disc_exchange@prenhall.com

Errata, updates of the book material and software, and additional information is available at www.bytechservices.com/verilog/